DREAM'S
EDGE

DREAM'S EDGE

Science Fiction Stories About
the Future of Planet Earth

Edited by **Terry Carr**

Sierra Club Books   **San Francisco**

The Sierra Club, founded in 1892 by John Muir, has devoted itself to the study and protection of the earth's scenic and ecological resources—mountains, wetlands, woodlands, wild shores and rivers, deserts and plains. The publishing program of the Sierra Club offers books to the public as a nonprofit educational service in the hope that they may enlarge the public's understanding of the Club's basic concerns. The point of view expressed in each book, however, does not necessarily represent that of the Club. The Sierra Club has some fifty chapters coast to coast, in Canada, Hawaii, and Alaska. For information about how you may participate in its programs to preserve wilderness and the quality of life, please address inquiries to Sierra Club, 530 Bush Street, San Francisco, CA 94108.

Acknowledgments for permission to reprint previously published material are found at the end of this book.

Library of Congress Cataloging in Publication Data:

Main entry under title:

Dream's edge

1. Science fiction, American.   I. Carr, Terry.
PS648.S3D7   813'.0876'08355   80-13389

ISBN 0-87156-232-4
ISBN 0-87156-238-3 (pbk.)

Cover and book design by Jon Goodchild
Cover illustration by Don Shields, courtesy of the Will Stone Collection, San Francisco

Printed in the United States of America

Contents

Science

Man, introverted man, having crossed
In passage and but a little with the nature of things this
    latter century
Has begot giants; but being taken up
Like a maniac with self-love and inward conflicts cannot
    manage his hybrids.
Being used to deal with edgeless dreams,
Now he's bred knives on nature turns them also inward:
    they have thirsty points though.
His mind forebodes his own destruction;
Actæon who saw the goddess naked among leaves and his
    hounds tore him.
A little knowledge, a pebble from the shingle,
A drop from the oceans: who would have dreamed this
    infinitely little too much?

Robinson Jeffers
from *Selected Poems*

Introduction

Terry Carr

ONCERN FOR THE PROBLEMS and prospects of our earthly environment comes naturally to the writers and readers of science fiction—it is as intrinsic to the genre as knowledge of physics, chemistry, the workings of politics and human psychology. Science fiction is literature about the future, telling stories of the marvels we hope to see—or for our descendants to see—tomorrow, in the next century, or in the limitless duration of time.

But though time is endless, there's no guarantee that humans will be around long. In order to tell a story of life on a future Earth, exploring the reaches of the solar system, or establishing colonies on the planets orbiting other stars, a writer must first believe we can get from here to there—and there are problems in that.

Will we manage to avoid a nuclear war that could kill most of the human race and leave the survivors only shattered societies and technologies? Can we check the disruption of Earth's ecological balance, on which human and all other life depends? If we do that much, can we manage to preserve enough energy resources to support the enormous requirements of an overpopulated world or of a sustained venture into space?

The answer to all of these questions is a qualified yes. We can do it; what's more, we must. The problem is how, and in recent years science fiction writers have increasingly concerned themselves with depicting the dangers and speculating about ways to avert them. There are no simple answers in science fiction, no brilliant inventions that will solve everything just as soon as an engineer works out the schematics. Many science fiction writers are scientists, but when they're writing their job is to tell stories.

Many go beyond that, of course; they sketch scenarios of the future to warn us and urge us to action. If that sounds like a trivial effort, remember that science fiction's stories of space travel were instrumental in the development of our space programs: most of the people now working for agencies like NASA acknowledge that their choice of career was sparked by science fiction. If science fiction can fulfill that role again, causing enough people to devote their working lives to solving environmental problems, it will make an even more important contribution to the world.

The development of the science fiction genre was a result of people's widespread realization, starting during the industrial revolution, that we have the ability to make vast changes through scientific planning. Early science fiction was optimistic and utopian, telling exciting tales of the wondrous futures science would make possible: in those years we seemed to have limitless opportunities, which scientists and industrialists were rapidly exploiting. But the results of technological profligacy are now alarmingly evident, and today's science fiction reflects that awareness.

We're rapidly exhausting the resources of our planet—burning the non-renewable energy sources, mining the finite mineral deposits, laying waste to agricultural land, depleting water tables. We're polluting what's left, further contributing to the disappearance of such basic necessities as atmospheric ozone and phytoplankton. Uncontrolled development continues to eradicate life forms and threatens the entire ecological web. And we're making sure all of this will get worse by continuing to reproduce in such numbers that tomorrow's food and energy needs will be even greater than today's.

Since science fiction has traditionally been about the future, and the "future" of early science fiction stories is our present, one might expect that we'd have had warnings of these problems long ago, in those strange, often fumbling stories from the late nineteenth and early twentieth centuries. But science fiction, like any other form of writing, has always been a product of the time in which it was written, so there are very few accurate warnings in early science fiction stories: the intellectual mood of the genre's early decades was very optimistic, and so were the stories.

Certainly there were exceptions. "The Doom of London" by Robert Barr, published in 1892, depicted the city suffocated by smog. W. H. Hudson's *A Crystal Age* (1887), and others of his works, considered how civilization might live in ecological balance with nature. But these and other exceptions merely prove the rule: examination of the probable origins of their ideas shows that they didn't come from scientific extrapolation. They were just mavericks that slipped into the science fiction mode by accident. Indeed, there *was* no science fiction mode as such in the nineteenth century; what "examples" there are have become visible only in hindsight.

Science fiction as a conscious genre did not begin until 1926, when the first science fiction magazine, *Amazing Stories,* commenced publication. Valuable environmental prediction in the early science fiction magazines is notable for its sparseness and naiveté. J. D. Beresford's "The Man Who Hated Flies" was published in 1929 and dealt with ecocatastrophe caused by an efficient pesticide, but it didn't appear in any science fiction magazine. Neither did E. M. Forster's "The Machine Stops," which depicted a future world of people living underground, served by a vast complex of machinery, when the surface of the planet had become incapable of supporting any kind of life.

The attitude of most people toward science and technology was simplistically positive—basically "faithful," especially during the worldwide depression of the 1920s and 1930s—and science fiction had nothing of importance to add. As late as 1940, when the science fiction genre was in the midst of its first great intellectual growth, Lester del Rey published this approving description (in *Astounding,* the pace-setter of the field) of a factory:

The smokestacks were throwing out their columns of inky oil smoke, telling of power feeding into the turbines that furnished the station with a steady, dependable supply of high-voltage direct current electricity.

Ironically, del Rey's story dealt with an experiment in atomic energy.

For the next decade, science fiction's worries centered around the possibilities of Earth being destroyed by world war, then the awesome and awful results that might come from nuclear fission. Such stories established the pattern for more recent "eco-doom" stories, depicting future worlds reduced to pre-technological levels and ravaged by diseases.

The science fiction of the 1950s began to concentrate on the dangers of overpopulation, with such writers as Isaac Asimov and C. M. Kornbluth producing stories about crowded future worlds. Kornbluth's "Shark Ship" (1958) presented a memorable image of a world so densely populated that large numbers of people were forced to abandon land and sail back and forth in established longitudes of the ocean, harvesting all the sea life in their lanes for food.

Not surprisingly, stories of ecological catastrophe also became common during this period. The most famous and influential was John Christopher's *No Blade of Grass* (1956), a best-selling science fiction novel that showed the results of a virus that destroyed the world's crops. There were many such dark visions in the science fiction that followed, as writers widened their concerns to include endangered species of life, the alarming rate at which wilderness areas are vanishing, and problems of finding enough energy to maintain civilization at its present level.

All these concerns came together in science fiction's holistic visions of the past two decades. Overpopulation was no longer seen simply as the problem of city dwellers finding apartments larger than four square feet, but also of having too little heat to keep them warm in winter, too little food to save them from hunger, air that was unhealthy, and no wilderness left to which they could escape.

Clearly, science fiction stories are still the product of their times: this awareness of the interdependence of humanity's welfare and that of the whole planet came from widespread public knowledge about complex environmental problems, spurred first by scientists' predictions and most effectively by concerned ecological groups. Most people listened to the warnings and then forgot them, since their day-to-day lives were still relatively unchanged. But the future is the province and livelihood of science fiction writers, so they remembered what they'd heard and thought about it.

The stories in this book present a wide range of their conclusions. Most of them are set within the next hundred years, and all of them on Earth, by editorial fiat: stories of humanity escaping the problems we face on this planet by establishing colonies in space or on hypothetical other worlds are peripheral to our present concerns. Moving to new environments is a possibility, but first we have to concern ourselves with living on the planet of our birth.

So here are twenty stories about energy depletion, endangered species, pollution, our vanishing wilderness, overpopulation, and alternative energy sources—problems of the immediate future. Science fiction still tells of wondrous futures far away and a long time from now (the dreams are still with us), but these are stories of the boundaries that lie immediately before us. We're coming to the edge of something—is it to be the death of our world, or an endless future?

Before we think about next week, we need to know there'll be a tomorrow.

The Green Marauder

Larry Niven

We begin at the beginning, with a story of the distant past. Never mind that the setting is a cocktail lounge of the future—there are beings from many worlds here, and some of them have extremely long memories. One even remembers the very first polluters of Earth.

Larry Niven has been one of science fiction's most popular writers for fifteen years. He won both the Nebula and Hugo awards for his novel Ringworld, and produced a best-seller (in collaboration with Jerry Pournelle) in Lucifer's Hammer. His most recent novel is Ringworld Engineers.

I WAS TENDING BAR alone that night. The chirpsithra interstellar liner that had left Earth four days earlier had taken most of my customers. The Draco Tavern was nearly empty.

The man at the bar was drinking gin and tonic. Two glig—gray and compact beings, wearing furs in three tones of green—were at a table with a chirpsithra guide. They drank vodka and consommé, no ice, no flavorings. Four farsilshree had their bulky, heavy environment tanks crowded around a bigger table. They smoked smoldering yellow paste through tubes. Every so often I got them another jar of paste.

The man was talkative. I got the idea he was trying to interview the bartender and owner of Earth's foremost multi-species tavern.

"Hey, not me," he protested. "I'm not a reporter. I'm Greg Noyes, with the *Scientific American* TV show."

"Didn't I see you trying to interview the glig, earlier tonight?"

"Guilty. We're doing a show on the formation of life on Earth. I thought maybe I could check a few things. The gligstith(click)optok—" He said that slowly, but got it right. "—have their own little empire out there, don't they? Earthlike worlds, a couple of hundred. They must know quite a lot about how a world forms an oxygenating atmosphere." He was careful with those polysyllabic words. Not quite sober, then.

"That doesn't mean they want to waste an evening lecturing the natives."

He nodded. "They didn't know anyway. Architects on vacation. They got me talking about my home life. I don't know how they managed that." He pushed his drink away. "I'd better switch to espresso. Why would a thing that *shape* be interested in my sex life? And they kept asking me about territorial imperatives—" He stopped, then turned to see what I was staring at.

Three chirpsithra, just coming in. One was in a floating couch with life support equipment attached.

"I thought they all looked alike," he said.

I said, "I've had chirpsithra in here for close to thirty years, but I can't tell them apart. They're all perfect physical specimens, after all, by their own standards. I never saw one like *that*."

I gave him his espresso, then put three sparkers on a tray and went to the chirpsithra table.

Two were exactly like any other chirpsithra; eleven feet tall, dressed in pouched belts and their own salmon-colored exoskeletons, and very much at their ease. The chirps claim to have settled the entire galaxy long ago—meaning the useful planets, the tidally locked oxygen worlds that happen to circle close around cool red dwarf suns—and they act like the reigning queens of wherever they happen to be. But the two seemed to defer to the third. She was a foot shorter than they were. Her exoskeleton was as clearly artificial as dentures: alloplastic bone worn on the outside. Tubes ran under the edges from the equipment in her floating couch. Her skin between the plates was more gray than red. Her head turned slowly as I came up. She studied me, bright-eyed with interest.

I asked, "Sparkers?" as if chirpsithra ever ordered anything else.

One of the others said, "Yes, and serve the ethanol mix of your choice to yourself and the other native. Will you join us?"

I waved Noyes over, and he came at the jump. He pulled up one of the floating chairs I keep around to put a human face on a level with a chirpsithra's. I went for another espresso and a Scotch and soda and (catching a soft imperative *hoot* from the farsilshree) a jar of yellow paste. When I returned they were deep in conversation.

"Rick Schumann," Noyes cried, "meet Ftaxanthir and Hrofilliss and Chorrikst. Chorrikst tells me she's nearly two *billion* years old!"

I heard the doubt beneath his exuberance. The chirpsithra could be the greatest liars in the universe, and how would we ever know? Earth didn't even have interstellar probes when the chirps came.

Chorrikst spoke slowly, in a throaty whisper, but her translator box was standard: voice a little flat, pronunciation perfect. "I have circled the galaxy numberless times, and taped the tales of my travels for funds to feed my wanderlust. Much of my life has been spent at the edge of lightspeed, under relativistic time-compression. So you see, I am not nearly so old as all that."

I pulled up another floating chair. "You must have seen wonders beyond counting," I said. Thinking: *My God, a short chirpsithra! Maybe it's true. She's a different color too, and her fingers are shorter. Maybe the species has actually changed since she was born!*

She nodded slowly. "Life never bores. Always there is change. In the time I have been gone, Saturn's ring has been pulled into separate rings, making it even more magnificent. Tides from the moons? And Earth has changed beyond recognition."

Noyes spilled a little of his coffee. "You were here? When?"

"Earth's air was methane and ammonia and oxides of nitrogen and carbon. The natives had sent messages across interstellar space . . . directing them toward yellow suns, of course, but one of our ships passed through a beam; and so we established contact. We had to wear life support," she rattled on, while Noyes and I sat with our jaws hanging, "and the gear was less comfortable then. Our spaceport was a floating platform, because quakes were frequent and violent. But it was worth it. Their cities—"

Noyes said, "Just a minute. Cities? We've never dug up any trace of, of nonhuman cities."

Chorrikst looked at him. "After seven hundred and eighty million years, I should think not. Besides, they lived in the offshore shallows in a not very salty ocean. If the quakes spared them, their tools and their cities still deteriorated rapidly. Their lives were short too, but their memories were inherited. Death and change were accepted facts for them, more than for most intelligent species. Their works of philosophy gained great currency among my people, and spread to other species too."

Noyes wrestled with his instinct for tact and good manners, and won. "How? How could anything have evolved that far? The Earth didn't even have any oxygen atmosphere! Life was just getting started; there weren't even trilobites!"

"They had evolved for as long as you have," Chorrikst said with composure. "Life began on Earth one and a half billion years ago. There were organic chemicals in abundance, from passage of lightning through the reducing atmosphere. Intelligence evolved, and eventually built an impressive civilization. They lived slowly, of course. Their biochemistry

7

was less energetic. Communication was difficult. They were not stupid, only slow. I visited Earth three times, and each time they had made more progress."

Almost against his will, Noyes asked, "What did they look like?"

"Small and soft and fragile, much more so than yourselves. I cannot say they were pretty, but I grew to like them. I would toast them according to your customs," she said. "They wrought beauty in their cities and beauty in their philosophies, and their works are in our libraries still. They will not be forgotten."

She touched her sparker, and so did her younger companions. Current flowed between her two claws, through her nervous system. She said, "Sssss . . ."

I raised my glass, and nudged Noyes with my elbow. We drank to our predecessors. Noyes lowered his cup and asked, "What happened to them?"

"They sensed worldwide disaster coming," Chorrikst said, "and they prepared; but they thought it would be quakes. They built cities to float on the ocean surface, and lived underneath. They never noticed the green scum growing in certain tidal pools. By the time they knew the danger, the green scum was everywhere. It used photosynthesis to turn carbon dioxide into oxygen, and the raw oxygen killed whatever it touched, leaving fertilizer to feed the green scum. The world was dying when we learned of the problem, and then what could we do? A photosynthesis-using scum growing beneath a yellow-white star? There was nothing in our libraries that would help. We tried, of course, but we were unable to stop it. The sky had turned an admittedly lovely transparent blue, and the tide pools were green, and the offshore cities were crumbling before we gave up the fight. There was an attempt to transplant some of the natives to a suitable world; but biorhythm upset made them sterile. I have not been back since, until now."

The depressing silence was broken by Chorrikst herself. "Well, the Earth is greatly changed, and of course your own evolution began with the green plague. I have heard tales of humanity from my companions. Would you tell me something of your lives?"

And we spoke of humankind, but I couldn't seem to find much enthusiasm for it. The anaerobic life that survived the advent of photosynthesis includes gangrene and botulism and not much else. I wondered what Chorrikst would find when next she came, and whether she would have reason to toast our memory.

East Wind, West Wind

Frank M. Robinson

Present-day pollution is largely caused by internal combustion engines; everyone knows it, but despite soaring fuel prices we keep on using them. Designs for new engines that would reduce or eliminate pollution are announced every year, but none of them is currently in production. Why not? Perhaps the following story, set in a near future when internal combustion engines have been outlawed, gives the right answer . . . but let's hope not.

Frank M. Robinson's novels include The Power, which was adapted for a television movie, and The Glass Inferno, a collaboration with Thomas N. Scortia that served as a basis for the film The Towering Inferno.

I T WASN'T GOING to be just another bad day; it was going to be a terrible one. The inversion layer had slipped over the city four days before and it had been like putting a lid on a kettle; the air was building up to a real Donora, turning into a chemical soup so foul I wouldn't have believed it if I hadn't been trying to breathe the stuff. Besides sticking in my throat, it made my eyes feel like they were being bathed in acid. You could hardly see the sun—it was a pale, sickly disc floating in a mustard-colored sky—but even so, the streets were an oven and the humidity was so high you could have wrung the water out of the air with your bare hands . . . dirty water, naturally.

On the bus a red-faced salesman with denture breath recognized my Air Central badge and got pushy. I growled that we didn't *make* the air—not yet, at any rate—and finally I took off the badge and put it in my pocket and tried to shut out the coughing and the complaints around me by concentrating on the faint, cheery sound of the "corn poppers" laundering the bus's exhaust. Five would have gotten you ten, of course, that their effect was strictly psychological, that they had seen more than twenty thousand miles of service and were now absolutely worthless. . . .

At work I hung up my plastic sportcoat, slipped off the white surgeon's mask (black where my nose and mouth had been), and filled my lungs with good machine-pure air that smelled only faintly of oil and electric motors; one of the advantages of working for Air Central was that our office air was the best in the city. I dropped a quarter in the coffee vendor, dialed it black, and inhaled the fumes for a second while I shook the sleep from my eyes and speculated about what Wanda would have for me at the Investigators' Desk. There were thirty-nine other investigators besides myself, but I was junior and my daily assignment card was usually just a listing of minor complaints and violations that had to be checked out.

Wanda was young and pretty and red-haired and easy to spot even in a secretarial pool full of pretty girls. I offered her some of my coffee and looked over her shoulder while she flipped through the assignment cards. "That stuff out there is easier to swim through than to breathe," I said. "What's the index?"

"Eighty-four point five," she said quietly. "And rising."

I just stared at her. I had thought it was bad, but hardly that bad, and for the first time that day I felt a sudden flash of panic. "And no alert? When it hits seventy-five this city's supposed to close up like a clam!"

She nodded down the hall to the Director's office. "Lawyers from Sanitary Pick-Up, Oberhausen Steel, and City Light and Power got an injunction—they were here to break the news to Monte at eight sharp. Impractical, unnecessary, money-wasting, and fifteen thousand employees would be thrown out of work if they had to shut down the furnaces and incinerators. They got an okay right from the top of Air Shed Number Three."

My jaw dropped. "How could they? Monte's supposed to have the last word!"

"So go argue with the politicians—if you can stand the hot air." She suddenly looked very fragile and I wanted to run out and slay a dragon or two for her. "The chickenhearts took the easy way out, Jim. Independent Weather's predicting a cold front for early this evening and rising winds and rain for tomorrow."

The rain would clean up the air, I thought. But Independent

Weather could be bought, and as a result it had a habit of turning in cheery predictions that frequently didn't come true. Air Central had tried for years to get I.W. outlawed, but money talks and their lobbyist in the capital was quite a talker. Unfortunately, if they were wrong this time, it would be as if they had pulled a plastic bag over the city's head.

I started to say something, then shut up. If you let it get to you, you wouldn't last long on the job. "Where's my list of small-fry?"

She gave me an assignment card. It was blank except for "See Me" written across its face. "Humor him, Jim, he's not feeling well."

This worried me a little because Monte was the father of us all—a really sweet old guy, which hardly covers it all because he could be hard as nails when he had to. There wasn't anyone who knew more about air control than he.

I took the card and started up the hall and then Wanda called after me. She had stretched out her long legs and hiked up her skirt. I looked startled and she grinned. "Something new—sulfur-proof nylons." Which meant they wouldn't dissolve on a day like today, when a measurable fraction of the air we were trying to breathe was actually dilute sulfuric acid. . . .

When I walked into his office, old Monte was leaning out the window, the fly ash clinging to his bushy gray eyebrows like cinnamon to toast, trying to taste the air and predict how it would go today. We had eighty Sniffers scattered throughout the city, all computerized and delivering their data in neat, graphlike forms, but Monte still insisted on breaking internal air security and seeing for himself how his city was doing.

I closed the door. Monte pulled back inside, then suddenly broke into one of his coughing fits.

"Sit down, Jim," he wheezed, his voice sounding as if it were being wrung out of him. "Be with you in a minute." I pretended not to notice while his coughing shuddered to a halt and he rummaged through the desk for his little bottle of pills. It was a plain office, as executive offices went, except for Monte's own paintings on the wall—the type I like to call Twentieth Century Romantic. A mountain scene with a crystal-clear lake in the foreground and anglers battling huge trout, a city scene with palm trees lining the boulevards, and finally, one of a man standing by an old automobile on a winding mountain road while he looked off at a valley in the distance.

Occasionally Monte would talk to me about his boyhood around the Great Lakes and how he actually used to go swimming in them. Once he tried to tell me that orange trees used to grow within the city limits of Santalosdiego and that the oranges were as big as tennis balls. It irritated me and I think he knew it; I was the youngest investigator for Air Central but that didn't necessarily make me naive.

When Monte stopped coughing I said hopefully, "I.W. claims a cold front is coming in."

He huddled in his chair and dabbed at his mouth with a handkerchief, his thin chest working desperately, trying to pump his lungs full of air. "I.W.'s a liar," he finally rasped. "There's no cold front coming in; it's going to be a scorcher for three more days."

I felt uneasy again. "Wanda told me what happened," I said.

He fought for a moment longer for his breath, caught it, then gave a resigned shrug. "The bastards are right, to an extent. Stop garbage pick-ups in a city this size and within hours the rats will be fighting us in the streets. Shut down the power plants and you knock out all the air conditioners and purifiers—right during the hottest spell of the year. Then try telling the yokels that the air on the outside will be a whole lot cleaner if only they let the air on the inside get a whole lot dirtier."

He hunched behind his desk and drummed his fingers on the top while his face slowly turned to concrete. "But if they don't let me announce an alert by tomorrow morning," he said quietly, "I'll call in the newspapers and. . . ." The coughing started again and he stood up, a gnomelike little man slightly less alive with every passing day. He leaned against the windowsill while he fought the spasm. "And we think this is bad," he choked, half to himself. "What happens when the air coming in is as dirty as the air already here? When the Chinese and the Indonesians and the Hottentots get toasters and ice-boxes and all the other goodies?"

"Asia's not that industrialized yet," I said uncomfortably.

"Isn't it?" He turned and sagged back into his chair, hardly making a dent in the cushion. I was bleeding for the old man but I couldn't let him know it. I said in a low voice, "You wanted to see me," and handed him the assignment card.

He stared at it for a moment, his mind still on the Chinese, then came out of it and croaked, "That's right, give you something to chew on." He pressed a button on his desk and the wall opposite faded into a map of the city and the surrounding area, from the ocean on the west to the low-lying mountains on the east. He waved at the section of the city that straggled off into the canyons of the foothills. "Internal combustion engine—someplace back there." His voice was stronger now, his eyes more alert. "It isn't a donkey engine for a still or for electricity; it's a private automobile."

I could feel the hairs stiffen on the back of my neck. Usually I drew minor offenses, like trash burning or secret cigarette smoking, but owning or operating a gasoline-powered automobile was a felony, one that was sometimes worth your life.

"The Sniffer in the area confirms it," Monte continued in a tired voice, "but can't pinpoint it."

"Any other leads?"

"No, just this one report. But—we haven't had an internal combustion engine in more than three years." He paused. "Have fun with it; you'll probably have a new boss in the morning." *That* was something I didn't even want to think about. I had my hand on the doorknob when he said quietly, "The trouble with being boss is that you have to play Caesar and his Legions all the time."

It was as close as he came to saying good-bye and good luck. I didn't know what to say in return, or how to say it, and found myself staring at one of his canvases and babbling, "You sure used a helluva lot of blue."

"It was a fairly common color back then," he growled. "The sky was full of it."

And then he started coughing again and I closed the door in a hurry; in five minutes I had gotten so I couldn't stand the sound.

I had to stop in at the lab to pick up some gear from my locker and ran into Dave Ice, the researcher in charge of the Sniffers. He was a chubby, middle-aged little man with small, almost feminine hands; it was a pleasure to watch him work around delicate machinery. He was our top-rated man, after Monte, and I think if there was anybody whose shoes I wanted to step into someday, it would have been Dave Ice. He knew it, liked me for it, and usually went out of his way to help.

When I walked in he was changing a sheet of paper in one of the smoke shade detectors that hung just outside the lab windows. The sheet he was taking out looked as if it had been coated with lampblack.

"How long an exposure?"

He looked up, squinting over his bifocals. "Hi, Jim—a little more than four hours. It looks like it's getting pretty fierce out there."

"You haven't been out?"

"No, Monte and I stayed here all night. We were going to call an alert at nine this morning but I guess you know what happened."

I opened my locker and took out half a dozen new masks and a small canister of oxygen; if you were going to be out in traffic for any great length of time, you had to go prepared. Allowable vehicles were buses, trucks, delivery vans, police electrics, and the like. Not all exhaust control devices worked very well and even the electrics gave off a few acid fumes. And if you were stalled in a tunnel, the carbon monoxide ratings really zoomed. I hesitated at the bottom of the locker and then took out my small Mark II gyrojet and shoulder holster. It was pretty deadly stuff; no recoil and the tiny pocket pellet had twice the punch of a .45.

Dave heard the clink of metal and without looking up asked quietly, "Trouble?"

"Maybe," I said. "Somebody's got a private automobile—gasoline—and I don't suppose they'll want to turn it in."

"You're right," he said, sounding concerned, "they won't." And then: "I heard something about it; if it's the same report, it's three days old."

"Monte's got his mind on other things," I said. I slipped the masks into my pocket and belted on the holster. "Did you know he's still on his marching Chinese kick?"

Dave was concentrating on one of the Sniffer drums slowly rolling beneath its scribing pens, logging a minute-by-minute record of the hydrocarbons and the oxides of nitrogen and sulfur that were sickening the atmosphere. "I don't blame him," he said, absently running a hand over his glistening scalp. "They've started tagging chimney exhausts in Shanghai, Djakarta, and Mukden with radioactives—we should get the first results in another day or so."

The dragon's breath, I thought. When it finally circled the globe it would mean earth's air sink had lost the ability to cleanse itself and all of us would start strangling a little faster.

I got the rest of my gear and just before I hit the door, Dave said: "Jim?" I turned. He was wiping his hands on a paper towel and frowning at me over his glasses. "Look, take care of yourself, huh, kid?"

"Sure thing," I said. If Monte was my professional father, then Dave was my uncle. Sometimes it was embarrassing but right then it felt good. I nodded good-bye, adjusted my mask, and left.

Outside it seemed like dusk; trucks and buses had turned on their lights and almost all pedestrians were wearing masks. In a lot across the street some kids were playing tag and the thought suddenly struck me that nowadays most kids seemed small for their age, but I envied them—the air never seemed to bother kids. I watched for a moment, then started up the walk. A few doors down I passed an apartment building, half hidden in the growing darkness, that had received a "political influence" exemption a month before. Its incinerator was going full blast now, only instead of floating upward over the city the small charred bits of paper and garbage were falling straight down the front of the building like a kind of oily black snow.

I suddenly felt I was suffocating and stepped out into the street and hailed a passing electricab. Forest Hills, the part of the city that Monte had pointed out, was wealthy and the homes were large, though not so large that some of them couldn't be hidden away in the canyons and gullies of the foothills. If you lived on a side road or at the end of one of the canyons it might even be possible to hide a car out there and drive it only at night. And if any of your neighbors found out . . . well, the people who lived up in the relative pure air of the highlands had a different view of things than those who lived down in the atmospheric sewage of the flats. *But where would a man get a gasoline automobile in the first place?*

And did it all really matter? I thought, looking out the window of the cab at the deepening dusk and feeling depressed. Then I shook my head and leaned forward to give the driver instructions. Some places could be checked out relatively easily.

The Carriage Museum was elegant—and crowded, considering that it was a weekday. The main hall was a vast cave of black marble housing a parade of ancient internal combustion vehicles shining under the subdued lights; most of them were painted a lustrous black though there was an occasional gray and burst of red and a few sparkles of old gold from polished brass headlamps and fittings.

I felt like I was in St. Peter's, walking on a vast sea of marble while all about me the crowds shuffled along in respectful silence. I kept my eyes to the floor, reading off the names on the small bronze plaques: *Rolls Royce Silver Ghost, Mercer Raceabout, Isotta-Fraschini, Packard Runabout, Hispano-Suiza, Model J Duesenberg, Flying Cloud Reo, Cadillac Imperial V16, Pierce Arrow,* the first of the *Ford V8s, Lincoln Zephyr, Chrysler Windsor Club Coup.* . . . And in small halls off to the side, the lesser breeds: *Hudson Terraplane, Henry J., Willys Knight,* something called a *Jeepster,* the *Mustang, Knudsen,* the 1986 *Volkswagen,* the last *Chevrolet.* . . .

The other visitors to the museum were all middle-aged or older; the look on their faces was something I had never seen before— something that was not quite love and not quite lust. It flowed across their features like ripples of water whenever they brushed a fender or stopped at a hood that had been opened so they could stare at the engine, all neatly chromed or painted. They were like my father, I thought. They had owned cars when they were young, before Turn-In Day and the same date a year later when even most private steam and electrics were banned because of congestion. For a moment I wondered what it had been like to own one, then canceled the thought. The old man had tried to tell me often enough, before I had stormed out of the house for good, shouting how could he love the damned things so much when he was coughing his lungs out. . . .

The main hall was nothing but bad memories. I left it and looked up the office of the curator. His secretary was on a coffee break so I rapped sharply and entered without waiting for an answer. On the door it had said "C. Pearson," who turned out to be a thin, over-dressed type, all regal nose and pencil moustache, in his mid-forties. "Air Central," I said politely, flashing my wallet I.D. at him.

He wasn't impressed. "May I?" I gave it to him and he reached for the phone. When he hung up he didn't bother apologizing for the double check, which I figured made us even. "I have nothing to do with the heating system or the air conditioning," he said easily, "but if you'll wait a minute I'll—"

"I only want information," I said.

He made a small tent of his hands and stared at me over his fingertips. He looked bored. "Oh?"

I sat down and he leaned toward me briefly, then thought better of it and settled back in his chair. "How easy would it be," I asked casually, "to steal one of your displays?"

His moustache quivered slightly. "It wouldn't be easy at all— they're bolted down, there's no gasoline in their tanks, and the batteries are dummies."

"Then none ever have been?"

A flicker of annoyance. "No, of course not."

I flashed my best hat-in-hand smile and stood up. "Well, I guess that's it, then, I won't trouble you any further." But before I turned away I said, "I'm really not much on automobiles but I'm curious. How did the museum get started?"

He warmed up a little. "On Turn-In Day a number of museums like this one were started up all over the country. Some by former dealers, some just by automobile lovers. A number of models were donated for public display and. . . ."

When he had finished I said casually, "Donating a vehicle to a museum must have been a great ploy for hiding private ownership."

"Certainly the people in your bureau would be aware of how strict the government was," he said sharply.

"A lot of people must have tried to hide their vehicles," I persisted.

Dryly. "It would have been difficult . . . like trying to hide an elephant in a playpen."

But still, a number would have tried, I thought. They might even have stockpiled drums of fuel and some spare parts. In the city, of course, it would have been next to impossible. But in remote sections of the country, in the mountain regions out west or in the hills of the Ozarks or in the forests of northern Michigan or Minnesota or in the badlands of South Dakota. . . . A few would have succeeded, certainly, and perhaps late at night a few weed-grown stretches of highway would have been briefly lit by the headlights of automobiles flashing past with muffled exhausts, tires singing against the pavement. . . .

I sat back down. "Are there many automobile fans around?"

"I suppose so, if attendance records here are any indication."

"Then a smart man with a place in the country and a few automobiles could make quite a bit of money renting them out, couldn't he?"

He permitted himself a slight smile. "It would be risky. I really don't think anybody would try it. And from everything I've read, I rather think the passion was for actual ownership—I doubt that rental would satisfy that."

I thought about it for a moment while Pearson fidgeted with a letter opener and then, of course, I had it. "All those people who were fond of automobiles, there used to be clubs of them, right?"

His eyes lidded over and it grew very quiet in his office. But it was too late and he knew it. "I believe so," he said after a long pause, his voice tight, "but . . ."

"But the government ordered them disbanded," I said coldly. "Air Control regulations thirty-nine and forty, sections three through seven, 'concerning the dissolution of all organizations which in whole or in part, intentionally or unintentionally, oppose clean air.'" I knew the regulations by heart. "But there still are clubs, aren't there? Unregistered clubs? Clubs with secret membership files?" A light sheen of perspiration had started to gather on his forehead. "You would probably make a very good membership secretary, Pearson. You're in the perfect spot for recruiting new members—"

He made a motion behind his desk, and I dove over it and pinned his arms behind his back. A small address book had fallen to the floor and I scooped it up. Pearson looked as if he might faint. I ran my hands over his chest and under his arms and then let him go. He leaned against the desk, gasping for air.

"I'll have to take you in," I said.

A little color was returning to his cheeks and he nervously smoothed down his damp black hair. His voice was on the squeaky side. "What for? You have some interesting theories but . . ."

"My theories will keep for court," I said shortly. "You're under arrest for smoking—section eleven thirty point five of the Health and Safety Code." I grabbed his right hand and spread the fingers so the tell-tale signs showed. "You almost offered me a cigarette when I came in, then caught yourself. I would guess that ordinarily you're pretty relaxed and sociable, you probably smoke a lot—and you're generous with your tobacco. Bottom right-hand drawer for the stash, right?" I jerked it open and they were there, all right. "One cigarette's a misdemeanor, a carton's a felony, Pearson. We can accuse you of dealing and make it stick." I smiled grimly. "But we're perfectly willing to trade, of course."

I put in calls to the police and Air Central and sat down to wait for the cops to show. They'd sweat Pearson for all the information he had but I couldn't wait around a couple of hours. The word would spread that Pearson was being held, and Pearson himself would probably start remembering various lawyers and civil rights that he had momentarily forgotten. My only real windfall had been the address book. . . .

I thumbed through it curiously, wondering exactly how I could use it. The names were scattered all over the city, and there were a lot of them. I could weed it down to those in the area where the Sniffer had picked up the automobile, but that would take time and nobody was going to admit that he had a contraband vehicle hidden away anyway. The idea of paying a visit to the club I was certain must exist kept recurring to me, and finally I decided to pick a name, twist Pearson's arm for anything he might know about him, then arrange to meet at the club and work out from there.

Later, when I was leaving the museum, I stopped for a moment just inside the door to readjust my mask. While I was doing it, the janitor showed up with a roll of weatherstripping and started attaching it to the edge of the doorway where what looked like thin black smoke was seeping in from the outside. I was suddenly afraid to go back out there. . . .

The wind was whistling past my ears and a curve was coming up. I feathered the throttle, downshifted, and the needle on the tach started to drop. The wheel seemed to have a life of its own and twitched slightly to the right. I rode high on the outside of the track, the leafy limbs of trees that lined the asphalt dancing just outside my field of vision. The rear started to come around in a skid and I touched the throttle again and then the wheel twitched back to center and I was away. My eyes were riveted on Number Nine, just in front of me. It was the last lap, and if I could catch him there would be nothing between me and the checkered flag. . . .

I felt relaxed and supremely confident, at one with the throbbing power of the car. I red-lined it and through my dirt-streaked goggles I could see I was crawling up on the red splash that was Number Nine and next I was breathing the fumes from his twin exhausts. I took him on the final curve and suddenly I was alone in the world of the straightaway with the countryside peeling away on both sides of me, placid cows and ancient barns flowing past and then the rails lined with people. I couldn't hear their shouting above the scream of my car. Then I was flashing under banners stretched across the track and thundering toward the finish. There was the smell of burning rubber and spent oil and my own perspiration, the heat from the sun, the shimmering asphalt, and out of the corner of my eye a blur of grandstands and cars and a flag swooping down. . . .

And then it was over and the house lights had come up and I was hunched over a toy wheel in front of me, gripping it with both hands, the sweat pouring down my face and my stomach burning because I could still smell exhaust fumes and I wanted desperately to put on my face mask. It had been far more real than I had thought it would be—the curved screen gave the illusion of depth and each chair had been set up like a driver's seat. They had even pumped in odors. . . .

The others in the small theatre were stretching and getting ready to leave and I gradually unwound and got to my feet, still feeling shaky. "Lucky you could make it, Jim," a voice graveled in my ear. "You missed Joe Moore and the lecture but the documentary was just great, really great. Next week we've got *Meadowdale '73,* which has its moments but you don't feel like you're really there and getting an eyeful of cinders, if you know what I mean."

"Who's Joe Moore?" I mumbled.

"Old-time racetrack manager—full of anecdotes, knew all the great drivers. Hey! You okay?"

I was finding it difficult to come out of it. The noise and the action and the smell, but especially the feeling of actually driving—it was more than just a visceral response. You had to be raised down in the flats where you struggled for your breath every day to get the same feeling of revulsion, the same feeling of having done something dirty. . . .

"Yeah, I'm okay," I said. "I'm feeling fine."

"Where'd you say you were from, anyway?"

"Bosnywash," I lied. He nodded and I took a breath and time out to size him up. Jack Ellis was bigger and heavier than Pearson and not nearly as smooth or as polished—Pearson perspired; my bulky friend sweated. He was in his early fifties, thinning brown hair carefully waved, the beginning of a small paunch well hidden by a lot of expensive tailoring, and a hulking set of shoulders that were much more than just padding. A business bird, I thought. The hairy-chested genial back-slapper. . . .

"You seen the clubrooms yet?"

"I just got in," I said. "First time here."

"Hey, great! I'll show you around!" He talked like he was pro-grammed. "A little fuel and a couple of stiff belts first, though—dining room's out of this world. . . ."

And it almost was. We were on the eighty-seventh floor of the new

Trans-America building and Ellis had secured a window seat. Above, the sky was almost as bright a blue as Monte had used in his paintings. I couldn't see the street below.

"Have a card," Ellis said, shoving the pasteboard at me. It read WARSHAWSKY & WARSHAWSKY, AUTOMOTIVE ANTIQUES, with an address in the Avenues. He waved a hand at the room. "We decorated all of this—pretty classy, huh?"

I had to give him that. The walls were covered with murals of old road races, while from some hidden sound system came a faint, subdued purring—the roaring of cars drifting through the esses of some long-ago race. In the center of the room was a pedestal holding a highly-chromed engine block that slowly revolved under a baby spot. While I was admiring the setting a waitress came up and set down a lazy Susan; it took a minute to recognize it as an old-fashioned wooden steering wheel, fitted with sterling silver hors d'oeuvre dishes between the spokes.

Ellis ran a thick thumb down the menu. "Try a Barney Oldfield," he suggested. "Roast beef and American cheese on pumpernickel."

While I was eating I got the uncomfortable feeling that he was looking me over and that somehow I didn't measure up. "You're pretty young," he said at last. "We don't get many young members—or visitors, for that matter."

"Grandfather was a dealer," I said easily. "Had a Ford agency in Milwaukee—I guess it rubbed off."

He nodded around a mouthful of sandwich and looked mournful for a moment. "It used to be a young man's game, kids worked on engines in their backyards all the time. Just about everybody owned a car. . . ."

"You, too?"

"Oh sure—hell, the old man ran a gas station until Turn-In Day." He was lost in his memories for a moment, then said, "You got a club in Bosnywash?"

"A few, nothing like this," I said cautiously. "And the law's pretty stiff." I nodded at the window. "They get pretty uptight about the air back east. . . ." I let my voice trail off.

He frowned. "You don't *believe* all that guff, do you? Biggest goddamn pack of lies there ever was, but I guess you got to be older to know it. Power plants and incinerators, they're the ones to blame, always have been. Hell, people too—every time you exhale you're polluting the atmosphere, ever think of that? And Christ, man, think of every time you work up a sweat."

"Sure," I nodded, "sure, it's always been blown up." I made a mental note that someday I'd throw the book at Ellis.

He finished his sandwich and started wiping his fat face like he was erasing a blackboard. "What's your interest? Mine's family sedans, the old family workhorse. Fords, Chevys, Plymouths—got a case of all the models from '50 on up, one-eighteenth scale. How about you?"

I didn't answer him, just stared out the window and worked with a toothpick for a long time until he began to get a little nervous. Then I let it drop. "I'm out here to buy a car," I said.

His face went blank, as if somebody had just pulled down a shade. "Damned expensive hobby," he said, ignoring it. "Should've taken up photography instead."

"It's for a friend of mine," I said. "Money's no object."

The waitress came around with the check and Ellis initialed it. "Damned expensive," he repeated vaguely.

"I couldn't make a connection back home," I said. "Friends suggested I try out here."

He was watching me now. "How would you get it back east?"

"Break it down," I said. "Ship it east as crates of machine parts."

"What makes you think there's anything for sale out here?"

I shrugged. "Lots of mountains, lots of forests, lots of empty space, lots of hiding places. Cars were big out here; there must have been a number that were never turned in."

"You're a stalking horse for somebody big, aren't you!"

"What do you think?" I said. "And what difference does it make anyway? Money's money."

If it's true that the pupil of the eye expands when it sees something that it likes, it's also true that it contracts when it doesn't—and right then his were in the cold buckshot stage.

"All right," he finally said. "Cash on the barrelhead and remember, when you have that much money changing hands, it can get dangerous." He deliberately leaned across the table so that his coat flapped open slightly. The small gun and holster were almost lost against the big man's girth. He sat back and spun the lazy Susan with a fat forefinger, spearing an olive as it slid past. "You guys run true to form," he continued quietly. "Most guys from back east come out to buy—I guess we've got a reputation." He hesitated. "We also try and take all the danger out of it."

He stood up and slapped me on the back as I pushed to my feet. It was the old Jack Ellis again, he of the instant smile and the sparkling teeth.

"That is, we try and take the danger out of it for *us,*" he added pleasantly.

It was late afternoon and the rush hour had started. It wasn't as heavy as usual—businesses had been letting out all day—but it was bad enough. I slipped on a mask and started walking toward the warehouse

21

section of town, just outside the business district. The buses were too crowded and it would be impossible to get an electricab that time of day. Besides, traffic was practically standing still in the steamy murk. Headlights were vague yellow dots in the gathering darkness and occasionally I had to shine my pocket flash on a street sign to determine my location.

I had checked in with Monte, who said the hospitals were filling up fast with bronchitis victims; I didn't ask about the city morgue. The venal bastards at Air Shed Number Three were even getting worried; they had promised Monte that if it didn't clear by morning, he could issue his alert and close down the city. I told him I had uncovered what looked like a car ring but he sounded only faintly interested. He had bigger things on his mind; the ball was in my court and what I was going to do with it was strictly up to me.

A few more blocks and the crowds thinned. Then I was alone on the street with the warehouses hulking up in the gloom around me, ancient monsters of discolored brick and concrete layered with years of soot and grime. I found the address I wanted, leaned against the buzzer by the loading dock door, and waited. There was a long pause, then faint steps echoed inside and the door slid open. Ellis stood in the yellow dock light, the smile stretching across his thick face like a rubber band. "Right on time," he whispered. "Come on in, Jim, meet the boys."

I followed him down a short passageway, trying not to brush up against the filthy whitewashed walls. Then we were up against a steel door with a peephole. Ellis knocked three times, the peephole opened, and he said, "Joe sent me." I started to panic. *For God's sake, why the act?* Then the door opened and it was as if somebody had kicked me in the stomach. What lay beyond was a huge garage with at least half a dozen ancient cars on the tool-strewn floor. Three mechanics in coveralls were working under the overhead lights; two more were waiting inside the door. They were bigger than Ellis and I was suddenly very glad I had brought along the Mark II.

"Jeff, Ray, meet Mr. Morrison." I held out my hand. They nodded at me, no smiles. "C'mon," Ellis said, "I'll show you the set-up." I tagged after him and he started pointing out the wonders of his domain. "Completely equipped garage—my old man would've been proud of me. Overhead hoist for pulling motors, complete lathe set-up . . . a lot of parts we have to machine ourselves, can't get the originals anymore, and of course the last of the junkers was melted down a long time ago." He stopped by a workbench with a large rack full of tools gleaming behind it. "One of the great things about being in the antique business, you hit all the country auctions and you'd be surprised at what you can pick up. Complete sets of torque wrenches, metric socket sets, spanner wrenches, feeler gauges, you name it."

22

I looked over the bench—he was obviously proud of the assortment of tools—then suddenly felt the small of my back grow cold. It was phony, I thought, the whole thing was phony. But I couldn't put my finger on just why.

Ellis walked over to one of the automobiles on the floor and patted a fender affectionately. Then he unbuttoned his coat so that the pistol showed, hooked his thumbs in his vest, leaned against the car behind him, and smiled. Someplace he had even found a broomstraw to chew on.

"So what can we do for you, Jim? Limited stock, sky-high prices, but never a dissatisfied customer!" He poked an elbow against the car behind him. "Take a look at this '73 Chevy Biscayne, probably the only one of its kind in this condition in the whole damned country. Ten thou and you can have it—and that's only because I like you." He sauntered over to a monster in blue and silver with grillwork that looked like a set of kitchen knives. "Or maybe you'd like a '76 Caddy convertible, all genuine simulated-leather upholstery, one of the last of the breed." He didn't add why but I already knew—in heavy traffic the high levels of monoxide could be fatal to a driver in an open car.

"Yours," Ellis was saying about another model, "for a flat fifteen"—he paused and shot me a friendly glance—"oh hell, for you, Jim, make it twelve and a half and take it from me, it's a bargain. Comes with the original upholstery and tires and there's less than ten thousand miles on it—the former owner was a little old lady from Pasadena who only drove it to weddings."

He chuckled at that, looking at me expectantly. I didn't get it. "Maybe you'd just like to look around. Be my guest, go right ahead." His eyes were bright and he looked very pleased with himself; it bothered me.

"Yeah," I said absently, "I think that's what I'd like to do." There was a wall phone by an older model and I drifted over to it.

"That's an early Knudsen two-seater," Ellis said. "Popular make for the psychedelic set; that paint job is the way they really came."

I ran my hand lightly down the windshield, then turned to face the cheerful Ellis. "You're under arrest," I said. "You and everybody else here."

His face suddenly looked like shrimp in molded gelatin. One of the mechanics behind him moved and I had the Mark II out winging a rocket past his shoulder. No noise, no recoil, just a sudden shower of sparks by the barrel and in the far end of the garage a fifty-gallon oil drum went *karrump* and there was a hole in it you could have stuck your head through.

The mechanic went white. *"Jesus Christ, Jack, you brought in some kind of nut!"* Ellis himself was pale and shaking, which surprised me; I thought he'd be tougher than that.

"Against the bench," I said coldly, waving the pistol. "Hands in front of your crotch and don't move them." The mechanics were obviously scared stiff and Ellis was having difficulty keeping control. I took down the phone and called in.

After I hung up, Ellis mumbled, "What's the charge?"

"Charges," I corrected. "Sections three, four, and five of the Air Control laws. Maintenance, sale, and use of internal combustion engines."

Ellis stared at me blankly. "You don't know?" he asked faintly.

"Know what?"

"I don't handle internal combustion engines." He licked his lips. "I really don't, it's too risky, it's . . . against the law."

The workbench, I suddenly thought. The goddamned workbench. I knew something was wrong then; I should have cooled it.

"You can check me," Ellis offered weakly. "Lift a hood, look for yourself."

He talked like his face was made of panes of glass sliding against one another. I waved him forward. *You* check it, Ellis, you open one up." Ellis nodded like a dipping duck, waddled over to one of the cars, jiggled something inside, then raised the hood and stepped back.

I took one glance and my stomach slowly started to knot up. I was no motor buff but I damned well knew the difference between a gasoline engine and a water boiler. Which explained the workbench—the tools had been window dressing. Most of them were brand-new because most of them had obviously never been used. There had been nothing to use them on.

"The engines are steam," Ellis said, almost apologetically. "I've got a license to do restoration work and drop in steam engines. They don't allow them in cities but it's different on farms and country estates and in some small towns." He looked at me. "The license cost me a goddamned fortune."

It was a real handicap being a city boy, I thought. "Then why the act? Why the gun?"

"This?" he asked stupidly. He reached inside his coat and dropped the pistol on the floor; it made a light thudding sound and bounced, a pot-metal toy. "The danger, it's the sense of danger, it's part of the sales pitch." He wanted to be angry now but he had been frightened too badly and couldn't quite make it. "The customers pay a lot of dough, they want a little drama. That's why—you know—the peephole and everything." He took a deep breath and when he exhaled it came out as a giggle, an incongruous sound from the big man. I found myself hoping

24

he didn't have a heart condition. "I'm well known," he said defensively. "I take ads. . . ."

"The club," I said. "It's illegal."

Even if it was weak, his smile was genuine and then the score became crystal clear. The club was like a speakeasy during the Depression, with half the judges and politicians in town belonging to it. Why not? Somebody older wouldn't have my bias. . . . Pearson's address book had been all last names and initials but I had never connected any of them to anybody prominent; I hadn't been around enough to know what connection to make.

I waved Ellis back to the workbench and stared glumly at the group. The mechanic I had frightened with the Mark II had a spreading stain across the front of his pants and I felt sorry for him momentarily.

Then I started to feel sorry for myself. Monte should have given me a longer briefing, or maybe assigned another investigator to go with me, but he had been too sick and too wrapped up with the politics of it all. So I had gone off half-cocked and come up with nothing but a potential lawsuit for Air Central that would probably amount to a million dollars by the time Ellis got through with me.

It was a black day inside as well as out.

I holed up in a bar during the middle part of the evening, which was probably the smartest thing I could have done. Despite their masks, people on the street had started to retch and vomit, and I could feel my own nausea grow with every step. I saw one man try and strike a match to read a street sign; it wouldn't stay lit, there simply wasn't enough oxygen in the air. The ambulance sirens were a steady wail now and I knew it was going to be a tough night for heart cases. They'd be going like flies before morning, I thought. . . .

Another customer slammed through the door, wheezing and coughing and taking huge gulps of the machine-pure air of the bar. I ordered another drink and tried to shut out the sound; it was too reminiscent of Monte hacking and coughing behind his desk at work.

And come morning, Monte might be out of a job, I thought. I for certain would be; I had loused up in a way that would cost the department money—the unforgivable sin in the eyes of the politicians.

I downed half my drink and started mentally reviewing the events of the day, giving myself a passing score only on figuring out that Pearson had had a stash. I hadn't known about Ellis's operation, which in one sense wasn't surprising. Nobody was going to drive something that looked like an old gasoline-burner around a city—the flatlanders would stone him to death.

But somebody still had a car, I thought. Somebody who was rich and immune from prosecution and a real nut about cars in the first place. . . . But it kept sliding away from me. Really rich men were too much in the public eye, ditto politicians. They'd be washed up politically if anybody ever found out. If nothing else, some poor bastard like the one at the end of the bar trying to flush out his lungs would assassinate him.

Somebody with money, but not too much. Somebody who was a car nut—they'd have to be to take the risks. And somebody for whom those risks were absolutely minimal. . . .

And then the lightbulb flashed on above my head, just like in the old cartoons. I wasn't dead certain I was right but I was willing to stake my life on it—and it was possible I might end up doing just that.

I slipped on a mask and almost ran out of the bar. Once outside, I sympathized with the guy who had just come in and who had given me a horrified look as I plunged out into the darkness.

It was smothering now, though the temperature had dropped a little so my shirt didn't cling to me in dirty, damp folds. Buses were being led through the streets; headlights died out completely within a few feet. The worst thing was that they left tracks in what looked like a damp, grayish ash that covered the street. Most of the people I bumped into—mere shadows in the night—had soaked their masks in water, trying to make them more effective. There were lights still on in the lower floors of most of the office buildings and I figured some people hadn't tried to make it home at all; the air was probably purer among the filing cabinets than in their own apartments. Two floors up, the buildings were completely hidden in the smoky darkness.

It took a good hour of walking before the sidewalks started to slant up and I knew I was getting out toward the foothills . . . . I thanked God the business district was closer to the mountains than the ocean. My legs ached and my chest hurt and I was tired and depressed but at least I wasn't coughing anymore.

The buildings started to thin out and the streets finally became completely deserted. Usually the cops would pick you up if they caught you walking on the streets of Forest Hills late at night, but that night I doubted they were even around. They were probably too busy ferrying cases of cardiac arrest to St. Francis. . . .

The Sniffer was located on top of a small, ancient building off on a side street. When I saw it I suddenly found my breath hard to catch again—a block down, the street abruptly turned into a canyon and wound up and out of sight. I glanced back at the building, just faintly visible through the grayed-down moonlight. The windows were boarded up and there was a For Rent sign on them. I walked over and flashed my light on the sign. It was old and peeling and had obviously been there for years; apparently nobody had ever wanted to rent the first floor. Ever? Maybe somebody had, I thought, but had decided to leave it boarded up. I ran my hand down the boards and suddenly paused at a knothole; I could feel heavy plate glass through it. I knelt and flashed my light at the hole and looked at a dim reflection of myself staring back. The glass had been painted black on the inside so it acted like a black marble mirror.

I stepped back and something about the building struck me. The boarded-up windows, I thought, the huge, oversized windows. . . . And the oversized, boarded-up doors. I flashed the light again at the concrete facing just above the doors. The words were there all right, blackened by time but still readable, cut into the concrete itself by order of the proud owner a handful of decades before. But you could still noodle them out: *RICHARD SIEBEN LINCOLN-MERCURY.*

Jackpot, I thought triumphantly. I glanced around—there was nobody else on the street—and listened. Not a sound, except for the faint murmur of traffic still moving in the city far away. A hot, muggy night in the core city, I thought, but this night the parks and the fire escapes would be empty and five million people would be tossing and turning in their cramped little bedrooms; it'd be suicide to try and sleep outdoors.

In Forest Hills it was cooler—and quieter. I glued my ear to the boards over the window and thought I could hear the faint shuffle of somebody walking around and, once, the faint clink of metal against metal. I waited a moment, then slipped down to the side door that had "Air Central" on it in neat black lettering. All Investigators had master keys and I went inside. Nobody was upstairs; the lights were out and the only sound was the soft swish of the Sniffer's scribing pens against the paper roll. There was a stairway in the back and I walked silently down it. The door at the bottom was open and I stepped through it into a short hallway. Something, maybe the smell of the air, told me it had been used recently. I closed the door after me and stood for a second in the darkness. There was no sound from the door beyond. I tried the knob and it moved silently in my grasp.

I cracked the door open and peered through the slit—nothing—then eased it open all the way and stepped out onto the showroom floor. There was a green-shaded lightbulb hanging from the ceiling, swaying slightly in some minor breeze so the shadows chased each other around the far corners of the room. Walled off at the end were two small offices where salesmen had probably wheeled and dealed long ago. There wasn't much else, other than a few tools scattered around the floor in the circle of light.

And directly in the center, of course, the car.

I caught my breath. There was no connection between it and Jack Ellis's renovated family sedans. It crouched there on the floor, a

27

mechanical beast that was almost alive. Sleek curving fenders that blended into a louvered hood with a chromed steel bumper curving flat around the front to give it an oddly sharklike appearance. The head-lamps were set deep into the fenders, the lamp wells outlined with chrome. The hood flowed into a windshield and that into a top which sloped smoothly down in back and tucked in neatly just after the rear wheels. The wheels themselves had wire spokes that gleamed wickedly in the light, and through a side window I could make out a neat array of meters and rocker switches, and finally bucket seats covered with what I instinctively knew was genuine black leather.

Sleek beast, powerful beast, I thought. I was unaware of walking up to it and running my hand lightly over a fender until a voice behind me said, "It's beautiful, isn't it?"

I turned like an actor in a slow-motion film. "Yeah, Dave," I said, "it's beautiful." Dave Ice of Air Central. In charge of all the Sniffers.

He must have been standing in one of the salesman's offices; it was the only way I could have missed him. He walked up and stood on the other side of the car and ran his left hand over the hood with the same affectionate motion a woman might use in stroking her cat. In his right hand he held a small Mark II pointed directly at my chest.

"How'd you figure it was me?" he asked casually.

"I thought at first it might be Monte," I said. "Then I figured you were the real nut about machinery."

His eyes were bright, too bright. "Tell me," he asked curiously, "would you have turned in Monte?"

"Of course," I said simple. I didn't add that it would have been damned difficult; that I hadn't even been able to think about that part of it.

"So might've I, so might've I," he murmured, "when I was your age."

"For a while the money angle threw me," I said.

He smiled faintly. "It's a family heirloom. My father bought it when he was young; he couldn't bring himself to turn it in." He cocked his head. "Could you?" I looked at him uneasily and didn't answer and he said casually, "Go ahead, Jimmy, you were telling me how you cracked the case."

I flushed. "It had to be somebody who knew—who was absolutely sure—that he wasn't going to get caught. The Sniffers are pretty efficient; it would have been impossible to prevent their detecting the car—the best thing would be to censor the data from them. And Monte and you were the only ones who could have done that."

Another faint smile. "You're right."

"You slipped up a few nights ago," I said.

He shrugged. "Anybody could've. I was sick, I didn't get to the office in time to doctor the record."

"It gave the game away," I said. "Why only once? The Sniffer should have detected it far more often than just once."

He didn't say anything and for a long moment both of us were lost in admiration of the car.

Then finally, proudly: "It's the real McCoy, Jim. Six-cylinder inline engine, 4.2 liters displacement, nine-to-one compression ratio, twin overhead cams, and twin Zenith-Stromberg carbs. . . ." He broke off. "You don't know what I'm talking about, do you?"

"No," I confessed, "I'm afraid not."

"Want to see the motor?"

I nodded and he stepped forward, waved me back with the Mark II, and opened the hood. To really appreciate it, of course, you had to have a thing for machinery. It was clean and polished and squatted there under the hood like a beautiful mechanical pet—so huge I wondered how the hood could close at all.

And then I realized with a shock that I hadn't been reacting like I should have, that I hadn't reacted like I should have ever since the movie at the club. . . .

"You can sit in it if you want to," Dave said softly. "Just don't touch anything." His voice was soft. "Everything works on it, Jim, everything works just dandy. It's oiled and greased and the tank is full and the battery charged and if you wanted to, you could drive it right off the showroom floor."

I hesitated. "People in the neighborhood—"

"—mind their own business," he said. "They have a different attitude, and besides, it's usually late at night and I'm out in the hills in seconds. Go ahead, get in." Then his voice hardened into command: "Get in!"

I stalled a second longer, then opened the door and slid into the seat. The movie was real now; I was holding the wheel and could sense the gearshift at my right, and in my mind's eye I could feel the wind and hear the scream of the motor. . . .

There was something hard pressing against the side of my head. I froze. Dave was holding the pistol just behind my ear and in the side mirror I could see his finger tense on the trigger and pull back a millimeter. *Dear God.* . . .

He relaxed. "You'll have to get out," he said apologetically. "It would be appropriate, but a mess just the same."

I got out. My legs were shaking and I had to lean against the car. "It's a risky thing to own a car," I chattered. "Feeling runs pretty high against cars. . . ."

He nodded. "It's too bad."

"You worked for Air Central for years," I said. "How could you do it, and own this, too?"

"You're thinking about the air," he said carefully. "But Jim"—his voice was patient—"machines don't foul the air, men do. They foul the air, the lakes, and the land itself. And there's no way to stop it." I started to protest and he held up a hand. "Oh sure, there's always a time when you care—like you do now. But time . . . you know, time wears you down, it really does, no matter how eager you are. You devote your life to a cause and then you find yourself suddenly growing fat and bald and you discover nobody gives a damn about your cause. They're paying you your cushy salary to buy off their own consciences. So long as there's a buck to be made, things won't change much. It's enough to drive you—" He broke off. "You don't *really* think that anybody gives a damn about anybody else, do you?" He stood there looking faintly amused, a pudgy little man whom I should've been able to take with one arm tied behind my back. But he was ten times as dangerous as Ellis had ever imagined himself to be. "Only suckers care, Jim. I . . ."

I dropped to the floor then, rolling fast to hit the shadows beyond the circle of light. His Mark II sprayed sparks and something burned past my shirt collar and squealed along the concrete floor. I sprawled flat and jerked my own pistol out. The first shot went low and there was the sharp sound of scored metal and I cursed briefly to myself—I must have brushed the car. Then there was silence and I scrabbled further back into the darkness. I wanted to pot the light but the bulb was still swaying back and forth and chances were I'd miss and waste the shot. Then there was the sound of running and I jumped to my feet and saw Dave heading for the door I had come in by. He seemed oddly defenseless—he was chubby and slow and knock-kneed and ran like a woman.

"Dave!" I screamed. "Dave! STOP!"

It was an accident, there was no way to help it. I aimed low and to the side, to knock him off his feet, and at the same time he decided to do what I had done and sprawled flat in the shadows. If he had stayed on his feet, the small rocket would have brushed him at knee level. As it was, it smashed his chest.

He crumpled and I ran up and caught him before he could hit the floor. He twisted slightly in my arms so he was staring at the car as he died. I broke into tears. I couldn't help that, either. I would remember the things Dave had done for me long after I had forgotten that one night he had tried to kill me. A threat to kill is unreal—actual blood and shredded flesh has its own reality.

I let him down gently and walked slowly over to the phone in the corner. Monte should still be in his office, I thought. I dialed and said, "The Director, please," and waited for the voice-actuated relay to connect me. "Monte, Jim Morrison here. I'm over at—" I paused. "I'm sorry, I thought it was Monte—" And then I shut up and let the voice at the other end of the line tell me that Monte had died with the window open and the night air filling his lungs with urban vomit. "I'm sorry," I said faintly, "I'm sorry, I'm very sorry," but the voice went on and I suddenly realized that I was listening to a recording and that there was nobody in the office at all. Then, as the voice continued, I knew why.

I let the receiver fall to the floor and the record started in again, as if expecting condolences from the concrete.

I should call the cops, I thought. I should—

But I didn't. Instead, I called Wanda. It would take an hour or more for her to collect the foodstuffs in the apartment and to catch an electricab but we could be out of the city before morning came.

And that was pretty funny because morning was never coming. The recording had said dryly that the tagged radioactive chimney exhausts had arrived, that the dragon's breath had circled the globe and the winds blowing in were as dirty as the air already over the city. Oh, it wouldn't happen right away, but it wouldn't be very long, either. . . .

Nobody had given a damn, I thought; not here nor any other place. Dave had been right, dead right. They had finally turned it all into a sewer and the last of those who cared had coughed his lungs out trying for a breath of fresh air that had never come, too weak to close a window.

I walked back to the car sitting in the circle of light and ran a finger down the scored fender where the small rocket had scraped the paint. Dave would never have forgiven me, I thought. Then I opened the door and got in and settled slowly back into the seat. I fondled the shift and ran my eyes over the instrument panel, the speedometer and the tach and the fuel and the oil gauges and the small clock. . . . The keys dangled from the button at the end of the hand brake. It was a beautiful piece of machinery, I thought again. I had never really loved a piece of machinery . . . until now.

I ran my hands around the wheel, then located the starter switch on the steering column. I jabbed in the key and closed my eyes and listened to the scream of the motor and felt its power shake the car and wash over me and thunder through the room. The movie at the club had been my only lesson but in its own way it had been thorough and it would be enough. I switched off the motor and waited.

When Wanda got there we would take off for the high ground. For the mountains and the pines and that last clear lake and that final glimpse of blue sky before it all turned brown and we gave up in final surrender to this climate of which we're so obviously proud. . . .

People's Park

Charles Ott

Our environmental problems go considerably beyond pollution; for instance, there's the fact that beautiful wilderness areas are being steadily eliminated by lumber companies and encroached on by our growing population. Even our national parks are suffering from "people pollution." If the government were to take drastic steps against this, what might happen?

Charles Ott is not a prolific writer, but the stories he does produce are thoughtful and thought-provoking.

THE HILLS WERE a glory. I shucked off my pack and lay down my rifle just to watch the evening dusk rise like tidewater through the golden forest. The autumn sky was steel blue, the trees like a hearth fire. It was the best time of the day, the best time of year. . . . I found I had been holding my breath.

A wood thrush sailed over my head and landed on a sapling across the stream I had been following. It did a little bouncing dance for me, singing against the water noise, and flew away when I laughed. I decided to make camp where I was; I had covered enough territory that day. I sat on a rock beetling over a deep, clear pool and pulled out the blue plastic notebook the Park Commission insisted I keep. It wasn't much more than makework, a record of areas inspected during the day. But I knew they would cheerfully fire me, in spite of all the money I had paid them to get this job, if I was slack in anything. There were ten dozen applicants for every place in the clearing program, but I intended to stay for the full six weeks by being careful. It meant a lot to me.

It was amber dusk and then blue evening before I had my tent set up and a fire laid. I was grilling a fresh caught trout for supper when the floater arrived.

It drifted in over the stream clearing, the little wake causing a flurry of sparks from the fire. It was a basketball-sized thing on its propeller platform, all lenses and antennas. The lenses shifted as it settled to the ground.

"Hullo, Peterson," it said. I knew by the voice it was Almack, the night-duty officer back at Park Headquarters. "Is that trout you're having? It looks good, I must say."

I was going to make some flip remark about the soy cutlet I knew Almack would have dined on, but I decided it would be cruel. "It is," I said simply. "What brings you out here at this hour?"

"You're not going to like this," he sighed, "but we want you to check up on a trace the trail sensors have reported."

"At night? I could get killed stumbling around in the dark. Let it go until morning, why don't you?"

"The trace is moving your way," he said patiently. "The infra-red picked it up and it's about the right size to be a hider. If so, he'll have to pass through here, because this is the only good pass through the hills in the area."

"He?" I snorted. "More likely, it's a brown bear with insomnia." But I added quickly, "I'll get set up." I certainly wasn't going to jeopardize my six weeks over one night's lost sleep.

"Good," said Almack. "I've got some other business to attend to, but he should arrive here in about an hour, and I'll try to return before then. Leave the radio beacon on." The floater took off quietly, rising lightly over the trees and pirouetting slowly while Almack located the moon just appearing in the east to get his bearings. Then it was gone.

I quickly doused the fire and threw the remains into the stream to kill the odor of burning wood. The tent folded easily and I brushed the ground with a bough to remove my tracks. In twenty minutes I was hidden in an outcropping of glacial rock looking down on the clearing and affording a good field of fire over the pass. After checking the clip of tranquilizer darts in my rifle, I set up the starlight scope and carefully considered every possible angle of approach. If it was a hider, he had probably left his hiding place to try to get to town, possibly for medical supplies or ammunition. If so, that made him a very stupid outlaw.

Almack returned some time later. Without the fire to guide him, the poor night vision of the floater obliged him to come in slowly, with much hesitation. Finally the floater settled near me and the fan rolled to a stop. The living silence of the forest returned. We waited.

There was a small sound. I saw the hider in the spectral glow of the starlight scope, a graying middle-aged man, bent low and sniffing the air like an uncertain wolf. He traveled quickly but lightly, and he stepped into the clearing suddenly. I had no thought of "fair warning," no halt-you-are-trespassing-in-a-public-park. I took quick aim at his torso and fired.

There was a splash of white liquid from his belt buckle as he whirled and leapt away without a sound. "That was a bit clumsy of you," said Almack, complacent and malicious. I was up with a curse, running with high dodging steps after him. His white head appeared momentarily between two trees and I loosed a shot without pausing. It went wide.

He vanished down a ravine and I knew I had lost him. I stood panting in the clearing until Almack's floater caught up with me. "Did you notice," he asked conversationally, "whether any of the liquid had splashed on his skin?" I told him it had. "Good," he said. "It's a contact-type drug. Even a small amount should begin to slow him up shortly, I should think."

It was an order. "All right," I answered, controlling my breathing, "I'll go find him." As I entered the dimly lit forest the floater rose and went into one of the automatic holding patterns. Probably Almack had gone out for coffee.

I set out for the point where I had last seen my quarry, straining for vision in the occasional scraps of moonlight. It was a thickly grown, steeply eroded little cut he had found. I decided against entering it and walked along the edge, peering into the viscous darkness below. Presently I sat down and pulled the starlight scope from its leg holster. I was sweeping with it when he jumped me from behind.

His hands were on my neck and his knees on my back and still he made no sound. I bucked and rolled desperately, trying to hit him with the scope. His face was demonic, lit in pale planes. He shifted weight just as I heaved and momentum carried us both over the edge of the ravine, sliding and tumbling in the raw yellow soil. We rolled and clutched at each other, scrabbling through falling sheets of rocks and grit, legs flapping. I came up against a branched stump with a painful jar and he careened into me and past, wrenching my leg. I heard him hit something solid, followed by a liquid splash. I blacked out.

Almack awoke me sometime later, the floater humming in front of me. "Are you all right?" he asked. "Where's the hider?"

"Down there," I grunted, motioning fuzzily, "I don't think I can move."

"Well, don't worry. We'll have a police ambulance copter in here shortly to pick you up. Just relax." The floater rose out of my vision, and I lost consciousness again.

When I awoke a second time it was to sounds of pain. The hider had dragged himself away from the stream, but he groaned with every move. Blood was glistening blackly on his pants as he came into my vision. I supposed he had broken some bones just as I had. "Take it easy, friend," I called. "There'll be an ambulance here shortly."

He cursed in a low voice, but gave up his efforts and settled back, looking at me sourly. His labored breathing slowed. After a while he hitched himself up to a sitting position and said, "I'll bet you're real proud of yourself, capturing a genuine desperado and getting injured in the line of duty and all. You can show off your medal to the kids back at home, right? You're a hero."

I shouldn't have been, but I was hurt. "Look, we don't hate you," I said. "My rifle's got nothing but tranquilizer darts in it. We just need to get you out of the park. It's closed right now."

He shook his head sadly. "You're as mealy-mouthed as the bureaucrats in Washington. The park isn't closed 'right now.' It's closed forever. You're not going to let anybody in here ever again. Then you wonder why some of us try to stay on here."

"Stop trying to act like a martyr. There'll be floater stations available to everybody for free."

"My God!" he cried. "Do you listen to yourself, ever? Floaters? Sitting in front of a TV screen, seeing what the machine sees, hearing the forest through a pair of earphones? You gadget-happy bastard, is that what the wilderness means to you?"

He continued into a long speech beginning with "Have you ever walked down a country road just to . . . ," but abruptly I couldn't listen. A sick realization had come to me: I would never walk in the woods again. The Park Commission wouldn't wait for me to heal. They would just hire the next man on the list to hunt down hiders, and by the time I got out of the hospital, this and every other national park in the country would be closed. I began to weep a little.

"Shut up!" I yelled suddenly, cutting off his sappy rhapsody. "You caused this; you brought this down on us!" I was shaking and gasping, angry at the world and angry at myself for loosing it at him. "You and your nature-lovers, and conservationists, and ecology freaks. You prattled for years about getting people back to the wilderness, and they *came,* my God, how they came. Backpacks and camper busses and tents and trailers and motorbikes. It's not enough for you to admire Mother Nature; you've got to be nature-lovers and sleep with her and live with her and piss in the streams. And when we finally close off the parks so that our kids will know at least what the wilderness is, you try to hide in here and spoil even that." I stopped, and I was ashamed.

"You're grandstanding," he commented, accurately. "You know you could just have restricted the park to hiking or something. Do you really think our children are going to be uplifted by pictures of beauty they can never share?"

I was long in answering. "You know better than that. There's three hundred million people in this country. If we let everyone into the park who wanted to come, even if they just walked around and didn't drop a single beer can, it wouldn't be wild anymore. It would just be a picnic grounds. The floaters are better—they're small, and quiet, and they don't even touch the ground. People will be able to see and hear the forest forever, even if they can't touch it, because the wilderness can survive the floaters. But the people would be the death of it."

We both were silent for a long time, nursing our pain and listening to the quiet spilling of the water in the bottom of the ravine. I thought of what a friend this man would have made, if I'd met him somewhere else. We were two alike, and I wanted to ask his name. But he spoke first: "The woods are beautiful tonight, aren't they?" he asked, a little indistinct with the drug.

They were. The moon was high now, and in its light the trees looked touched with old pewter. There was a breeze, gentle with the scent of pine and rich moss, tasting like mineral water. "It's a shame," he said, "that the kids growing up now won't be able to smell this."

In the distance, I heard the beat of the helicopters approaching. "They're developing an olfactory unit for the floaters," I said.

Last Hunt

Eric Vinicoff
and Marcia Martin

Of the many endangered species on this planet, probably the best known are the whales, which are still being hunted to extinction. Neither the giant corporations that make enormous profits from whale hunting nor the individual hunters who make a marginal living are willing to abandon their ways. But perhaps it will be different when human predators realize there will soon be no more whales to kill. Perhaps.

Eric Vinicoff and Marcia Martin, who always write together, began their joint career only a few years ago.

I T WAS COLD beyond the skim field, starry clear, knifing antarctic cold. Killing cold, and it had claimed its due enough times to earn the name. Large bergs floated near the horizon, black cutouts against the faint northern lights. Water ran freely around the hull, but bergy-bits shattering on the alloy made a musical sound like shoveling broken glass.

"Clear ahead." Claire tapped the scopes for emphasis. "Sonar and radar."

Pinkoski nodded. He stood at the prow, eyes ever outward. His upper body jutted beyond the skim field, so his long black hair and bushy mustache were attacked by wind and spray. *Rorqual* was cruising at its fifty knots max, lifted half out of the water on its hydrofoil wing.

"Range and distance?" His words, precious jewels that he shared sparingly, were precise and so deep as to seem felt rather than heard.

I jerked my gaze back to the computer displays, where it should have been. "Fade-out on buoy A6, pickup on B13 and 14. That programs out to range thirty kilometers, course 233. Speed—six knots."

Claire's hands typewrote across her board. "Locked in, Chan. Captain, we're closing. E.T.—twelve minutes."

He nodded.

It was just the three of us and S.E.'s best boat, a thirty-meter converted sea racer. Claire was the pilot, and likewise S.E.'s best. But she wasn't captain this run, because Pinkoski was aboard.

Me? I had been happily monitoring fish-tracking buoys at Cal Tech's Hilo station when S.E. bought my contract. Then I was dropping buoys from a jetcopter in a wide grid of Antarctic waters. Finally I ended up here.

"Bergs ahead!" Claire shouted. "Range three kilometers! Intersect in approximately two and a half minutes!"

"Any channels near our course?" Pinkoski asked calmly.

She wanted desperately to say no, but couldn't lie to him. "A damned narrow one, Captain. And shallow, though we might be able to hop it on the wing."

I shivered. I had heard enough tales of Antarctic shipwrecks to know that if we went up on the ice we would never get home to spend our hazard pay. "Captain," I cut in, "if we swing around the bergs we'd only lose—"

"Time, and maybe the trail." He turned to look at me briefly, and saw down to my bedrock of terror. "Don't worry, lad. We'll come through it."

I was almost convinced. "But it's not worth the risk."

"Bloody blast it's not! How long have we been out? Five, six months? And this the only strike we've had! Veer for the channel, lass!"

"Aye, aye," Claire responded. "Six degrees to port."

Rorqual actually banked with the sudden change in direction. Straps held the two of us in our chairs. Pinkoski had ridden wave-slicked decks in hurricane winds; he adjusted his stance automatically.

The bergs ahead began to swell. They were flat-topped, indicating that they had but recently broken off from the great ice sheet covering Antarctica. When they aged, they would resemble Norman fortresses with many turrets and spires.

A pencil shaft of night between two of them also grew, but not quickly enough. Claire hyped the turbines to emergency, and *Rorqual* rose even higher. The normal slight bouncing of the hull against wavelets became trip-hammer pounding that loosened teeth. Yet Pinkoski didn't return to the cockpit.

Claire looked frankly scared. I'm sure I did too.

"Fifteen seconds to intersect!" she shouted.

"Keep a weather eye on your displays," Pinkoski said to me over his shoulder. "I don't want to lose the trail during the passage. It may be a bit rough."

That, from him, was like a pronouncement of doom.

The bergs reached from sea to sky in front of us, and the channel was still microscopic. Ice dark with volcanic ash towered a hundred meters or more. Thunder rolled across the water as it cracked internally, and small flat pieces slid down from the main masses to form growler bergs.

Spray was an all but solid sheet battering the boat and Pinkoski. I couldn't see how he kept from being knocked overboard, even with adhesive deck shoes. But there he stood, vague in the night, as implacable as the immense shapes he faced.

"Five seconds!" Claire's voice broke. "Brace for possible collision!"

Then we were in the channel, moving so fast that the icy walls were a close rushing presence.

"We're clear below," Claire whispered, "but the cliffs are so irreg—"

CRAAAAANG!

I waited for the world to go away. The sound and feel of ice tearing through metal was a terrible thing that shredded the soul. But seconds later, finding myself still alive, I opened my eyes.

Pinkoski was gone from the prow.

I looked around wildly, unbelievingly. We were beyond the bergs, in open water again, and floating in the silence of stilled turbines. Claire was frantically struggling with her emergency systems board. She had no time for anything else, not even the blood flowing down her cheek from a long scalp wound.

Strange creaking noises were coming from below, and I imagined I could feel the boat settling. It didn't bother her.

"Bloody blast this misbegotten patch of bilgewater!" The faint words drifted up from beyond the deck about five meters back from the prow on the starboard side. I stared, and made out two black-gloved hands hanging onto the railing. As I watched, Pinkoski pulled himself back on board. His black warmsuit dripped profusely, and his face stretched with effort into strange ridges and valleys. The skim field didn't make his task any easier.

I realized with shock that he was *old*.

I wobbled over to help, but he made it up before I reached him. His worn face was sweaty but welded into its usual grim mask. "Jesus," I babbled, "you were almost—"

He pushed by me and jumped down into the cockpit. "How badly are we breached?" he demanded of Claire even as he read the displays over her shoulder.

She wiped blood away from her right eye. "Took a hit starboard, tore us open along three meters of seam. Pumps at full, but losing ground. We're taking water fast."

"How about patching it, lass?"

"Too big for the autopatch system, and welding one on from either inside or outside would take a day in drydock."

"What does that leave?"

She punched a button marked EMERG FLOTATION—STARBOARD BILGE. A dull thud shot through the hull, and *Rorqual* rose and righted itself. She scanned the displays again and began trembling. "We're okay now, I think."

I pulled the med kit from under her chair and did what I could for her cut. Meanwhile Pinkoski went below to make sure the pressurized gasbags were holding against the water and not abrading on torn hull alloy. I could hear plastic foam gurgling into the bags. When it hardened in a few minutes we would be safer.

He quickly rejoined us, but Claire had managed to get the turbines idling in the interim.

"We'll float," he reported.

"Good," I said. "Just as long as it gets us home."

"All in good time, lad. Get back to your board and find me my whale."

I couldn't believe it. "This isn't a jihad, Captain. We can go home, refit, and come back. We'll find another one."

He came over and stared at me. I was *homo urbanis* and had encountered many tough city dudes. But they were civilized tough, artificial, and therefore vulnerable. Pinkoski had a different type of toughness; salt and sea, wind and water. Unstoppable. "We're seaworthy. Get back to your board."

I wilted. The computer was still working, sad to say. "It's still out there, Captain. Near the surface. It just came up from a deep dive, so I think it'll play on top a bit. Range three kilometers. Course 059."

Claire set up a course on her board. Her eyes were shining, and there was no question in her. The way she looked at him said it all.

"I want that whale," Pinkoski said to no one in particular. "It's one of the last. The hunt is up, after so many searching years. I'll have it ended. Now."

Rorqual jumped ahead and climbed on its wing, which had somehow come through the crash intact. A small boat in a big, big ocean.

Pinkoski went back to the stern bay and unlatched it. "We've got to close before it dives, lass."

"We will," she promised.

This was all crazy. We didn't belong here, and wouldn't be here but for an old seaman who had given his life to a dream, and another old man who owned Santee Enterprises and could lend substance to any dream he shared.

Out there somewhere in the black water swam their dream. *Balaenoptera Musculus*. The great blue whale. Largest living being ever on Earth, at the doorway leading from reality to myth.

The one out there probably wasn't the last. Estimates put the survivors at a few dozen. But this would be the last generation. They wandered individually in vast migratory paths, and mated when males encountered females. With so few left, it wasn't likely any would so meet.

Thus the dream. The last hunt.

"E.T. one minute!" Claire shouted. "Slowing to stalk!"

Pinkoski began pulling equipment from the bay. He donned a black plastic headlamp and goggles. The jetski was heavy, but he managed to manhandle it to the stern, ready for jump-off.

Finally he drew the harpoon from its nest of electronic gear. It sang of cold silver pain in the reflected cockpit light. It was long and spectrally slender in the shaft, with an icepick tip and a stubby haft. I winced.

Like everything else out here, S.E.'s best. This obsession was costing Mister Santee big bucks. That didn't bother me, but throwing lives into the pot did.

The turbines slowed until *Rorqual* moved ahead at a mere crawl. "Thar she blows!" Claire shouted. "Ten points to starboard!"

The big prow searchlight flared to life and swung around under sonar slaving. A thin wedge of ocean was dimly illuminated, a stage in the center of the night.

And there it was. A long, low, mottled blue-gray island flippering slowly away from us. It spanned over thirty-five meters from black baleen to flukes. White showed on the undersides of the flippers, and the tiny dorsal fin was barely visible. Spray shot up from its blowhole.

But the main thing was it was *big*. Bigger than any other whale, and I had seen some huge ones up close during my studies. Humpbacks. Right whales, so called because they were the ones the whalers were looking for. Sperm whales.

But this was their king, last and greatest, hunted into oblivion to the shame of humanity. I recognized it from photos, of course—of us only Pinkoski had ever seen a living blue whale, fleetingly and far away, from the deck of the *James Bay* just before the accident that focused his life.

"Beautiful," he whispered, and I barely heard him over the lapping of water against the hull. "At last . . . an ending."

He moved the harpoon thoughtfully, staring at it, into the jetski's rack. Then he swung into the saddle.

"Luck, Captain!" Claire waved frantically.

It should have been ludicrously melodramatic. Ahab after his whale. Gary Cooper striding out to his gunfight. Only it wasn't. Loneliness and desperation clotted the air. Why was he here, really? Claire and I couldn't ever know, and that left us on the outside. Alone in an environment that hated us. A part of someone else's destiny. Trapped.

He kicked the jetski and himself over the side, splashing into the water, then bobbing back up. He said nothing to us. We were out of it now.

The whale was diving, then rising again several hundred meters further away. Claire moved *Rorqual* slowly to keep up. Wanting to or not, we would see what there was to see.

Pinkoski rode the jetski in a wide arc to come up on the whale's port flank. The tiny craft almost disappeared in the broth of wake the flukes kicked up.

A commercial deck gun could have blown a harpoon into the whale from up to two kilometers away. But this harpoon had to be planted in exactly the right place. Which required precision.

Proximity.

Confrontation.

Which might have been a part of the white-heat in Pinkoski.

"He's making his run," Claire said unnecessarily.

I nodded. He was a small figure in the distance, frail and pointless, coming up alongside the great whale. It ignored him. How could it know the transcendental power of human emotion?

The harpoon came out of its rack, rose high in his right hand while his left remained on the jetski's handlebar. That right hand—and arm—seemingly normal, was a prosthesis, no less artificial than the harpoon. It formed an electromechanical symbiosis between technology and biology, between weapon and wielding flesh.

Two young men had been aboard the *James Bay* during its days of heroism, a seaman and an industrialist, diverse types brought together by ideals. In the midst of the struggle, between trawlers and prey, a lifelong friendship began. One lost an arm when a steel prow sheared through a wooden lifeboat. The other replaced it as best he could.

Pinkoski closed until the side wake of the whale threatened to knock him from the saddle. He came to within meters of the patch of parasite-covered hide that had been selected for the lack of vital organs under it.

Suddenly the whale's broad head dipped beneath the water. Up came the twin-mattress tail. It was about to dive.

Pinkoski stood up on the jetski's footrests. The harpoon cast a last gleam of light back our way. Then he flung it into the whale's flank.

The whale slid under its white wake. Froth slammed the side of the jetski. Before Pinkoski could sit down or regain his balance, it tipped over.

Pinkoski vanished.

The tail came down flat on the jetski. A cracking sound reached us. Then everything was gone from the surface of the ocean.

Claire and I just kept staring.

Something started beeping on my board. Flashing redness caught the corner of my eye.

Pinkoski wasn't there anymore.

Then I noticed the sound and light. I pointed to the board. Claire saw, and dully locked in a new course. We were acting instinctively. Routine was an escape from thought.

Rorqual swung to port and closed on the source of the radio beacon signal.

I took a boathook to the prow and stared down. The big searchlight had targeted the flotation balloon for me. I speared it with the hook.

Pinkoski was gone. The last part of his hunt was left to us.

Claire killed the turbines.

I hauled the balloon aboard, then reeled in the line hanging from it.

Up came the harpoon.

I used my pocket vibraknife to cut it free from the line. I shivered at its cold metallic touch. The ocean had wiped it clean of blood. I looked it over. Everything seemed to have gone perfectly.

Except for one detail.

I detached the tip and also the haft, which was now hollow since the flotation balloon had ejected and pulled the harpoon out of the whale. That left about two meters of glistening silver shaft. I checked a tiny indicator on one end—it was glowing green.

"How does it look?" Claire was staring over my shoulder.

"The cryo-unit light is green. I think it's a go."

"Great." But she said it with no enthusiasm.

I walked slowly sternward to the equipment bay. The harpoon unit was purely a temporary measure. I slid the shaft back into its electronic auxiliaries, made the necessary connections, and nodded when green lights flashed amid the gear. The boat computer had taken over caring for our prize.

"Ahoy there! Did you net it?"

Claire and I whirled. She stifled a scream, then began crying softly. I almost had a heart seizure.

Pinkoski, streaming water but apparently in one piece, was pulling himself over the deck railing. If he had looked old before, he now resembled death resurrected. But he stood rigidly upright. His voice was controlled.

"How—?" I choked. Even a warmsuit couldn't save a person from that much time in 6°C Antarctic water. Not to mention the battering he must have taken from the flukes, or the time spent underwater.

Claire rushed him into the cockpit. He refused first aid, but let her make him a cup of coffee.

"You haven't answered my question," he said to us.

"We got it," I replied as I studied my board. "And the whale is about 250 meters below us, alive and well."

"Good."

He took the steaming cup from Claire and put it to his lips. "Then it's time we set a homeward course."

I nodded gratefully. Claire returned to her board and began plotting a safe route back through the bergs. I stared at Pinkoski as he stared out at the dark water. All I could figure was that he gripped life a lot tighter than the rest of us, and therefore was that much harder to kill.

"Fare you well," he said to the deeps. "Live in peace. You won't be the last. Your children will live as long as there are oceans."

So they would. The thousands of its living cells in the cryogenically preserved sample would go to the S.E. genetic labs. DNA would be subtly altered to produce chromosome chains for both sexes and the many trait differences that made up a genetic pool. Clones would be raised in neoembryonic fluid tanks to young adulthood, then introduced with care into their natural environment. Now that they would face only natural dangers—whaling was a part of the bad old days—they would grow and multiply.

The greatest living beings on Earth would survive.

Rorqual swung around and rose on its wing, rushing northeast, toward home.

I smiled weakly at Pinkoski. "Now what?"

"For me?" He laughed—a deep, rich music I hadn't heard before. "There are other species in danger of being lost. Other whales. Porpoises. Even fish. We'll be back, lad."

If he meant we as in me too, he was crazy. Or was he?

Greenslaves

Frank Herbert

No species in existence today is totally lacking in defenses, of which adaptability must certainly be the most important. (Ask any virus.) Generally speaking, the larger the creature the more specialized the defenses it will have evolved, while the smaller ones rely on adapting to change. But every year humanity produces new ways of killing insect pests; in order to survive, their ultimate adaptation may be something like the one described in this story.

Frank Herbert's concern with ecological problems goes well beyond having written Dune, the most famous of ecological science fiction novels. He is an active campaigner for environmental awareness, and his own home is powered by windmills.

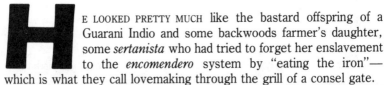

H E LOOKED PRETTY MUCH like the bastard offspring of a Guarani Indio and some backwoods farmer's daughter, some *sertanista* who had tried to forget her enslavement to the *encomendero* system by "eating the iron"— which is what they call lovemaking through the grill of a consel gate.

The type-look was almost perfect except when he forgot himself while passing through one of the deeper jungle glades.

His skin tended to shade down to green then, fading him into the background of leaves and vines, giving a strange disembodiment to the mud-grey shirt and ragged trousers, the inevitable frayed straw hat and rawhide sandals soled with pieces cut from worn tires.

Such lapses became less and less frequent the farther he got from the Parana headwaters, the *sertao* hinterland of Goyaz where men with his bang-cut black hair and glittering eyes were common.

By the time he reached *bandeirantes* country, he had achieved almost perfect control over the chameleon effect.

But now he was out of the jungle growth and into the brown dirt tracks that separated the parceled farms of the resettlement plan. In his own way, he knew he was approaching the *bandeirante* checkpoints, and with an almost human gesture, he fingered the *cedula de gracias al sacar,* the certificate of white blood, tucked safely beneath his shirt. Now and again, when humans were not near, he practiced speaking aloud the name that had been chosen for him—"Antonio Raposo Tavares."

The sound was a bit stridulant, harsh on the edges, but he knew it would pass. It already had. Goyaz Indios were notorious for the strange inflection of their speech. The farm folk who had given him a roof and fed him the previous night had said as much.

When their questions had become pressing, he had squatted on the doorstep and played his flute, the *qena* of the Andes Indian that he carried in a leather purse hung from his shoulder. He had kept the sound to a conventional, non-dangerous pitch. The gesture of the flute was a symbol of the region. When a Guarani put flute to nose and began playing, that was a sign words were ended.

The farm folk had shrugged and retired.

Now, he could see red-brown rooftops ahead and the white crystal shimmering of a *bandeirante* tower with its aircars alighting and departing. The scene held an odd hive-look. He stopped, finding himself momentarily overcome by the touch of instincts that he knew he had to master or fail in the ordeal to come.

He united his mental identity then, thinking, *We are greenslaves subservient to the greater whole.* The thought lent him an air of servility that was like a shield against the stares of the humans trudging past all around him. His kind knew many mannerisms and had learned early that servility was a form of concealment.

Presently, he resumed his plodding course toward the town and the tower.

The dirt track gave way to a two-lane paved market road with its footpaths in the ditches on both sides. This, in turn, curved alongside a four-deck commercial transport highway where even the footpaths were paved. And now there were groundcars and aircars in greater number, and he noted that the flow of people on foot was increasing.

Thus far, he had attracted no dangerous attention. The occasional snickering side-glance from natives of the area could be safely ignored, he knew. Probing stares held peril, and he had detected none. The servility shielded him.

The sun was well along toward mid-morning and the day's heat was beginning to press down on the earth, raising a moist hothouse stink from the dirt beside the pathway, mingling the perspiration odors of humanity around him.

And they were around him now, close and pressing, moving slower and slower as they approached the checkpoint bottleneck. Presently, the forward motion stopped. Progress resolved itself into shuffle and stop, shuffle and stop.

This was the critical test now and there was no avoiding it. He waited with something like an Indian's stoic patience. His breathing had grown deeper to compensate for the heat, and he adjusted it to match that of the people around him, suffering the temperature rise for the sake of blending into his surroundings.

Andes Indians didn't breathe deeply here in the lowlands.

Shuffle and stop.

Shuffle and stop.

He could see the checkpoint now.

Fastidious bandeirantes in sealed white cloaks with plastic helmets, gloves, and boots stood in a double row within a shaded brick corridor leading into the town. He could see sunlight hot on the street beyond the corridor and people hurrying away there after passing the gantlet.

The sight of that free area beyond the corridor sent an ache of longing through all the parts of him. The suppression warning flashed out instantly on the heels of that instinctive reaching emotion.

No distraction could be permitted now; he was into the hands of the first bandeirante, a hulking blonde fellow with pink skin and blue eyes.

"Step along now! Lively now!" the fellow said.

A gloved hand propelled him toward two bandeirantes standing on the right side of the line.

"Give this one an extra treatment," the blonde giant called. "He's from the upcountry by the look of him."

The other two bandeirantes had him now, one jamming a breather mask over his face, the other fitting a plastic bag over him. A tube trailed from the bag out to machinery somewhere in the street beyond the corridor.

"Double shot!" one of the bandeirantes called.

Fuming blue gas puffed out the bag around him, and he took a sharp, gasping breath through the mask.

Agony!

The gas drove through every multiple linkage of his being with needles of pain.

We must not weaken, he thought.

But it was a deadly pain, killing. The linkages were beginning to weaken.

"Okay on this one," the bag handler called.

The mask was pulled away. The bag was slipped off. Hands propelled him down the corridor toward the sunlight.

"Lively now! Don't hold up the line."

The stink of the poison gas was all around him. It was a new one—a dissembler. They hadn't prepared him for this poison!

Now, he was into the sunlight and turning down a street lined with fruit stalls, merchants bartering with customers or standing fat and watchful behind their displays.

In his extremity, the fruit beckoned to him with the promise of life-saving sanctuary for a few parts of him, but the integrating totality fought off the lure. He shuffled as fast as he dared, dodging past the customers, through the knots of idlers.

"You like to buy some fresh oranges?"

An oily dark hand thrust two oranges toward his face.

"Fresh oranges from the green country. Never been a bug anywhere near these."

He avoided the hand, although the odor of the oranges came near overpowering him.

Now, he was clear of the stalls, around a corner down a narrow side street. Another corner and he saw far away to his left the lure of greenery in open country, the free area beyond the town.

He turned toward the green, increasing his speed, measuring out the time still available to him. There was still a chance. Poison clung to his clothing, but free air was filtering through the fabric—and the thought of victory was like an antidote.

We can make it yet!

The green drew closer and closer—trees and ferns beside a river bank. He heard the running water. There was a bridge thronging with foot traffic from converging streets.

No help for it; he joined the throng, avoided contact as much as possible. The linkages of his legs and back were beginning to go, and he knew the wrong kind of blow could dislodge whole segments. He was over the bridge without disaster. A dirt track led off the path and down toward the river.

He turned toward it, stumbled against one of two men carrying a pig in a net slung between them. Part of the shell on his right upper leg gave way and he could feel it begin to slip down inside his pants.

The man he had hit took two backward steps, almost dropped the end of the burden.

"Careful!" the man shouted.

The man at the other end of the net said: "Damn drunks."

The pig set up a squirming, squealing distraction.

In this moment, he slipped past them onto the dirt track leading down toward the river. He could see the water down there now, boiling with aeration from the barrier filters.

Behind him, one of the pig carriers said: "I don't think he was drunk, Carlos. His skin felt dry and hot. Maybe he was sick."

The track turned around an embankment of raw dirt dark brown with dampness and dipped toward a tunnel through ferns and bushes. The men with the pig could no longer see him, he knew, and he grabbed at his pants where the part of his leg was slipping, scurried into the green tunnel.

Now, he caught sight of his first mutated bee. It was dead, having entered the barrier vibration area here without any protection against that deadliness. The bee was one of the butterfly type with iridescent yellow and orange wings. It lay in the cup of a green leaf at the center of a shaft of sunlight.

He shuffled past, having recorded the bee's shape and color. They had considered the bees as a possible answer, but there were serious drawbacks to this course. A bee could not reason with humans, that was the key fact. And humans had to listen to reason soon, else all life would end.

There came the sound of someone hurrying down the path behind him, heavy footsteps thudding on the earth.

Pursuit? . . .

He was reduced to a slow shuffling now and soon it would be only crawling progress, he knew. Eyes searched the greenery around him for a place of concealment. A thin break in the fern wall on his left caught his attention. Tiny human footprints led into it—children. He forced his way through the ferns, found himself on a low narrow path along the embankment. Two toy aircars, red and blue, had been abandoned on the path. His staggering foot pressed them into the dirt.

The path led close to a wall of black dirt festooned with creepers, around a sharp turn, and onto the lip of a shallow cave. More toys lay in the green gloom at the cave's mouth.

He knelt, crawled over the toys into the blessed dankness, lay there a moment, waiting.

The pounding footsteps hurried past a few feet below.

Voices reached up to him.

"He was headed toward the river. Think he was going to jump in?"

"Who knows? But I think me for sure he was sick."

"Here; down this way. Somebody's been down this way."

The voices grew indistinct, blended with the babbling sound of the river.

The men were going on down the path. They had missed his hiding place. But why had they pursued him? He had not seriously injured the one by stumbling against him. Surely they did not suspect.

Slowly, he steeled himself for what had to be done, brought his specialized parts into play, and began burrowing into the earth at the end of the cave. Deeper and deeper he burrowed, thrusting the excess dirt behind and out to make it appear the cave had collapsed.

Ten meters in he went before stopping. His store of energy contained just enough reserve for the next stage. He turned on his back, scattering the dead parts of his legs and back, exposing the queen and her guard cluster to the dirt beneath his chitinous spine. Orifices opened at his thighs, exuded the cocoon foam, the soothing green cover that would harden into a protective shell.

This was victory; the essential parts had survived.

Time was the thing now—ten and one-half days to gather new energy, go through the metamorphosis, and disperse. Soon, there would be thousands of him—each with its carefully mimicked clothing and identification papers and appearance of humanity.

Identical—each of them.

There would be other checkpoints, but not as severe; other barriers, lesser ones.

This human copy had proved a good one. They had learned many things from study of their scattered captives and from the odd crew directed by the red-haired human female they'd trapped in the *sertao*. How strange she was: like a queen and not like a queen. It was so difficult to understand human creatures, even when you permitted them limited freedom . . . almost impossible to reason with them. Their slavery to the planet would have to be proved dramatically, perhaps.

The queen stirred near the cool dirt. They had learned new things this time about escaping notice. All of the subsequent colony clusters would share that knowledge. One of them—at least—would get through to the city by the Amazon "River Sea" where the death-for-all originated. One had to get through.

Senhor Gabriel Martinho, prefect of the Mato Grosso Barrier Company, paced his study, muttering to himself as he passed the tall, narrow window that admitted the evening sunlight. Occasionally, he paused to glare down at his son, Joao, who sat on a tapir-leather sofa beneath one of the tall bookcases that lined the room.

The elder Martinho was a dark wisp of a man, limb-thin, with grey hair and cavernous brown eyes above an eagle nose, slit mouth, and boot-toe chin. He wore old-style black clothing as befitted his position, his linen white against the black, and with golden cuffstuds glittering as he waved his arms.

"I am an object of ridicule!" he snarled.

Joao, a younger copy of the father, his hair still black and wavy, absorbed the statement in silence. He wore a bandeirante's white coverall suit sealed into plastic boots at the calf.

"An object of ridicule!" the elder Martinho repeated.

It began to grow dark in the room, the quick tropic darkness hurried by thunderheads piled along the horizon. The waning daylight carried a hazel blue cast. Heat lightning spattered the patch of sky visible through the tall window, sent dazzling electric radiance into the study. Drumming thunder followed. As though that were the signal, the house sensors turned on lights wherever there were humans. Yellow illumination filled the study.

The Prefect stopped in front of his son. "Why does my own son, a bandeirante, a jefe of the Irmandades, spout these Carsonite stupidities?"

Joao looked at the floor between his boots. He felt both resentment and shame. To disturb his father this way, that was a hurtful thing, with the elder Martinho's delicate heart. But the old man was so blind!

"Those rabble farmers laughed at me," the elder Martinho said. "I told them we'd increase the green area by ten thousand hectares this month, and they laughed. 'Your own son does not even believe this!' they said. And they told me some of the things you had been saying."

"I am sorry I have caused you distress, father," Joao said. "The fact that I'm a bandeirante . . ." He shrugged. "How else could I have learned the truth about this extermination program?"

His father quivered.

"Joao! Do you sit there and tell me you took a false oath when you formed your Irmandades band?"

"That's not the way it was, father."

Joao pulled a sprayman's emblem from his breast pocket, fingered it. "I believed it . . . then. We could shape mutated bees to fill every gap in the insect ecology. This I believed. Like the Chinese, I said: 'Only the useful shall live!' But that was several years ago, father, and since then I have come to realize we don't have a complete understanding of what usefulness means."

"It was a mistake to have you educated in North America," his father said. "That's where you absorbed this Carsonite heresy. It's all well and good for *them* to refuse to join the rest of the world in the Ecological Realignment; they do not have as many million mouths to feed. But my own son!"

Joao spoke defensively: "Out in the red areas you see things, father. These things are difficult to explain. Plants look healthier out there and the fruit is . . ."

"A purely temporary thing," his father said. "We will shape bees to meet whatever need we find. The destroyers take food from our mouths. It is very simple. They must die and be replaced by creatures which serve a function useful to mankind."

"The birds are dying, father," Joao said.

"We are saving the birds! We have specimens of every kind in our sanctuaries. We will provide new foods for them to . . ."

"But what happens if our barriers are breached . . . before we can replace the population of natural predators? What happens then?"

The elder Martinho shook a thin finger under his son's nose. "This is nonsense! I will hear no more of it! Do you know what else those *mameluco* farmers said? They said they have seen bandeirantes reinfesting the green areas to prolong their jobs! That is what they said. This, too, is nonsense—but it is a natural consequence of defeatist talk just such as I have heard from you tonight. And every setback we suffer adds strength to such charges!"

"Setbacks, father?"

"I have said it: setbacks!"

Senhor Prefect Martinho turned, paced to his desk and back. Again, he stopped in front of his son, placed hands on hips. "You refer to the Piratininga, of course?"

"You accuse me, father?"

"Your Irmandades were on that line."

"Not so much as a flea got through us!"

"Yet, a week ago the Piratininga was green. Now, it is crawling. Crawling!"

"I cannot watch every bandeirante in the Mato Grosso," Joao protested. "If they . . ."

"The IEO gives us only six months to clean up," the elder Martinho said. He raised his hands, palms up; his face was flushed. "Six months! Then they throw an embargo around all Brazil—the way they have done with North America." He lowered his hands. "Can you imagine the pressures on me? Can you imagine the things I must listen to about the bandeirantes and especially about my own son?"

Joao scratched his chin with the sprayman's emblem. The reference to the International Ecological Organization made him think of Dr. Rhin Kelly, the IEO's lovely field director. His mind pictured her as he had last seen her in the A' Chigua nightclub at Bahia—red-haired, green-eyed . . . so lovely and strange. But she had been missing almost six weeks now—somewhere in the *sertao*, and there were those who said she must be dead.

Joao looked at his father. If only the old man weren't so excitable. "You excite yourself needlessly, father," he said. "The Piratininga was not a full barrier, just a . . ."

53

"Excite myself!"

The Prefect's nostrils dilated; he bent toward his son. "Already we have gone past two deadlines. We gained an extension when I announced you and the bandeirantes of Diogo Alvarez had cleared the Piratininga. How do I explain now that it is reinfested, that we have the work to do over?"

Joao returned the sprayman's emblem to his pocket. It was obvious he'd not be able to reason with his father this night. Frustration sent a nerve quivering along Joao's jaw. The old man had to be told, though; someone had to tell him. And someone of his father's stature had to get back to the Bureau, shake them up there, and make *them* listen.

The Prefect returned to his desk, sat down. He picked up an antique crucifix, one that the great Aleihadinho had carved in ivory. He lifted it, obviously seeking to restore his serenity, but his eyes went wide and glaring. Slowly, he returned the crucifix to its position on the desk, keeping his attention on it.

"Joao," he whispered.

It's his heart! Joao thought.

He leaped to his feet, rushed to his father's side. "Father! What is it?"

The elder Martinho pointed, hand trembling.

Through the spiked crown of thorns, across the agonized ivory face, over the straining muscles of the Christ figure crawled an insect. It was the color of the ivory, faintly reminiscent of a beetle in shape, but with a multi-clawed fringe along its wings and thorax, and with furry edging to its abnormally long antennae.

The elder Martinho reached for a roll of papers to smash the insect, but Joao put out a hand restraining him. "Wait. This is a new one. I've never seen anything like it. Give me a handlight. We must follow it, find where it nests."

Senhor Prefect Martinho muttered under his breath, withdrew a small permalight from a drawer of the desk, handed the light to his son.

Joao peered at the insect, still not using the light. "How strange it is," he said. "See how it exactly matches the tone of the ivory."

The insect stopped, pointed its antennae toward the men.

"Things have been seen," Joao said. "There are stories. Something like this was found near one of the barrier villages last month. It was inside the green area, on a path beside a river. Two farmers found it while searching for a sick man." Joao looked at his father. "They are very watchful of sickness in the newly green regions, you know. There have been epidemics . . . and that is another thing."

"There is no relationship," his father snapped. "Without insects to carry disease, we will have less illness."

"Perhaps," Joao said, and his tone said he did not believe it.

Joao returned his attention to the insect. "I do not think our ecologists know all they say they do. And I mistrust our Chinese advisors. They speak in such flowery terms of the benefits from eliminating useless insects, but they will not let us go into their green areas and inspect. Excuses. Always excuses. I think they are having troubles they do not wish us to know."

"That's foolishness," the elder Martinho growled, but his tone said this was not a position he cared to defend. "They are honorable men. Their way of life is closer to our socialism than it is to the decadent capitalism of North America. Your trouble is you see them too much through the eyes of those who educated you."

"I'll wager this insect is one of the spontaneous mutations," Joao said. "It is almost as though they appeared according to some plan. Find me something in which I may capture this creature and take it to the laboratory."

The elder Martinho remained standing by his chair. "Where will you say it was found?"

"Right here," Joao said.

"You will not hesitate to expose me to more ridicule?"

"But father . . ."

"Can't you hear what they will say? In his own home this insect is found. It is a strange new kind. Perhaps he breeds them there to reinfest the green."

"Now *you* are talking nonsense, father. Mutations are common in a threatened species. And we cannot deny there is a threat to insect species—the poisons, the barrier vibrations, the traps. Get me a container, father. I cannot leave this creature, or I'd get a container myself."

"And you will tell where it was found?"

"I can do nothing else. We must cordon off this area, search it out. This could be . . . an accident. . . ."

"Or a deliberate attempt to embarrass me."

Joao took his attention from the insect, studied his father. *That* was a possibility, of course. The Carsonites had friends in many places . . . and some were fanatics who would stoop to any scheme. Still . . .

Decision came to Joao. He returned his attention to the motionless insect. His father had to be told, had to be reasoned with at any cost. Someone whose voice carried authority had to get down to the Capitol and make them listen.

"Our earliest poisons killed off the weak and selected out those insects immune to this threat," Joao said. "Only the immune remained to breed. The poisons we use now . . . some of them, do not leave such loopholes, and the deadly vibrations at the barriers. . . ." He shrugged. "This is a form of beetle, father. I will show you a thing."

Joao drew a long, thin whistle of shiny metal from his pocket. "There was a time when this called countless beetles to their deaths. I had merely to tune it across their attraction spectrum." He put the whistle to his lips, blew while turning the end of it.

No sound audible to human ears came from the instrument, but the beetle's antennae writhed.

Joao removed the whistle from his mouth.

The antennae stopped writhing.

"It stayed put, you see," Joao said. "And there are indications of malignant intelligence among them. The insects are far from extinction, father . . . and they are beginning to strike back."

"Malignant intelligence, pah!"

"You must believe me, father," Joao said. "No one else will listen. They laugh and say we are too long in the jungle. And where is our evidence? And they say such stories could be expected from ignorant farmers but not from bandeirantes. You must listen, father, and believe. It is why I was chosen to come here . . . because you are my father and you might listen to your own son."

"Believe what?" the elder Martinho demanded, and he was the Prefect now, standing erect, glaring coldly at his son.

"In the sertao of Goyaz last week," Joao said, "Antonil Lisboa's bandeirante lost three men who . . ."

"Accidents."

"They were killed with formic acid and oil of copahu."

"They were careless with their poisons. Men grow careless when they . . ."

"Father! The formic acid was a particularly strong type, but still recognizable as having been . . . or being of a type manufactured by insects. And the men were drenched with it. While the oil of copahu . . ."

"You imply that insects such as this . . ." The Prefect pointed to the motionless creature on the crucifix. ". . . blind creatures such as this . . ."

"They're not blind, father."

"I did not mean literally blind, but without intelligence," the elder Martinho said. "You cannot be seriously implying that these creatures attacked humans and killed them."

"We have yet to discover precisely how the men were slain," Joao said. "We have only their bodies and the physical evidence at the scene. But there have been other deaths, father, and men missing, and we grow more and more certain that . . ."

He broke off as the beetle crawled off the crucifix onto the desk. Immediately, it darkened to brown, blending with the wood surface.

"Please, father. Get me a container."

The beetle reached the edge of the desk, hesitated. Its antennae curled back, then forward.

"I will get you a container only if you promise to use discretion in your story of where this creature was found," the Prefect said.

"Father, I . . ."

The beetle leaped off the desk far out into the middle of the room, scuttled to the wall, up the wall, into a crack beside a window.

Joao pressed the switch of the handlight, directed its beam into the hole which had swallowed the strange beetle.

"How long has this hole been here, father?"

"For years. It was a flaw in the masonry . . . an earthquake, I believe."

Joao turned, crossed to the door in three strides, went through an arched hallway, down a flight of stone steps, through another door and short hall, through a grillwork gate, and into the exterior garden. He set the handlight to full intensity, washed its blue glare over the wall beneath the study window.

"Joao, what are you doing?"

"My job, father," Joao said. He glanced back, saw that the elder Martinho had stopped just outside the gate.

Joao returned his attention to the exterior wall, washed the blue glare of light on the stones beneath the window. He crouched low, running the light along the ground, peering behind each clod, erasing all shadows.

His searching scrutiny passed over the raw earth, turned to the bushes, then the lawn.

Joao heard his father come up behind.

"Do you see it, son?"

"No, father."

"You should have allowed me to crush it."

From the outer garden that bordered the road and the stone fence, there came a piercing stridulation. It hung on the air in almost tangible waves, making Joao think of the hunting cry of jungle predators. A shiver moved up his spine. He turned toward the driveway where he had parked his airtruck, sent the blue glare of light stabbing there.

He broke off, staring at the lawn. "What is that?"

The ground appeared to be in motion, reaching out toward them like the curling of a wave on a beach. Already, they were cut off from the house. The wave was still some ten paces away, but moving in rapidly.

Joao stood up, clutched his father's arm. He spoke quietly, hoping not to alarm the old man further. "We must get to my truck, father. We must run across them."

"Them?"

"Those are like the insect we saw inside, father—millions of them. Perhaps they are not beetles, after all. Perhaps they are like army ants. We must make it to the truck. I have equipment and supplies there. We will be safe inside. It is a bandeirante truck, father. You must run with me. I will help you."

They began to run, Joao holding his father's arm, pointing the way with the light.

Let his heart be strong enough, Joao prayed.

They were into the creeping wave of insects then, but the creatures leaped aside, opening a pathway which closed behind the running men.

The white form of the airtruck loomed out of the shadows at the far curve of the driveway about fifteen meters ahead.

"Joao . . . my heart," the elder Martinho gasped.

"You can make it," Joao panted. "Faster!" He almost lifted his father from the ground for the last few paces.

They were at the wide rear door into the truck's lab compartment now. Joao yanked open the door, slapped the light switch, reached for a spray hood and poison gun. He stopped, stared into the yellow-lighted compartment.

Two men sat there—sertao Indians by the look of them, with bright glaring eyes and bang-cut black hair beneath straw hats. They looked to be identical twins—even to the mud-grey clothing and sandals, the leather shoulder bags. The beetle-like insects crawled around them, up the walls, over the instruments and vials.

"What the devil?" Joao blurted.

One of the pair held a qena flute. He gestured with it, spoke in a rasping, oddly inflected voice: "Enter. You will not be harmed if you obey."

Joao felt his father sag, caught the old man in his arms. How light he felt! Joao stepped up into the truck, carrying his father. The elder Martinho breathed in short, painful gasps. His face was a pale blue and sweat stood out on his forehead.

"Joao," he whispered. "Pain . . . my chest."

"Medicine, father," Joao said. "Where is your medicine?"

"House," the old man said.

"It appears to be dying," one of the Indians rasped.

Still holding his father in his arms, Joao whirled toward the pair, blazed: "I don't know who you are or why you loosed those bugs here, but my father's dying and needs help. Get out of my way!"

"Obey or both die," said the Indian with the flute.

"He needs his medicine and a doctor," Joao pleaded. He didn't like the way the Indian pointed that flute. The motion suggested the instrument was actually a weapon.

"What part has failed?" asked the other Indian. He stared curiously at Joao's father. The old man's breathing had become shallow and rapid.

"It's his heart," Joao said. "I know you farmers don't think he's acted fast enough for . . ."

"Not farmers," said the one with the flute. "Heart?"

"Pump, said the other.

"Pump." The Indian with the flute stood up from the bench at the front of the lab, gestured down. "Put . . . father here."

The other one got off the bench, stood aside.

In spite of fear for his father, Joao was caught by the strange look of this pair, the fine, scale-like lines in their skin, the glittering brilliance of their eyes.

"Put father here," repeated the one with the flute, pointing at the bench. "Help can be . . ."

"Attained," said the other one.

"Attained," said the one with the flute.

Joao focused now on the masses of insects around the walls, the waiting quietude in their ranks. They *were* like the one in the study.

The old man's breathing was now very shallow, very rapid.

He's dying, Joao thought in desperation.

"Help can be attained," repeated the one with the flute. "If you obey, we will not harm."

The Indian lifted his flute, pointed it at Joao like a weapon. "Obey."

There was no mistaking the gesture.

Slowly, Joao advanced, deposited his father gently on the bench.

The other Indian bent over the elder Martinho's head, raised an eyelid. There was a professional directness about the gesture. The Indian pushed gently on the dying man's diaphragm, removed the Prefect's belt, loosened his collar. A stubby brown finger was placed against the artery in the old man's neck.

"Very weak," the Indian rasped.

Joao took another, closer look at this Indian, wondering at a sertao backwoodsman who behaved like a doctor.

"We've got to get him to a hospital," Joao said. "And his medicine in . . ."

"Hospital," the Indian agreed.

"Hospital?" asked the one with the flute.

A low, stridulant hissing came from the other Indian.

"Hospital," said the one with the flute.

That stridulant hissing! Joao stared at the Indian beside the Prefect. The sound had been reminiscent of the weird call that had echoed across the lawn.

The one with the flute poked him, said: "You will go into front and maneuver this . . ."

"Vehicle," said the one beside Joao's father.

"Vehicle," said the one with the flute.

"Hospital?" Joao pleaded.

"Hospital," agreed the one with the flute.

Joao looked once more to his father. The other Indian already was strapping the elder Martinho to the bench in preparation for movement. How competent the man appeared in spite of his backwoods look.

"Obey," said the one with the flute.

Joao opened the door into the front compartment, slipped through, feeling the other one follow. A few drops of rain spattered darkly against the curved windshield. Joao squeezed into the operator's seat, noted how the Indian crouched behind him, flute pointed and ready.

A dart gun of some kind, Joao guessed.

He punched the igniter button on the dash, strapped himself in while waiting for the turbines to build up speed. The Indian still crouched behind him, vulnerable now if the airtruck were spun sharply. Joao flicked the communications switch on the lower left corner of the dash, looked into the tiny screen there giving him a view of the lab compartment. The rear doors were open. He closed them by hydraulic remote. His father was securely strapped to the bench now, Joao noted, but the other Indian was equally secured.

The turbines reached their whining peak. Joao switched on the lights, engaged the hydrostatic drive. The truck lifted six inches, angled upward as Joao increased pump displacement. He turned left onto the street, lifted another two meters to increase speed, headed toward the lights of a boulevard.

The Indian spoke beside his ear: "You will turn toward the mountain over there." A hand came forward, pointing to the right.

The Alejandro Clinic is there in the foothills, Joao thought.

He made the indicated turn down a cross street angling toward the boulevard.

Casually, he gave pump displacement another boost, lifted another meter, and increased speed once more. In the same motion, he switched on the intercom to the rear compartment, tuned for the spare amplifier and pickup in the compartment beneath the bench where his father lay.

The pickup, capable of making a dropped pin sound like a cannon, gave forth only a distant hissing and rasping. Joao increased amplification. The instrument should have been transmitting the old man's heartbeats now, sending a noticeable drum-thump into the forward cabin.

There was nothing.

Tears blurred Joao's eyes, and he shook his head to clear them.

My father is dead, he thought. *Killed by these crazy backwoodsmen.*

He noted in the dash screen that the Indian back there had a hand under the elder Martinho's back. The Indian appeared to be massaging the dead man's back, and a rhythmic rasping matched the motion.

Anger filled Joao. He felt like driving the airtruck into an abutment, dying himself to kill these crazy men.

They were approaching the outskirts of the city, and ring-girders circled off to the left giving access to the boulevard. This was an area of small gardens and cottages protected by over-fly canopies.

Joao lifted the airtruck above the canopies, headed toward the boulevard.

To the clinic, yes, he thought. *But it is too late.*

In that instant, he realized there were no heartbeats at all coming from that rear compartment—only the slow, rhythmic grating, a faint susurration, and a cicada-like hum up and down scale.

"To the mountains, there," said the Indian behind him.

Again, the hand came forward to point off to the right.

Joao, with that hand close to his eyes and illuminated by the dash, saw the scale-like parts of a finger shift position slightly. In that shift, he recognized the scale-shapes by their claw fringes.

The beetles!

The finger was composed of linked beetles working in unison!

Joao turned, stared into the *Indian's* eyes, seeing now why they glistened so: they were composed of thousands of tiny facets.

"Hospital, there," the creature beside him said, pointing.

Joao turned back to the controls, fighting to keep from losing composure. They were not Indians . . . they weren't even human. They were insects—some kind of hive-cluster shaped and organized to mimic a man.

The implications of this discovery raced through his mind. How did they support their weight? How did they feed and breathe?

How did they speak?

Everything had to be subordinated to the urgency of getting this information and proof of it back to one of the big labs where the facts could be explored.

Even the death of his father could not be considered now. He had to capture one of these things, get out with it.

He reached overhead, flicked on the command transmitter, set its beacon for a homing call. *Let some of my Irmaos be awake and monitoring their sets,* he prayed.

"More to the right," said the creature behind him.

Again, Joao corrected course.

The moon was high overhead now, illuminating a line of bandeirante towers off to the left. The first barrier.

They would be out of the green area soon and into the grey—then, beyond that, another barrier and the great red that stretched out in reaching fingers through the Goyaz and the Mato Grosso. Joao could see scattered lights of Resettlement Plan farms ahead, and darkness beyond.

The airtruck was going faster than he wanted, but Joao dared not slow it. They might become suspicious.

"You must go higher," said the creature behind him.

Joao increased pump displacement, raised the nose. He levelled off at three hundred meters.

More bandeirante towers loomed ahead, spaced at closer intervals. Joao picked up the barrier signals on his meters, looked back at the *Indian*. The dissembler vibrations seemed not to affect the creature.

Joao looked out his side window and down. No one would challenge him, he knew. This was a bandeirante airtruck headed *into* the red zone . . . and with its transmitter sending out a homing call. The men down there would assume he was a band leader headed out on a contract after a successful bid—and calling his men to him for the job ahead.

He could see the moon-silvered snake of the Sao Francisco winding off to his left, and the lesser waterways like threads ravelled out of the foothills.

I must find the nest—where we're headed, Joao thought. He wondered if he dared turn on his receiver—but if his men started reporting in . . . No. That could make the creatures suspect; they might take violent counter-action.

My men will realize something is wrong when I don't answer, he thought. *They will follow.*

If any of them hear my call.

Hours droned past.

Nothing but moonlighted jungle sped beneath them now, and the moon was low on the horizon, near setting. This was the deep red region where broadcast poisons had been used at first with disastrous results. This was where the wild mutations had originated. It was here that Rhin Kelly had been reported missing.

This was the region being saved for the final assault, using a mobile barrier line when that line could be made short enough.

Joao armed the emergency charge that would separate the front and rear compartments of the truck where he fired it. The stub wings of the front compartment and its emergency rocket motors could get him back into bandeirante country.

With the *specimen* sitting behind him safely subdued, Joao hoped.

He looked up through the canopy, scanned the horizon as far as he could. Was that moonlight glistening on a truck far back to the right? He couldn't be sure.

"How much farther?" Joao asked.

"Ahead," the creature rasped.

Now that he was alert for it, Joao heard the modulated stridulation beneath that voice.

"But how long?" Joao asked. "My father . . ."

"Hospital for . . . the father . . . ahead," said the creature.

It would be dawn soon, Joao realized. He could see the first false line of light along the horizon behind. This night had passed so swiftly. Joao wondered if these creatures had injected some time-distorting drug into him without his knowing. He thought not. He was maintaining himself in the necessities of the moment. There was no time for fatigue or boredom when he had to record every landmark half visible in the night, sense everything there was to sense about these creatures with him.

How did they coordinate all those separate parts?

They appeared conscious. Was that mimicry, too? What did they use for a brain?

Dawn came, revealing the plateau of the Mato Grosso. Joao looked out his windows. This region, he knew, stretched across five degrees of latitude and six degrees of longitude. Once, it had been a region of isolated *fazendas* farmed by independent blacks and by *sertanistos* chained to the *encomendero* plantation system. It was hardwood jungles, narrow rivers with banks overgrown by lush trees and ferns, savannahs, and tangled life.

Even in this age it remained primitive, a fact blamed largely on insects and disease. It was one of the last strongholds of *teeming* insect life, if the International Ecological Organization's reports could be believed.

Supplies for the bandeirantes making the assault on this insect stronghold would come by way of São Paulo, by air and by transport on the multi-decked highways, then on antique diesel trains to Itapira, on river runners to Bahus and by airtruck to Registo and Leopoldina on the Araguaya.

This area crawled with insects: wire worms in the roots of the savannahs, grubs digging in the moist black earth, hopping beetles, dart-like angita wasps, chalcis flies, chiggers, sphecidae, braconidae, fierce hornets, white termites, hemipteric crawlers, blood roaches, thrips, ants, lice, mosquitoes, mites; moths, exotic butterflies, mantidae—and countless unnatural mutations of them all.

This would be an expensive fight—unless it were stopped—because it already had been lost.

I musn't think that way, Joao told himself. *Out of respect for my father.*

Maps of the IEO showed this region in varied intensities of red. Around the red ran a ring of grey with pink shading where one or two persistent forms of insect life resisted man's poisons, jelly flames, astringents, sonitoxics—the combination of flamant couroq and supersonics that drove insects from their hiding places into waiting death—and all the mechanical traps and lures in the bandeirante arsenal.

A grid map would be placed over this area and each thousand-acre square offered for bid to the independent bands to deinfest.

We bandeirantes are a kind of ultimate predator, Joao thought. *It's no wonder these creatures mimic us.*

But how good, really, was the mimicry? he asked himself. And how deadly to the predators?

"There," said the creature behind him, and the multi-part hand came forward to point toward a black scarp visible ahead in the grey light of morning.

Joao's foot kicked a trigger on the floor releasing a great cloud of orange dye-fog beneath the truck to mark the ground and forest for a mile around under this spot. As he kicked the trigger, Joao began counting down the five-second delay to the firing of the separation charge.

It came in a roaring blast that Joao knew would smear the creature behind him against the rear bulkhead. He sent the stub wings out, fed power to the rocket motors, and backed hard around. He saw the detached rear compartment settling slowly earthward above the dye cloud, its fall cushioned as the pumps of the hydrostatic drive automatically compensated.

I will come back, father, Joao thought. *You will be buried among family and friends.*

He locked the controls, twisted in the seat to see what had happened to his captive.

A gasp escaped Joao's lips.

The rear bulkhead crawled with insects clustered around something white and pulsing. The mud-grey shirt and trousers were torn, but insects already were repairing it, spinning out fibers that meshed and sealed on contact. There was a yellow sac-like extrusion near the pulsing white, and a dark brown skeleton with familiar articulation.

It looked like a human skeleton—but chitinous.

Before his eyes, the thing was reassembling itself, the long, furry antennae burrowing into the structure and interlocking.

The flute-weapon was not visible, and the thing's leather pouch had been thrown into a rear corner, but its eyes were in place in their brown sockets, staring at him. The mouth was reforming.

The yellow sac contracted, and a voice issued from the half-formed mouth.

"You must listen," it rasped.

Joao gulped, whirled back to the controls, unlocked them, and sent the cab into a wild, spinning turn.

A high-pitched rattling buzz sounded behind him. The noise seemed to pick up every bone in his body and shake it. Something crawled on his neck. He slapped at it, felt it squash.

All Joao could think of was escape. He stared frantically out at the earth beneath, seeing a blotch of white in a savannah off to his right and, in the same instant, recognizing another airtruck banking beside him, the insignia of his own Irmandades band bright on its side.

The white blotch in the savannah was resolving itself into a cluster of tents with an IEO orange and green banner flying beside them.

Joao dove for the tents, praying the other airtruck would follow.

Something stung his cheek. They were in his hair—biting, stinging. He stabbed the braking rockets, aimed for open ground about fifty meters from the tents. Insects were all over the inside of the glass now, blocking his vision. Joao said a silent prayer, hauled back on the control arm, felt the cab mush out, touch ground, skidding and slewing across the savannah. He kicked the canopy release before the cab stopped, broke the seal on his safety harness, and launched himself up and out to land, sprawling in grass.

He rolled through the grass, feeling the insects bite like fire over every exposed part of his body. Hands grabbed him and he felt a jelly hood splash across his face to protect it. A voice he recognized as Thome of his own band said: "This way, Johnny! Run!" They ran.

He heard a spraygun fire: "Whoooosh!"

And again.

And again.

Arms lifted him and he felt a leap.

They landed in a heap and a voice said, "Mother of God! Would you look at that!"

Joao clawed the jelly hood from his face, sat up to stare across the savannah. The grass seethed and boiled with insects around the uptilted cab and the airtruck that had landed beside it.

Joao looked around him, counted seven of his Irmaos with Thome, his chief sprayman, in command.

Beyond them clustered five other people, a red-haired woman slightly in front, half turned to look at the savannah and at him. He recognized the woman immediately: Dr. Rhin Kelly of the IEO. When they had met in the A' Chigua nightclub in Bahia, she had seemed exotic and desirable to Joao. Now, she wore a field uniform instead of gown and jewels, and her eyes held no invitation at all.

"I see a certain poetic justice in this . . . traitors," she said.

Joao lifted himself to his feet, took a cloth proffered by one of his men, wiped off the last of the jelly. He felt hands brushing him, clearing dead insects off his coveralls. The pain of his skin was receding under the medicant jelly, and now he found himself dominated by puzzled questioning as he recognized the mood of the IEO personnel.

They were furious and it was directed at him . . . and at his fellow Irmandades.

Joao studied the woman, noting how her green eyes glared at him, the pink flush to her skin.

"Dr. Kelly?" Joao said.

"If it isn't Joao Martinho, jefe of the Irmandades," she said, "the traitor of the Piratininga."

"They are crazy, that is the only thing, I think," said Thome.

"Your pets turned on you, didn't they?" she demanded. "And wasn't that inevitable?"

"Would you be so kind as to explain," Joao said.

"I don't need to explain," she said. "Let your friends out there explain." She pointed toward the rim of jungle beyond the savannah.

Joao looked where she pointed, saw a line of men in bandeirante white standing untouched amidst the leaping, boiling insects in the jungle shadow. He took a pair of binoculars from around the neck of one of his men, focused on the figures. Knowing what to look for made the identification easy.

"Tommy," Joao said.

His chief sprayman, Thome, bent close, rubbing at an insect sting on his swarthy cheek.

In a low voice, Joao explained what the figures at the jungle edge were.

"Aieee," Thome said.

An Irmandade on Joao's left crossed himself.

"What was it we leaped across coming in here?" Joao asked.

"A ditch," Thome said. "It seems to be filled with couroq jelly . . . an insect barrier of some kind."

Joao nodded. He began to have unpleasant suspicions about their position here. He looked at Rhin Kelly. "Dr. Kelly, where are the rest of your people? Surely there are more than five in an IEO field crew."

Her lips compressed, but she remained silent.

"So?" Joao glanced around at the tents, seeing their weathered condition. "And where is your equipment, your trucks and lab huts and jitneys?"

"Funny thing you should ask," she said, but there was uncertainty atop the sneering quality of her voice. "About a kilometer into the trees over there . . . ," she nodded to her left, ". . . is a wrecked jungle truck containing most of our . . . equipment, as you call it. The track spools of our truck were eaten away by acid."

"Acid?"

"It smelled like oxalic," said one of her companions, a blonde Nordic with a scar beneath his right eye.

"Start from the beginning," Joao said.

"We were cut off here almost six weeks ago," said the blonde man. "Something got our radio, our truck—they looked like giant chiggers and they can shoot an acid spray about fifteen meters."

"There's a glass case containing three dead specimens in my lab tent," said Dr. Kelly.

Joao pursed his lips, thinking. "So?"

"I heard part of what you were telling your men there," she said. "Do you expect us to believe that?"

"It is of no importance to me what you believe," Joao said. "How did you get here?"

"We fought our way in here from the truck using *caramuru* cold-fire spray," said the blonde man. "We dragged along what supplies we could, dug a trench around our perimeter, poured in the couroq powder, and topped it off with all our copahu oil . . . and here we sat."

"How many of you?" Joao asked.

"There were fourteen of us," said the man.

Joao rubbed the back of his neck where the insect stings were again beginning to burn. He glanced around at his men, assessing their condition and equipment, counted four spray rifles, saw the men carried spare charge cylinders on slings around their necks.

"The airtruck will take us," he said. "We had better get out of here."

Dr. Kelly looked out to the savannah, said: "I think it has been too late for that since a few seconds after you landed, bandeirante. I think in a day or so there'll be a few less traitors around. You're caught in your own trap."

Joao whirled to stare at the airtruck, barked: "Tommy! Vince! Get

. . ." He broke off as the airtruck sagged to its left.

"It's only fair to warn you," said Dr. Kelly, "to stay away from the edge of the ditch unless you first spray the opposite side. They can shoot a stream of acid at least fifteen meters . . . and as you can see . . . ," she nodded toward the airtruck, ". . . the acid eats metal."

"You're insane," Joao said. "Why didn't you warn us immediately?"

"Warn you?"

Her blonde companion said: "Rhin, perhaps we . . ."

"Be quiet, Hogar," she said, and turned back to Joao. "We lost nine men to your playmates." She looked at the small band of Irmandades. "Our lives are little enough to pay now for the extinction of eight of you . . . traitors."

"You *are* insane," Joao said.

"Stop playing innocent, bandeirante," she said. "We have seen your companions out there. We have seen the new playmates you bred . . . and we understand that you were too greedy; now your game has gotten out of hand."

"You've not seen my Irmaos doing these things," Joao said. He looked at Thome. "Tommy, keep an eye on these insane ones." He lifted the spray rifle from one of his men, took the man's spare charges, indicated the other three armed men. "You—come with me."

"Johnny, what do you do?" Thome asked.

"Salvage the supplies from the truck," Joao said. He walked toward the ditch nearest the airtruck, laid down a hard mist of foamal beyond the ditch, beckoned the others to follow, and leaped the ditch.

Little more than an hour later, with all of them acid burned—two seriously—the Irmandades retreated back across the ditch. They had salvaged less than a fourth of the equipment in the truck, and this did not include a transmitter.

"It is evident the little devils went first for the communications equipment," Thome said. "How could they tell?"

Joao said: "I do not want to guess." He broke open a first aid box, began treating his men. One had a cheek and shoulder badly splashed with acid. Another was losing flesh off his back.

Dr. Kelly came up, helped him treat the men, but refused to speak, even to answering the simplest question.

Finally, Joao touched up a spot on his own arm, neutralizing the acid and covering the burn with fleshtape. He gritted his teeth against the pain, stared at Rhin Kelly. "Where are these chigua you found?"

"Go find them yourself!" she snapped.

"You are a blind, unprincipled megalomaniac," Joao said, speaking in an even voice. "Do not push me too far."

Her face went pale and the green eyes blazed.

Joao grabbed her arm, hauled her roughly toward the tents. "Show me these chigua!"

She jerked free of him, threw back her red hair, stared at him defiantly. Joao faced her, looked her up and down with a calculating slowness.

"Go ahead, do violence to me," she said. "I'm sure I couldn't stop you."

"You act like a woman who wants . . . needs violence," Joao said. "Would you like me to turn you over to my men? They're a little tired of your raving."

Her face flamed. "You would not dare!"

"Don't be so melodramatic," he said. "I wouldn't give you the pleasure."

"You insolent . . . you . . ."

Joao showed her a wolfish grin, said: "Nothing you say will make me turn you over to my men!"

"Johnny."

It was Thome calling.

Joao turned, saw Thome talking to the Nordic IEO man who had volunteered information. What had she called him? Hogar.

Thome beckoned.

Joao crossed to the pair, bent close as Thome signaled secrecy.

"The gentleman here says the female doctor was bitten by an insect that got past their barrier's fumes."

"Two weeks ago," Hogar whispered.

"She has not been the same since," Thome said. "We humor her, jefe, no?"

Joao wet his lips with his tongue. He felt suddenly dizzy and too warm.

"The insect that bit her was similar to the ones that were on you," Hogar said, and his voice sounded apologetic.

They are making fun of me! Joao thought.

"I give the orders here!" he snapped.

"Yes, jefe," Thome said. "But you . . ."

"What difference does it make who gives the orders?"

It was Dr. Kelly close behind him.

Joao turned, glared at her. How hateful she looked . . . in spite of her beauty.

"What's the difference?" she demanded. "We'll all be dead in a few days anyway." She stared out across the savannah. "More of your friends have arrived."

Joao looked to the forest shadow, saw more human-like figures arriving. They appeared familiar and he wondered what it was—something at the edge of his mind, but his head hurt. Then he realized they looked like sertao Indians, like the pair who had lured him here. There were at least a hundred of them, apparently identical in every visible respect.

More were arriving by the second.

Each of them carried a qena flute.

There was something about the flutes that Joao felt he should remember.

Another figure came advancing through the *Indians,* a thin man in a black suit, his hair shiny silver in the sunlight.

"Father!" Joao gasped.

I'm sick, he thought. *I must be delirious.*

"That looks like the Prefect," Thome said. "Is it not so, Ramon?"

The Irmandade he addressed said: "If it is not the Prefect, it is his twin. Here, Johnny. Look with the glasses."

Joao took the glasses, focused on the figure advancing toward them through the grass. The glasses felt so heavy. They trembled in his hands and the figure coming toward them was blurred.

"I cannot see!" Joao muttered and he almost dropped the glasses.

A hand steadied him, and he realized he was reeling.

In an instant of clarity, he saw that the line of Indians had raised their flutes, pointing to the IEO camp. That buzzing-rasping that had shaken his bones in the airtruck cab filled the universe around him. He saw his companions begin to fall.

In the instant before his world went blank, Joao heard his father's voice calling strongly: "Joao! Do not resist! Put down your weapons!"

The trampled grassy earth of the campsite, Joao saw, was coming up to meet his face.

It cannot be my father, Joao thought. *My father is dead and they've copied him . . . mimicry, nothing more.*

Darkness.

There was a dream of being carried, a dream of tears and shouting, a dream of violent protests and defiance and rejection.

He awoke to yellow-orange light and the figure who could not be his father bending over him, thrusting a hand out, saying: "Then examine my hand if you don't believe!"

But Joao's attention was on a face behind his father. It was a giant face, baleful in the strange light, its eyes brilliant and glaring with pupils within pupils. The face turned, and Joao saw it was no more than two centimeters thick. Again, it turned, and the eyes focused on Joao's feet.

Joao forced himself to look down, began trembling violently as he saw he was half enveloped in a foaming green cocoon, that his skin shared some of the same tone.

"Examine my hand!" ordered the old-man figure beside him.

"He has been dreaming." It was a resonant voice that boomed all around him, seemingly coming from beneath the giant face. "He has been dreaming," the voice repeated. "He is not quite awake."

With an abrupt, violent motion, Joao reached out, clutched the proffered hand.

It felt warm . . . human.

For no reason he could explain, tears came to Joao's eyes.

"Am I dreaming?" he whispered. He shook his head to clear away the tears.

"Joao, my son," said his father's voice.

Joao looked up at the familiar face. It *was* his father and no mistake. "But . . . your heart," Joao said.

"My pump," the old man said. "Look." And he pulled his hand away, turned to display where the back of his black suit had been cut away, its edges held by some gummy substance, and a pulsing surface of oily yellow between those cut edges.

Joao saw the hair-fine scale lines, the multiple shapes, and he recoiled.

So it was a copy, another of their tricks.

The old man turned back to face him. "The old pump failed and they gave me a new one," he said. "It shares my blood and lives off me and it'll give me a few more years. What do you think our bright IEO specialists will say about the *usefulness* of that?"

"Is it really you?" Joao demanded.

"All except the pump," said the old man. "They had to give you and some of the others a whole new blood system because of all the corrosive poison that got into you."

Joao lifted his hands, stared at them.

"They know medical tricks we haven't even dreamed about," the old man said. "I haven't been this excited since I was a boy. I can hardly wait to get back and . . . Joao! What is it?"

Joao was thrusting himself up, glaring at the old man. "We're not human anymore if . . . We're not human!"

"Be still, son!" the old man ordered.

"If this is true," Joao protested, "they're in control." He nodded toward the giant face behind his father. "They'll *rule* us!"

He sank back, gasping. "We'll be their slaves."

"Foolishness," rumbled the drum voice.

Joao looked at the giant face, growing aware of the fluorescent insects above it, seeing that the insects clung to the ceiling of a cave, noting finally a patch of night sky and stars where the fluorescent insects ended.

"What is a slave?" rumbled the voice.

Joao looked beneath the face where the voice originated, saw a white mass about four meters across, a pulsing yellow sac protruding from it, insects crawling over it, into fissures along its surface, back to the ground beneath. The face appeared to be held up from that white mass by dozens of round stalks, their scaled surfaces betraying their nature.

"Your attention is drawn to our way of answering your threat to us," rumbled the voice, and Joao saw that the sound issued from the pulsing yellow sac. "This is our brain. It is vulnerable, very vulnerable, weak, yet strong . . . just as your brain. Now, tell me, what is a slave?"

Joao fought down a shiver of revulsion, said: "I'm a slave now; I'm in bondage to you."

"Not true," rumbled the voice. "A slave is one who must produce wealth for another, and there is only one true wealth in all the universe—living time. Are we slaves because we have given your father more time to live?"

Joao looked up to the giant, glittering eyes, thought he detected amusement there.

"The lives of all those with you have been spared or extended as well," drummed the voice. "That makes us your slaves, does it not?"

"What do you take in return?"

"Ah, hah!" the voice fairly barked. "Quid pro quo! You are, indeed, our slaves as well. We are tied to each other by a bond of mutual slavery that cannot be broken—never could be."

"It is very simple once you understand it," Joao's father said.

"Understand what?"

"Some of our kind once lived in greenhouses and their cells remembered the experience," rumbled the voice. "You know about greenhouses, of course?" It turned to look out at the cave mouth where dawn was beginning to touch the world with grey. "That out there, that is a greenhouse, too." Again, it looked down at Joao, the giant eyes glaring. "To sustain life, a greenhouse must achieve a delicate balance—enough of this chemical, enough of that one, another substance available when needed. What is poison one day can be sweet food the next."

"What's all this to do with slavery?" Joao demanded.

"Life has developed over millions of years in this greenhouse we call Earth," the voice rumbled. "Sometimes it developed in the poison excrement of other life . . . and then that poison became necessary to it. Without a substance produced by the wire worm, that savannah grass out there would die . . . in time. Without substances produced by

. . . insects, your kind of life would die. Sometimes, just a faint trace of the substance is needed, such as the special copper compound produced by the arachnids. Sometimes, the substance must subtly change each time before it can be used by a life form at the end of the chain. The more different forms of life there are, the more life the greenhouse can support. This is the lesson of the greenhouse. The successful greenhouse must grow many times many forms of life. The more forms of life it has, the healthier it is."

"You're saying we have to stop killing insects," Joao said. "You're saying we have to let you take over."

"We say you must stop killing yourselves," rumbled the voice. "Already, the Chinese are . . . I believe you would call it *reinfesting* their land. Perhaps they will be in time, perhaps not. Here, it is not too late. There . . . they were fast and thorough . . . and they may need help."

"You . . . give us no proof," Joao said.

"There will be time for proof, later," said the voice. "Now, join your woman friend outside; let the sun work on your skin and the chlorophyll in your blood, and when you come back, tell me if the sun is your slave."

Incased in Ancient Rind

R. A. Lafferty

Humans, like other creatures, are seriously threatened by the deteriorating condition of our world but are likewise adaptable—so what changes might we make in the difficult centuries ahead? What differences might those changes make in the basic physiology and psychology of humanity?

R. A. Lafferty is generally considered a writer of science fiction whimsy, despite such thoughtful novels as Past Master and The Devil Is Dead. He maintains, however, that humor and seriousness can be very similar. See below.

I

The eye is robbed of impetus
By Fogs that stand and shout:
And swiftness all goes out from us
And all the stars go out.

—O'HANLON, "Lost Skies"

WEAR A MASK or die," the alarmists had been saying louder and louder; and now they were saying, "Wear a mask and die anyhow." And why do we so often hold the alarmists in contempt? It isn't always a false alarm they sound and this one wasn't. The pollution of air and water and land had nearly brought the world to a death halt, and crisis was at hand as the stifling poison neared critical mass.

"Aw, dog dirt, not another air pollution piece," you say.

Oh, come off of it. You know us better than that. This is not such an account as you might suppose. It will not be stereotype, though it may be stereopticon.

"The lights are burning very brightly," said Harry Baldachin, "this club room is sealed off as tightly as science can seal it, the air conditioning labors faithfully, the filters are the latest perfection, this is the clearest day in a week—likely a clearer day than any that will ever follow—yet we have great difficulty in seeing each other's face across the table. And we are in Mountain Top Club out in the high windy country beyond the cities. It is quite bad in the towns, they say. Suffocation victims are still lying unburied in heaps."

"There's a curious thing about that though," Clement Flood said. "The people are making much progress on the unburied heaps. People aren't dying as fast as they were even a month ago. Why aren't they?"

"Don't be so truculent about it, Clement," Harry said. "The people will die soon enough. All the weaker ones have already died, I believe, and the strong ones linger awhile; but I don't see how any of us can have lungs left. There'll be another wave of deaths, and then another and another. And all of us will go with it."

"I won't," said Sally Strumpet. "I will live forever. It doesn't bother me very much at all, just makes my nose and eyes itch a little bit. What worries me, though, is that I don't test fertile yet. Do you suppose that the pollution has anything to do with my not being fertile?"

"What are you chattering about, little girl?" Charles Broadman asked. "Well, it is something to think about. Gathering disasters usually increase fertility, as did the pollution disaster at first. It has always been as though some cosmic wisdom was saying, 'Fast and heavy fruit now for the fruitless days ahead.' But now it seems as if the cosmic wisdom is saying 'Forget it, this is too overmuch.' But fertility now is not so much inhibited as delayed," Broadman continued almost as if he knew what he was talking about.

Sally Strumpet was a bright-eyed (presently red-eyed) seventeen-year-old actress, and that was her stage name only. Her real name was Joan Struthio, and she was met for club dinner with Harry Baldachin, Clement Flood, and Charles Broadman, all outstanding in the mentality set, because she had a publicity man who arranged such things. Sally herself belonged to the mentality set by natural right, but not many suspected this fact: only Charles Broadman of those present, only one in a hundred of those who were entranced by Sally's rather lively simpering, hardly any of the mucous-lunged people.

"This may be the last of our weekly dinners that I am able to attend," Harry Baldachin coughed. "I'd have taken to my bed long ago except that I can't breathe at all lying down anymore. I'm a dying man now, as are all of us."

"I'm not, neither the one nor the other," Sally said.

"Neither is Harry," Charles Broadman smiled snakishly, "not the first, surely, and popular doubt has been cast on the second. You're not dying, Harry. You'll live till you're sick of it."

"I'm sick of it now. By my voice you know that I'm dying."

"By your voice I know that there's a thickening of the pharynx," Charles said. "By your swollen hands I know that there is already a thickening of the metacarpals and phalanges, not to mention the carpals themselves. Your eyes seem unnaturally deep-set now, as though they had decided to withdraw into some interior cave. But I believe that it is the thickening of your brow ridges that makes them seem so, and the new bulbosity of your nose. You've been gaining weight, have you not?"

"I have, yes, Broadman. Every pound of poison that I take in adds a pound to my weight. I'm dying, and we're all dying."

"Why Harry, you're coming along amazingly well. I thought I would be the first of us to show the new signs, and instead it is yourself. No, you will be a very, very long time dying."

"The whole face of the earth is dying," Harry Baldachin maintained.

"Not dying. Thickening and changing," said Charles Broadman.

"There's a mortal poison on everything," Clement Flood moaned. "When last was a lake fish seen not floating belly upward? The cattle are poisoned and all the plants, all dying."

"Not dying. Growing larger and weirder," said Broadman.

"I am like a dish that is broken" said the Psalmist. "My strength has failed through affliction, and my bones are consumed. I am forgotten like the unremembered dead."

"Your dish is made thicker and grosser, but it is not broken," Broadman insisted. "Your bones are not consumed but altered. And you are forgotten only if you forget."

"Poor Psalmist," said Sally. This was startling, for the Psalmist had always been a private joke of Charles Broadman's, but now Sally was aware of him also. "Why, your strength hasn't failed at all," she said. "You come on pretty strong to me. But my own nose is always itching; that's the only bad part of it. I feel as though I were growing a new nose. When can I come to another club supper with you gentlemen?"

"There will be no more," Harry Baldachin hacked through his thickened pharynx. "We'll all likely be dead by next week. This is the last of our meetings."

"Yes, we had better call our dinners off," Clement Flood choked. "We surely can't hold them every week now."

"Not every week," said Charles Broadman, "but we will still hold them. This all happened before, you know."

"I want to come however often they are," Sally insisted.

"How often will we hold them, dreamer, and we all near dead?"

Harry asked. "You say that this has happened before, Broadman? Well then, didn't we all die with it before?"

"No. We lived an immeasurably long time with it before," Charles Broadman stated. "What, can you not read the signs in the soot yet, Harry?"

"Just how often would you suggest that we meet then, Charles?" Clement Flood asked with weary sarcasm.

"Oh, how about once every hundred years, gentlemen and Sally. Would that be too often?"

"Fool," Harry Baldachin wheezed and peered out from under his thickening orbital ridges.

"Idiot," Clement Flood growled from his thickening throat.

"Why, I think a hundred years from today would be perfect," Sally cried. "That will be a wednesday, will it not?"

"That was fast," Broadman admired. "Yes, it will be a wednesday, Sally. Do be here, Sally, and we will talk some more of these matters. Interesting things will have happened in the meanwhile. And you two gentlemen will be here?"

"No, don't refuse," Sally cut in. "You are so unimaginative about all this. Mr. Baldachin, say that you will dine with us here one hundred years from today if you are alive and well."

"By the emphyseman God that afflicts us, and me dying and gone, yes, I will be here one hundred years from today if I am alive and well," Harry Baldachin said angrily. "But I will not be alive this time next week."

"And you say it also, Mr. Flood," Sally insisted.

"Oh, stop putting fools' words in people's mouths, little girl. Let me die in my own phlegm."

"Say it, Mr. Flood," Sally insisted. "Say that you will dine with us all here one hundred years from this evening if you are alive and well."

"Oh, all right," Clement Flood mumbled as he bled from his rheumy eyes. "Under those improbable conditions I will be here."

But only Sally and Charles Broadman had the quick wisdom to understand that the thing was possible.

Fog, smog, and grog, and the people perished. And the more stubborn ones took a longer time about perishing than the others. But a lethal mantle wrapped the whole globe now. It was poison utterly compounded, and no life could stand against it. There was no possibility of improvement; there was no hope of anything. It could only get worse. Something drastic had to happen.

And of course it got worse. And of course something drastic happened. The carbon pollution on earth reached trigger mass. But it didn't work out quite as some had supposed that it might.

2

We shamble thorough our longish terms
Of Levalloisian mind
Till we be ponderous Pachyderms
Incased in ancient rind.

—O'HANLON, "Lost Skies"

Oh, for one thing, no rain, or almost no rain fell on the earth for that next hundred years. It was not missed. Moisture was the one thing that was in abounding plenty.

"But a mist rose from the earth and watered all the surface of the ground."

Rainless rain forests grew and grew. Ten million cubic miles of seawater rose to the new forming canopy and hung there in a covering world-cloud no more than twenty miles up. Naturally the sun and moon and stars were seen no more on the earth for that hundred years; and the light that did come down through the canopy seemed unnatural. But plants turned into giant plants and spread over the whole earth, gobbling the carbon dioxide with an almost audible gnashing.

So there was more land, now, and wetter land. There was a near equipoise of temperature everywhere under the canopy. The winds were all gathered up again into that old leather bag and they blew no more on the earth. Beneath the canopy it was warm and humid and stifling from pole to pole and to the utmost reaches of the earth.

It was a great change and everything felt it. Foot-long saurians slid out of their rocks that were warm and moist again, and gobbled and grew, and gobbled and grew, and gobbled and grew. Old buried fossil suns had been intruded into the earth air for a long time, and now the effect of their carbon and heat was made manifest. Six-foot-diameter turtles, having been ready to die, now postponed that event; and in another hundred years, in two hundred, they would be ten-foot-diameter turtles, thirteen-foot-diameter turtles.

The canopy, the new lowering copper-colored sky, shut out the direct sun and the remembered blue sky, and it shut out other things that had formerly trickled down: hard radiation, excessive ultraviolet rays and all the actinic rays, and triatomic oxygen. These things had been the carriers of the short and happy life, or the quick and early death; and these things were no longer carried down.

There was a thickening of bone and plate on all boned creatures everywhere, as growth continued for added years. There were new inhibitors and new stimulants; new bodies for old—no, no—older bodies for old. Certain teeth in certain beasts had always grown for all the beast life. Now the beast life was longer, and the saber-tooths appeared again.

It was murky under the new canopy, though. It took a long time to get used to it—and a long time was provided. It was a world filled with fogs, and foggy phrases.

"A very ancient and fishlike smell."

"Just to keep her from the foggy foggy dew."

"There were giants on the earth in those days."

"When Enos was ninety years old, he became the father of Cainan. Enos lived eight hundred and fifteen years after the birth of Cainan, and had other sons and daughters."

"Behold now Behemoth, which I have made with thee."

"And beauty and length of days."

"There Leviathan . . . stretched like a promontory sleeps or swims."

"I will restore to you the years that the locust has eaten."

"A land where the light is as darkness," said Job.

"Poor Job," said Sally Strumpet.

"This is my sorrow, that the right hand of the Most High is changed," said the Psalmist.

"Poor Psalmist," said Sally Strumpet.

The world that was under the canopy of the lowering sky was very like a world that was under water. Everything was incomparably aged and giantized and slow. Bears grew great. Lizards lengthened. Human people broadened and grew in their bones, and lengthened in their years.

"I suppose that we are luckier than those who come before or after," Harry Baldachin said. "We had our youths, we had much of our proper lives, and then we had this."

This was a hundred years to a day (a wednesday, was it not?) since that last club dinner, and the four of them, Harry Baldachin, Clement Flood, Charles Broadman, and Sally Strumpet were met once more in the Mountain Top Club. Two of them, it will be remembered, hadn't expected to be there.

"What I miss most in these last nine or ten decades is colors," Clement Flood mused. "Really, we haven't colors, not colors as we had when I was young. Too much of the sun is intercepted now. Such aviators as still go up (the blue-sky hobbyists and such) say that there are still true colors above the canopy, that very ordinary objects may be taken up there and examined, and that they will be in full color as in ancient times. I believe that the loss of full color was understood by earlier psychologists and myth makers. In my youth, in my pre-canopy youth, I made some studies of very ancient photography. It was in black and white and gray only, just as most dreams were then in black and white and gray only. It is strange that these two things nearly anticipated the present world; we are so poor in color that we nearly fall back to the old predictions. No person under a hundred years old, unless he has flown above the canopy, has ever seen real color. But I will remember it."

"I remember wind and storm," said Harry Baldachin, "and these cannot now be found in their real old form even by going above the canopy. I remember frost and snow, and these are very rare everywhere on earth now. I remember rain, that most efficient thing ever—but it's pleasant in memory."

"I remember lightning," said Charles Broadman, "and thunder. Ah, thunder."

"Well, it's more than made up for in amplitude," Clement smiled. "There is so much more of the earth that is land now, and all the land is gray and growing—I had almost used the old phrase 'green and growing,' but the color green can be seen now only by those who ascend above the canopy. But the world is warm and moist from pole to pole now, and filled with giant plants and giant animals and giant food. The canopy above, and the greenhouse diffusion effect below, it makes all the world akin. And the oceans are so much more fertile now—one can almost walk on the backs of the fish. There is such a lot more carbon in the carbon cycle than there used to be, such a lot more life on the earth. And more and more carbon is being put into the cycle every year."

"That's true," said Harry Baldachin. "That's about the only industrialism that is still being carried out, the only industrialism that is still needed: burning coal and petroleum to add carbon to the cycle, burning it by the tens of thousands of cubic miles. Certain catastrophes of the past had buried great amounts of this carbon, had taken it out of the cycle, and the world was so much poorer for it. It was as if the fruit of whole suns had been buried uselessly in the earth. Now, in the hundred years since the forming or the reforming of the canopy, and to a lesser extent during the two hundred years before its forming, these buried suns have been dug up and put to use again."

"The digging up of buried suns has caused all manner of mischief," Charles Broadman said.

"You are an old fogy, Charles," Clement Flood told him. "A hundred years of amplitude have made no change at all in you."

The hundred years had really made substantial changes in all of them. They hadn't aged exactly, not in the old way of aging. They had gone on growing in a new, or a very old way. They had thickened in face and body. They had become more sturdy, more solid, more everlasting. Triatomic oxygen, that old killer, was dense in the world canopy, shutting out the other killers; but it was very rare at ground level, a perfect arrangement. There was no wind under the canopy, and things held their levels well. How long persons might live now could only be guessed. It might be up to a thousand years.

"And how is the—ah—younger generation?" Harry Baldachin asked. "How are you, Sally? We have not seen you for a good round century."

"I am wonderful, and I thought you'd never ask. People take so much longer to get to the point now, you know. The most wonderful news is that I now test fertile. When I was seventeen I worried that I didn't test out. The new times had already affected me, I believe. But now my term has come around, and about time I'd say. I'm a hundred and seventeen and there are cases of girls no more than a hundred who are ready. I will marry this very week and will have sons and daughters. I will marry one of the last of the aviators who goes above the canopy. I myself have gone above the canopy and seen true colors and felt the thin wind."

"It's not a very wise thing to do," said Harry. "They are going to put a stop to flights above the canopy, I understand. They serve no purpose; and they are unsettling."

"Oh, but I want to be unsettled," Sally cried.

"You should be old enough not to want any such thing, Sally," Clement Flood advised. "We are given length of days now, and with them wisdom should come to us."

"Well, *has* wisdom come?" Charles Broadman asked reasonably. "No, not really. Only slowness has come to us."

"Yes, wisdom, we have it now," Harry Baldachin insisted. "We enter the age of true wisdom. Long wisdom. Slow wisdom."

"You are wrong, and unwise," Charles Broadman said out of his thickened and almost everlasting face. "There is not, there has never been, any such name or thing as unqualified Wisdom. And there surely are not such things as Long Wisdom or Slow Wisdom."

"But there *is* a thing named Swift Wisdom," Sally stated with great eagerness.

"There was once, there is not now, we lost it," Charles Broadman said sadly.

"We almost come to disagreement," Baldachin protested, "and that is not seemly for persons of the ample age. Ah well, we have lingered five hours over the walnuts and the wine, and perhaps it were the part of wisdom that we leave each other now. Shall we make these dinners a regular affair?"

"I want to," Sally said.

"Yes, I'd rather like to continue the meetings at regular intervals," Clement Flood agreed.

"Fine, fine," Charles Broadman murmured. "We will meet here again one hundred years from this evening."

3

And some forget to leave or let
And some forget to die:
But may my right hand wither yet
If I forget the sky.

—O'HANLON, "Lost Skies"

We are not so simple as to say that the Baluchitherium returned. The Baluchitherium was of an earlier age of the earth and flourished under an earlier canopy. Something that looked very like the Baluchitherium did appear, however. It was not even of the rhinoceros family. It was a horse grown giant and gangly. Horses of course, being artificial animals like dogs, are quite plastic and adaptable. A certain upper-lippiness quickly appeared when this new giant animal had turned into a giant leaf eater and sedge eater ("true" grass had about disappeared: how could it compete with the richer and fuller plants that flourished under the canopy?); a certain spreading of the hoofs, a dividedness more of appearance than of fact, was apparent after this animal had become a swamp romper. Well, it was a giant horse and a mighty succulent horse, but it looked like the Baluchitherium of old.

We are not so naive as to accept that the brontosaurus came back. No. But there was a small flatfooted lizard that quickly became a large flatfooted lizard and came to look more and more like the brontosaurus. It came to look like this without changing anything except its size and its general attitude toward the world. Put a canopy over any creature and it will look different without much intrinsic change.

We surely are not gullible enough to believe that the crinoid plants returned to the ponds and the slack water pools. Well, but certain conventional long-stemmed water plants had come to look and behave very like the crinoids.

All creatures and plants had made their peace with the canopy, or they had perished. The canopy, in its two hundredth year, was a going thing; and the blue-sky days had ended forever.

There was still vestigial organic nostalgia for the blue-sky days, however. Most land animals still possessed eyes that would have been able to see full colors if there were such colors to be seen; man himself still possessed such eyes. Most food browsers still possessed enough crown to their teeth to have grazed grass if such an inefficient thing as grass had remained. Many human minds would still have been able to master the mathematics of stellar movements and positions, if ease and the disappearance of the stellar content had not robbed them of the inclination and opportunity for such things. (There was, up to about two hundred years ago, a rather cranky pseudo-science named astronomy.)

There were other vestiges that hung like words in the fog and rank dew of the world.

"And the name of the star is called Wormwood."

"In the brightness of the saints, before the day-star."

"It was the star-eater who came, and then the sky-eater."

"And the stars are not clear in his sight," said Job.

"Poor Job," said Sally.

The second hundred years had gone by, and the diners had met at Mountain Top Club again. And an extra diner was with them.

"Poor Sally," said Harry Baldachin. "You are still a giddy child, and you have already had sons and daughters. But you should not have brought your husband to this dinner without making arrangements. You could have proposed it this time, and had him here the next time. After all, it would only be a hundred years."

We are not so soft-headed as to say that the Neanderthal men had returned. But the diners at Mountain Top Club, with that thickening of their faces and bones and bodies that only age will bring, had come to look very like Neanderthals—even Sally a little.

"But I wanted him here this time," Sally said. "Who knows what may happen in a hundred years?"

"How could anything happen in a hundred years?" Harry Baldachin asked.

"Besides, your husband is in ill repute," Clement Flood said with some irritation. "He's said to be an outlaw flyer. I believe that a pickup order for his arrest was put out some six years ago, so he may be picked up at any time. In the blue-sky days he would have been picked up within twenty-four hours, but we move more graciously and slowly under the canopy."

"It's true that there's a pickup order out for me," said the husband. "It's true that I still fly above the canopy, which is now illegal. I doubt if I'll be able to do it much longer. I might be able to get my old craft up one more time, but I don't believe I would be able to get it down. I'll leave if you want me to."

"You will stay," Charles Broadman said. "You are a member of the banquet now, and you and I and Sally have them outnumbered."

The husband of Sally was a slim man. He did not seem to be properly thickened to joint and bone. It was difficult to see how he could live a thousand years with so slight a body. Even now he showed a certain nervousness and anxiety, and that did not bode a long life.

"Why should anyone want to go above the canopy?" Harry Baldachin asked crossly. "Or rather, why should anyone want to claim to do it, since it is now assumed that the canopy is endless and no one could go above it?"

"But we do go above it," Sally stated. "We go for the sun and the stars; for the thin wind there, which is a type of the old wind; for the rain even—do you know that there is sometimes rain passing between one part of the canopy and another?—for the rainbow—do you know that we have actually seen a rainbow?"

"I know that the rainbow is a sour myth," Baldachin said.

"No, no, it's real," Sally swore. "Do you recall the lines of the old Vachel Lindsay: 'When my hands and my hair and my feet you kissed / When you cried with your love's new pain / What was my name in the dragon mist / In the rings of rainbowed rain?' Is that not wonderful?"

Harry Baldachin pondered it a moment.

"I give it up, Sally," he said then. "I can't deduce it. Well, what's the answer to the old riddle? What is the cryptic name that we are supposed to guess?"

"Forgive him," Charles Broadman murmured to the husband and to Sally. "We have all of us been fog-bound for too long a time below the canopy."

"It is now believed that the canopy has always been there," Baldachin said stiffly.

"Almost always, Harry, but not always," Charles Broadman answered him. "It was first put there very early, on the second day, as a matter of fact. You likely do not remember that the second day is the one that God did not call good. It was surely a transient and temporary backdrop that was put there to be pierced at the proper times by early death and by grace. One of the instants it was pierced was just before this present time. It had been breached here and there for short ages. Then came the clear instant, which has been called glaciation or flood or catastrophe, when it was shattered completely and the blue sky was seen supreme. It was quite a short instant; some say it was not more than ten thousand years, some say it was double that. It happened, and now it is gone. But are we expected to forget that bright instant?"

"The law expects you to forget that instant, Broadman, since it never happened, and it is forbidden to say that it happened," Baldachin stated stubbornly. "And you, man, the outlaw flyer, it is rumored that you have your craft hidden somewhere on this very mountain. Ah, I must leave you all for a moment."

They sat for some five hours over the walnuts and wine. It is the custom to sit for a long time after eating the heavy steaks of any of the neo-saurians. Baldachin returned and left several times, as did Flood. They seemed to have something going between them. They might even have been in a hurry about it if hurry were possible to them. But mostly the five persons spent the after-dinner hours in near-congenial talk.

"The short and happy life, that is the forgotten thing," the husband of Sally was saying. "The blue-sky interval—do you know what that was? It was the bright death sword coming down in a beam of light. Do you know that in the blue-sky days hardly one man in ten lived to be even a hundred years old? But do you know that in the blue-sky days it wasn't sealed off? The sword stroke was a cutting of the bonds. It was a release and an invitation to higher travel. Are you not tired of living in this prison for even two hundred years or three hundred?"

"You are mad," Harry Baldachin said.

Well of course the young man was mad. Broadman looked into the young man's eyes (this man was probably no older than Sally; he likely was no more than two hundred and twenty) and was startled by the secret he discovered there. The color could not be seen under the canopy, of course; the eyes were gray to the canopy world. But if he were above the canopy, Broadman knew, in the blue-sky region where the full colors could be seen, the young man's eyes would have been sky-blue.

"For the short and happy life again, and for the infinite release," Sally's husband was saying. "For those under the canopy there is no release. The short and happy life and scorching heat and paralyzing cold. Hunger and disease and fever and poverty, all the wonderful things! How have we lost them? These are not idle dreams. We have them by the promise—the Bow in the Clouds and the Promise that we be no more destroyed. But you destroy yourselves under the canopy."

"Mad, mad. Oh, but they are idle dreams, young man, and now they are over," Harry Baldachin smiled an old saurian smile. And the room was full of ponderous guards.

"Take the two young ones," Clement Flood said to the thickened guards.

But the laughter of Sally Strumpet shivered their ears and got under their thick skins.

"Take us?" she hooted. "How would they ever take us?"

"Girl, there are twenty of them; they will take you easily," Baldachin said slowly. But the husband of Sally was also laughing.

"Will twenty creeping turtles be able to catch two soaring birds on the high wing?" he laughed. "Would two hundred of them be able to?

But your rumor is right, Baldachin. I do have my craft hidden somewhere on this very mountain. Ah, I believe I will be able to get the old thing up one more time."

"But we'll never be able to get it down again," Sally whooped. "Coming, Charles?"

"Yes," Charles Broadman cried eagerly. And he meant it, he meant it.

Those guards were powerful and ponderous, but they were just too slow. Twenty creeping turtles were no way able to catch those two soaring birds in their high flight. Crashing through windows with a swift tinkle of glass, then through the uncolored dark of the canopy world, to the rickety craft named Swift Wisdom that would go up one more time but would never be able to come down again, the last two flyers escaped through the pachydermous canopy.

"Mad," said Harry Baldachin.

"Insane," said Clement Flood.

"No," Charles Broadman said sadly. "No." And he sank back into his chair once more. He had wanted to go with them and he couldn't. The spirit was willing but the flesh was thickened and ponderous.

Two tears ran down his heavy cheeks but they ran very slowly, hardly an inch a minute. How should things move faster on the world under the canopy?

Occam's Scalpel

Theodore Sturgeon

It's very difficult to believe that beings as smart as humans would deliberately maintain societies that destroy the world in which they live. Is there some unknown factor at work that causes such obviously irrational behavior? Theodore Sturgeon suggests an answer.

Sturgeon's is a name to conjure with in science fiction. Though his stories are often strongly philosophical (More Than Human and Venus Plus X are examples), he always puts human reactions foremost in his stories.

I

JOE TRILLING HAD a funny way of making a living. It was a good living, but of course he didn't make anything like the bundle he could have in the city. On the other hand he lived in the mountains a half mile away from a picturesque village in clean air and piney-birchy woods along with lots of mountain laurel and he was his own boss. There wasn't much competition for what he did; he had his wife and kids around all the time and more orders than he could fill. He was one of the night people and after the family had gone to bed he could work quietly and uninterruptedly. He was happy as a clam.

One night—very early morning, really—he was interrupted. *Bup, bup, bup, bup.* Knock at the window, two shorts, two longs. He froze, he whirled, for he knew that knock. He hadn't heard it for years but it had been a part of his life since he was born. He saw the face outside and filled his lungs for a whoop that would have roused them at the fire station on the village green, but then he saw the finger on the lips and let the air out. The finger beckoned and Joe Trilling whirled again, turned down a flame, read a gauge, made a note, threw a switch, and joyfully but silently dove for the outside door. He slid out, closed it carefully, peered into the dark.

"Karl?"

"Shh."

There he was, edge of the woods. Joe Trilling went there and, whispering because Karl had asked for it, they hit each other, cursed, called each other the filthiest possible names. It would not be easy to explain this to an extra-terrestrial; it isn't necessarily a human thing to do. It's a cultural thing. It means, I want to touch you, it means I love you; but they were men and brothers, so they hit each other's arms and shoulders and swore despicable oaths and insults, until at last even those words wouldn't do and they stood in the shadows, holding each other's biceps and grinning and drilling into each other with eyes. Then Karl Trilling moved his head sidewards toward the road and they walked away from the house.

"I don't want Hazel to hear us talking," Karl said. "I don't want her or anyone to know I was here. How is she?"

"Beautiful. Aren't you going to see her at all—or the kids?"

"Yes, but not this trip. There's the car. We can talk there. I really am afraid of that bastard."

"Ah," said Joe. "How is the great man?"

"Po'ly," said Karl. "But we're talking about two different bastards. The great man is only the richest man in the world, but I'm not afraid of him, especially now. I'm talking about Cleveland Wheeler."

"Who's Cleveland Wheeler?"

They got into the car. "It's a rental," said Karl. "Matter of fact, it's the second rental. I got out of the executive jet and took a company car and rented another—and then this. Reasonably sure it's not bugged. That's one kind of answer to your question, who's Cleve Wheeler. Other answers would be the man behind the throne. Next in line. Multifaceted genius. Killer shark."

"Next in line," said Joe, responding to the only clause that made any sense. "The old man is sinking?"

"Officially—and an official secret—his hemoglobin reading is four. That mean anything to you, Doctor?"

"Sure does, Doctor. Malnutritive anemia, if other rumors I hear are true. Richest man in the world—dying of starvation."

"And old age—and stubbornness—and obsession. You want to hear about Wheeler?"

"Tell me."

"Mister Lucky. Born with everything. Greek coin profile. Michelangelo muscles. Discovered early by a bright-eyed elementary school principal, sent to a private school, used to go straight to the teachers' lounge in the morning and say what he'd been reading or thinking about. Then they'd tell off a teacher to work with him or go out with him or whatever. High school at twelve, varsity track, basketball, football, and high diving—three letters for each—yes, he graduated in three years, *summa cum*. Read all the textbooks at the beginning of each term, never cracked them again. More than anything else he had the habit of success.

"College, the same thing: turned sixteen in his first semester, just ate everything up. Very popular. Graduated at the top again, of course."

Joe Trilling, who had slogged through college and medical school like a hod carrier, grunted enviously. "I've seen one or two like that. Everybody marvels; nobody sees how easy it was for them."

Karl shook his head. "Wasn't quite like that with Cleve Wheeler. If anything was easy for him it was because of the nature of his equipment. He was like a four-hundred-horsepower car moving in sixty-horsepower traffic. When his muscles were called on he used them, I mean really put it down to the floor. A very willing guy. Well—he had his choice of jobs—hell, choice of careers. He went into an architectural firm that could use his math, administrative ability, public presence, knowledge of materials, art. Gravitated right to the top, got a partnership. Picked up a doctorate on the side while he was doing it. Married extremely well."

"Mister Lucky," Joe said.

"Mister Lucky, yeah. Listen. Wheeler became a partner and he did his work and he knew his stuff—everything he could learn or understand. Learning and understanding are not enough to cope with some things like greed or unexpected stupidity or accident or sheer bad breaks. Two of the other partners got into a deal I won't bother you with—a high-rise apartment complex in the wrong place for the wrong residents and land acquired the wrong way. Wheeler saw it coming, called them in, and talked it over. They said yes-yes and went right ahead and did what they wanted anyway—something that Wheeler never in the world expected. The one thing high capability and straight morals and a good education don't give you is the end of innocence. Cleve Wheeler was an innocent.

"Well, it happened, the disaster that Cleve had predicted, but it happened far worse. Things like that, when they surface, have a way of exposing a lot of other concealed rot. The firm collapsed. Cleve Wheeler had never failed at anything in his whole life. It was the one thing he had no practice in dealing with. Anyone with the most rudimentary intelligence would have seen that this was the time to walk away—

lie down, even. Cut his losses. But I don't think these things even occurred to him."

Karl Trilling laughed suddenly. "In one of Philip Wylie's novels is a tremendous description of a forest fire and how the animals run away from it, the foxes and the rabbits running shoulder to shoulder, the owls flying in the daytime to get ahead of the flames. Then there's this beetle, lumbering along on the ground. The beetle comes to a burned patch, the edge of twenty acres of hell. It stops, it wiggles its feelers, it turns to the side, and begins to walk around the fire—" He laughed again. "That's the special thing Cleveland Wheeler has, you see, under all that muscle and brain and brilliance. If he had to—and were a beetle—he wouldn't turn back and he wouldn't quit. If all he could do was walk around it, he'd start walking."

"What happened?" asked Joe.

"He hung on. He used everything he had. He used his brains and his personality and his reputation and all his worldly goods. He also borrowed and promised—and he worked. Oh, he worked. Well, he kept the firm. He cleaned out the rot and built it all up again from the inside, strong and straight this time. But it cost.

"It cost him time—all the hours of every day but the four or so he used for sleeping. And just about when he had it leveled off and starting up, it cost him his wife."

"You said he'd married well."

"He'd married what you marry when you're a young block-buster on top of everything and going higher. She was a nice enough girl, I suppose, and maybe you can't blame her, but she was no more used to failure than he was. Only he could walk around it. He could rent a room and ride the bus. She just didn't know how—and of course with women like that there's always the discarded swain somewhere in the wings."

"How did he take that?"

"Hard. He'd married the way he played ball or took examinations—with everything he had. It did something to him. All this did things to him, I suppose, but that was the biggest chunk of it.

"He didn't let it stop him. He didn't let anything stop him. He went on until all the bills were paid—every cent. All the interest. He kept at it until the net worth was exactly what it had been before his ex-partners had begun to eat out the core. Then he gave it away. Gave it away! Sold all right and title to his interest for a dollar."

"Finally cracked, hm?"

Karl Trilling looked at his brother scornfully. "Cracked. Matter of definition, isn't it? Cleve Wheeler's goal was zero—can you understand that? What is success anyhow? Isn't it making up your mind what you're going to do and then doing it, all the way?"

"In that case," said his brother quietly, "suicide is success."

Karl gave him a long penetrating look. "Right," he said, and thought about it a moment.

"Anyhow," Joe asked, "why zero?"

"I did a lot of research on Cleve Wheeler, but I couldn't get inside his head. I don't know. But I can guess. He meant to owe no man anything. I don't know how he felt about the company he saved, but I can imagine. The man he became—was becoming—wouldn't want to owe it one damned thing. I'd say he just wanted out—but on his own terms, which included leaving nothing behind to work on him."

"Okay," said Joe.

Karl Trilling thought, *The nice thing about old Joe is that he'll wait. All these years apart with hardly any communication beyond birthday cards—and not always that—and here he is, just as if we were still together every day. I wouldn't be here if it weren't important; I wouldn't be telling him all this unless he needed to know; he wouldn't need any of it unless he was going to help. All that unsaid—I don't have to ask him a damn thing. What am I interrupting in his life? What am I going to interrupt? I won't have to worry about that. He'll take care of it.*

He said, "I'm glad I came here, Joe."

Joe said, "That's all right," which meant all the things Karl had been thinking. Karl grinned and hit him on the shoulder and went on talking.

"Wheeler dropped out. It's not easy to map his trail for that period. It pops up all over. He lived in at least three communes—maybe more, but those three were a mess when he came and a model when he left. He started businesses—all things that had never happened before, like a supermarket with no shelves, no canned music, no games or stamps, just neat stacks of open cases, where the customer took what he wanted and marked it according to the card posted by the case, with a marker hanging on a string. Eggs and frozen meat and fish and the like, and local produce were priced a flat 2 percent over wholesale. People were honest because they could never be sure the checkout counter didn't know the prices of everything—besides, to cheat on the prices listed would have been just too embarrassing. With nothing but a big empty warehouse for overhead and no employees spending thousands of man-hours marking individual items, the prices beat any discount house that ever lived. He sold that one too, and moved on. He started a line of organic baby foods without preservatives, franchised it, and moved on again. He developed a plastic container that would burn without polluting and patented it and sold the patent."

"I've heard of that one. Haven't seen it around, though."

"Maybe you will," Karl said in a guarded tone. "Maybe you will.

91

Anyway, he had a CPA in Pasadena handling details, and just did his thing all over. I never heard of a failure in anything he tried."

"Sounds like a junior edition of the great man himself, your honored boss."

"You're not the only one who realized that. The boss may be a ding-a-ling in many ways, but nobody ever faulted his business sense. He has always had his tentacles out for wandering pieces of very special manpower. For all I know he had drawn a bead on Cleveland Wheeler years back. I wouldn't doubt that he'd made offers from time to time, only during that period Cleve Wheeler wasn't about to go to work for anyone that big. His whole pattern is to run things his way, and you don't do that in an established empire."

"Heir apparent," said Joe, reminding him of something he had said earlier.

"Right," nodded Karl. "I knew you'd begin to get the idea before I was finished."

"But finish," said Joe.

"Right. Now what I'm going to tell you, I just want you to know. I don't expect you to understand it or what it means or what it has all done to Cleve Wheeler. I need your help, and you can't really help me unless you know the whole story."

"Shoot."

Karl Trilling shot: "Wheeler found a girl. Her name was Clara Prieta and her folks came from Sonora. She was bright as hell—in her way, I suppose, as bright as Cleve, though with a tenth of his schooling—and pretty as well, and it was Cleve she wanted, not what he might get for her. She fell for him when he had nothing—when he really wanted nothing. They were a daily, hourly joy to each other. I guess that was about the time he started building this business and that, making something again. He bought a little house and a car. He bought two cars, one for her. I don't think she wanted it, but he couldn't do enough—he was always looking for more things to do for her. They went out for an evening to some friends' house, she from shopping, he from whatever it was he was working on then, so they had both cars. He followed her on the way home and had to watch her lose control and spin out. She died in his arms."

"Oh, Jesus."

"Mister Lucky. Listen: a week later he turned a corner downtown and found himself looking at a bank robbery. He caught a stray bullet— grazed the back of his neck. He had seven months to lie still and think about things. When he got out he was told his business manager had embezzled everything and headed south with his secretary. Every-thing."

92

"What did he do?"

"Went to work and paid his hospital bill."

They sat in the car in the dark for a long time, until Joe said, "Was he paralyzed, there in the hospital?"

"For nearly five months."

"Wonder what he thought about."

Karl Trilling said, "I can imagine what he thought about. What I can't imagine is what he decided. What he concluded. What he determined to be. Damn it, there are no accurate words for it. We all do the best we can with what we've got, or try to. Or should. He *did*—and with the best possible material to start out with. He played it straight; he worked hard; he was honest and lawful and fair; he was fit; he was bright. He came out of the hospital with those last two qualities intact. God alone knows what's happened to the rest of it."

"So he went to work for the old man."

"He did—and somehow that frightens me. It was as if all his qualifications were not enough to suit both of them until these things happened to him—until they made him become what he is."

"And what is that?"

"There isn't a short answer to that, Joe. The old man has become a modern nymph. Nobody ever sees him. Nobody can predict what he's going to do or why. Cleveland Wheeler stepped into his shadow and disappeared almost as completely as the boss. There are very few things you can say for certain. The boss has always been a recluse and in the ten years Cleve Wheeler has been with him he has become more so. It's been business as usual with him, of course—which means the constantly unusual—long periods of quiet, and then these spectacular unexpected wheelings and dealings. You assume that the old man dreams these things up and some high-powered genius on his staff gets them done. But it could be the genius that instigates the moves—who can know? Only the people closest to him—Wheeler, Epstein, me. And I don't know."

"But Epstein died."

Karl Trilling nodded in the dark. "Epstein died. Which leaves only Wheeler to watch the store. I'm the old man's personal physician, not Wheeler's and there's no guarantee that I ever will be Wheeler's."

Joe Trilling recrossed his legs and leaned back, looking out into the whispering dark. "It begins to take shape," he murmured. "The old man's on the way out, you very well might be, and there's nobody to take over but this Wheeler."

"Yes, and I don't know what he is or what he'll do. I do know he will command more power than any single human being on Earth. He'll have so much that he'll be above any kind of cupidity that you or I could imagine—you or I can't think in that order of magnitude. But you see, he's a man who, you might say, has had it proved to him that being good and smart and strong and honest doesn't particularly pay off. Where will he go with all this? And hypothesizing that he's been making more and more of the decisions lately, and extrapolating from that—where is he going? All you can be sure of is that he will succeed in anything he tries. That is his habit."

"What does he want? Isn't that what you're trying to figure out? What would a man like that want, if he knew he could get it?"

"I knew I'd come to the right place," said Karl almost happily. "That's it exactly. As for me, I have all I need now and there are plenty of other places I could go. I wish Epstein were still around, but he's dead and cremated."

"Cremated?"

"That's right—you wouldn't know about that. Old man's instructions. I handled it myself. You've heard of the hot and cold private swimming pools—but I bet you never heard of a man with his own private crematorium in the second sub-basement."

Joe threw up his hands. "I guess if you can reach into your pocket and pull out two billion real dollars, you can have anything you want. By the way, was that legal?"

"Like you said—if you have two billion. Actually, the county medical examiner was present and signed the papers. And he'll be there when the old man pushes off too—it's all in the final instructions. Hey—wait, I don't want to cast any aspersions on the M.E. He wasn't bought. He did a very competent examination on Epstein."

"Okay—we know what to expect when the time comes. It's afterward you're worried about."

"Right. What has the old man—I'm speaking of the corporate old man now—what has he been doing all along? What has he been doing in the last ten years, since he got Wheeler—and is it any different from what he was doing before? How much of this difference, if any, is more Wheeler than boss? That's all we have to go on, Joe, and from it we have to extrapolate what Wheeler's going to do with the biggest private economic force this world has ever known."

"Let's talk about that," said Joe, beginning to smile.

Karl Trilling knew the signs, so he began to smile a little, too. They talked about it.

II

The crematorium in the second sub-basement was purely functional, as if all concessions to sentiment and ritual had been made elsewhere, or canceled. The latter most accurately describes what had happened when at last, at long long last, the old man died. Everything was done precisely according to his instructions immediately after he was certifiably dead and before any public announcements were made—right up to and including the moment when the square mouth of the furnace opened with a startling clang, a blare of heat, a flare of light—the hue the old-time blacksmiths called straw color. The simple coffin slid rapidly in, small flames exploding into being on its corners, and the door banged shut. It took a moment for the eyes to adjust to the bare room, the empty greased track, the closed door. It took the same moment for the conditioners to whisk away the sudden smell of scorched soft pine.

The medical examiner leaned over the small table and signed his name twice. Karl Trilling and Cleveland Wheeler did the same. The M.E. tore off copies and folded them and put them away in his breast pocket. He looked at the closed square iron door, opened his mouth, closed it again, and shrugged. He held out his hand.

"Good night, Doctor."

"Good night, Doctor. Rugosi's outside—he'll show you out."

The M.E. shook hands wordlessly with Cleveland Wheeler and left.

"I know just what he's feeling," Karl said. "Something ought to be said. Something memorable—end of an era. Like 'One small step for man—'"

Cleveland Wheeler smiled the bright smile of the college hero, fifteen years after—a little less wide, a little less even, a great deal less in the eyes. He said in the voice that commanded, whatever he said, "If you think you're quoting the first words from an astronaut on the moon, you're not. What he said was from the ladder, when he poked his boot down. He said, 'It's some kind of soft stuff. I can kick it around with my foot.' I've always liked that much better. It was real; it wasn't rehearsed or memorized or thought out and it had to do with that moment and the next. The M.E. said good night and you told him the chauffeur was waiting outside. I like that better than anything anyone could say. I think he would, too," Wheeler added, barely gesturing, with a very strong, slightly cleft chin, toward the hot black door.

"But he wasn't exactly human."

"So they say." Wheeler half smiled and, even as he turned away, Karl could sense himself tuned out, the room itself become of secondary importance—the next thing Wheeler was to do, and the next and the one after, becoming more real than the here and now.

Karl put a fast end to that.

He said levelly, "I meant what I just said, Wheeler."

95

It couldn't have been the words, which by themselves might have elicited another half smile and a forgetting. It was the tone, and perhaps the "Wheeler." There is a ritual about these things. To those few on his own level, and those on the level below, he was Cleve. Below that he was mister to his face and Wheeler behind his back. No one of his peers would call him mister unless it was meant as the herald of an insult; no one of his peers or immediate underlings would call him Wheeler at all, ever. Whatever the component, it removed Cleveland Wheeler's hand from the knob and turned him. His face was completely alert and interested. "You'd best tell me what you mean, Doctor."

Karl said, "I'll do better than that. Come." Without gestures, suggestions, or explanations he walked to the left rear of the room, leaving it up to Wheeler to decide whether or not to follow. Wheeler followed.

In the corner Karl rounded on him. "If you ever say anything about this to anyone—even me—when we leave here, I'll just deny it. If you ever get in here again, you won't find anything to back up your story." He took a complex four-inch blade of machine stainless steel from his belt and slid it between the big masonry blocks. Silently, massively, the course of blocks in the corner began to move upward. Looking up at them in the dim light from the narrow corridor they revealed, anyone could see that they were real blocks and that to get through them without that key and the precise knowledge of where to put it would be a long-term project.

Again Karl proceeded without looking around, leaving go, no-go as a matter for Wheeler to decide. Wheeler followed. Karl heard his footsteps behind him and noticed with pleasure and something like admiration that when the heavy blocks whooshed down and seated themselves solidly behind them, Wheeler may have looked over his shoulder but did not pause.

"You've noticed we're alongside the furnace," Karl said, like a guided-tour bus driver. "And now, behind it."

He stood aside to let Wheeler pass him and see the small room.

It was just large enough for the tracks which protruded from the back of the furnace and a little standing space on each side. On the far side was a small table with a black suitcase standing on it. On the track stood the coffin, its corners carboned, its top and sides wet and slightly steaming.

"Sorry to have to close that stone gate that way," Karl said matter-of-factly. "I don't expect anyone down here at all, but I wouldn't want to explain any of this to persons other than yourself."

Wheeler was staring at the coffin. He seemed perfectly composed, but it was a seeming. Karl was quite aware of what it was costing him.

Wheeler said, "I wish you'd explain it to *me.*" And he laughed. It was the first time Karl had ever seen this man do anything badly.

"I will. I am." He clicked open the suitcase and laid it open and flat on the little table. There was a glisten of chrome and steel and small vials in little pockets. The first tool he removed was a screwdriver. "No need to use screws when you're cremating 'em," he said cheerfully and placed the tip under one corner of the lid. He struck the handle smartly with the heel of one hand and the lid popped loose. "Stand this up against the wall behind you, will you?"

Silently Cleveland Wheeler did as he was told. It gave him something to do with his muscles; it gave him the chance to turn his head away for a moment; it gave him a chance to think—and it gave Karl the opportunity for a quick glance at his steady countenance.

He's a mensch, Karl thought. *He really is. . . .*

Wheeler set up the lid neatly and carefully and they stood, one on each side, looking down into the coffin.

"He—got a lot older," Wheeler said at last.

"You haven't seen him recently."

"Here and in there," said the executive. "I've spent more time in the same room with him during the past month than I have in the last eight, nine years. Still, it was a matter of minutes, each time."

Karl nodded understandingly. "I'd heard that. Phone calls, any time of the day or night, and then those long silences two days, three, not calling out, not having anyone in—"

"Are you going to tell me about the phony oven?"

"Oven? Furnace? It's not a phony at all. When we've finished here it'll do the job, all right."

"Then why the theatricals?"

"That was for the M.E. Those papers he signed are in sort of a never-never country just now. When we slide this back in and turn on the heat they'll become as legal as he thinks they are."

"Then why—"

"Because there are some things you have to know."

Karl reached into the coffin and unfolded the gnarled hands. They came apart reluctantly and he pressed them down at the sides of the body. He unbuttoned the jacket, laid it back, unbuttoned the shirt, unzipped the trousers. When he had finished with this he looked up and found Wheeler's sharp gaze, not on the old man's corpse, but on him.

"I have the feeling," said Cleveland Wheeler, "that I have never seen you before."

Silently Karl Trilling responded: *But you do now.* And, *Thanks, Joey. You were dead right.* Joe had known the answer to that one plaguing question, *How should I act?*

97

Talk just the way he talks, Joe had said. *Be what he is, the whole time. . . .*

Be what he is. A man without illusions (they don't work) and without hope (who needs it?), who has the unbreakable habit of succeeding. And who can say it's a nice day in such a way that everyone around snaps to attention and says: *Yes, SIR!*

"You've been busy," Karl responded shortly. He took off his jacket, folded it, and put it on the table beside the kit. He put on surgeon's gloves and slipped the sterile sleeve off a new scalpel. "Some people scream and faint the first time they watch a dissection."

Wheeler smiled thinly. "I don't scream and faint." But it was not lost on Karl Trilling that only then, at the last possible moment, did Wheeler actually view the old man's body. When he did he neither screamed nor fainted; he uttered an astonished grunt.

"Thought that would surprise you," Karl said easily. "In case you were wondering, though, he really was a male. The species seems to be oviparous. Mammals too, but it has to be oviparous. I'd sure like a look at a female. That isn't a vagina. It's a cloaca."

"Until this moment," said Wheeler in a hypnotized voice, "I thought that 'not human' remark of yours was a figure of speech."

"No, you didn't," Karl responded shortly.

Leaving the words to hang in the air, as words will if a speaker has the wit to isolate them with wedges of silence, he deftly slit the corpse from the sternum to the pubic symphysis. For the first-time viewer this was always the difficult moment. It's hard not to realize viscerally that the cadaver does not feel anything and will not protest. Nerve-alive to Wheeler, Karl looked for a gasp or a shudder; Wheeler merely held his breath.

"We could spend hours—weeks, I imagine, going into the details," Karl said, deftly making a transverse incision in the ensiform area, almost around to the trapezoid on each side, "but this is the thing I wanted you to see." Grasping the flesh at the juncture of the cross he had cut, on the left side, he pulled upward and to the left. The cutaneous layers came away easily, with the fat under them. They were not pinkish, but an off-white lavender shade. Now the muscular striations over the ribs were in view. "If you'd palpated the old man's chest," he said, demonstrating on the right side, "you'd have felt what seemed to be normal human ribs. But look at this."

With a few deft strokes he separated the muscle fibers from the bone on a mid-costal area about four inches square, and scraped. A rib emerged and, as he widened the area and scraped between it and the next one, it became clear that the ribs were joined by a thin flexible layer of bone or chitin.

"It's like baleen—whalebone," said Karl. "See this?" He sectioned out a piece, flexed it.

"My God."

III

"Now look at this." Karl took surgical shears from the kit, snipped through the sternum right up to the clavicle and then across the lower margin of the ribs. Slipping his fingers under them, he pulled upward. With a dull snap the entire ribcage opened like a door, exposing the lung.

The lung was not pink, nor the liverish-brownish-black of a smoker, but yellow—the clear, bright yellow of pure sulfur.

"His metabolism," Karl said, straightening up at last and flexing the tension out of his shoulder, "is fantastic. Or was. He lived on oxygen, same as us, but he broke it out of carbon monoxide, sulfur dioxide and trioxide, and carbon dioxide mostly. I'm not saying he could—I mean he had to. When he was forced to breathe what we call clean air, he could take just so much of it and then had to duck out and find a few breaths of his own atmosphere. When he was younger he could take it for hours at a time, but as the years went by he had to spend more and more time in the kind of smog he could breathe. Those long disappearances of his and that reclusiveness—they weren't as kinky as people supposed."

Wheeler made a gesture toward the corpse. "But—what is he? Where—?"

"I can't tell you. Except for a good deal of medical and biochemical details, you now know as much as I do. Somehow, somewhere, he arrived. He came, he saw, he began to make his moves. Look at this."

He opened the other side of the chest and then broke the sternum up and away. He pointed. The lung tissue was not in two discrete parts, but extended across the median line. "One lung, all the way across, though it has these two lobes. The kidneys and gonads show the same right-left fusion."

"I'll take your word for it," said Wheeler a little hoarsely. "Damn it, what *is* it?"

"A featherless biped, as Plato once described homo sap. *I* don't know what it is. I just know *that* it is—and I thought you ought to know. That's all."

"But you've seen one before. That's obvious."

"Sure. Epstein."

"Epstein?"

"Sure. The old man had to have a go-between—someone who could, without suspicion, spend long hours with him and hours away. The old man could do a lot over the phone, but not everything. Epstein

99

was, you might say, a right arm that could hold its breath a little longer than he could. It got to him in the end, though, and he died of it."

"Why didn't you say something long before this?"

"First of all, I value my own skin. I could say reputation, but skin is the word. I signed a contract as his personal physician because he needed a personal physician—another bit of window dressing. But I did precious little doctoring—except over the phone—and nine-tenths of that was, I realized quite recently, purely diversionary. Even a doctor, I suppose, can be a trusting soul. One or the other would call and give a set of symptoms and I'd cautiously suggest and prescribe. Then I'd get another call that the patient was improving and that was that. Why, I even got specimens—blood, urine, stools—and did the pathology on them and never realized that they were from the same source as what the medical examiner checked out and signed for."

"What do you mean, same source?"

Karl shrugged. "He could get anything he wanted—anything."

"Then—what the M.E. examined wasn't—" he waved a hand at the casket.

"Of course not. That's why the crematorium has a back door. There's a little pocket sleight-of-hand trick you can buy for fifty cents that operates the same way. This body here was inside the furnace. The ringer—a look-alike that came from God knows where; I swear to you I don't—was lying out there waiting for the M.E. When the button was pushed the fires started up and that coffin slid in—pushing this one out and at the same time drenching it with water as it came through. While we've been in here, the human body is turning to ashes. My personal, private secret instructions, both for Epstein and for the boss, were to wait until I was certain I was alone and then come in here after an hour and push the second button, which would slide this one back into the fire. I was to do no investigations, ask no questions, make no reports. It came through as logical but not reasonable, like so many of his orders." He laughed suddenly. "Do you know why the old man—and Epstein too, for that matter, in case you never noticed—wouldn't shake hands with anyone?"

"I presumed it was because he had an obsession with germs."

"It was because his normal body temperature was a hundred and seven."

Wheeler touched one of his own hands with the other and said nothing.

When Karl felt that the wedge of silence was thick enough he asked lightly, "Well, boss, where do we go from here?"

Cleveland Wheeler turned away from the corpse and to Karl slowly, as if diverting his mind with an effort.

"What did you call me?"

"Figure of speech," said Karl and smiled. "Actually, I'm working for the company—and that's you. I'm under orders, which have been finally and completely discharged when I push that button—I have no others. So it really is up to you."

Wheeler's eyes fell again to the corpse. "You mean about him? This? What we should do?"

"That, yes. Whether to burn it up and forget it—or call in top management and an echelon of scientists. Or scare the living hell out of everyone on Earth by phoning the papers. Sure, that has to be decided, but I was thinking on a much wider spectrum than that."

"Such as—"

Karl gestured toward the box with his head. "What was he doing here, anyway? What has he done? What was he trying to do?"

"You'd better go on," said Wheeler; and for the very first time said something in a way that suggested diffidence. "You've had a while to think about all this; I—" and almost helplessly, he spread his hands.

"I can understand that," Karl said gently. "Up to now I've been coming on like a hired lecturer and I know it. I'm not going to embarrass you with personalities except to say that you've absorbed all this with less buckling of the knees than anyone in the world I could think of."

"Right. Well, there's a simple technique you learn in elementary algebra. It has to do with the construction of graphs. You place a dot on the graph where known data put it. You get more data, you put down another dot and then a third. With just three dots—of course, the more the better, but it can be done with three—you can connect them and establish a curve. This curve has certain characteristics and it's fair to extend the curve a little farther with the assumption that later data will bear you out."

"Extrapolation."

"Extrapolation. X axis, the fortunes of our late boss. Y axis, time. The curve is his fortunes—that is to say, his influence."

"Pretty tall graph."

"Over thirty years."

"Still pretty tall."

"All right," said Karl. "Now, over the same thirty years, another curve: change in the environment." He held up a hand. "I'm not going to read you a treatise on ecology. Let's be more objective than that. Let's just say changes. Okay: a measurable rise in the mean temperature because of CO_2 and the greenhouse effect. Draw the curve. Incidence of heavy metals, mercury, and lithium in organic tissue. Draw a curve. Likewise chlorinated hydrocarbons, hypertrophy of algae due to phosphates, incidence of coronaries . . . All right, let's superimpose all these curves on the same graph."

"I see what you're getting at. But you have to be careful with that kind of statistics game. Like, the increase of traffic fatalities coincides with the increased use of aluminum cans and plastic-tipped baby pins."

"Right. I don't think I'm falling into that trap. I just want to find reasonable answers to a couple of otherwise unreasonable situations. One is this: if the changes occurring in our planet are the result of mere carelessness—a more or less random thing, carelessness—then how come nobody is being careless in a way that benefits the environment? Strike that. I promised, no ecology lessons. Rephrase: how come all these carelessnesses promote a change and not a preservation?

"Next question: What is the direction of the change? You've seen speculative writing about 'terra-forming'—altering other planets to make them habitable by humans. Suppose an effort were being made to change this planet to suit someone else? Suppose they wanted more water and were willing to melt the polar caps by the greenhouse effect? Increase the oxides of sulfur, eliminate certain marine forms from plankton to whales? Reduce the population by increases in lung cancer, emphysema, heart attacks, and even war?"

Both men found themselves looking down at the sleeping face in the coffin. Karl said softly, "Look what he was into—petrochemicals, fossil fuels, food processing, advertising, all the things that made the changes or helped the changers—"

"You're not blaming him for all of it."

"Certainly not. He found willing helpers by the million."

"You don't think he was trying to change a whole planet just so he could be comfortable in it."

"No, I don't think so—and that's the central point I have to make. I don't know if there are any more around like him and Epstein, but I can suppose this: if the changes now going on keep on—and accelerate—then we can expect them."

Wheeler said, "So what would you like to do? Mobilize the world against the invader?"

"Nothing like that. I think I'd slowly and quietly reverse the changes. If this planet is normally unsuitable to them, then I'd keep it so. I don't think they'd have to be driven back. I think they just wouldn't come."

"Or they'd try some other way."

"I don't think so," said Karl. "Because they tried this one. If they thought they could do it with fleets of spaceships and super-zap guns, they'd be doing it. No—this is their way and if it doesn't work, they can try somewhere else."

Wheeler began pulling thoughtfully at his lip. Karl said softly, "All it would take is someone who knew what he was doing, who could command enough clout, and who had the wit to make it pay. They might even arrange a man's life—to get the kind of man they need."

And before Wheeler could answer, Karl took up his scalpel.

"I want you to do something for me," he said sharply in a new, commanding tone—actually, Wheeler's own. "I want you to do it because I've done it and I'll be damned if I want to be the only man in the world who has."

Leaning over the head of the casket, he made an incision along the hairline from temple to temple. Then, bracing his elbows against the edge of the box and steadying one hand with the other, he drew the scalpel straight down the center of the forehead and down on to the nose, splitting it exactly in two. Down he went through the upper lip and then the lower, around the point of the chin and under it to the throat. Then he stood up.

"Put your hands on his cheeks," he ordered. Wheeler frowned briefly (how long had it been since anyone had spoken to him that way?), hesitated, then did as he was told.

"Now press your hands together and down."

The incision widened slightly under the pressure, then abruptly the flesh gave and the entire skin of the face slipped off. The unexpected lack of resistance brought Wheeler's hands to the bottom of the coffin and he found himself face to face, inches away, with the corpse.

Like the lungs and kidneys, the eyes—eye?—passed the median, very slightly reduced at the center. The pupil was oval, its long axis transverse. The skin was pale lavender with yellow vessels and in place of a nose was a thread-fringed hole. The mouth was circular, the teeth not quite radially placed; there was little chin.

Without moving, Wheeler closed his eyes, held them shut for one second, two, and then courageously opened them again. Karl whipped around the end of the coffin and got an arm around Wheeler's chest. Wheeler leaned on it heavily for a moment, then stood up quickly and brushed the arm away.

"You didn't have to do that."

"Yes, I did," said Karl. "Would you want to be the only man in the world who'd gone through that—with nobody to tell it to?"

And after all, Wheeler could laugh. When he had finished he said, "Push that button."

"Hand me that cover."

Most obediently Cleveland Wheeler brought the coffin lid and they placed it.

Karl pushed the button and they watched the coffin slide into the square of flame. Then they left.

Joe Trilling had a funny way of making a living. It was a good living, but of course he didn't make anything like the bundle he could have made in the city. On the other hand, he lived in the mountains a half mile away from a picturesque village, in clean air and piney-birchy woods along with lots of mountain laurel, and he was his own boss. There wasn't much competition for what he did.

What he did was to make simulacra of medical specimens, mostly for the armed forces, although he had plenty of orders from medical schools, film producers, and an occasional individual, no questions asked. He could make a model of anything inside, affixed to or penetrating a body or any part of it. He could make models to be looked at, models to be felt, smelled, and palpated. He could give you gangrene that stunk or dewy thyroids with real dew on them. He could make one-of-a-kind or he could set up a production line. Dr. Joe Trilling was, to put it briefly, the best there was at what he did.

"The clincher," Karl told him (in much more relaxed circumstances than their previous ones; daytime now, with beer), "the real clincher was the face bit. God, Joe, that was a beautiful piece of work."

"Just nuts and bolts. The beautiful part was your idea—his hands on it."

"How do you mean?"

"I've been thinking back to that," Joe said. "I don't think you yourself realize how brilliant a stroke that was. It's all very well to set up a show for the guy, but to make him put his hands as well as his eyes and brains on it—that was the stroke of genius. It's like—well, I can remember when I was a kid coming home from school and putting my hand on a fence rail and somebody had spat on it." He displayed his hand, shook it. "All these years I can remember how that felt. All these years couldn't wear it away, all those scrubbings couldn't wash it away. It's more than a cerebral or psychic thing, Karl—more than the memory of an episode. I think there's a kind of memory mechanism in the cells themselves, especially on the hands, that can be invoked. What I'm getting to is that no matter how long he lives, Cleve Wheeler is going to feel that skin slip under his palms and that is going to bring him nose to nose with that face. No, you're the genius, not me."

"Na. You knew what you were doing. I didn't."

"Hell you didn't." Joe leaned far back in his lawn chaise—so far he could hold up his beer and look at the sun through it from the underside. Watching the receding bubbles defy perspective (because they swell as they rise), he murmured, "Karl?"

"Yuh."

"Ever hear of Occam's Razor?"

"Um. Long time back. Philosophical principle. Or logic or something. Let's see. Given an effect and a choice of possible causes, the simplest cause is always the one most likely to be true. Is that it?"

"Not too close, but close enough," said Joe Trilling lazily. "Hm. You're the one who used to proclaim that logic is sufficient unto itself and need have nothing to do with truth."

"I still proclaim it."

"Okay. Now, you and I know that human greed and carelessness are quite enough all by themselves to wreck this planet. We didn't think that was enough for the likes of Cleve Wheeler, who can really do something about it, so we constructed him a smog-breathing extra-terrestrial. I mean, he hadn't done anything about saving the world for our reasons, so we gave him a whizzer of a reason of his own. Right out of our heads."

"Dictated by all available factors. Yes. What are you getting at, Joe?"

"Oh—just that our complicated hoax is simple, really, in the sense that it brought everything down to a single cause. Occam's Razor slices things down to simplest causes. Single causes have a fair chance of being right."

Karl put down his beer with a bump. "I never thought of that. I've been too busy to think of that. *Suppose we were right?*"

They looked at each other, shaken.

At last Karl said, "What do we look for now, Joe—space ships?"

The Spirit Who Bideth by Himself in the Land of Mist and Snow

Susan Janice Anderson

If we are to solve the twin problems of dwindling resources and mounting world population, we'll have to come up with some new ideas. One plan that's been seriously suggested to help feed millions of people who would otherwise starve is to irrigate Australia's vast interior for food production. But this would require a great deal of fresh water. Might it be possible to send tugs to the Antarctic and bring back icebergs?

It's a bold idea, and not the least of its attractions is the thought of how awesome those icebergs would look being towed into port. Struck by this vision, Susan Janice Anderson wrote the following lyrical and imaginative story.

Susan Janice Anderson teaches courses in science fiction at the university level, and was coeditor (with Vonda N. McIntyre) of the science fiction anthology Aurora: Beyond Equality.

"ICEBERG'S IN," said Ruth-parent.

"Come on!" yelled Margalit, jumping up from the lawn.

Chuck-parent gave his low gentle laugh. "You go. We've seen bergs come in since before you were born."

Leaving the eight adults sprawled over the grass, Margalit ran through the garden. Tall eucalypti and pines swayed in the wind and the air was heavy with the fragrance of blossoms. Her sandal strap came loose and flapped against her ankle but she didn't stop to fasten it. She followed the wood-chip path to the cliff overlooking the ocean. At first, all she could see was sun sparkling in the warm Australian sea. Then one of the sparkles broadened and grew more substantial. From a distance, it reminded her of a magnified snowflake that had just fallen on a glassy lake. But instead of melting, this snowflake grew. First it became a tiny lump of ice, then a small hill—furrowed on the sides but flat on top. Trying not to slip on the crumbly soil, Margalit edged her way down the cliff.

Squinting, she could make out the silvery form of what looked like a toy boat—the supertug that had towed the berg from Antarctica. The tug turned and the berg skewed to the side. Outlined against the azure sky, its flat top slanted downward, marking the ice it had lost on its long journey.

"How big was the berg when the tuggers got it?" Margalit wondered.

Half closing her eyes, she tried to imagine the berg floating in the cold water of the South Pole. She could almost see it calving from the ice shelf, joining other bergs as the current carried them into the open sea.

"Years ago," Ruth-parent had said, "nothing was done about the bergs. While places like Australia desperately needed their water, they were left to melt at sea. That was before the supertugs were built."

Margalit imagined herself in a tugger's red parka, firing the bolt into the berg. Then she would circle as the helicopter fed out the line. Anchored to the supertug, the iceberg would begin its long journey to Australia. Back in port, she would assist in the melting—a process non-tuggers were forbidden to watch. Finally she would discover why.

"Margalit!"

Just a few more years and she would be old enough to take the exams.

"Margalit, time to practice your flute. The berg's not going to melt overnight."

Reluctantly, she started back up the cliff. At the top, Chuck-parent waited for her.

"Next thing we know, you'll want to be a tugger."

"I do already," she said.

Chuck-parent shook his head. "Take it from an ex-tugger, child. It's a hard and lonely life. Stick to your music and stay in Australia."

Margalit frowned. "But you and Anna-parent kept at it for five years. There must have been something you liked about tugging."

Chuck-parent's eyes grew far-away. "Sun never sets that time of year so the berg floats behind you glistening like it's on fire. And you've got all the time in the world to watch it. Bergs got a low frictional resistance, so you have to watch your speed on the way back. And on the return, you've got the winds to do most of your work for you."

"Did you ever get bored on the way back?"

"Not among tuggers. To get selected, you have to be a lot more than just a passable oceanographer. Why, a tugger can discuss almost any subject from Baroque music to science fiction. That's the way Maria set up the selection process."

"Why aren't non-tuggers allowed to watch the melting? And why don't tuggers ever come ashore? Don't they get tired after such a long trip?"

"So many questions," said Chuck-parent, lifting Margalit off the ground. Trees and flowers spun around in a wild kaleidoscope. Laughing, she scrambled to her feet, but she refused to be distracted.

"Why don't they ever come ashore?"

Chuck-parent's eyes grew sad. "They used to, child, but people didn't treat them very nicely."

"Why not?"

"Because they're different."

"How are they different?"

Chuck-parent shook his head. "Just take my word for it, Margalit, you don't want to be a tugger."

As they walked towards the house, Margalit glanced over her shoulder. In the late afternoon sun, the iceberg gleamed pinkish-gold, like a mountain on fire.

Despite her red parka, twenty-year-old Margalit shivered as she watched the ice shelf come into view. All the pictures she had seen as a child hadn't prepared her for this—an enormous field of ice, much larger than she had imagined. Sharply outlined against the sky was the white line of the ice barrier. Like a gleaming serpent, it twisted its way down the length of the shelf. As the supertug, the *Seelye-Coryell,* pulled in closer, she made out jagged crevices that marked where icebergs had calved. Several tabular bergs were floating in the waters around the shelf. Though their shapes were familiar, their size overwhelmed her. And soon her sub-team would attempt to encircle one of the giant masses.

"They make you realize just how small you are, don't they? Even after all my years of tugging, I can't get over that feeling."

Misty Dawn, senior member of the team, stood close by her shoulder. A fine net of wrinkles covered the older woman's face but her dark eyes were bright and alert as a girl's. Her voice carried a slight accent of her native Pueblo tongue.

Margalit's eyes were moist. "They're even more beautiful than I had imagined."

"So they are, child, and even more so when you make contact with them." The older woman looked over at the helicopter. The other member of the sub-team, Jan David, his fingers twisting a strand of his blond hair, was perusing some satellite photos. They walked over to join him.

His Eurasian eyes squinted in the sun as he looked up at them.

"Can't tell enough from the photos. We'd better examine the bergs up close."

Misty Dawn nodded and they sat down next to Jan David in the craft. Margalit glanced over her shoulder as they pulled away from the *Seelye-Coryell*. Compared to the supertug, the helicopter seemed no bigger than a fly, and she and her companions microorganisms. And those microorganisms would soon do battle with white giants. She could sense her companions' confidence in their movements as they maneuvered the helicopter—a confidence she herself did not yet fully share. But they had been through many more tuggings than she. She read unspoken communications in their alert eyes. So many variables had to be taken into consideration in selecting a berg, not just size but also proper shape so it wouldn't melt too fast in transit. Satellite photos helped to a certain extent but once they were at the shelf, tuggers had to develop a kind of intuition to guide them the rest of the way. Margalit wondered how long it would take until she too could sense which bergs to choose.

"That group of five over there," said Misty Dawn. "Should be one we could use."

Jan David headed the craft in the direction she was pointing. Margalit's heart leaped as they wove their way around the ice islands. So easy for the craft to crash straight into a wall of ice and be pulled under by churning waves. Darting through the frozen obstacle course, they headed for a berg floating some distance from the group. Misty Dawn touched Margalit's shoulder.

"You release the line."

"Are you sure?" she said, her heart pounding.

"You'll do fine."

The helicopter edged towards the berg. The ice mountain loomed below them, its flattened top casting an elongated shadow over the water. So large it could engulf them in an instant. Pulse quickening, Margalit pushed the line release. The line shot through the air, heading towards the berg's heart.

"Begin circling," said Misty.

As the craft started up, the line wound its way around the berg like a huge serpent uncoiling. Slowly, it covered every inch of the enormous circumference. Not until the line was firmly anchored to the *Seelye-Coryell* did Margalit begin to relax. Back on board, talking excitedly, members of other sub-teams greeted them. For a while now, their part of the work was done. Others would continue the task of preparing the berg for the long journey home.

"Not hard at all, was it?" said Misty, as the three rested on the sun deck.

Margalit laughed. "I've got a lot more tugging to do until I can feel as calm about it as you do."

"Everything comes in time."

"Talking about time, we'll have a hell of a lot on our hands now," said Margalit. "How do you keep yourselves from going nuts on the trip back when the wind's doing most of the work?"

Neither Misty Dawn nor Jan David seemed to hear her question.

"Don't you get bored going so slowly?" she asked.

"No, the trip back's the really important part," said Misty.

She was about to ask why, but something in the older woman's face stopped her. A far-away look, a tightening of the facial muscles that suggested that Misty didn't want to explore the subject any further.

Suddenly Margalit remembered what Chuck-parent had told her about tuggers being different. What exactly had he meant? The people she had met on the ship seemed pleasant and interesting though they did tend to stick fairly closely to their sub-teams. Sometimes, she thought, it was uncanny just how harmoniously the sub-teams worked together, almost as if they were part of some larger organic whole.

Margalit yawned, sleepiness overcoming curiosity. Through half-closed eyes, she glanced back at their newly captured companion. Sunlight reflecting off the berg's sides transformed it into a glistening jewel. And its visible surface, though gigantic, was dwarfed by the five-sixths hidden beneath the ocean. Just before she closed her eyes, the shadow of a bird's wings darkened the perfect whiteness.

"Tuggers are different." The phrase kept circling through Margalit's mind. Drumming her fingers against the railing, she watched the waves slap against the sides of the supertug. Every day, as they neared Australia, the water grew steadily warmer. Already, the berg was showing signs of its long journey. Streams of meltwater were beginning to carve hollows in its smooth sides. Sun and velocity were taking their toll. All the way back, the tuggers fought to maintain a delicate equilibrium with time.

Maybe it was the constant pressure of time, the presence of the berg that made tuggers so intense. In that way they were different, their every waking thought dominated by the image of the berg. And even in sleep, they were followed by their enormous companion. Margalit brushed a strand of hair off her forehead. Sometimes the images in her dreams were so vivid they seemed more real than the waking reality. She wondered if the same thing happened to other tuggers.

She glanced over at Misty Dawn and Jan David sunning themselves on the deck. For several days now, she had wanted to tell them about her dreams. But remembering the look on Misty's face when she had asked about the trip back, she was afraid she would upset the older woman. Yet every day, the compulsion to talk about her dreams grew stronger. Taking a deep breath, she walked across the deck and sat down cross-legged between them.

"Misty, Jan David, are you asleep?"

"Not really," said Misty, sitting up. Jan David yawned and shook himself awake.

"There's something I wanted to talk to you about."

"You're not feeling sick, are you?" asked Jan David, looking concerned.

"Physically, no. Mentally—sometimes I'm not so sure."

"How so?" said Misty.

Margalit shrugged. "This dream I've been having. The same one over and over."

The muscles in Misty's face tightened. "Describe it," she said softly.

"I dream we've finally reached port and it's almost time for the melting to begin. At first, everything goes smoothly: we attach the heating device; the gatherer and pipeline are in place. But when it's time to begin, nothing happens. The berg remains frozen and compact as ever; it simply refuses to begin melting. We recheck our equipment but everything's in order. Then . . ." Margalit frowned and touched her forehead.

"Then what?" said Jan David, leaning forward.

"I feel this tremendous pressure in my head—like some kind of energy is trying to break loose. I can hardly bear it. You both feel it too, I can tell by the pain in your faces. Then it spreads to the other subteams."

"And then?"

"That's where it's always ended. Until last night, that is."

Misty looked at her intently. "What happened last night?"

"All of a sudden, I could see inside your minds. And at the moment we shared each other's consciousnesses, the berg began to melt."

Misty and Jan David exchanged glances.

Margalit laughed self-consciously. "You probably think I'm nuts."

"No," said Misty slowly, "not really."

"You mean it's not just me?"

"Not at all. Nearly every tugger has had dreams like that on the way back. And even before the days of tugging, early explorers of the South Pole recorded their strange visions."

"I wonder why it happens?"

"It's all part of being different. Tuggers aren't like other people."

Something in Misty's tone, in her expression, made Margalit shiver.

"What," she said, "do you mean by 'different?'"

An unspoken question passed between Misty and Jan David.

"In time you'll get used to it, child. You'll experience the pain and loneliness, but also the joy."

"Get used to what?" said Margalit, not completely sure she wanted to know.

"To this," said Misty, speaking into Margalit's mind.

"The telepathic link is strongest when we reach port," said Misty Dawn. "Until then, it's sporadic."

Hundreds of questions circled through Margalit's mind once she had recovered from her initial shock. "How? And why only tuggers? Why don't non-tuggers know about it?"

"A long story, and a sad one. How much we owe to Maria."

"Who was she?"

"A first generation tugger. A psychologist, originally, by profession. From the few articles that had appeared on the subject, she'd become interested in the tugger neurosis. Somehow, she wasn't satisfied with the conventional explanations of paranoia and mass hallucination caused by boredom. So she signed up with a tugging crew to investigate the matter firsthand."

"What did she discover?"

"First of all, that one personality type in particular was most susceptible to the neurosis. Generally, more intelligent individuals, those with multiplex visions of reality. And when Maria herself came down with the 'disorder,' she was able to examine it from the inside. Though her findings ran contrary to established scientific data, she could determine only one explanation for the deep insights she was making into the minds of her fellow crew members. Somehow, under conditions of enforced monotony, those tuggers with the most active imaginations had developed telepathy. The berg too, she thought, might also have something to do with it, but this possibility was never fully investigated."

"Why not?"

Misty's face grew sad. "When Maria presented her data, her colleagues refused to believe her and all her funding was cut. Sometimes, for a sensitive person, laughter is a crueler weapon than outright persecution. But those tuggers who'd experienced what she described believed her. And those tuggers were able to influence the selection process for future tuggers, choosing those with greater psi potential."

"But why didn't they spread their knowledge to non-tuggers?"

"At first, many of them tried during their time in port. At best, they were laughed at, at worst . . ."

"But were people really that prejudiced?"

Misty's eyes grew moist. "I'm afraid people haven't changed that much since they killed off my Pueblo ancestors. They fear what's different."

"But if only they could be made to see that they too have the potential. . . ."

"One day, perhaps," said Misty softly. "Until then, we're condemned to a lonely life. Only with our fellow tuggers are we able to communicate on the deepest level."

Margalit remembered Chuck-parent's words: "It's a hard and lonely life. Stick to your music and stay in Australia."

Had she known, would she have made the same choice? Margalit looked back at the berg. The same shiver of delight ran through her that she had experienced as a child watching the bergs come into port. She thought of her parents' garden filled with blossoming trees and winding paths. How she would lie for hours on end in the grass, playing her flute, breathing in the fragrant air. But without the icebergs' water, the garden would never have existed. Even as a child, she had known she must follow the water to its source. As she watched the trailing berg, she thought of all the energy its frozen crystals contained—energy that would make the desert bloom. And she knew her choice would have been the same.

Margalit watched the heating device burrow its way into the mountain's heart. A pinkish-red glow spread through the berg. Small streams of meltwater trickled down, widening into rushing brooks. Each precious drop flowed into the gathering hemisphere, then made its way into the pipe which pumped back to shore.

Then, just as in the dream, she felt a pressure in her head. Images of other meltings superimposed themselves on what she now saw. Other men and women appeared in her mind, who had shared with Misty and Jan David as she did now. Even clearer than their faces, she could sense the feelings they had shared, their fears and anxieties but also their joys.

She watched the berg grow smaller. Eventually, the melting would reach the five-sixths that lay hidden under the warm Australian sea. With Misty, she traveled back to a far-away Pueblo set in red earth.

Together, they watched dark clouds gather behind the black mountain. The legends told that the spirits of the ancestors went to dwell on the mountain after death. And after the thundering rain, a double rainbow spread across the azure sky. Then she followed Jan David to the cold climate of his native Sweden. She climbed, with him, down the rocky hillsides and listened to the wind call through the barren trees.

The iceberg grew smaller and cast a pinkish-orange glow over the water. Margalit led her companions through her parents' garden. Oblique rays of sun bathed down on them. Breathing in the fragrance of the flowers, they ran through the grass. By a large rhododendron, they stopped. Magenta blossoms burst forth like stars. From a distance, they looked like one single flower—up close they divided into fourteen separate blossoms. Each flower branched into five petals. Diamond-shaped dots marked the topmost petal. Then the colors started pulsating and the blossoms fused into a mountain of magenta.

In the late afternoon sun, the outlines of the berg were growing faint. Tightly, Margalit clasped her two companions to her breast. In the distance, the lights of the port city were beginning to flash on, like miniature stars. And she thought of her group parents, of all the inhabitants of the city in which she had grown up. How much she longed to share with them the beauty of what she had just experienced.

The telepathic link was growing weaker but still she heard Misty's thought: "They wouldn't understand, child. They would fear and envy you."

And she remembered the sadness in Chuck-parent's face whenever he spoke about tugging. Sadness for what must remain unsaid. For several days now, the iceberg would melt. The tears of its dissolution would bring life to the parched land.

When Petals Fall

Sydney J. Van Scyoc

A complicating factor in our population problem is the fact that unlike past centuries, when human deaths roughly equaled births, current medical science is steadily extending the lifetimes of most people. There's even an experimental system for freezing the bodies of terminally ill patients with the hope that they can be revived at some time in the future when cures have been discovered for their illnesses. Should this become widespread and feasible, it would add further to overpopulation. This dramatic and moving story posits a backlash to such efforts.

Sydney Joyce Van Scyoc's science fiction novels include Salt Flower, Starmother **and** Cloudcry.

T WAS 2:00 A.M. when Kelta pushed the night buzzer at the personnel entrance. A minute later a narrow night face, male variety, appeared at the opening door. Kelta palmed her credentials at him. "Federal Inspector." Quickly she stepped past into the corridor, a tall, lean girl with straight brows and purpose in her voice. "Take me to the desk."

The orderly stared at her incredulously. "You can't come in here."

"I have. Now examine my credentials again and take me to the desk."

"You—" He frowned at the credential case in her hand, shook his head, and reluctantly surrendered to her authority.

The corridor turned, branched, and they approached a broad counter behind which appeared another night face, female variety, sandwiched unpalatably between a stiff white collar and a bun of rusty hair.

"Miss Hastings, this—"

"This Federal Inspector is bumping the aide on Ward Seven for the remainder of the shift," Kelta finished for him, presenting her credentials and sliding out of her coat. Beneath she wore white.

Hastings gaped at the emergent uniform and at the tall young woman inside it. She turned the credentials, digesting them biliously. Her face pulled itself together. "You can't enter this facility at this hour. Inspections are scheduled through Director Behrens herself. For daylight hours."

"Well, my approach is a little different. I'm Inspector West, transferred out of Federal District Four six months ago."

Intelligence invaded the stony eyes. "So."

"So," Kelta agreed, confident her reputation had preceded her. "I'm sure you know that if a Federal Inspector is denied entry, the facility may find its license suspended upon twenty-four hours' notice. That would involve relocating a number of patients very rapidly."

Hastings's face underwent a second unpleasant arrangement. She moved to the end of the counter, punched at the commset there. She molded the privacy receiver against her ear. "Director, I'm sorry to disturb you at home, but there is a Federal Inspector here. West. She is trying to enter Seven." Her glance returned to Kelta. "Director wants the name of your superior."

"I'm sure she knows Pallan Holmes has been Supervising Inspector in this district for several years. But she may not know that if I'm not conducted to Seven within five minutes, my report to Holmes will reflect your lack of cooperation. Combined with what happened here three nights ago, that could have a deleterious effect upon the licensure of this institution."

Quickly Hastings relayed the ultimatum. A moment later she proffered the receiver. "Director Behrens will speak with you herself."

Kelta shook her head. "Tomorrow, after I've completed my inspection." She retrieved her credentials and dropped them into her bag. Deftly she flipped her dark hair off her collar, rolled it, and pinned it to her head.

She waited.

Five minutes later the door of Ward Seven slid and Kelta stepped in. Her eyes swung up the steep walls. Tiers of care cradles, serviced by narrow, railed catwalks, reached to the ceiling. A deserted monitor desk commanded a view of both cradle walls of Ward Seven.

Hastings's voice rattled up the walls. "Ames?"

A face appeared upon an upper catwalk, eyes large.

"Inspection. You're dismissed for the night."

The aide's eyes slid to Kelta. She pattered down the stairs, stepped quickly behind the desk to retrieve her coat, and vanished through the sliding door.

Kelta stepped to the desk. Her eyes moved across the display of monitor panels. Over half those panels were dark tonight. The ones that were illuminated, indicating occupied cradles, were scattered randomly. "I see you haven't consolidated the survivors on the lower tiers."

Hastings glanced at the display without comment.

"Didn't it strike you at the time of the raid that there was an unusually high survival rate? Normally when a Messenger strikes, 95 percent of the patients are lost. In this case, better than 40 percent were salvaged."

Hastings's eyes were impenetrable. "Evidently the girl failed to pull the tubes early enough in her shift."

Kelta nodded. "Possible." She dropped her coat over the back of the seat. "But I'm very interested in that survival rate." Her mouth moved in a quick, impersonal smile. "Please don't let anyone interrupt me tonight."

Hastings moved to fortify her position. "Director Behrens instructed me—"

"To see that I don't turn in an unfavorable report. I know. And I'm telling you I don't want to be annoyed by anyone while I'm at work. I will sign out when the day shift arrives at 6:00 A.M."

There was a recoiling in the stony eyes. "Night shift terminates at 4:00 A.M. on these wards."

Kelta's eyebrows rose. "Oh? Who takes the load between four and six?"

"Monitor readout is switched to the central desk. I take it myself."

Kelta's eyes narrowed. "I see. Well, I'll relieve you of this one ward tonight."

The rocky eyes turned briefly to lava. Then Hastings withdrew.

Alone, Kelta dropped her bag beside the desk. She sat and touched the surface of the desk. Here, only three nights before, a Messenger of Mercy had sat watching these readout panels while her patients died in their cradles. Then, shortly before her shift ended, she had disappeared into the night. She hadn't been seen since.

Not by anyone who hunted her.

Kelta stood, mounted the catwalks, and walked the tiers. The old lay in their cradles swaddled in senility, entubed at every orifice, gaping eyes deserted, lax mouths wordless. Forty-two of them doggedly fighting out the last moments of personal existence; blood circulated by machinery, minds erased by age, they waited for the miracle that could restore them to function, however minimal. Waited for someone, somewhere, to make the immortality breakthrough before their bodies deteriorated to the point where even the machinery of Ward Seven would be useless to them.

But these particular patients seemed to have an edge on the elderly in other nursing homes around the country. Because when the Messenger had disentubed this ward three nights before, forty-two of these patients had resisted death. Forty-two of a hundred had remained warm and breathing.

Now Kelta examined those forty-two. In most she found several unusual conditions. The skin that stretched across the wasted muscles and prominent bones was leathery, lacking the typical fragility of age. Turning the patients she found no sign of bedsores. In these same patients, Kelta found the surfaces of the eyeballs subtly mottled. In most there were perceptible deformities of the limbs, bones of the forearms and forelegs oddly bent.

When Kelta had examined all the present occupants of the ward, she selected her three tests cases. Grimly she disconnected them from the equipment that maintained them, leaving their tubes arcing loose like so many strands of half-cooked spaghetti. Then she returned to the monitor desk and sat.

Waiting.

Watching.

In all three cases, blood pressure fell—and stabilized. Heart action appeared—and stabilized. Temperature fell, four degrees—and stabilized. No distress lights flashed. Within their cradles the three patients drew breath without artificial aid.

Just as they had three nights before.

Kelta frowned and bobbed up to make a visual check. She found respiration barely perceptible, pulse light but steady, skin surfaces slightly cool, but not with the chill of death. This was the chill of life.

Unnatural life. The lines of Kelta's face lengthened. Her lips set.

At 5:50 A.M. she reconnected her three subjects and settled behind the desk again. At 6:00 the door slid. A thirtyish woman in white stepped through, eyes anxious. Kelta stood. "Day duty?"

"I'm—yes, I'm Fisher." Fisher's eyes moved nervously up the tiers.

"How long have you been on Seven, Fisher?"

Fisher probed dry lips with a pale tongue. "Three years."

"Have you ever noticed anything unusual about the patients who survived the Messenger call?"

Again Fisher's eyes made the anxious trip up the tiers. "They're—well, they're different. They're—" Her voice died uncertainly.

Kelta nodded. "Do you have any idea whether they're on special medication?"

Fisher shook her head. "A registered nurse administers medications. I'm not qualified."

Kelta nodded again, stood, and flipped her coat off the back of the chair. "Well, I think you'll find everything in order. There were no emergencies."

Upstairs Hastings waited stiffly behind the desk while her relief moved busily behind her. "What time does Director Behrens normally sign in?" Kelta asked.

"Director arrives at 9:30."

"Good. Leave word that I'll be in to speak with her then."

Outside the world was dim, the walks almost empty. Kelta plunged through the dawn-fogged loneliness toward the transit stop, preoccupied. At the hotel she shelled out a dozen water tokens and showered. It refreshed her little.

Immortality. Someone was on the verge of the breakthrough, perhaps had already penetrated the barrier. There could be no other explanation. But she was not helpless in the face of this development. Not if the patients on Ward Seven, and probably on other wards as well, had been used in the way she suspected they had.

At 8:30 she hit the commset and reached the district headquarters. "Supervisor Holmes, please."

Pallan Holmes appeared upon the faceplate immediately, a big man with curly locks that tumbled over his forehead and a vague expression. It became less vague when he met Kelta's eyes. "West," he acknowledged painfully.

"I've run across something a little unusual in my present assignment. I'm scheduling the day to deal with it. I may have to requisition someone to back me up later in the day."

Alarmed, Holmes pawed at his desklog. "You're at Leisure Gardens in Cincinnati?"

"No. Taylor-Welsh Home in Cleveland. I rearranged my schedule. I wanted to observe the aftermath of the Messenger strike three nights ago."

Holmes's voice rose in alarm. "West, Taylor-Welsh is one of the higher caliber homes in our district. We've never had cause for complaint there. Management has always been fully cooperative with the department, and the department in turn—"

"The department has always been fully cooperative with management. You've even allowed Director Behrens to schedule 'impromptu' inspections at her own convenience."

Holmes swept at his curls, his eyes lost in agony. "West, it's our policy to cooperate with reputable facilities whenever we can. Particularly when they're as ably administered as Taylor-Welsh. I've known

Director Behrens personally—"

"A convenient arrangement for everyone, though sometimes I think that philosophy has something to do with the way I'm bounced from district to district. I'll call later if I need help. I'd appreciate it if you would hold Napp available."

Holmes's face twisted. "West, you're not—"

"You'll probably have a call from Director Behrens later this morning. I haven't interviewed her yet." Quickly Kelta broke connection and retreated from the commset.

It summoned a moment later. Kelta did not answer. Somehow she recognized the wounded tone of its cry.

At 9:35 she was admitted to Director Behrens's private office.

Director Behrens was a middle-aged woman with glossy green hair. Matching green-lacquered fingernails lay upon her desk. "The type of off-hours inspection you subjected this facility to last night would be far more appropriate to some undercapitalized vegetable farm," she snapped, green nails tapping the desktop once in sharp emphasis.

"Well, I guess you've already heard that I don't tailor my visits to suit management," Kelta said, sitting. "And I thought the Messenger raid unusual enough a circumstance to warrant an unusual type of visit."

Director Behrens's face creased bitterly. "Inspector, no home in the nation is invulnerable to these fanatics. I learned that three nights ago. Despite every precaution, they slipped through to work their devastation upon our business."

"And not upon your patients?"

Behrens's face colored slightly. "Our patients *are* our business. They've entrusted their future to us. In the past years, our district association has watched this scourge concentrate first upon one district, then upon another. Now apparently it is our turn. Seven homes ravaged in a bare four months. I completely fail to understand why the authorities have not prosecuted these people."

"The fact that none of them have ever been apprehended may have something to do with it."

"And *why* have none been apprehended? Over a period of five years? After thousands of deaths?"

Kelta shrugged. "The operation appears to be very well managed. The Messenger appears with an apparently valid certificate from a local aide training school. She works for a day, maybe for two or three days, even four. Then, before anyone on the staff has had time to become acquainted with her, she pulls the plug and disappears, never to be seen again. It later develops it was another Messenger who actually attended the training course, having borrowed the name and background of some local woman for enrollment purposes. This false identity was, of course, passed on to the strike Messenger at graduation. The local woman whose identity was usurped is always found to be in complete ignorance of the double-barreled impersonation. Presumably both Messengers change their appearance and resume their former lives.

"The leaders of the movement issue periodic statements of philosophy and intent—but never in such a way as to point to the identity of any member of the organization. You know, I've heard it suggested that any member who has delivered her Message is immediately and permanently disaffiliated."

Behrens nodded impatiently. "Oh yes, I've heard all the theories. And I feel it should be made adequately clear to the public that when an incident of this nature occurs, the home is in no way at fault. Despite all my media releases, this home is losing patients at the rate of two dozen a day."

"Unfortunate." Kelta's tone became remote from the topic. "Now. My first question concerns the two-hour gap between night shift and day shift on the wards."

Behrens's green nails disappeared beneath whitening knuckles. "During those two hours all monitor systems are read at the central desk, Inspector. The nurse on duty can attend to any emergency within moments. Out patients are in no way endangered by this simple economy measure."

Kelta nodded. "I see. But I wonder why you economize in that particular way when no other reputable home leaves wards unattended during the early morning hours."

"Inspector, there is nothing within regulations to prohibit this particular practice."

"No. As a matter of fact, there isn't. Now, I'm interested in the patients who survived the Messenger raid. Have you examined them yourself?"

"I never enter the wards."

"But I'm sure you know those patients show some interesting physical manifestations. A difference in skin texture and thickness, a mottling of the ocular surfaces, limb deformities. Are these attributable to some medication these patients receive?"

"You may speak with our staff physician tomorrow. He is out today."

Kelta shook her head. "I think I will learn just as much by examining your patient files."

Behrens stared at her. Her face whitened. "The condition of the patients on our wards is testimony enough to the care we render here."

"Well, I'm going to see the files anyway, Director. Immediately."

Director Behrens sat, stark and still. Then, abruptly, she stood, her eyes fierce. She stalked out.

Kelta sat back in the chair to wait. There would be a delay, she knew, while Director Behrens called Pallan Holmes. In a few cases, Kelta's Supervising Inspector had actually summoned her back to district headquarters before she had completed inspection. But she doubted that Pallan Holmes would respond that vigorously or directly.

Ten minutes later the door opened. A secretary tapped across the floor, pressed the control that brought the microviewer up from Director Behrens's desktop, inserted a plate of microrecords. "You'll be able to view better from this chair."

"Thank you." Kelta installed herself in the Director's chair. "Do these include files on the patients who died in the raid?"

"Why, no. These only include patients who are on Seven now."

"I want the others too."

The secretary wheeled and addressed a silent question to Director Behrens, who stood at the door. Tight-lipped, Behrens nodded.

Kelta flashed through the files in half an hour. Then she stacked the two plates. "Wrapping paper and tape, Director?"

Behrens stared at her, grappling for voice. "For what purpose?"

"I'm going to take these records with me. They're quite interesting."

"They're—you can't."

Kelta stood, tapping the plates. "I don't find any mention here of the medication being administered to the patients who survived the raid and not to the others on Seven. Something else I don't find is signed consent forms."

"Consent? For what?"

"For the drug that obviously *is* being dispensed to those patients sometime between 4:00 and 6:00 A.M. It's a criminal offense, you know, to use experimental drugs on patients who haven't been apprised of all details and who haven't signed consent forms while in clear mind."

"This home—Inspector, Taylor-Welsh would never risk the welfare of its patients in the fashion you intimate."

Kelta shook her head. "I'm not intimating. I'm stating. Studying these records, I see that the patients who survived the Messenger strike are actually on the average older than the patients who died. I disconnected several of the survivors myself this morning—for three hours. From their medical records, and from my personal observation, I can say they should have expired almost immediately. They didn't, any more than they expired when the Messenger disentubed them. They're receiving a drug that enables them to survive. But there's no such drug on the market. Therefore it's experimental. And there are no signed consent forms in these files."

Director Behrens's eyes flashed. "Young woman, it would be much more to the point for you to attempt to find the person who killed over fifty of our patients than to persecute the administration of a reputable home."

"I'm a Facility Inspector, Director. My job is to police the management of nursing homes. The local and state police forces will have to track the Messenger for you."

"And they'll never catch her! They never do! These children—they come into our facilities, devastate our business, and then they drop from sight! Idealists they call themselves!"

Kelta's brows rose. "Well, there *are* a lot of ways the time and money you expend here could be put to better use."

"These children might think differently if they were old themselves."

Kelta shrugged. "Wrapping paper and tape?"

There was another delay. Then the requested items appeared. Kelta secured the two plates into a small package. "I'm filing departmental action immediately to insure that those patients aren't removed from the facility. If you need me, I'll be at the Southside Hotel for the rest of the day."

Before proceeding there, however, she locked the microplates into a security box in a bank vault. The key to the box she mailed to herself at district headquarters.

Reaching her room, she called Pallan Holmes again. He flashed on screen in a state of agitation, curls bobbing distraught. "West, I've had two calls from Director Behrens at Taylor-Welsh in the past hour."

"I'll fill you in later," Kelta said quickly. "I have some very interesting evidence in safekeeping, but I need a backup agent immediately. Is Napp available?"

"West, Taylor-Welsh is one of the most respected homes for the aged in our district. I've known Director Behrens—"

"Yes—personally for a number of years. Is Napp available? I want sound equipment with him, and I want him now."

Discussion ensued. Kelta prevailed. Napp was scheduled on the next flash west.

He arrived an hour later and appeared at Kelta's door, a burly young man with reddish-blond hair receding from a high, bulbous forehead. "You jarred me off write-up on a week's work. You're offering thrills?"

Kelta grinned. "I'm offering. You have the sound equipment?"

Napp nodded, stepping into the room and glancing around. "Here?"

Kelta chewed her lower lip. "No, elsewhere, I think. I want a remote button."

Napp nodded, setting down his case and rummaging in it. Kelta studied the top of his head, hoping her evaluation of him had been accurate. "How much stock do you hold, Napp?"

Napp's eyebrows furnished brief warmth to his balding upper forehead. "Pardon?"

"Stock. United Textiles East. Singer Diversified. General Paper and Plastics."

Napp's grin cleared a dozen and a half solid white teeth. "You know, West, I've observed that ownership of stock tends to interfere with pursuit of duty. So I don't own any stock. But I hear others in the department own a little. I guess you've run into that, as much as you've bounced districts."

"Repeatedly. Now I think I'm about to be offered some myself." She accepted the small blue sound button along with his appraising glance. She clipped the button into the hair at the base of her neck. "Has this equipment been checked out recently?"

"I checked everything while I was waiting for flash time."

The call came minutes later. A smooth masculine voice, a matter of mutual interest to be discussed, a rendezvous arranged.

A rendezvous kept. Kelta arrived at the hotel bar, where a reserved booth awaited her, five minutes early. She wore a brief dress with buttercup skirt strips that flapped across her long thighs. She had touched her lips with color, but her brows remained straight and uncompromising.

That fact she obscured temporarily with an effusive smile when two sleek men in business blue were conducted to the booth, suits glossy, smiles glassy. "Miss West?"

"Yes," she agreed brightly.

Manifestly prosperous, patently shrewd, they were Patrick and Nussman. "Our colleague, Dr. Vincinzi, will meet us in a few moments," Nussman reassured Kelta smoothly. "I think we may order without him."

They ordered. Drinks arrived.

Nussman leaned earnestly across the table. "Now, Miss West, it has been suggested that you are an excellent prospect for investment counseling. You hold a civil service position with good salary and security prospects. You're young, dedicated, very much involved with your profession. Too involved, I'm sure, to make careful analysis of the market yourself or to spend much time watching your stocks as they must be watched to derive maximum benefit from your investment program."

Kelta tilted her drink, examined the bottom of the glass through it, nodding. "My time is so completely filled I've never gotten around to investing at all. Which counseling service do you represent?"

"Ah." Nussman flourished an embossed card. "Actually, we represent Robard Wheels East, a diversified industrial and service firm. Casters, utility wheels, rubber products—"

"Nursing homes."

Nussman's glib attempt to gloss over Kelta's interruption was interrupted in turn by the arrival of an elderly man, slight and visibly withdrawn. Patrick and Nussman bobbed up. "Dr. Vincinzi, Inspector Kelta West. We were just discussing Miss West's investment program."

"Which is currently non-existent," Kelta added, her eyes on the older man. He joined them with obvious reluctance. "Do you represent Robard East too, Dr. Vincinzi?"

Vincinzi's forehead creased faintly. "Not in the way Patrick and Nussman do." His eyes met Kelta's briefly, then moved away, avoiding his associates.

Nussman reasserted himself. "Miss West, we're here because a mutual acquaintance suggested you might appreciate being introduced to a new investment plan. Our plan, you see—it's still in the pilot stage—is designed to help responsible younger citizens find their way into the market by granting them substantial blocks of Robard at very nominal prices. In addition, you will be introduced to one of the investment firms we have found reliable in our own trading. They will handle your account without fee. In fact, it might be possible to arrange an extended program, a certain number of shares of Robard East being entered into your account semi-annually over a decade. Of course, you would be in no way obliged to retain the stock. You could trade or sell, although your counselors would advise you that Robard is a diversified concern with many excellent prospects."

Kelta nodded gravely. "Are you in the pharmaceutical line, Dr. Vincinzi?"

The older man's eyes came up, faded, wary.

Nussman hastened into the gap. "Now, Miss West, we can't discuss certain aspects of our enterprise at all. Pharmaceuticals are a very touchy field. If the nature or direction of certain researches are leaked too soon, the opportunity to sweep the market—at enormous profit— could be lost forever. That would certainly diminish considerably what you might otherwise expect to realize from your own block of Robard."

"I see. How many nursing homes does Robard hold?"

Nussman's smooth forehead was briefly marred by irritation. "Robard holds half a dozen of the better homes in this state."

"And in how many of those are experiments in extended longevity being conducted?"

The three men were silent. Perspiration appeared upon Nussman's forehead.

"Only in the Taylor-Welsh home and Walden Gardens," Dr. Vincinzi said quietly, finally meeting and holding Kelta's eye.

"And how far has the research progressed, Doctor?"

Vincinzi's pale eyes were troubled. "With the help of my staff, I have developed a serum that produces, as nearly as we can determine, virtual immortality. Unfortunately it does nothing to deter the progress of senility. It does not delay the onset or ameliorate the more distressing manifestations of senility even slightly. Virtually all it does is enable the body to survive as a body, not as a viable personality."

"Are your subjects vulnerable to accidental death?"

Vincinzi nodded slowly. "They are. Severe blood loss—loss amounting to 80 percent or more—will produce death. Incineration of body tissues likewise will produce death." He shrugged. "Little else will. I have in my possession mice who are up to twenty years old. They are helpless. Hopeless. But alive."

"Like the patients I examined this morning on Ward Seven."

Nussman moved uneasily. "Inspector, this is no place to discuss these matters. We made this appointment in order—"

Kelta's eyes were grave. "This is where we are going to discuss them. Doctor, have you considered the social aspects of your serum?"

"Present? Or future? I've considered both. I'm still considering them." Vincinzi shook his head. "When I went into this branch of research, I was a young man on the trail of conquest. Immortality—the unexplored frontier. If a breakthrough came in my time, it was my ticket to the future, to the centuries that lie ahead. My personality could survive, participate, contribute.

"Now I'm old. I see my development purely as a holding measure. There are hundreds of thousands of my generation in homes across this country, waiting. Most of them, if there were no startling development within the next few years, would die despite everything. But if my serum is marketed soon, they can continue to live. They can continue to wait—for the miracle that may someday restore them to consciousness and function." His eyes were suddenly intense. "Perhaps they will never contribute much to the future—perhaps *I* never will. But the sun shines. Water flows. Children play and roses bloom. The simple pleasures continue. Can we deny ourselves them? Could you deny yourself, after your productive years are past?"

Kelta was aware of Nussman and Patrick's alert silence. She frowned. The personal case, always the personal case. The two entrepreneurs hoped Dr. Vincinzi's personal case would persuade her.

She could only give the personal answer. She reached for her bag, flipped out a handful of tokens, and spread them before her. "Water flows, Dr. Vincinzi? This represents my water allowance for next week.

It will get me through two showers, some personal laundry, and hopefully I'll be able to wash my face each morning. Of course, I don't drink from the tap. I don't like to use sick leave unnecessarily.

"Personal Exhibit #2, a photograph. My brother. He's twenty-two years old. He doesn't leave the apartment. That's because he's allergic to air—or to what passes for air. My parents have invested thousands of dollars in air filtration devices so he can survive inside the apartment.

"Exhibit #3, my radiation badge." She slipped it from around her neck. "It registers normal now. That's because I was reissued fourteen years ago, after the Dallas pile disaster. You'd be surprised how many young women are dedicating themselves to social causes because they'll never bear normal children."

She shook her head. "Your generation invested its time in a number of worthwhile purposes and in a number of frivolous ones. It created a number of problems we've all had to live with. Now, instead of passing on and leaving the heritage any generation can leave—a clear field for the next generation to deal with those problems—it wants to linger. It wants present and future generations to maintain it indefinitely in thousands of storage homes all over the country. It wants precious resources expended upon it—water, power, pharmaceuticals, rubber, plastic, and metal products."

Kelta smiled grimly. "You're not asking just for moral support. You're asking for our drinking water, our oxygen, our children playing. I say no. You've had your roses, Doctor. I hope you enjoyed them. You've had your time on Earth too. Now it's our turn."

Nussman's features contracted ominously. "That sounds like the Messenger line."

"Is there anyone in the country who hasn't heard the Messenger line by now?"

Vincinzi touched Kelta's hand, his face grave. "You've answered my question, the one I've been asking myself—and sometimes these gentlemen—with increasing frequency these past few years. No man wants to go. But several mornings ago I stood on Ward Seven and saw fifty-eight dead. Fifty-eight, stiff and cold in their cradles. And a strange thought, an alien thought almost, entered my mind: death *is* a part of life."

"The rose petal drops." Kelta swung her head to meet two other pairs of eyes. They glittered, stark and cold. "As I see it, Robard has a choice. It can face charges of illegal experimentation upon human subjects and attempting to bribe a Federal officer—I have a sound man upstairs recording this conversation—or it can close down its immortality project. Immediately."

Nussman and Patrick sat very still. Finally Nussman creaked back to life. "You can't prove anything. Even with sound tracks."

"I can prove a lot. I *will* prove a lot if I have to. You can make your stock offer to every member of the district staff—and it won't keep *me* quiet." Kelta stood. "The reason the department keeps me bouncing from district to district is that I don't silence."

"But we have a massive investment in this project!" Patrick exploded. "We've dropped billions into this!"

Kelta smiled tautly. "Now you're going to lose billions. Either way. If the government prosecutes, your chance to grab the market dissolves. Along with your corporate image. If you turn off the project, you might salvage at least the image."

Nussman shook his head stubbornly. "No. You misread public climate. Federal funds support our nursing homes. The old have public sympathy. Our serum will have public sympathy too, even if there has been some infraction of the law."

"Oh! Which public? For how long? Nursing homes originally drew public funds because their clients were human beings. Now the nursing homes have created a clientele of objects, and I see public sympathy changing. I see the public resenting the flow of money and resources into the maintenance of corpses. I see the public beginning to realize, with each Messenger strike, that the only parties who benefit from the present arrangement are the owners of these homes." She shook her head. "You have a choice. Dr. Vincinzi, I think maybe you've made yours."

The older man spoke through dry lips. "I believe I have, now."

Upstairs Napp repacked his equipment. Kelta twitched the remote sound button out of her hair, dropped it into his palm, and sagged into a chair. "I want the sound tracks dropped directly into a security box."

"Done." Napp's eyes were bright. "What do you think? Which light will they blink?"

Kelta shook her head. "I don't know. But I think we have them either way."

"You do?" Napp's brows went north, surprised. "Well, I can see Nussman and Patrick wading right through your charges and going ahead with their project, even from prison. There's still profit in corpses, even if it has to be shared."

Kelta shrugged. "In that case, I can see Messengers doing more than pulling tubes. I can see Messengers reversing blood flow back into the circulating equipment. Or creating a series of funeral pyres. And releasing more public statements, especially on the subject of the increased costs of maintaining the tubers.

"And I can see Vincinzi publicly denouncing the project if necessary. Maybe even delivering a Message to his experimental subjects himself. As a public demonstration of his feelings."

Napp's eyes widened. "Ah." His legs folded, and he sat on the floor.

"That *was* the Messenger line you were unwinding downstairs."

Kelta's eyes rested upon him. The normally decisive line of her mouth drooped with weariness.

"The Messenger line—you've been in this district what? Five months?"

"Six."

"And four months ago we began getting heavy Messages. As many in a few months as we'd gotten in two years before."

Kelta's expression remained opaque.

Napp frowned intently. "You know, a Facility Inspector would be an ideal coordinator for Messenger operations. A Facility Inspector has access to everything: schedules, floor plans, personnel records, the facilities themselves. A Facility Inspector—"

Kelta unfolded from her chair and rummaged in her bag. She came out with a handful of water tokens. "Napp, would you mind if I took a shower?"

Slowly Napp shook his head. "No. No, I'll go rent a security box." He grinned. "On the way back maybe I'll pick up a rose."

Kelta smiled. "All right. Buy a yard of sunshine too. We'll spread it on the floor."

"And a puddle of rainwater? Enjoy it while we can."

"And one child playing." She touched her radiation badge, trying to keep the smile on her lips.

How Can We Sink
When We Can Fly?

Alexei Panshin

Sometimes it's impossible for a conscientious science fiction writer to produce a hopeful picture of the future in view of the number of serious problems we face and the fact that we're doing far too little about them. Alexei Panshin, asked to write a story about a future world he couldn't really believe in, found himself in this difficult position. After much thought he produced the following ingeniously constructed story-within-a-story, in which his auctorial dilemma, the problems of our world, and the solution to both finally come together. The operative word is faith.

Alexei Panshin's first novel, Rite of Passage, won the Nebula Award. Singly and later in collaboration with his wife Cory, he has since produced four more novels, several short stories, and two books of science fiction criticism.

In the final analysis civilization can be saved only if we are willing to change our ways of life. We have to invent utopias not necessarily to make them reality but to help us formulate worthwhile human goals.

—RENÉ DUBOS

1

ENDINGS OF STORIES come easy. It is the beginnings, when anything is still possible, that come hard.

To think yourself into somewhere strange and someone new, and then to live it, takes the nerve of a revolutionary or a bride. If writers had that kind of nerve, they wouldn't be writers. They would be starting revolutions and getting married, like everyone else. As it is, we tend to cultivate our gardens and mull a lot.

When the beginnings come harder than usual and when the only news that penetrates the Pennsylvania outback is of lost causes and rumors of lost causes, I give a call to Rob to grab whoever he can find between Springfield, Massachusetts and here, and come on down for the weekend. The people around here are good people, but all they know is what they hear on the evening news. And they can't talk shop. Rob talks good shop, and he has a completely unique set of rumors. His news is no better, but it isn't the common line.

It does him good to come, too. Springfield is no place to live. In a sense I feel responsible for Rob. Springfield was founded by William Pynchon, who was an ancestor of mine. He wrote a book in Greek called *The Meritorious Price of Our Redemption*, which was burned on Boston Common in 1650 as religiously unsound, and he went back to England. He stayed long enough to found Springfield and a branch of my mother's family, and make me responsible for Rob.

If I ever meet Thomas Pynchon, who wrote *V.*, I intend to ask him how he feels about Springfield, Mass. In the meantime Rob has some leeway with me, which he takes advantage of on occasion.

I was expecting Rob and Leigh, but when we picked them up on Friday morning at the lunch-counter bus stop across the river in New Jersey, they had a kid with them. Leigh is in her thirties, good silent strong plain people. She writes Westerns. Rob had collected her in New York. Where he'd gotten the kid I didn't know.

"This is Juanito," Rob said.

The kid was blond as Maytime, dressed in worn blue jeans and a serape. He was wishing for a beard. I didn't know him, but he looked like a member of the tribe.

"I'm Alex and this is Cory," I said, and he nodded. Then the five of us headed for our 1951 Plymouth, our slow beast.

"I'm just as glad to get out of here," Rob said, looking back as we headed onto the bridge to Pennsylvania. "It reminds me of Springfield."

It is a depressing battered little town. A good place to leave behind.

Cory said, "And you know, there are people who commute to work in New York from here every day. Two hours each way."

"It's a long way to come for flaking paint and tumble-down houses," Rob said. "But I suppose if that's the way you like to live . . ."

He turned to look at the brighter prospect of the Pennsylvania hills. "Well," he said, "let's get going. Bring on your sheep and geese and cats."

I said, "There are a couple of ducks now, and Gemma had three kittens."

131

The only part of the livestock that belongs to us is two of the cats. There are two stray tomcats on the place and some independent bullfrogs. The sheep and their lambs are the farmer's. The rest belongs to our landlady up in the big house.

Leigh said, "How old are the kittens?"

Cory turned and said over the seat back, "They haven't even got their eyes open."

Across the Delaware in Pennsylvania we passed a broad field full of dead auto bodies rusting into the land, crossed the shortest covered bridge in the county, and headed up into the hills.

"Well," said Rob. "How badly are you stuck?"

"Stuck," I said. "I'm doing a story based on an idea by Isaac Asimov, for an anthology of new stories."

"You're a hack," said Rob. "You work for money."

"Right," I said. "I work to live and live to work. No, my problem is that I want to respect Asimov's idea without following it to the letter. I guess the problem is that I can't see any way to get from our now to his future. When I listen to the news, I wonder about any future at all. So I sit in front of the typewriter, but I don't write. I'll find the story, I'll see the way, but right now I'm still trying to find my beginning."

"Don't brood about it," said Leigh. "Sit down and write it the simplest way." Kind advice, because in spite of what Leigh may sometimes say about her own work, that's not the way she writes.

"Seen any movies lately?" Rob asked. Not an idle question.

"None," I said. The movies they've been bringing around here haven't been the ones I'm planning to catch. Not Anthony Quinn and Ingrid Bergman in a love story for the ages. Besides, I couldn't take the chance of getting that far from the typewriter. Not with the birth of a story imminent.

"I know you've stopped answering your mail," he said.

"Do I owe you a letter?"

"Of course."

"It must have gotten lost in the mail strike," I said, though in fact I hadn't written. "Our mail hasn't yet gotten back to normal. I'm keeping a list of things that haven't come, starting with a check from Henry." Henry is the agent of all of us. Henry is the agent of half the writers I know.

"Hey, you had a sale?" Automatic question.

"My first this year, and just in time, too. We need the money. They're supposed to pay at the end of the month, and today is already the tenth."

"What about letters?" Rob asked. "Have you really been answering your mail?"

"Letters? I'm busy. All my time goes to writing—that is, not writing."

"Travel? Have you been anyplace recently?"

The size of a mental block can be fairly estimated by the writer's list of austerities. It is less a matter of income than an inability to put anything ahead of writing—that is, not writing. If a writer does nothing whatsoever but sit very very still and pretend to think, you know he is up the creek without a paddle.

Cory answered that one. "Not since Christmas," she said.

"Fine," said Rob, like any doctor in possession of a juicy symptom. "Are you able to read?"

"I never stop reading," I said. "I've never been that petrified."

"Name a good novel you read recently."

"Does it have to be good?"

"Name a novel," Rob said. "It doesn't have to be good."

"All right," I said. "I'm not reading fiction. *Creative Mythology,* the fourth volume of *The Masks of God.*"

"Is that as heavy as it sounds?"

Cory said, "I lost momentum half through it."

"That one is for inspiration," I said. "Then *Personal Knowledge,* by Polanyi. That's food for thought. And *Heroes and Heretics: A Social History of Dissent.* That's for the times. I pick one or the other up in the morning, read a paragraph or a page, and then I think about the Asimov story."

"Oh, you lucky writers," Leigh said. "Your time is your own."

Rob finally let me off the hook. "Let me see what Asimov wrote when we get to your place. Maybe we can talk it out."

A deer suddenly flashed onto the road ahead of us, showed tail, and bounded off through the wooded hillside. Only Cory and I in the front and Juanito in the back got a good look. Leigh caught just a glimpse and Rob missed it entirely. I try to bring people by the scenic route, but they have to be prepared to look at things fast. Rob never bothers.

"Nice," said Leigh.

"We sat at sunset over on Geigel Hill Road the other week and watched a whole herd—twelve or more, and even more down in the draw—cross the road and stream up the long open hillside," I said. "And when our landlady's daughter was here for Easter from England, she said there was a herd in the woods on the State Park land just behind the farm."

"Just behind the farm?" Leigh said. "How far would it be?"

Cory said, "Not far. A ten-minute walk. We could go up this afternoon and look."

Rob said, "Not me. I've been up for thirty hours. I need sack time."

"I'll go," said Juanito.

This Pennsylvania countryside offers you just about anything you want. We've been here the better part of a year and still discover surprises within five miles, and even within one, or within three hundred yards: wild onion, wild strawberries, poison ivy. In the space of a mile on a single road you can find high-speed intersection, three-hundred-year-old farmstead, random suburbia, crossroad community, and woodland in any order and combination you like, strung across little valleys, hidden in hollows, up and over hills. There are even pockets of industry.

"What is that?" Juanito asked.

It's part of the scenery, but you have to be particularly quick to see it. If you could see more of it, perhaps it would have been closed down sooner.

I stopped our old Plymouth tank and backed up the hill to the curve. In early April, with the trees still bare or only barely budding, you can see it from one vantage on the road. Tinny prefab buildings and the half a dozen chemical lagoons perched overlooking the creek with blue and yellow gullies staining the hillside.

"Every time it rains there's overflow," I said. "That's the Revere Chemicals dump. It was put in in 1965, and the State Health people said at the time that it was going to do this, and it took them five years to close it down. Now it just sits there and leaks. The manager is trying to start a new operation in the next township."

"I hope the deer doesn't drink from that stream," Leigh said.

"He has to take his chances the same as the rest of us," Rob said. Growing up in Springfield has left Rob with more than a little sourness.

When we got to the farm, I stopped the car at the head of the long gravel drive. "Somebody hop out and check the mailbox," I said.

Rob made no move. I said, "Rob, it's your side."

"I've been up for thirty hours," he said.

Juanito said, "I'll look."

He dropped the door on the big white mailbox with the blue and red hex sign matching the white hexes on the barn. I could see that it was empty—and the mail truck not in sight yet.

Juanito hesitated in order to let a semi pass, the wind by-blow whipping his hair and his serape, and then he came back to the car. He had a nonreturnable beer bottle in his hand, one of the little squat ones. It had been on the roadside long enough for the label to wash free, but then it has been a wet spring.

"What about this?" he said.

I was irritated. I had expected the mail to be there when we got back from the run to Frenchtown.

"Oh, throw it back!" I said. "Unless you mean to pick up all the trash along the frontage. Start with the chrome and the broken headlights up at the second phone pole."

The kid looked slightly bewildered at my vehemence. I was immediately sorry.

I switched the engine off, set the brake, and hopped out. "I'll tell you what," I said. "We'll strike a blow."

I walked to the back of the car and opened up the humpback trunk. Then I said, "Throw your bottle in there," and the kid did.

I stepped down into the front field and picked up the black and raddled truck-tire carcass I'd been meaning to police up ever since it was abandoned there. I lugged it up the grade and slung it into the trunk.

"There," I said.

The geese set up their automatic clank and clatter when we drove into the yard. Phoebe is the goose, Alexander the gander. Alexander is the main squawk of the barnyard, Phoebe just the harmony, but when they trudge around the farm, it is Phoebe who leads and Alexander who walks behind attempting to look impressive.

Fang skirted the geese and came skittering past us, tail briefly raised in acknowledgment, a miniature panther in penguin clothes. We followed her into the house for lunch.

The house was once a carriage house. The original beams, marked with the holes and gouges of the gear used to raise and lower carriages, cross the twelve-foot ceiling of the living room, and a glass chandelier hangs from the lowest beam. The kitchen behind and the bedrooms upstairs in the original building and the library and study in the addition are cut to less heroic proportion. It's a tidy small house with an overwhelming living room. It has all the charms of Frank Lloyd Wright without the dim constricted little hallways Wright insisted on designing.

During lunch Cory took me aside and said, "We're going to need more bacon and a dozen eggs."

"I'll go to the Elephant this afternoon," I said.

"Get a couple of half gallons of milk, too." Then she said, "Who is this boy, Alexei? He keeps looking around, but he doesn't say much."

I said, "He seems within the normal range of Rob's friends."

"Well, Rob's strange."

"True. I don't suppose I'd want to put this Juanito to a vote of the neighbors."

Then Cory said, "Alexei, what are we going to do about the taxes if the money doesn't come?"

I said, "We know it's coming. If worse comes to worst, I'll mail our check, and we can deposit Henry's check as soon as it comes. Don't

135

brood."

I don't worry about the money except when I absolutely have to. I juggle without thinking, and the money usually comes from somewhere when it has to be found. If I worried about money, I'd be too busy to stare at my typewriter.

After lunch, Rob said, "All right. Let me have a look at that Asimov idea before I collapse."

Cory and Leigh and Juanito went walking back toward the State Park land to look for the deer herd. Two lambs clowning in the plowed lands went ducking urgently under the wire fencing looking for mama at the passage of the people.

Rob and I went back inside the house and into the study. It's a small room. The people before us used it for a nursery. Now it holds our desks, two small armchairs, three small bookcases of reference books, including our prize, the eleventh-edition *Britannica* we bought for $50 in Doylestown, and a catbox in the closet to keep us humble.

I scooped Wolf, our lesser cat, out of my easy chair. She's a tortoiseshell, pine needles and shadow, with an orange nose and a wide black greasepaint moustache. She keeps me company when I write. At five months she is still small enough to curl up to sleep in my typing-paper box like a mouse tucked up for winter inside a Swiss cheese. I sat down with her on my lap.

Rob said, "How's the collaboration with Cory coming?"

Cory and I have a contract for a fantasy novel in four books.

I said, "Cory has just been reading the novel I did at eighteen to give herself encouragement. She found it very encouraging."

"It's pretty bad?"

"I don't remember it too well, fortunately. Cory says it's about an incredibly narrow and suspicious young man whose only distinguishing feature is that he wants a way to leave."

"That's all?"

"That's all. I made the story up as I went along. I remember that much."

That wasn't all, but that's the way I talk to Rob. I remember there was a galactic empire in the story that did nasty things, and my hero wanted a way to leave it. If I were writing the story now, I suppose he'd try to change it.

"Hmmm," said Rob. He wrote a novel at eighteen, too, making it up as he went along. The difference is that his was published and mine wasn't, so he has more to regret. "Let me see what Asimov has to say."

I searched through the clutter on the right-hand corner of my desk. While I was searching, Rob looked through the books on the opposite corner. He came up with *Personal Knowledge* by Michael Polanyi and began to thumb it.

"You weren't kidding about this, were you?" he said. "What do you get out of all of this?" It's a crabbed book in small type with heavy footnotes.

"I don't generally recommend it," I said. "It's epistemology. The nature and limits of knowledge."

"What have you gotten out of it?"

"The power of mind to shape the world. The need for responsible belief," I said. "Not that the idea is new. One of my ancestors . . ."

"I know. One of your ancestors founded Springfield." Rob isn't too sure whether I'm lying in whole or in part about William Pynchon. We do work at misleading each other. I like to tell the truth so that it comes out sounding like a lie for the pure artistic beauty of doing it, and I don't know how much to make of the stories Rob tells me.

"I was about to say, one of my ancestors was the brother of Hosea Ballou, who founded the Universalists. 'The Father of American Universalism.'"

"What's that?"

"They amalgamated with the Unitarians. They're all Unitarian Universalists now. And another ancestor was a cousin of Sam Adams. The point is, they were men of conscience."

"For whatever that means."

"For whatever that means." I handed him the Asimov proposal. "Here, read. This is the relevant part."

Rob read it several times. It said:

The Child as Young God. *In this one we picture the society as possessing few children. If the average life expectancy has reached five hundred years, let us suppose, then the percentage of children should be, say, one-twentieth what it is now. In such a society biologic parenthood gives a person immense social prestige but no special rights in the child one has created. All children are children of society in general, with everyone anxious to share in the rights of mothering and fathering. The child is the Golden Boy/Girl of the neighborhood, and there is considerable distress if one of these children approaches adulthood without another child being born to take its place. This story can be poignant and young, for I see it told from the viewpoint of a child who is approaching adulthood and who doesn't want to lose the Goldenness of his position and is perhaps jealous of another child on the way: sibling rivalry on a grand scale.*

I stroked Wolf while Rob read. Wolf was purring but not lying quietly. She batted at my hand. I picked up a pipe cleaner and wrapped it into a coil around my little finger and dropped it on the floor. Wolf pushed off my lap, seized the little woolly spring in her jaws, growled fiercely, and ran out of the study. When she isn't batting them under the bookcases in the library and then fishing them out again, she loves to run from room to room with a pipe cleaner in her mouth, growling all the while. She's very fierce.

Rob finished reading, looked up, and said, "It's like something you've done, isn't it?"

"What's that?"

"Rite of Passage."

Rite of Passage was my first novel. It's about a girl, a bright super-child on the verge of adulthood in a low-population future society. Otherwise it's not much the same.

"Hmm. I guess I see what you mean, but I don't think the similarity has to be close enough to be any problem. The thought of repeating myself is not what's hanging me up. What do you think of the proposal?"

"Well," said Rob, "when did you say the story is supposed to take place?"

I flipped to the front page of the proposal to check. "The next century. The only date mentioned is 2025. After 2025, I guess."

"Fifty years from now? Where do all the five-hundred-year-olds come from?"

I waved that aside. "I'm willing to make it one hundred or one hundred and fifty plus great expectations."

"These people would have to be alive now," Rob said.

"True," I said. "It's something to think about."

It was a good point, just the sort of thing I wanted Rob to come up with. It raised possibilities.

"Are there any restrictions on what you write?"

"Fifteen thousand words and no nasty language."

"What about nasty ideas?"

"Nothing said about that, but I don't supposed they are worried. Everybody knows I never had a nasty idea in my life."

"Oh, yes. Um-hmm," said Rob. "Look, I know this is a radical suggestion, but what's wrong with writing the idea as it stands? There is a story there."

"I know," I said. "I thought of writing it for a long time, but then when I tried I just couldn't do it. That's where I got hung up. I like the opening phrase. I like it—'the child as young god.' That's provocative. It speaks to me. But what a distance to come for nothing. Sibling rivalry? Sibling rivalry? Why write it as science fiction? Why write it at all?"

"What's the matter, Alex?" Rob said. "Are you yearning for relevance again?"

It's a point of philosophical contention between us. Rob believes that all a story has to do is be entertaining.

I said, "Just read this." And I picked the *Whole Earth Catalog* off Cory's desk. I showed him their statement of purpose:

We are as gods and might as well get good at it. So far, remotely done power and glory—as via government, big business, formal education, church—has succeeded to the point where gross defects obscure actual gains. In response to this dilemma and to these gains a realm of intimate personal power is developing—power of the individual to conduct his own education, find his own inspiration, shape his own environment, and share his adventure with whoever is interested. Tools that aid this process are sought and promoted by the Whole Earth Catalog.

"I'd like to speak to that," I said. "I don't have any final solutions. In fifteen thousand words I'm not going to lay out a viable and functioning and uncriticizable utopia, but for God's sake, Rob, shouldn't I at least try to say something relevant? As it is, I don't think the chances are overwhelming that any of us are going to be alive in twenty years, let alone live to five hundred."

"I know. You've said that before."

"Not in print. If the society has solved the problems Asimov says—and we're going to have to—that's what I ought to write about, isn't it? At the price of being relevant and not just entertaining. There is a story in the Asimov proposal that I want to write. Somewhere. And it isn't about a kid who doesn't want to grow up. I just have to find it."

Rob said, "How do you propose to do it?"

"Sit and stare at the typewriter until it comes to me, I guess. Or putter in the garden."

"Do you really have a garden?"

"Of course," I said. "Tom Disch tells me that a half hour in the garden every day keeps the soul pure." Tom's another writer. We tend to pass basic tips like this around our little circles. "I'm going to try it and see what good it does me."

"You do that," said Rob. "And good luck. But I've got to hit the sack now. I'm about to drop off."

I turned off my desk lamp. As I got up, I said, "By the way, just who is this kid, Juanito?"

Rob said, "He's no kid. He's your age."

I wouldn't have thought it. I'm pushing thirty. I said, "Who is he?"

"Who is he?" Rob grinned. He grins like that when he is about to say something that's more entertaining than relevant. "He's Juanito the Watcher. He's your test of relevance. He's watching and assessing. If you're okay, that's cool. But if you aren't right, he'll split without a word. Take your chances."

"Thanks a lot, friend," I said.

Rob went upstairs to flake out, and I walked down to the road to see if the mail had come. It had. My check hadn't. Junk mail.

I sorted the mail as I walked up the long gravel drive to the farm, and I stopped off at the main house to leave Mrs. S. her share of the bills and fliers. I collected ducklings and a spade and set to work on the garden.

I was unhappy about the check not coming, so I lit into the work with a vengeance, turning sod and earth. The ducklings, twice their Easter-morning size but still clothed in yellow down, went *reep-a-cheep* and *peep-a-deep* around my heels and gobbled happily when I turned up worms for their benefit. They knew there was someone looking out for their welfare. I was wishing I knew as much.

Spring this year was wet and late, and the only thing in bloom was the weeping willow in the back yard with its trailing yellow catkins. The trees spread over the running hills to the next farm were still winter sticks. The day was cool enough for a light jacket in spite of the work, and the sky was partly overcast. Gardening was an act of faith that the seasons would change and warmth and flower come. Gardening is an act of faith. I'm a pessimist, but still I garden.

It's much like the times.

Our society is imperfect. That's what we say, and we shrug and let it go at that. Societies change in their own good time, and there isn't much that individuals can do to cause change or direct it. Most people don't try. They have a living to make, and whatever energies are left over, they know how to put to good use. They leave politics to politicians.

But let's be honest. Our society is not just imperfect. Our society is an unhappy shambles. And leaving politics to politicians is proving to be as dangerous a business as leaving science to scientists, war to generals, and profits to profiteers.

I read. I watch. I listen. And I judge by my own experience.

The best of us are miserable. We all take drugs—alcohol, tobacco, and pills by the handful. We do work in order to live and live in order to work—an endless unsatisfying round. The jobs are no pleasure. Employers shunt us from one plastic paradise to another. One quarter of the country moves each year. No roots, no stability.

We live our lives in public, with less and less opportunity to know each other. To know anybody.

Farmers can't make a living farming. Small businessmen can't make a living anymore, either. Combines and monoliths take them over or push them out. And because nobody questions the ways of a monolith and stays or rises in one, the most ruthless monoliths survive, run by the narrowest and hungriest and most self-satisfied among us.

The results: rivers that stink of sewage, industrial waste, and dead fish. City air that's the equivalent of smoking two packs of cigarettes a day. Countryside turned to rubble. Chemical lagoons left to stain hillsides with their overflow. Fields of rusting auto bodies.

And all the while, the population is growing. Progress. New consumers. But when I was born in 1940, there were 140 million people in this country, and now there are more than 200 million, half of them born since 1940. Our institutions are less and less able to cope with the growth. Not enough houses. Not enough schools. Not enough doctors or teachers or jobs. Not enough room at the beach. Not enough beaches.

Not enough food. The world is beginning to starve, and for all the talk of Green Revolutions, we no longer have surplus food. We are importing lamb from Australia and beef from Argentina now. How soon before we all start pulling our belts a notch tighter?

And our country acts like one more self-righteous monolith. Policing the world in the name of one ideal or another. In practice, supporting dictators, suppressing people who want fresh air to breathe as much as any of us with just as much right. In practice, taking, taking, taking, with both hands. Our country has 6 percent of the world's population. We consume 50 percent of the world's production. How long will we be allowed to continue? Who will we kill to continue?

And as unhappiness rises, crime rises. Women march. Blacks burn their slums and arm themselves. Kids confront. And nobody is sure of his safety. I'm not sure of mine.

All of us are police, or demonstrators, or caught in between. And there is more of the same to come.

Our society may be worse than a shambles. Certainly, in spite of the inventions, the science, the progress, the magic at our command, our problems are not growing less. Each year is more chaotic than the one before. Marches. Demonstrations. Riots. Assassinations. Crime. Frustration. Malaise. General inability to cope.

We are in a hell of a mess. And nobody has any solutions.

Head-beatings and suppression are not solutions. Barricades are no solution. Bloody revolutions merely exchange one set of power brokers for another.

But the problems we have are real and immediate. Those who are hungry, unskilled, jobless, homeless, or simply chronically unhappy, cannot be told to shut up. The 100 million of us who are young cannot be told to go away. The 100 million of us who are old cannot be ignored. The 20 million of us who are black cannot be killed, deported, or subjugated longer at any cost short of our total ruin as human beings. And so far we have no solutions. Merely the same old knee-jerk reactions of confrontation and suppression.

There may in fact be no solutions.

We may be on the one-way trip to total destruction. These may be the last years of the human race or the last bearable ones that any of us will know.

In times like these, gardening is an act of faith. That the seasons will change and warmth and flower come. But it is the best thing I know to do. We do garden.

So I worked and thought—and thought about my story. And how we might get from this now of ours to a brighter future. I'd like to believe in one.

And so I worked. As wet as the spring had been, the ground I was turning was muddy, and I was up to my knees in it. And down on my knees. And up to my elbows. Finding worms for the ducklings when I could. Some of the mud—or its cousin—appears on the fourth page of this manuscript. If our printer is worth his salt, I trust it will appear in true and faithful reproduction when you read this. When and wherever you read this, a touch of garden.

After a time, Alexander the gander came waddling over to investigate us, me and the ducklings. There is truth to the adage "cross as a goose." There is also truth to the adage "loose as a goose," but that is of no moment. Alexander lowers his head, opens his beak, and hisses like an angry iguana. He and I have struck a truce. When he acts like an iguana, I act like an iguana back, and I am bigger than he is, so Alexander walks away.

The ducklings don't have my advantages, and Alexander began to run them around in circles. They peeped and ran, peeped and ran. Alexander was doing them no harm, but he was upsetting them mightily. They were too upset to eat worms, and that is upset.

After a few minutes of this I put down my spade and grabbed an armful of disgruntled goose. I held Alexander upside down and began to stroke his belly feathers. Stroke. Stroke. Stroke. After a moment he became less angry. He ceased to hiss. His eyes glazed and he began to tick, every few seconds a wave passing through like the wake behind a canoe. At last I set him back on his feet and Alexander walked dazedly away. He seemed bewildered, not at all certain of what had happened to him. He shook his little head and then reared back and flapped his wings as though he were stretching for the morning. At last he found a place in the middle of the gravel drive and stood there like a sentinel, muttering to himself in goose talk.

It's what I call Upgraded Protective Reaction. I'd like to try it on our so-called leaders.

A sudden stampede of lambs back under the fence announced the return of Cory, Leigh, and Juanito from their walk to the State Park.

"Hello, love," I said. "Did you see anything?"

Cory smiled widely. "We set up the whole herd down by Three Mile Run. They bounded across the valley, and then one last one like an afterthought trying to catch up."

"Oh, fine," I said in appreciation.

Leigh nodded, smiling too. She doesn't talk a lot. She isn't verbal. I am, so we talk some, just as Rob and I talk. But when she and Rob talk, she gestures and he nods, and then he gestures and she nods. She found a worm in my well-turned mud and held it at a dangle for the smaller duckling, who gobbled it down.

Cory said, "We're going to have a look at Gemma's kittens."

"Good," I said. "I think I've put in my half hour here. I'll come along."

"Have you gone to the Elephant yet?"

"Oh," I said. "It slipped my mind. I checked on the mail, though. The mail came."

"What?"

"Nothing good," I said. "Juanito, want to go to the Elephant with me?"

He really didn't look my age. But then I don't look my age, either.

"All right," he said.

Cory and Leigh walked off toward the main house to have their look at the kittens. The ducklings hesitated and then went pell-melling after them, wagging their beam ends faster than a boxer puppy.

"Now's our chance," I said.

But when Juanito and I got to the car, I remembered the truck tire.

"Just a minute," I said, and took it out of the trunk. "Let me put this away while I think of it. Grab your bottle."

He fished the beer bottle from behind the spare tire where it had rolled. Then he followed me as I hefted the tire and carried it through the machine shop and into the tractor shed. I dumped the tire by the great heavy trash cans.

"Bottle there," I said, pointing to a can, and Juanito set it on top of the trash like a careful crown.

"What's going to happen to it?" he asked.

"When the ground dries, the farmer will take it all down and dump it in the woods." Out of sight, out of mind.

"Oh," he said.

We lumbered off to the Elephant in the old Plymouth. It was once a hotel, a wayside inn. Now it's a crossroads store and bar. We shop there when we need something in a hurry. It's a mile down the road.

Everything else is five miles or more. Mostly more.

Juanito said, "Do you drive alone much?"

"Not much," I said. "Cory can't drive yet, so we go shopping together about twice a week." I'm conscious of the trips to Doylestown and Quakertown because they so often cut into my writing.

"Whereabouts you from, Juanito?" I asked.

"Nowhere in particular these days," he said. "I pretty much keep on the move. I stay for a while, and then I move on to the next place."

"Always an outside agitator?" I asked, maneuvering to avoid a dead possum in the road. Possums like to take evening walks down the center of the highway.

"Something like that, I guess," he said.

"I couldn't do it," I said. "I hitched across the country when I was eighteen, but I couldn't take the uncertainty of always being on the move. I couldn't work without roots and routine."

On our right as we drove up the winding hill to the Elephant was a decaying set of grandstands.

"What is that?" asked Juanito.

"The Vargo Dragway," I said. "On a Sunday afternoon you could hear them winding up and gearing down all the way back at the farm. They finally got it shut down last year. It took five years. It always seems to take them five years."

I swung into the gravel parking lot beside the bar. They kept the bacon, eggs, and milk in the refrigerator behind the bar, so we went inside there rather than around to the store. There were two men drinking, but there was no one behind the bar, so we waited. Behind the bar are pictures and an old sign that says, "Elephant Hotel—1848," around the silhouette of an elephant.

One of the drinkers looked us over. A wrinkled pinch-face in working clothes.

He said in a loud voice to no one in particular, "Hippies! I don't like 'em. Dirty hippies. Ruining the country. We don't want 'em moving in around here. Bums."

The man sitting at the other end of the bar seemed acutely uncomfortable and looked away from him. I leaned back against the pool table. This sort of thing doesn't happen to me often enough that I know what to do about it.

The drinker kept up the comments. At last I took two steps toward him and said something inane like, "Look, do you want everybody to dress and think like you?" It was inane because he and I were dressed much the same.

He threw his hands up in front of his face and said anxiously, "Get away from me! Get away from me!"

So I stopped and shut up and moved back to the pool table. And he returned to his comments to no one.

"Creeps! Making trouble."

From the doorway to the store, Mrs. Lokay said, "Mr. Pinchen," and I turned, grateful for the interruption. She hasn't got my name straight, and she knows nothing of William Pynchon or *The Meritorious Price of Our Redemption,* but at times when I've come in for the Sunday *New York Times* and found no change in my jeans, they've put me down in the book on trust.

We followed her into the store. She said, "Don't mind him. He's mad about his stepson. He shouldn't talk to you that way. Thank you for not making trouble. We'll talk to him."

I shrugged and said, "That's all right," because I didn't know what else to say. I was calm, but I was upset.

Juanito and I waited in the store while Mrs. Lokay went back into the bar for our order. I carried the sack all the way around the building rather than walk back through and set him off again.

I don't really like trouble much, and I'll go out of my way to avoid violence. I clutched the wheel tightly. Instead of driving directly home, I turned off into East Rockhill where the farm country plays out and the woods take over. I set my jaw and drove and thought about all the things I might have said.

I could have said, "That's all right, buddy. I've got a license to look like this. They call it the Constitution."

I could have said, "Have you seen Lyndon Johnson's hair hanging over his collar lately?"

I could have said, "What's the matter? Can't you tell a simple country boy when you see one?"

But I hadn't.

Juanito said, "What you ought to do is get a big plastic sack with a zipper and rig it up. You have two controls. One for warm saline solution, the other for your air line. Spend the night in that. It's very calming."

I said, "It sounds like what I've read about Barry Goldwater falling alseep on the bottom of his swimming pool. Never mind, I have something as good."

I stopped the car, pulling it off to the side of the road. On that side were woods. On the other were fountains, fieldstone walkways, planting, dogwoods, and two scaled-down pyramids, one six feet tall, the other twenty.

"What's this place?" Juanito asked.

"It's the Rosicrucian Meditation Garden," I said, and got out of the car.

The signs say it is open from 8:30 every morning. I've never seen anyone else walking there, but no one has ever come out to ask me to prove that I was meditating.

After I walked around for a time and looked at the tadpoles swimming in the pool around the smaller pyramid—just like the Great Pyramid in Egypt—I got a grip on myself. Thank the Rosicrucians.

As we drove back to the farm, we passed the rock quarry. "Rock quarry," I said in answer to Juanito's question. They don't call it East Rockhill for nothing.

"It won't always be that ugly," I said. "When they have the dam in, all this will be under water. Until the valley silts up, all we'll have to worry about is an invasion and speedboats."

They don't have lakes in this part of Pennsylvania, so they propose to make them.

"I know about that," Juanito said. "Cory mentioned it."

The lake will run through the State Park land. Where the deer herd is now. I don't relish the trade. Ah, but progress.

After dinner, after dark, we all gathered in the living room. Cory collected me from the study where I was taking ten minutes after dinner to stare at my typewriter.

"Are you getting anywhere?" she asked.

I shook my head. "Nothing written. Great and fleeting ideas only."

"Alexei, what are we going to do about the money?"

I said, "Henry said he mailed the check. We just have to trust it to come."

I opened my desk drawer and took out the checkbook with the undernourished balance. I wrote a check out to Internal Revenue for $371.92—more than we had to our name.

"Here," I said. "Put this in the envelope with the return. We'll mail it when the check comes from Henry or on the fifteenth, whichever comes sooner."

Cory tucked the check under the flap of the envelope but left it unsealed. She set it on top of the phonograph speaker by the front door.

When we came into the living room, Rob said, "Oh, hey. I almost forgot. I brought something for you."

He fished in his bag while I waited. I like presents, even if I don't lie awake on Christmas Eve in anticipation anymore. He came up with a paperback and handed it to me. It was *The Tales of Hoffman,* portions of the transcript of the Chicago Eight trial.

"Thank you," I said. "I'll read it tomorrow."

It was just the book for Rob to give me. His idea of the most pressing urgency in this country is court reform. Which is needed, as anybody who has been through the agonies of waiting in jails and courtrooms can attest. I'm more bothered by the debasement of thought and language—starting with calling the War Department the Department of Defense and proceeding down the line from there. One thumbing of the book told me Rob and I had a common meeting ground.

Rob said, "What about your story?"

I said, "I'll read the book in the bathtub."

"Are you going to spend the day in the bathtub?"

"If I have to."

We turned off the lights except for the chandelier, dim and yellow, and Cory brought out a candle and set it to pulsing in its wine-colored glass. Four of us sat on the floor around the candle, and Leigh sat in the easy chair. The light from the chandelier played off the dark veneer and outlined the carriage beams. The candlelight made the rug glow like autumn.

We talked of one thing and another, and I played records. Great Speckled Bird. Crosby, Stills, Nash and Young. The new Baez. Rob pulled out *Highway 61 Revisited,* and I got into it as I never had before.

Wolf and Fang went freaking in the candlelight, chasing each other round and round the room. I put on Quicksilver Messenger Service, the first album, and when "The Fool" reached its peak, Wolf went dashing in and out of the room, ending on the deep window ledge with the last bent note.

And sitting there into the night, we speculated.

Rob, sitting tailor-fashion, said, the conversation having carried him there in some drifting fashion, "Is there really a Mafia?"

"I don't know," I said. "You're closer to it than I am."

"I'm in daily contact with people who think there is," he said thoughtfully. "They think they belong. I could get myself killed. But what I'm asking is, is there *really* a Mafia? Or are there only a lot of people pretending?"

It's a good question. Is there really such a thing as the United States, or just a lot of people pretending?

I said, "Is there really a Revolution?"

Last summer, just before Cory and I left Cambridge to move down here, in fact the day before we moved, I got a call from William James Heckman. Bill had been my roommate my senior year in prep school, and I hadn't heard from him since the day we graduated. He and I had never been friends and never seen much of interest in each other. But I told him, sure, come on over.

I was curious. In the spring, eleven years after we graduated, they'd gotten around to throwing a tenth reunion of my class. I'd had a book to finish and had to miss it, and been sorry. I'd been an outsider at Mount Hermon and I was curious to know what had become of all the

Golden People. I like to know the ending to stories, and eleven years later is a good place to put a period to high school. Bill hadn't been Golden People, either, but under the circumstances I was willing to let him serve as a substitute for the reunion.

Bill had changed. Fair enough—I've changed, too. His hair was starting to thin. He wore a moustache with droopy ends, sideburns, and a candystripe shirt.

We traded neutralities and ate chips and dip. He was in Cambridge to visit his former wife. He was studying theater at Cornell. He'd taken a course from Joanna Russ, a writer friend of mine, and mentioned that he had known me, and she had given him my address.

We spoke about relevance. He said that he wanted to do more than just entertain, too.

Then, in the hallway as he was leaving, he said suddenly and with more than a little pride, "I'm really a revolutionary. I'm working for the Revolution."

"So am I," I said. As he disappeared around the curve in the hallway, I called, with a certain sense of joy, "So are we all."

Is there really a Revolution, or are there just a lot of people pretending? What will happen when enough people pretend hard enough, long enough?

The five of us and the two cats gathered around our candle late on a spring night. If there really is a Revolution, are we its leaders? What if we pretended to be long enough, hard enough?

And I wondered in how many other rooms people were gathered around a flame thinking the same things, dreaming the same dreams. There have to be new ways, there have to be better ways, and we all know it.

Later that night, when we were in bed, Cory said, "Did you find out anything about Juanito? I asked Leigh while you were gone and Rob was sleeping, but she didn't know anything. He was with Rob when Rob showed up."

I said, "All I got from Rob was a put-on." And I told her about it. We laughed and we fell asleep.

But when we got up in the morning, Juanito was gone.

I went outside to look for him. There was a full-grown ewe nibbling on the rosebush by the barn, and I waved my arms and stampeded her back under the wire, kneeling and humping to get through and leaving wool behind. But no Juanito.

There was a trash can by the front door that I hadn't left there. It was full of beer cans, soft-drink cans, rusty oil tins riddled by shot, beer bottles, plastic ice-cream dishes and spoons, cigarette butts, cigarette packs, a partly decayed magazine, and plastic, glass, and chrome from the last auto accident.

I hauled the trash can away, thinking. Cory was standing by the front door when I came back.

"I've got my story," I said. "I've got my story."

"At last," she said.

2

At the age of thirty Little John was still a child, with a child's impatience to be grown. More than anything—more than the long study and the slow ripening that his Guide assured him were the true road to his desires, as indeed they were, in part—he wished to be finished now, matured now, set free from the eternal lessons of the past now. He was a child, one of the chosen few, favored, petted, and loved just for living. On the one hand, he accepted it as his proper due; on the other, he found it a humiliation. It meant he was still only one of the Chosen, only a boy, and he wished to be a grown-up god like everyone else.

It was not that he lacked talent for it. People even more ordinary than he had made Someone of themselves. He simply hadn't yet gotten the idea. Chosen, but not yet called.

He conceived progress in his lessons to be his road to grace. It was what Samantha had taught him to believe, and believing it, he was impatient to gulp down one lesson and be on to the next. He had been led to believe that sheer accumulation was sufficient in itself, and he had closets full of notes. He had also been taught not to believe everything he was told and to think for himself, but this information was lost somewhere on note cards in one of his closets.

Impatient though he was, he tried to conceal his impatience from Samantha. He was awed by his Guide. He was awed by her age, by her reputation, by her impenetrability, and by the sheer living distance between the two of them, her and him. At the same time he accepted as right and proper that someone like her should be his Guide, for, after all, he was one of the Chosen.

Samantha encouraged his awe. Awe, like impatience, was a mark of his greenness, a measure of the distance he had to travel to reach the insight that lessons are to be applied, not merely amassed—that one thing in all the world that she could not tell him but could only leave him to discover for himself in his own time. Behind her impenetrable expression, however, she sighed at his awe, shook her head at his pride in advancement, and smiled at his wriggling impatience. And then tried his patience all the harder.

When he returned from his trip to 1381, she gave him a week to think about the experience before they began to discuss it.

"I could live in 1381 and be a god," Little John said. "It wouldn't be easy, but I saw enough. It takes endurance. That's the chief thing."

They talked about it for a month, day after day. The problems of being a peasant in those times, and still a god, relating as a god should to his fellow men. The problems of overcoming ignorance. And all the while, Little John visibly eager to be done and on to the next trip.

At last she sent him on one. She sent him back to 1381 for another look from a new perspective. It is, after all, one problem to be a powerless peasant courting godhood, and quite another, as Buddha knew, to be a noble aiming for the same end. Little John didn't really see that. All he recognized was 1381 come 'round again when he felt he ought to be off to a new time and new problems of godhood. As though godliness could be measured in trips and not in what was made of them.

So he said again, "I could live in 1381 and be a god. Endurance. That's the main thing. Isn't it?"

She told him to think it over. So they talked about it for another month. And in time he finally said something about the psychological difficulty of shedding power when power is held to be a birthright.

He said, "You could give your money and property to the Church. That's a way."

"Is it a godly way?"

"Well, it could be," he said. "They thought it could."

"Do you think so?"

"I met a very decent Franciscan."

"Organized godliness?"

So they talked further about the times and how it might have been possible to live well in them when your fellow wolves were ready to stay wolves until they died and ready to die to stay wolves. And Little John saw that it was indeed a very different problem than being the godly victim of wolves.

He felt that the last juice had been squeezed from the trip and was ready for the next long before Samantha was ready to send him. And when that trip was back to 1381 again for a stay in a monastery, he felt—well, not cheated, but distinctly disappointed. And he took nothing away from the experience, except for the usual stack of notes.

And after a week of discussion his impatience finally got the better of him.

He said, "Keats died at twenty-five. Masaccio died at twenty-seven, and so did Henry Gwyn-Jeffreys Moseley." He had memorized a long series of people like that, from Emily Brontë to Mikhail Yurievich Lermontov. "I'm nearly thirty. I want to do what I have to do and be done, and be out in the world."

He didn't understand the point. If you are going to do, you do. Those who want for freedom are never free.

And Samantha, who had a reputation for tartness, said, "Yes, and Christopher Marlowe died at twenty-nine and still wrote all of Shakespeare. Do you think forty or fifty years are too many to spend in preparation for a life as long as you have ahead of you?"

"Oh, no," he said. "Oh, no." But in his heart he did. "It's just that I'm tired of 1381. It's easy to be a god then. It's too easy. I want something harder. Send me to 1970. I'm ready. Really I am."

1970 had a reputation. If you could be a god then, you could be a god anytime. Little John looked on it as a final examination of sorts, and he wanted nothing more than to go.

"Do you believe you're ready to handle 1970?" Samantha asked.

"Oh, yes," he said. "Please."

He was sitting cross-legged before her. They were on the hilltop circle standing high above the community buildings and the flowering fields. The outdoor theater was here, and convocation when decisions had to be made. It was a good place to watch sunset and moonrise. His walks with Samantha often brought them here.

He was more than a little apprehensive at making his request, and he watched Samantha's face closely as she considered, anxious for the least sign of the nature of her answer, impatient for the first clue. And, as usual, her face was composed and gave him no hint.

Little John waited so long and her face was so still that he was half afraid that she would fall asleep. He tried to make a still center of himself no less than three times before she spoke, and each time fell victim to wonder and lost the thread. He managed silence and reasonable stillness, and that was all.

At last, she said, "This is not a matter for haste. I think we've spoken enough for today. Walk, meditate, consider your lessons."

"And then?"

"Why, come tomorrow to my chambers at the regular time." And she gave him the sign of dismissal.

So he rose, and gathered his notes, and went down the hill, leaving Samantha still sitting. He turned for a look where the stony path made a corner and she was still sitting, looking over the valley.

Shelley Anne Fenstermacher, the other Chosen, who was ten years old and half his size and used him as a signpost as he had used Hope Saltonstall when he was younger, was waiting for him. She emptied her bucket of garbage into the hog trough, climbed down from the fence, and came running.

"Did you ask? Did you ask? What did she say?"

"She said I was to walk and meditate," said Little John.

"What do you think it means?"

"I know."

He went into his room and got his latest notes from the closet. He didn't know what Samantha had in mind, but if it made the slightest difference, he meant to follow her advice. He always followed her advice to the best of his understanding.

"Can I come?" Shelley asked when he came outside.

"Not today," he said. "Today I'd better walk alone."

"Oh," she said.

"I'm sorry."

So he walked in the woods and meditated and read his note cards, anxious to stuff the least and last of it into his head. If it made a difference, if she quizzed him, he meant to be ready. He had every word she had said to him down on paper. Ask him anything, he'd show he was ready.

And the next day when he and Samantha met, he was ready, that is, ready for anything except what he received, which was nothing. Samantha acted as though he had never spoken. She took up the discussion where he had broken it the day before, and they walked and they talked as usual and she never said a word about his request.

And Little John, afraid to speak, said never a word, either. He did wriggle a lot, though.

At the end of the two hours, however, she said, "A fruitful session, was it not?"

And dumbly, he nodded. And then he said, "Please ma'am, have you made a decision?"

"Yes," she said. "I brought you something." She reached into her pants pocket and brought out an embroidered pouch. "It's a present. Take this grass up on Roundtop tonight, and when the moon is two full hands above the horizon, smoke it and meditate."

That night he sat up on Roundtop on his favorite log. He watched the sun set and he watched the moon rise. And he measured with his hands. When the moon was two full hands above the horizon, he filled his pipe and smoked. And he thought, and his thoughts filled the night to its conclusion. They were good thoughts, but they were all of 1970 and of graduation to godhood. It was good grass.

In gratitude he brought Samantha the best apple he could pick. He searched the whole orchard before he made a choice.

His teacher was pleased with the apple. "Thank you, Little John," she said. She ate it as they walked and wrapped up the core for the pigs.

"What conclusions did you come to last night?" she asked.

His thoughts had been ineffable, so what he said was, "Novalis died at twenty-eight."

"So he did," Samantha said.

They walked on in silence. They walked in silence for two hours. For someone her age Samantha was a brisk and sturdy walker. They circled Roundtop. The day was heavy and hot. There was a skyhawk wheeling high overhead, drifting on the current, and Little John envied it. He wanted to fly free, too.

When they reached home, walking up the lane between the ripe fields, Samantha finally spoke. "Spend the night in Mother," she said. "Then see me tomorrow."

"Without Tempus?" he asked.

"Yes, without Tempus."

"But I've never done that."

She said, "We had Mother before we had Tempus. Try it and see."

"Yes, ma'am," he said.

He had kept Shelley Anne apprised of his progress. When she sought him out after dinner sitting on the porch in the warm and quiet of the evening, he told her what Samantha wished him to do.

"Really?" she said. "I never heard of that. Does she expect you to change your mind?"

"I don't know," he said. "But I have to do it if she wants me to."

While they were talking, Lenny came out on the porch. "Hi, children," he said. "Are you going to the convo tonight?"

Shelley Anne said she was. Little John said he was busy and had other plans. When Lenny left, Shelley Anne went with him, and Little John was left alone in the evening. He could see the fire up on Roundtop and hear the voices.

At last he went inside and set up Mother, just as though he were going on a trip, but without the drug. He checked the air line. He checked the solution line. And he set the alarm to rouse himself.

He undressed himself and kicked his clothes into the corner. It was something he'd been known to do since he had decided that it wasn't necessarily ungodlike. He picked them up himself sometime, and as long as he did that eventually he figured it was all right.

Then he unzipped Mother and climbed inside. It was overcool on his bare skin until he got used to it, like settling down on a cold toilet seat. He fitted the mouthpiece of the air line into place. He didn't close the bag until he was breathing comfortably.

As the warm saline solution rose in the bag, he cleared his mind. He basked and floated. He had never used Mother except on official trips and had never thought to wonder why it was called Mother. Now he leaned back, drifted and dreamed in Mother's warm arms and she was very good to him.

Strange undirected dreams flitted through his mind. Pleasant dreams. He saw Shelley Anne Fenstermacher as an old woman and she nodded, smiled and said, "Hi," just like she always did. He saw Samantha as a ten-year-old with a doll in her arms. He saw his old friends in the monastery in 1381, making their cordials and happily sampling them. And he wheeled through the blue skies along with his friend the skyhawk, coasting on the summer breeze high above the temperate world.

And then he passed beyond dreams.

In the morning, the cool, calm morning, he sat in the slanting sunlight listening to the song of a mockingbird shift and vary, and tried to pick it out with his eye in the leaf-cloaked branches of a walnut tree. At last Samantha came out to join him. He thought he could see the ten-year-old in her, even without the doll.

She said, "How did the night pass?"

Though his skin was prunish, he didn't think to mention it. "Well," he said. "I never spent a night like that before." But already he planned to again. "It was very soothing."

"Ah, was it?" And then, without further preamble, she said, "Do you still want to travel to 1970?"

"Yes, ma'am," he said. "I'm ready for it. I'll show you I am. What else do you want me to do first?"

"Nothing. If you still want to go, if you're still determined to go, I'll send you."

Little John nearly jumped up and gave her a hug, but awe restrained him. If Samantha had been asked, perhaps she would have had him retain that much awe.

So Little John got his trip to 1970, his chance to graduate. Mother was readied again, not for general wandering, but for a directed dream. Samantha calculated the mix of Tempus herself.

She said, "This won't be like any other time you've been."

"Oh, I know that."

"Do you? I almost remember it myself, and it wasn't like now."

"I can handle it."

"Let us hope," she said. "I'm going to see that you are in good hands. Nothing too serious should happen to you."

"Please," he said. "Don't make it too easy."

"Say that again after you've returned. I'm going to give you a mnemonic. If you want to abort the trip and come back before the full period, then concentrate on the mnemonic. Do you understand?"

"I understand," he said.

She checked him out on all points, once, twice, and then again before she was satisfied. Then, at last, he climbed inside Mother and drank the draft she handed him.

"Have a good trip," she said.

"Oh, I will, ma'am. Don't worry about that," Little John said as the sack filled and he drifted away from her, back in time, back in his mind. "I expect to have a *good* time."

That's what he said. Nothing hard about being a god in 1970. They had had all the materials, and by now he had had experience in godhood. He was ready.

But he came back early. And he didn't have a *good* time.

In fact, he was heartsick, subdued, drained. He wouldn't speak to Shelley Anne Fenstermacher. And without prompting by Samantha or anyone he disappeared into the woods to be by himself, and he didn't come back for two days.

He spent the whole time thinking, trying to make sense of what he had seen, and he wasn't able to do it. He missed two whole sessions with Samantha. And when he did turn up at last, he didn't apologize for being missing.

"You were right," he said simply. "I wasn't ready. Send me back to 1381 again. Please."

"Perhaps," Samantha said.

"I don't understand. I don't understand. I knew things weren't right then, but I didn't think they would be like that. Taxes was what they cared about. They didn't even see what was going on. Not really. And it was just before the Revolution. Are things always that bad before they change?"

"Yes," she said. "Always. The only difference this time is the way things changed. And you didn't see the worst of it. Not by half, Little John."

"I didn't?" he said in surprise. "I thought it must be."

She was too kind to laugh. "No."

"But it was so awful. So ruthless. So destructive."

Samantha said, "Those people weren't so bad. As it happens, they were my parents."

"Oh, I'm sorry, ma'am," he said.

"And your grandparents weren't so different. And they did learn better. That's the important thing to remember. If you take away nothing else, remember that. If they hadn't changed, none of us would be here now."

He cried out, "But they had so much power. They all had the power of gods, and they used it so badly."

Little John may have been stupid, abysmally stupid, he may have been green, and he may have had more years ahead of him than little Shelley Anne Fenstermacher before he was fit to be let out in the world, but there were some things he was able to recognize. Some things are writ plain.

3

Endings of stories come easy. It is the beginnings, when anything is still possible, that come hard.

Start now.

Three Tinks on the House

F. M. Busby

It's possible for governments to legislate against large families in order to slow or eliminate population rise. But most people are emotionally resistant to such measures, so even when the resources-versus-consumers equation clearly passes into the negative, politicians who wish to be reelected will probably limit themselves to purely economic sanctions. These may, however, be augmented by peer pressure—which can have violent and sad results, as in the story below.

F. M. Busby is the author of The Demu Trilogy, Rissa Kerguellen, **and** Zelde M'Tana.

"**F**OUR O'CLOCK in the morning! Why do you have to work such crazy hours?" Stuffing the thirty-hour week into three days cuts commuter traffic a lot, but it doesn't do much for my wife's disposition. "If I didn't have to ride in with you for this damned dentist's appointment . . ."

Normally, Linda's a good-looking woman—big green eyes, shiny black hair in a monkey-fur cut, skin holding up better than most. After eighteen years of marriage I still like to look at her, especially when she smiles. But when she's feeling hacked about something, she can look like a witch.

"More coffee?" I said, and poured for her. "Good breakfast, honey." I'd finished my egg, toast, and juice and was relaxing over coffee.

"Wouldn't be so bad, Johnny, if it didn't take so long to get to town."

"All right! Let's get out where there's room to breathe, you said. Okay, here we are. Out of the high-rise jungle—no apartments over fourteen stories. Of course, they're *all* fourteen, but what the hell. Use of the pool Tuesdays and Fridays if we want. Our own parking slot in the secured area. So it takes a little longer to get to work; you win some, you lose some."

"I suppose. If I just had my own car again . . ." She stopped, and smiled a little. Not much, but a little. Breakfast was beginning to help. "Look, I know it's not practical—the double tax on second cars and all. It's only that I had a lot more fun when I had my own job and my own car."

"Sure, I know, Linda." A computer took her job and the Eco Laws took her car. I was glad she hadn't rubbed my nose in one bet I'd lost; when the first big Eco crunch had hit, the color-coded routes and the Federal horsepower tax, I'd had to sell the one car to pay for propane conversion on the newer one. I'd thought propane was a safe bet, and only a five-dollar tax per horse instead of the twenty for Diesel or gashogs. Not to mention the saving on fuel tax . . .

So what happened? The Enumclaw Freeway, my best route to Seattle, had been coded yellow—*no* internal combustion. Commuterwise, I was up the creek. But to convert to an outside-burner I'd have had to put a second mortgage on the apartment. Well, I'd taken the chance, and lost.

She made a grimace, a little one-sided grin. "Maybe Metro Transit really will run the Renton line down here, complete the loop to Kent. They keep promising. You know, with all the taxes we pay . . ."

"Yeah. The taxes." I sipped the dregs and stood. "Ready?"

"*Un momento.* Better safe than sorry." She went into the bathroom.

I had to smile, remembering her story of the last time she'd stopped at a service station to exchange the left-hand propane tank for a full one. First there was a guy in the john who stayed a long time, and when he came out he let the door go locked. Any decent fellow would have held it for her, with the attendant not watching. Then it turned out she wasn't carrying that company's credit card, and the door scanner wasn't programmed to recognize her bank card. The station attendant couldn't be bothered to help.

"Unlock this Goddamned door," she'd said, "or I'll piddle right here in front of it!"

But he'd told her, "Go ahead, lady. The fifty bucks for littering, you *can* put on your bank card." There wasn't any other place handy, so she'd had to hold it until she got home.

On second thought, it wasn't funny. Those things used to be free, part of the service—not a gimmick to promote a company's own credit cards.

Linda was ready to go. I cut the alarms, checked the hallway, and motioned for her to come out. I made sure to thumb the ten-second reset button before closing the door behind us. The building hadn't had a successful break-in during the four years we'd lived there, and only one killing and two rapes in the halls. But still I think it pays to stick to the routine.

We showed I.D. to the guard by the elevators, to the one in the elevator itself and at our parking sub-deck. The man on duty there handed me our car keys. As we walked away he was alerting the outside guard over the intercom.

The car was an '82 VW Matador, remodeled slightly for the propane. Even if I couldn't drive it on the yellow-coded freeway, I still liked it. For one thing, it covered only seventy-five square feet of ground space; the size kept my surcharge down to $225. The Matador started on the first try; I drove slowly through the well-lighted aisles.

The inner doors were open. I drove through them into the security pocket, waited for them to close behind me and then for the outer gates to open. We were on our way. The smog wasn't at all bad; I could see the sun.

Old Route 516 was still coded blue, barred only to gasoline and Diesel. It was slow, a four-lane back road crowded with freeway-rejects like myself, but it was the best route available.

"Do you know if Marise came home last night, Linda?"

"No. I mean she didn't. She and Sydni were going to stay with Ali and George." I felt relief—Marise and her girlfriend, at seventeen, were still satisfied with the young studs in our own safe building.

"Ali and George, again? She could do worse. Anything serious, do you think?" We were approaching the interchange to I-5 North; I switched lanes. By rights, I suppose, I-5 should be yellow. But it's the only good secondary route north into Seattle, so most of the time it stays blue. Luckily for me.

"Marise says she and Syd would like to try a four-marriage there for a while, if they could pry the two boys out of each others' arms long enough. Not for children, yet; you know Marise is in no hurry to make paternity choices."

I swung into the interchange and merged onto I-5 North. Not far ahead, I could see high-rise country looming. But my mind was on our kids.

"Yes, she'll be all right," I said. "George doesn't have much in the way of brains, but those four aren't likely to hurt each other much. And since the abortion, Marise gets her implants renewed, right on schedule. But . . ."

"It's Les that bothers you, isn't it?"

I didn't answer immediately. I was trying to think it out—how I felt, and how much of what I felt was leftover from cultural conditioning.

We passed the first Sea-Tac exit. The old airport wouldn't handle anything bigger than a 747. But as long as the FAA still defined flight-paths in piston-engine terms, Sea-Tac held the high-rises at bay.

"Yeah, Les," I said, finally. "I'm not arguing against adolescent bisexuality—for one thing, it holds down the abortion rate. But when a fifteen-year-old boy can't see a girl at all, for his boy friend's ass, I think maybe the schools and the media are pushing it a little too much. When I was his age—"

High-rise country began, about where Boeing Field used to be. Not much diluted sunlight from there on—the tall boxes cut off all but an occasional shaft.

Linda laughed. "I know. When you were his age you were in love with the *Playboy* centerfold and got your sex in the bathroom with the door locked." She patted my thigh, high and inside; not expecting the touch, I jumped a little. "But didn't you ever—"

"A little. Playing around, experimenting, I guess. But not much."

Billy Jordal and I, maybe twelve. Excited as hell from talking about how it would be with a girl. Trying some things that were as close as we could think of to the real bit. Not doing too well at them. Then, when somebody else got caught, not us, learning what other people called what we'd done, and what they thought of it. After that, Billy and I weren't friends anymore. We stayed away from each other. At least, I thought, Les wasn't getting loaded down with all that guilt crap.

"Oh, Johnny—isn't that the tunnel exit? I'll look . . . no, no enforcement behind, that I can see."

The waterfront tunnel exit was a permanent gripe of mine. Naturally, the tunnel itself was coded red—*no* combustion cars. But the exit ramp went several hundred yards in open air to get to the tunnel, and halfway along it was a second exit that saved me twenty minutes of dumb stop-and-go traffic. Because some moron ran his red pencil further up his map than necessary, all the way to I-5, I was not supposed to use that shortcut.

I did, though, habitually—except when I spotted enforcement in position to see me. I'd caught three tickets in four years; I figured I was ahead of the game. But it still pissed me. I'd written a letter to the morning paper once. It wasn't printed.

I won again—no pursuing tweeter, no pullover, no citation. But it still frosted me, having to take that chance for no good reason.

The thing is, I have better things to do with any twenty minutes of my life than to sit looking at red lights.

We drove west along the south edge of downtown. White-coded, to my right—no private vehicles at all. I let Linda off near a Transit station, about a dozen blocks from my parking area. We kissed. I was glad I'd married a woman who didn't forget how. "You want to wait and ride home with me," I said, "or go earlier?"

"No," she shook her head. "I'll take Transit to Renton and chances from there." I knew what she meant. The electric buses were regular, but we lived two miles from the nearest. The freelance jitneys were more flexible—if you could find one. Private cars would give rides sometimes, but a woman couldn't be too careful. Or a man, either, for that matter. Linda has a good instinct for safety, though. She'd had only one bad scare—a freak in a Rotarian suit; they'll fool you—and she'd gotten out of that one okay.

As soon as she entered the station, I drove on. The parking area at work handles eight or ten plants and hasn't enough security to plug your nosebleed. We get by because everybody knows there's nothing much to steal or mug in an industrial parking lot, outside of the Executive Section. There are a lot of rapes, though, mostly by employees. No security system can prevent all of those.

I got lucky, and parked only about half a mile from the plant. I decided the hell with the respirator; even down in industrial territory the smog was light. I brought it along, though; the afternoon could be different. The shuttle wasn't in sight or hearing, but the walk was good exercise; I could use it.

I found the office shorthanded. That's par when it's not our regular workday, when we're shifted so that the high-pollution plants can operate on a low-smog day. It happens so irregularly that routine-bound types aren't braced for it and are apt to miss work.

Ten hours makes a long day; everyone gets irritable. Franzen over in Expediting tried to bend me once too often. I told him to freak out; it was time he knew I don't work for him. I came close to asking him to sign waivers with me and have it out: any limits he wanted, or none. He's big, all right, but not *that* big.

Being still chugged at Franzen was my only excuse, if any, for bumming Leda Robarge when she came around at the afternoon break. I knew her trick; everybody did, around there. Why she doesn't find a new hunting ground, I'll never know.

I have nothing against a little healthy seduction, or most forms of sexual freedom, in moderation. Linda and I will swing a little with good friends and don't begrudge each other an occasional night out. The time we tried a four-marriage, it broke up over such things as garlic and wet towels. But Leda's scene was not healthy.

She'd collected for help on two abortions—"My doctor has no *idea* how it could have happened"—before a third guy checked and found she'd drawn her Federal sterilization bonus when she was twenty.

My problem was that my skull was running at half speed, same as the air-conditioning. When she began to put it on me, fluttering her eyelids to emphasize the fashionable gold foil that covered them, I said, "Leda, I expect you're one hell of a good spread. But we have to think of the future."

"The future, Johnny? Why, I don't know what you mean."

"Well, if anything should go wrong—if you were to, say, get pregnant—don't worry about a thing, Leda. *I'll* have the baby for you."

She threw a mean coffee cup, but her aim was off. I felt a little guilty, but not much. People Pollution is bad enough; people who try to collect on it are even worse.

That day couldn't end too soon, and it didn't. Trudging back to the car, I knew I'd been someplace. The smog was high; I should have used the respirator, but I was too pooped to bother.

And GodDAMN! Not thinking, I'd driven the little Matador all the way into the parking stall, leaving room for some ass to sneak a Midgie in behind me, crosswise inside the spotter-beam, blocking me. *You sonofasow!*

Midgie had chosen badly; I carry a dolly-jack in the rear-hood. Up and out with the heavy thing, under the braked back wheels; raise it. Now, where to put it?

Franzen's stall was close; I was tempted to dump it on him. He's a mechanical moron; he'd probably try to kick it to death. But I settled for leaving the Midge directly in the spotter-beam at the back of an empty stall. Not unhappily, I drove away. Midgie would probably pay about fifty for that one. *That'll teach you to screw around with the Green Hornet!*

A few blocks ahead of the on-ramp to I-5 South, I saw the blinker signals. Access had been cut from blue to yellow: external combustion, yes; me and my propane, no. For a while, until the smog level dropped and the signal changed back again, I was stuck.

I could cut over to old Route 99, like crawling on hands and knees. Or I could wait for I-5 South to shift back to blue. If it shifted within the hour, I was better off to wait. And more comfortable. . .

Yeah. Joe's Stoneboat Bar was off to the right, not far. I stopped there sometimes, knew a few of the people. For instance, one of the doctors from the nearby hospital was an engraved character.

I turned right, and three blocks later pulled the Matador into the shady side of Joe's parking lot. I hated to button up the car in the heat.

The Stoneboat was cool inside. The back room, away from the TV-juke, was quiet except for the crowd noise. I figure that's why Joe usually works that room himself and lets his hired help handle the front.

"A live one, Johnny?" said Joe. I nodded. Live-yeast beer is my favorite low-high; sometimes I wonder how we ever got along without it.

Even after three years a bar doesn't smell right to me without stale cigarette smoke; the Stoneboat smelled only of beer and last month's repainting.

I knew the two men at the table next to the end of the bar. We said "Hi" and I sat with them.

Artie Rail was singing it down about his stupid car some more. "I just dunno what I'm going to do, fellas." He said it with his usual whine. "I'm about ready to turn it in for the demolition bonus. Except I can't afford to buy anything I *can* afford—if you see what I mean."

Sure, I saw what he meant. Artie was paying three, four hundred in horsepower tax, and close to the same for the area of his Detroit parade-float. He was in a tight knot, all right.

Hollis MacIlwain wasn't wasting his sympathy, if he had any. "Oh hell, Artie, it's your own fault. You bought that Cadillac when the taxes you bitch about were already in the talk stage. It was a damn fool trick, and you know it."

"Yeah?" Artie bit back. "*You* weren't all that happy, Hollis, when you had to put in short pistons to cut your compression for no-lead gas. Anyway, my brother-in-law gave me a real good deal on that Cad."

"So sue your brother-in-law." Hollis's gravel voice was weary. "Don't load me with your grotches."

I wasn't much interested, either; I'd heard it all before. We'd each had to make our choices. I'd made my bet two years ago, good or not, and got it over with. But here they were, still at it.

"What ya think's the best pick in the new stuff coming out?" Artie said. "Joe, you got any upper ideas on that?"

"Hard to tell. General Ford's selling its little electrics a lot, for short-haul. The ones with the plug-in packs."

"Yeah," I said, "but you use 20 percent of the charge just lugging the pack around. Okay if you don't use a car much, I guess."

"Hey, Joe," said Hollis, "gimme a tink and tonic." He had bills on the table, and his card for Joe to punch. "You know what *I* think?" We did, but he went ahead with it anyway.

"Until somebody without an expense account can afford one of those fuel-cell jobbies, you're not going to beat the little Japanese outside-burners, like the hot-air Honda my nephew got." He went on with it, but I wasn't listening. He always says it just about the same, Hollis does, as if it were real news.

A new customer came in, a young fat little guy, letting the TV-juke noise come with him as he opened the door. It was the *Stucco Crocodile*, doing "Baby, You're a Sidewiser." I didn't notice anyone inviting him, but he came and sat with us anyway.

The three of us gave each other the look that said that none of us knew him. The Stoneboat got trade from people hanging around the hospital waiting-rooms up the next block. Usually, though, they stayed in the front room with the juke to take their minds off their worries.

"Tink and soda," the new guy said. Joe waited until the man remembered and got his card out, to go with his money. "It's all right, bartender. First one today." So Joe punched the card, counted the drops of tincture he shook into the glass, and added the ice and soda. The man didn't get the extra drop, I noticed, that Joe usually gave his regular customers, law or no law. His first sip went long and deep; he grimaced at the bitterness. Personally I like a mix that covers the taste.

"Aah! That's what I needed." He smiled, then apparently thought better of it. "Oh, bartender! I'm expecting a call. From the hospital. They'll ask for Mr. Anstruther. If you don't mind."

"Sure," said Joe, "no trouble. Bleeding for some news?"

"Yes." Anstruther looked embarrassed. "My wife is—er, having a baby."

We were all careful not to look at him. Then I thought, what the hell; it happens sometimes. And he was pretty young; maybe it was his first. Couldn't blame a man for that, even now. I had two myself, but they dated from when nobody knew any better. Now, there wasn't that excuse.

More to break the silence than anything else, I said, "Hey, Joe! Throw a tink in a live one for me, will you?" That's the way I like tink; I can't taste it through live beer. Joe inspected the card with a straight face before he punched it—I mean, he knows I seldom tink up and hardly ever take the limit of three in one day.

He gave me the extra drop for being a regular, though. Someday, I thought, he's going to get narked off for that. I hoped Anstruther was only a would-be daddy-boy and not something else.

"You know?" said Anstruther. "They had tink over in Britain and Europe for years, before most of us here ever heard of it. Say, I might as well have another one." He pushed forward his card and money. Joe obliged him. Anstruther, I saw, still didn't get the extra drop.

"Anyway," he went on, "I think the administration made a good compromise, legalizing only the liquid form. Makes it a lot easier to control."

"Hell," said Artie Rail, "all they wanted was to get reelected, just like always. Any campaign's a snow job; what makes this year any different?"

Well, who could argue? Give one side a little, but not enough to grotch the other side. That's politics and always will be.

The phone chimed. Anstruther stood and moved to the bar. Joe picked up the handpiece, listened, and handed it over. He faced the console piece toward the other man. By habit—the visual was off; someone at the other end was saving money on the call.

"Yes?" said Anstruther. "I'll be right over." He came back to the table and gulped his second tink, which is not a good idea. Then he bolted out.

Hollis smiled. "That guy has a point. Who would have figured that when pot got legal, we'd be drinking it instead of smoking it?"

I wished he hadn't said that. I still miss tobacco. Not enough to bootleg it, though. Then I relaxed, beginning to stone-up from the tink. It *is* nice, once in a while. It was a little while before I started to listen again.

Artie was off and running, about his kid, this time. "They're trying to turn the boy queer or something in them schools," he said. "Other day I caught him and his buddy—you wouldn't believe it! And he had the bowels to say to his own father . . ."

I didn't bother to argue. I had my own misgivings to argue with, and I wished I knew which side of me was right.

When I tuned in again, Artie was still going. "And you know what else? He asked, did I rather he went and got his sterilization bonus? At *his* age? Hell, I want grandchildren, like anybody else." He grinned, looking uneasy. "Not too many, o' course. But, freakin' Jeez—*one,* anyway. I believe in Zero Population Growth, but not Zero Population."

Nobody answered Artie; he didn't ask questions that *had* good answers. He went back to creeping about his car; every place he wanted to go, the routes were more and more coded-out against him. Green-code routes, no restrictions, were getting hard to come by.

So what *else* was top-line news? I could see the handwriting on the wall, too. The only difference between Artie and me was that I believed it meant what it said.

The door to the front swung open; it was Anstruther again. The blast we caught from the TV-juke was *Lefty and the Seven Feeps,* striding on "Up Your Taxes."

"Tink and soda," he said, waving his card. This time he didn't sit with us, but climbed onto the nearest barstool. "Yes, I know," he said, "last for the day." Joe nodded, he hadn't argued. "But fitting, you know," the man continued. "Very fitting."

"Yeah?" said Hollis MacIlwain. "What fits it so nice?"

Anstruther didn't answer right away. He sipped on his tink while Artie began the next chapter of how the whole damn world wasn't set up for his personal tastes. I can listen to that all night without ever hearing much of it. Not that I hang in at Joe's that heavy; I wasn't even late home for dinner yet.

Anstruther raised his glass. "Three tinks," he said, "And three—"

"And three what?" Hollis said. Anstruther didn't say anything. I got a hunch.

"Three, uh—kids, maybe?" I said. "Three *kids,* you have?"

Whatever Anstruther wanted to say, it wouldn't come out. He tried to shake his head, but all it did was wobble a little.

"Three kids," said Artie Rail. For once, he wasn't whining. "You Goddamn *breeder!*"

"All right, three kids!" Anstruther blurted. He pulled his head up, sat straight. "It's not a crime. Not yet . . ." True, but still . . . Then he threw it. "And maybe we'll have another, too, if we happen to want to!"

Silence. Then the sound of chairs being pushed back. Joe was the first to speak up. "Whatever you do, do it *outside!*"

I didn't really feel like it, being stoned, and I don't suppose Hollis did, either. But it was too much. Anstruther hadn't made an apology, much less an excuse, and then he'd said maybe he'd do it again. Hollis got him by the neck and one arm; I had the other arm. We took him out the back way, to the alley.

We used to say, "Up against the wall," and Anstruther sure as hell was. But he didn't fight, or even try to. All he said was, "Not all three of you, for God's sakes!" That was fine with Hollis and me; we stepped back. And Anstruther did get his hands up, looking fairly competent.

Still it was no fair fight; Artie was Golden Gloves once. He faked Anstruther's hands high and slammed him in the gut, then threw his hard one.

Anstruther's head cracked back against the bricks; he collapsed.

Artie knelt beside him. "Jeez; I didn't mean to *kill* the bastard. Just to show him how the cow ate the cabbage." Artie looked scared. "You think he's all right?"

The man was still breathing; Artie relaxed a little. Hollis was looking into Anstruther's wallet; he showed it to Artie and me, then stuffed it back into the man's pocket.

"We might as well go back in," he said.

Inside, on our table, three tinks were set up. Our usuals, on the house and no cards punched. Joe had one, too. We all drank a little off the top. I don't think anybody thought it was a toast.

"Call an ambulance for that guy," said Hollis.

"Sure thing," said Joe. "In about an hour."

"No," said Artie. "Now. We did wrong on him."

"What the hell you mean?" said Joe.

Artie sure didn't like to have to say it. "He has a ZPG card. Sterilization bonus, a little over a year ago."

"Bullshit!" Joe said. "His wife just had her kid today."

"Yeah, sure," I said. "But whose?"

"Jesus! No wonder he—" Joe didn't finish it.

You don't waste a tink; we drank them, then left before the ambulance could get there. It's one thing to admit you screwed up, and something else to stay around and pay for it. Tough world, little brother.

I-5 South was blue again; I got home before my warmed-over dinner was too tired to eat. Marise and Les were both out someplace. I didn't feel much like talking.

"Anthing special happen today?" Linda asked.

I thought about it. "Well, yes. Joe at the Stoneboat set up three tinks on the house."

Fortune Hunter

Poul Anderson

If we allow irreplaceable wilderness areas to disappear, the quality of life in the future will be seriously diminished. Perhaps we're living in the last Golden Age right now; if so, imagine how nostalgic and envious future generations may feel about our time. And if they should develop a means of time travel . . .?

Poul Anderson is one of the major authors of science fiction. His best works combine scientific knowledge with human concerns and evocative writing, as in the following story.

AFTER CLEANING UP indoors, I stepped outside for a look at the evening. I'd only moved here a few days ago. Before, I'd been down in the woods. Now I was above timberline, and there'd just been time to make my body at home—reassemble the cabin and its furnishings, explore the area, deploy the pickups, let lungs acquire a taste for thinner air. My soul was still busy settling in.

I missed sun-flecks spattered like gold on soft shadow-brown duff, male ruggedness and woman-sweet odor of pines and their green that speared into heaven, a brook that glittered and sang, bird calls, a splendidly antlered wapiti who'd become my friend and took food from my hand. (He was especially fond of cucumber peels. I dubbed him Charlie.) You don't live six months in a place, from the blaze of autumn through the iron and white of winter, being reborn with the land when spring breathes over it—you don't do this and not keep some of that place ever afterward inside your bones.

Nevertheless, I'd kept remembering high country, and when Jo Modzeleski said she'd failed to get my time extended further, I decided to go up for what remained of it. That was part of my plan; she loved the

168

whole wilderness as much as I did, but she kept her heart on its peaks and they ought to help make her mood right. However, I myself was happy to return.

And as I walked out of the cabin, past my skeletal flitter, so that nothing human-made was between me and the world, suddenly the whole of me was again altogether belonging where I was.

This base stood on an alpine meadow. Grass grew thick and moist, springy underfoot, daisy-starred. Here and there bulked boulders the size of houses, grayness scored by a glacier which had once gouged out the little lake rippling and sparkling not far away; a sign to me that I also was included in eternity. Everywhere around, the Wind River Mountains lifted snow crowns and the darker blues of their rock into a dizzyingly tall heaven where an eagle hovered. He caught on his wings the sunlight which slanted out of the west. Those beams seemed to fill the chilliness, turning it somehow molten; and the heights were alive with shadows.

I smelled growth, more austere than in the forest but not the less strong. A fish leaped, I saw the brief gleam and an instant later, very faintly through quietness, heard the water clink. Though there was no real breeze, my face felt the air kiss it.

I buttoned my mackinaw, reached for smoking gear, and peered about. A couple of times already, I'd spied a bear. I knew better than to try a Charlie-type relationship with such a beast, but surely we could share the territory amicably; and if I could learn enough of his ways to plant pickups where they could record his life—or hers, in which case she'd be having cubs—

No. You're bound back to civilization at the end of this week. Remember?

Oh, but I may be returning.

As if in answer to my thought, I heard a whirr aloft. It grew, till another flitter hove into sight. Jo was taking me up on my invitation at an earlier hour than I'd expected when I said, "Come for dinner about sundown." Earlier than I'd hoped? My heart knocked. I stuck pipe and tobacco pouch back in my pockets and walked fast to greet her.

She landed and sprang out of the bubble before the airpad motors were silent. She always had been quick and graceful on her feet. Otherwise she wasn't much to look at: short, stocky, pug nose, pale round eyes under close-cropped black hair. For this occasion she'd left off the ranger's uniform in favor of an iridescent clingsuit; but it couldn't have done a lot for her even if she had known how to wear it.

"Welcome," I said, took both her hands, and gave her my biggest smile.

"Hi." She sounded breathless. Color came and went across her

169

cheeks. "How are you?"

"Okay. Sad at leaving, naturally." I turned the smile wry, so as not to seem self-pitiful.

She glanced away. "You'll be going back to your wife, though."

Don't push too hard. "You're ahead of yourself, Jo. I meant to have drinks and snacks ready in advance. Now you'll have to come in and watch me work."

"I'll help."

"Never, when you're my guest. Sit down, relax." I took her arm and guided her toward the cabin.

She uttered an uncertain laugh. "Are you afraid I'll get in your way, Pete? No worries. I know these knockdown units—I'd better, after three years—"

I was here for four, and that followed half a dozen years in and out of other wildernesses, before I decided that this was the one I wanted to record in depth, it being for me the loveliest of the lovely.

"—and they only have one practical place to stow any given kind of thing," she was saying. Then she stopped, which made me do likewise, turned her head from side to side, drank deep of air and sunglow. "Please, don't let me hurry you. This is such a beautiful evening. You were out to enjoy it."

Unspoken: And you haven't many left, Pete. The documentation project ended officially last year. You're the last of the very few mediamen who got special permission to stay on and finish their sequences; and now, no more stalling, no more extra time; the word is Everybody Out.

My unspoken reply: Except you rangers. A handful of you, holding degrees in ecology and soil biotics and whatnot—a handful who won in competition against a horde—does that give you the right to lord it over all this?

"Well, yes," I said, and segued to: "I'll enjoy it especially in present company."

"Thank you, kind sir." She failed to sound cheery.

I squeezed her arm. "You know, I am going to miss you, Jo. Miss you like hell." This past year, as my plan grew within me, I'd been cultivating her. Not just card games and long conversations over the sensiphone; no in-the-flesh get-togethers for hikes, rambles, picnics, fishing, birdwatching, deerwatching, starwatching. A mediaman gets good at the cultivation of people, and although this past decade had given me scant need to use that skill, it hadn't died. As easy as breathing. I could show interest in her rather banal remarks, her rather sappy sentimental opinions. . . . "Come see me when you get a vacation."

"Oh, I'll—I'll call you up . . . now and then . . . if Marie won't . . .

mind."

"I mean come in person. Holographic image, stereo sound, even scent and temperature and every other kind of circuit a person might pay for the use of—a phone isn't the same as having a friend right there."

She winced. "You'll be in the city."

"It isn't so bad," I said in my bravest style. "Pretty fair-sized apartment, a lot bigger than that plastic shack yonder. Soundproofed. Filtered and conditioned air. The whole conurb fully screened and policed. Armored vehicles available when you sally forth."

"And a mask for my nose and mouth!" She nearly gagged.

"No, no, that hasn't been needed for a long while. They've gotten the dust, monoxide, and carcinogens down to a level, at least in my city, which—"

"The stinks. The tastes. No, Pete, I'm sorry, I'm no delicate flower but the visits to Boswash I make in line of duty are the limit of what I can take . . . after getting to know this land."

"I'm thinking of moving into the country myself," I said. "Rent a cottage in an agrarea, do most of my business by phone, no need to go downtown except when I get an assignment to document something there."

She grimaced. "I often think the agrareas are worse than any 'tropolis."

"Huh?" It surprised me that she could still surprise me.

"Oh, cleaner, quieter, less dangerous, residents not jammed elbow to elbow, true," she admitted. "But at least those snarling, grasping, frenetic city folk have a certain freedom, a certain . . . *life* to them. It may be the life of a ratpack, but it's real, it has a bit of structure and spontaneity and— In the hinterlands, not only nature is regimented. The people are."

Well, I don't know how else you could organize things to feed a world population of fifteen billion.

"All right," I said. "I understand. But this is a depressing subject. Let's saunter for a while. I've found some gentian blooming."

"So early in the season? Is it in walking distance? I'd like to see."

"Too far for now, I'm afraid. I've been tramping some mighty long days. However, let me show you the local blueberry patch. It should be well worth a visit, come late summer."

As I took her arm again, she said, in her awkward fashion, "You've become an expert, haven't you, Pete?"

"Hard to avoid that," I grunted. "Ten years, collecting sensie material on the Wilderness System."

"Ten years . . . I was in high school when you began. I only knew the regular parks, where we stood in line on a paved path to see a redwood or a geyser, and we reserved swimming rights a month in advance. While you—" Her fingers closed around mine, hard and warm. "It doesn't seem fair to end your stay."

"Life never was fair."

Too damn much human life. Too little of any other kind. And we have to keep a few wildernesses a necessary reserve for what's left of the planet's ecology; a source of knowledge for researchers who're trying to learn enough about that ecology to shore it up before it collapses altogether; never mentioned, but present in every thinking head, the fact that if collapse does come, the wilderness will be Earth's last seedbeds of hope.

"I mean," Jo plodded, "of course areas like this were being destroyed by crowds—loved to death, as somebody wrote—so the only thing to do was close them to everybody except a few caretakers and scientists, and that was politically impossible unless 'everybody' meant *everybody*." Ah, yes, she was back to her habit of thumbing smooth-worn clichés. "And after all, the sensie documentaries that artists like you have been making, they'll be available and—" The smoothness vanished. "*You* can't come back, Pete! Not ever again!"

Her fingers remembered where they were and let go of me. Mine followed them and squeezed, a measured gentleness. Meanwhile my pulse fluttered. It was as well that words didn't seem indicated at the moment, because my mouth was dry.

A mediaman should be more confident. But such a God damn lot was riding on this particular bet. I'd gotten Jo to care about me, not just in the benevolent way of her colleagues, isolated from mankind so they can afford benevolence, but about me, this Pete-atom that wanted to spend the rest of its flickering days in the Wind River Mountains. Only how deeply did she care?

We walked around the lake. The sun dropped under the peaks— for minutes, the eastern snows were afire—and shadows welled up. I heard an owl hoot to his love. In royal blue, Venus kindled. The air sharpened, making blood run faster.

"Br-r-r!" Jo laughed. "Now I do want that drink."

I couldn't see her features through the dusk. The first stars stood forth infinitely clear. But Jo was a blur, a warmth, a solidness, no more. She might almost have been Marie.

If she had been! Marie was beautiful and bright and sexy and— Sure, she took lovers while I was gone for months on end; we'd agreed that the reserves were my mistresses. She'd had no thought for them on my returns. . . . Oh, if only we could have shared it all!

Soon the sky would hold more stars than darkness, the Milky Way would be a white cataract, the lake would lie aglow with them, and when

Jupiter rose there would be a perfect glade across the water. I'd stayed out half of last night to watch that.

Already the shining was such that we didn't need a penflash to find the entrance to my cabin. The insulation layer yielded under my touch. We stepped through, I zipped the door and closed the main switch, fluoros awoke as softly as the ventilation.

Jo was correct; those portables don't lend themselves to individuality. (She had a permanent cabin, built of wood and full of things dear to her.) Except for a few books and the like, my one room was strictly functional. True, the phone could bring me the illusion of almost anything or anybody, anywhere in the world, that I might want. We city folk learn to travel light. This interior was well proportioned, pleasingly tinted, snug; a step outside was that alpine meadow. What more did I need?

Out of hard-earned habit, I checked the nucleo gauge—ample power—before taking dinner from the freezer and setting it to cook. Thereafter I fetched nibblies, rum, and fruit juice, and mixed drinks the way Jo liked them. She didn't try to help after all, but settled back into the airchair. Neither of us had said much while we walked. I'd expected chatter out of her—a bit nervous, a bit too fast and blithe—once we were here. Instead, her stocky frame hunched in its mother-of-pearl suit that wasn't meant for it, and she stared at the hands in her lap.

No longer cold, I shucked my mackinaw and carried her drink over to her. "Revelry, not reverie!" I ordered. She took it. I clinked glasses. My other hand being then free, I reached thumb and forefinger to twitch her lips at the corners. "Hey you, smile. This is supposed to be a jolly party."

"Is it?" The eyes she raised to me were afloat in tears.

"Sure, I hate to go—"

"Where's Marie's picture?"

That rocked me back. I hadn't expected so blunt a question. "Why, uh—" *Okay. Events are moving faster than you'd planned on, Peter. Move with them.* I took a swallow, squared my shoulders, and said manfully: "I didn't want to unload my troubles on you, Jo. The fact is, Marie and I have broken up. Nothing's left but the formalities."

"What?"

Her mouth is open, her look lost in mine; she spills some of her drink and doesn't notice— Have I really got it made? This soon?

I shrugged. "Yeah. The notice of intent to dissolve relationship arrived yesterday. I'd seen it coming, of course. She'd grown tired of waiting around."

"Oh, Pete!" She reached for me.

I was totally aware—walls, crowded shelves, night in a window, murmur and warm gusting from the heat unit, monitor lamp on the radionic oven and meat fragrances seeping out of it, this woman whom I must learn to desire—and thought quickly that at the present stage of things, I'd better pretend not to notice her gesture. "No sympathy cards," I said in a flat tone. "To be quite honest, I'm more relieved than otherwise."

"I thought—" she whispered. "I thought you two were happy."

Which we have been, my dear, Marie and I, though a sophisticated mediaman does suspect that considerable of our happiness, as opposed to contentment, has been due to my long absences this past decade. They've added spice. That's something you'll always lack, whatever happens, Jo. Yet a man can't live only on spices.

"It didn't last," I said as per plan. "She's found someone more compatible. I'm glad of that."

"You, Pete?"

"I'll manage. C'mon, drink your drink. I insist that we be merry."

She gulped. "I'll try."

After a minute: "You haven't even anyone to come home to!"

"'Home' doesn't mean a lot to a city man, Jo. One apartment is like another; and we move through a big total of 'em in a lifetime." The liquor must have touched me a bit, since I rushed matters: "Quite different from, say, these mountains. Each patch of them is absolutely unique. A man could spend all his years getting to know a single one, growing into it— Well."

I touched a switch and the armchair expanded, making room for me to settle down beside her. "Care for some background music?" I asked.

"No." Her gaze dropped—she had stubby lashes—and she blushed—blotchily—but she got her words out with a stubbornness I had come to admire. Somebody who had that kind of guts wouldn't be too bad a partner. "At least, I'd not hear it. This is just about my last chance to talk . . . really talk . . . to you, Pete. Isn't it?"

"I hope not." *More passion in that voice, boy.* "Lord, I hope not!"

"We have had awfully good times together. My colleagues are fine, you know, but—" She blinked hard. "You've been special."

"Same as you to me."

She was shivering a bit, meeting my eyes now, lips a bare few centimeters away. Since she seldom drank alcohol, I guessed that what I'd more or less forced on her had gotten a good strong hold, under these circumstances. *Remember, she's no urbanite who'll hop into bed and scarcely remember it two days later. She went directly from a small town to a tough university to here, and may actually be a virgin. However, you've worked toward this moment for months, Pete, old chum. Get started!*

It was the gentlest kiss I think I have ever taken.

"I've been, well, afraid to speak," I murmured into her hair, which held an upland sunniness. "Maybe I still am. Only I don't, don't, don't want to lose you, Jo."

Half crying, half laughing, she came back to my mouth. She didn't really know how, but she held herself hard against me, and I thought: *May she end up sleeping with me, already this night?*

No matter, either way. What does count is, the Wilderness Administration allows qualified husband-and-wife teams to live together on the job; and she's a ranger and I, being skilled in using monitoring devices, would be an acceptable research assistant.

And then-n-n:

I didn't know, I don't know to this day what went wrong. We'd had two or three more drinks, and a good deal of joyous tussling, and her clothes were partly off her, and dinner was beginning to scorch in the oven when

I was too hasty

she was too awkward and/or backward-holding, and I got impatient and she felt it.

I breathed out one of those special words which people say to each other only, and she being a bit terrified anyway decided it wasn't mere habit-accident but I was pretending she was Marie because in fact my eyes were shut

she wasn't as naive as she, quite innocently, had led me to believe, and in one of those moments which (contrary to fantasy) are forever coming upon lovers asked herself, "Hey, what the hell is really going on?"

or whatever. It makes no difference. Suddenly she wanted to phone Marie.

"If, if, if things are as you say, Pete, she'll be glad to learn—"

"Wait a minute! Wait one damn minute! Don't you trust me?"

"Oh, Pete, darling, of course I do, but—"

"But nothing." I drew apart to register offense.

Instead of coming after me, she asked, as quietly as the night outside: "Don't you trust *me?*"

Never mind. A person can't answer a question like that. We both tried, and shouldn't have. All I truly remember is seeing her out the door. A smell of charred meat pursued us. Beyond the cabin, the air was cold and altogether pure, sky wild with stars, peaks aglow. I watched her stumble to her flitter. The galaxy lit her path. She cried the whole way. But she went.

However disappointed, I felt some relief, too. It would have been a shabby trick to play on Marie, who had considerable love invested in me. And our apartment is quite pleasant, once it's battened down against the surroundings; I belong to the fortunate small minority. We had an appropriate reunion. She even babbled about applying for a childbearing permit. I kept enough sense to switch that kind of talk immediately.

Next evening there was a rally which we couldn't well get out of attending. The commissioners may be right as far as most citizens go. "A sensiphone, regardless of how many circuits are tuned in, is no substitute for the physical togetherness of human beings uniting under their leaders for our glorious mass purposes." We, though, didn't get anything out of it except headaches, ears ringing from the cadenced cheers, lungs full of air that had passed through thousands of other lungs, and skins which felt greasy as well as gritty. Homebound, we encountered smog so thick it confused our vehicle. Thus we got stopped on the fringes of a riot and saw a machine gun cut a man in two before the militia let us move on. It was a huge relief to pass security check at our conurb and take a transporter which didn't fail even once, up and across to our own place.

There we shared a shower, using an extravagant percentage of our monthly water ration, and dried each other off, and I slipped into a robe and Marie into something filmy; we had a drink and a toke which Haydn lilted, and got relaxed to the point where she shook her long tresses over her shoulders and her whisper tickled my ear: "Aw, c'mon, hero, the computers've got to've edited your last year's coverage by now. I've looked forward all this while."

I thought fleetingly of Jo. Well, she wouldn't appear in a strictly wilderness-experience public-record documentary; and I myself was curious about what I had actually produced, and didn't think a revisit in an electronic dream would pain me, even this soon afterward.

I was wrong.

What hurt most was the shoddiness. Oh yes, decent reproduction of a primrose nodding in the breeze, a hawk a-swoop, spuming whiteness and earthquake rumble of a distant avalanche, fallen leaves brown and baking under the sun, their smell and crackle, the laughter of a gust which flirted with my hair, suppleness incarnate in a snake or a cougar, flamboyance at sunset and shyness at dawn—a competent show. Yet it wasn't real; it wasn't what I had loved.

Marie said, slowly, in the darkness where we sat, "You did better before. Kruger, Mato Grosso, Baikal, your earlier stays in this region —I almost felt I was at your side. You weren't a recorder there; you were an artist, a great artist. Why is this different?"

"I don't know," I mumbled. "My presentation is kind of mechanical, I admit. I suppose I was tired."

"In that case—" she sat very straight, half a meter from me, fingers gripped together, "—you didn't have to stay on. You could have come home to me long before you did."

But I wasn't tired rammed through my head. *No, now is when I'm drained; then, there, life flowed into me.*

That gentian Jo wanted to see . . . it grows where the land suddenly drops. Right at the cliff edge those flowers grow, oh, blue, blue, blue against grass green and daisy white and the strong gray of stone; a streamlet runs past, leaps downward, ringing, cold, tasting of glaciers, rocks, turf, the air which also blows everywhere around me, around the high and holy peaks beyond . . .

"Lay off!" I yelled. My fist struck the chair arm. The fabric clung and cloyed. A shade calmer, I said, "Okay, maybe I got too taken up in the reality and lost the necessary degree of detachment." *I lie, Marie, I lie like Judas. My mind was never busier, planning how to use Jo and discard you.* "Darling, those sensies, I'll have nothing but them for the rest of my life." *And none of the gentians. I was too busy with my scheme to bother with anything small and gentle and blue.* "Isn't that penalty enough?"

"No. You did have the reality. And you did not bring it back." Her voice was like a wind across the snows of upland winter.

My Lady of the Psychiatric Sorrows

Brian W. Aldiss

"The quality of life" naturally means different things to different people. If our resources dwindle to the point of being unable to support a technological society, no doubt many of us will scarcely miss it. But many will. This story suggests what might happen to a married couple with sharply divergent reactions to change.

Brian W. Aldiss is a widely accomplished writer who has dealt with apocalyptic futures in such novels as Greybeard and Earthworks. He is also the author of the best book to date on the history of science fiction, Billion Year Spree.

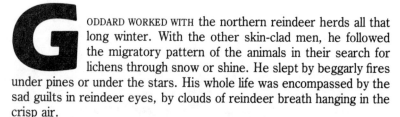 ODDARD WORKED WITH the northern reindeer herds all that long winter. With the other skin-clad men, he followed the migratory pattern of the animals in their search for lichens through snow or shine. He slept by beggarly fires under pines or under the stars. His whole life was encompassed by the sad guilts in reindeer eyes, by clouds of reindeer breath hanging in the crisp air.

The herd consisted of some hundred thousand beasts. They moved in good mild order, with their attendant pest-army of mosquitoes and bloodsucking flies. Their antlers appeared like a moving forest.

For Goddard, it was a Pleistocene way of life. But when spring came he was paid off and began to walk south, back to Scally and the children, with his dog Gripp at his side.

He walked for sixteen days, steadily. The climate grew warmer. The steaks in his pack began to stink, but still he ate them. Every now and then, he came to villages or mills; always he avoided them.

At last, he was among the vales of the Gray Horse. He walked through sparse forests, where the beech, birch, and hazel bushes were putting forth green leaves. Through the trees, standing by the old highway, was his home. His father was working in the garden. Goddard called to him, and the guard dogs, Chase and Setter, started furious barking.

"How are the children?" Goddard asked his father, embracing the old man. His father was still upright, though the winter months seemed to have shrunk him.

"Come and see. They aren't half growing big!"

"You've made out?"

"Fine, Tom. And I've not heard of a case of plague all winter."

"Good."

"It'll mean that people will be coming back. . . ." As they spoke, they walked together, close, to the rear of the house, where the windmill stood on the rise above their small stream. Gripp kept to Goddard's heel.

The children were there—Derek wading in the stream, June kneeling on the bank. Both were picking reeds. They dropped them and ran with cries of delight into their father's embrace. He rolled on the ground with them, all three of them laughing and crying.

"You don't half smell animal, Dad!"

"I've been an animal. . . ." He was proud of them, both so big and strong, neither older than seven, their eyes clear, their glance candid—as their mother's once had been.

Granddad roasted one of the rotting steaks and they all ate, throwing gristle and bone to the dogs. After, Goddard slept in a downstairs room. He woke once. The sun had gone. His father and the children were in the other room, weaving hurdles from willow sticks by the light of two candles. They called to him affectionately; but when he had urinated outside, he staggered back to his cot and slept again.

In the morning they swarmed over him once more. He kissed and hugged them, and they screamed at his rough lips and beard.

"It's a holiday today. What shall we do?"

"Go and see Mother, of course. Let's feed the animals first."

The goat, the two sows, the chickens, the rabbits were fed. Leaving the dogs on guard, they all set out along the vale to see Mother. The children snatched up sticks from ditches, leaning heavily on them and saying in their clear voices, "Now we are *old* children." Their laughter seemed to settle about Goddard's heart.

A stramineous sun broke through the mists. Where the track

turned, they saw the bulk of the planetoid ahead, and the children set up a muted cheer.

Goddard said to his father, turning from that shadow-shrouded form, "I don't reckon I could bear life without the kids and all their happiness. I dread when they'll turn into adults and go their way."

"It'll be different then. Don't look ahead." But the old man turned his head away sorrowfully.

"They seem to have a purpose, over and above keeping alive—just like the reindeer."

His father had no answer.

The planetoid was so immense that it blocked the valley. It had created its own ecoclimate. On this side, the northern side, dark hardy bushes had grown at its base, rock and stone had piled up, and a stream dashed from it. The top of the planetoid's shell showed serrated through thinning cloud.

Derek and June dropped back in awe. June took her father's hand. "Don't it look huge this morning! Tell us how it came here, Dad."

They always liked the drama of the old story. Goddard said, "As the reindeer roam in search of food, men used to roam in search of energy. When the local supplies ran out, they built a mass of little planets, like this one, called zeepees. The zeepees circled about in space, getting energy from the sun. But some of the planetoids got in trouble, just like people. This one—I think it was called Fragrance, or something fancy—it crashed here. Another one went into the sun. Another one drifted off toward the stars."

"Was that years and years ago, Dad?" Derek asked. He took up a stone and flung it, to show he was not scared.

"Not so long ago. Only, let's see, only six years ago. The zeepee was empty by then. All the people in it had come back to Earth, so nobody was hurt."

"Did Mother go to live there as soon as it crashed?"

"After a bit, yes."

They climbed up a steeply winding path to one side, where the soil had been flung back by the impact. Broom and nettles grew now. The enormous hull was plastic. Its fall through the atmosphere had caused blisters to erupt, so that its sides were warted and striped like a toad.

"I bet it came down with a great big CRASH!" June said.

"It split right open like an egg," her granddad told her.

Goddard led them in through the broken hatch, going cautiously. There had been looting at first. Now all was deserted.

The children fell silent as they walked. The amazing, jumbled maze which had once been a city, a world, was no longer lit, except by daylight filtering in through the ruptured hull. They walked not on floors and roads but on sides of tunnels and walls of corridors. The stress of impact had caused fractures and crazy distortions of the structure. Defunct lights and signs sprouted underfoot. Doorways had become hatches leading to dry wells. Once-busy intersections produced shafts leading up into nothingness. Dummies stared down at them from overhead tanks which had been shop windows. They tramped across the hitherto inaccessible, where stairways had become abstract bas-reliefs.

"It's cold—I shouldn't like to live here," June said. "Not unless I was a polar bear."

They waded through a riverlet. Cracked and broken, the planetoid lay open to the elements. The rains of autumn, the snows of winter, all blew in among Fragrance's complex structures, turning yesterday's apartments into today's reservoirs. Slowly the water leaked downward through the upturned city, draining at last into native ground. Plants and fungi were getting a grasp on the ruined precincts. Small animals had taken over the defunct sewage system. Sparrows and starlings built their nests in what had once been an underground railway several thousand miles above Earth. After the birds came smaller life forms. Flies and spiders and wasps and beetles and moths. Change worked at everything. What had been impregnable to the rigors of space fell to the ardors of a mild spring.

"Dad, why does Mother want to live here?" Derek asked.

"She liked the old times. She couldn't take to the new."

Goddard never forgot the way to the spot where Scally had settled in. She had indulged her sybaritic tastes and ensconced herself in what had been Fragrance's chief hotel, the Astral. Goddard had found only one way of entering the hotel, which had stood in a block on its own, and that was by way of a metal ladder which an early looter had propped up against a fire exit overhead. Goddard leading, the four of them climbed the ladder and worked their way into the foyer, whose elaborate reception area now projected from one wall. Loose debris had provided the wall on which they stood with a carpet.

Scally had barricaded herself into the old bar. They climbed up a pile of tumbled desks, calling her name through the shattered doors.

He remembered the dirty, tomblike smell of her lair. The smell of dead hope, he told himself.

In her first year there, Goddard had come up often from the Vale of the Gray Horse—for sex, for love, or for pity. Scally had not wanted the outside world and had slowly, almost against her own will, rejected him as a symbol of it. He had helped her make herself comfortable here. So she lived in aspic, in dowdy magnificence, the great cracked mirrors of her ceiling reflecting every torpid move she made.

As her husband and children appeared, she rose from a chair. Instead of coming toward them, she retreated to the far wall. She was tall and soft; the last few indoor years had turned her all gray. As she smiled at them, a long pallid hand crept up to cover her lips.

"Mother, look, Dad's back from the North!" Derek said, running over and clutching her, making her bend over and kiss him and June. "He's been with reindeer."

"You're getting so big and rough," Scally said, letting go of them and backing away, until she could lean against a piano in a self-conscious attitude.

Conscious of his coarse skins, Goddard went over and took her in his arms. She was thinner and drier than previously, while all around her compartments bulged with the rich damps of decay. Her expression as she searched his face wounded him.

"It's spring again, Scally," he said. "Come out with us. Come home. We'll fix the roof, Dad and I, and get one of the upstairs rooms done specially for you."

"This is my place," she said.

"The children need you." But the children had lost interest in their mother, and were questing about the room and adjacent corridors. They had found two rods to walk with; June was laughing and calling, "Now we're a couple of old children again!"

"I'm a hundred years old."

"I'm a thousand and sixty hundred years old."

"I'm even older than Mum."

Goddard's father was embarrassed. He looked about and eventually left the room too, to follow the children.

"He hates me!" Scally said, pointing at the closing door.

"No, he doesn't. He just doesn't have anything to say. He hates this prison."

"He thinks I should come back and look after you and the children."

"Why don't you? We need you. You could take some of this furniture."

"Huh! I'd only be a liability to you."

"Scally, you're my wife. I'd gladly have you back. This place is no good. Why do you stay here?"

She looked away, waved a hand in dismissal. "You ask such fool questions."

Angry, he grasped her wrist. "Come on, then, we take the trouble to come and see you! Tell me why you want to live in this muddy ruin, come on—tell me!"

Through the dim, upturned light, a glow crept into her features. "Because I can't take reality the way you can! You're so stupidly insensitive, you don't mind the beastly pig-reality of the present. But some of us live by myth, by legend. Just as the children do, until you turn them out of it and make them grow up before their time."

He said sullenly, "You only came here because you thought you'd be a bit more comfortable. It's nothing to do with myth."

"While I'm here, I'm in the remains of an age when men lived by their myths, when they created machines and looked outward, when they didn't wallow in every muddy season and grovel on the ground as you do! This room once sailed among the stars—and all you can imagine is that I'm after comfort."

She laughed bitterly.

Goddard scratched his head. "I know it's kind of uncomfortable back at home. But honest, if you can face up to it, life's better than it used to be in the old days. It's more real. Less of all that waffle, all those things we didn't really need."

She folded her arms, no longer looking as faded as she had five minutes earlier. "You were born to be a farmer, Tom, to walk behind cattle and reindeer, tramping through their droppings. Of course you rejoice at the death of the consumer society. But that wasn't all we had, was it? Remember the other things the Catastrophe killed off? The hope that we were moving toward a better world, the feeling that mankind might come to some sort of ethical maturity as he left his home planet? I resent being kicked back into the Dark Ages, if you don't."

He did not know what to say. He shook his head. "Resentment's no way to shape your life."

"There *is* no shape to life, Tom. Not any more. Style died along with everything else. Why, when I look at you . . ." She turned away. "To think you were a top sports-clothes designer! In six years, you've become nothing but a peasant."

The children were screaming with feigned terror in one of the upside-down corridors.

"I'll try and make you comfortable if you come home," Goddard said. She could always confuse him. Half aware that he was only infuriating her, he put out a hand pleadingly, but she turned away toward the table and chair at which she had been sitting when they entered.

"At least I can read here, at least my mind is free." She had picked a book up from the table.

He shook his head. "All that old world is dead and gone, my dear. Books are where you get your sick notions from. Throw it away and come into the light of day. The plague has gone and things'll be better."

The children were screaming with delight outside.

"Today or yesterday, I was reading about the scientific basis for the legend of the Golden Fleece," Scally told Goddard. "Did you ever hear of the Greek legend of the Golden Fleece, and how Jason and the

Argonauts went in search of it? The story has always related to the Black Sea area. When this book was published, researchers had analyzed pieces of cloth from the tomb of an old king of that area, Tumulus I, who lived in the fifth century B.C. That was the period of Jason and his crew. Do you know what the researchers found?"

He tried to escape from the conversation, but she went on remorselessly, although the children had come back hooting into the room.

"They found that the cloth from the tomb was composed of extremely fine fibers, with mean diameters of—I forget the exact measurements—about sixteen micrometers, I believe. That is the earliest appearance of true fine-wooled sheep by several centuries. So you see that all that golden legend was generated by Jason and his friends going in search of more comfortable underwear." She laughed.

The children had tied sticks around their heads with old fabric.

"Look, Dad, Mother! We're reindeer. We've gone wild! We're going to head north and we'll never let anyone milk us again!"

Puzzled by her story, Goddard said to her over the racket, "I don't understand you properly. Whatever happened to those Argonauts can't affect us, can it?"

She looked at him wearily, with her eyelids lowered. "Take these young reindeer away," she said. "One day soon their myths will break down. Don't you see, there's a prosaic reality to every legend, but people like you beat legends into prosaic reality."

"I never beat you!"

"Have you got remarkably thick in the head, or is that meant to be funny?"

"You're sick, Scally, really you are. Come away and let me look after you!"

"Never say that again! You oaf, if you didn't believe that I was sick, can't you see that I might come with you willingly?"

Goddard scratched his head. "Since you can always get the better of me in words, I can't think why you're afraid to come with me." Then he turned away.

The next day was mild and springlike. Goddard stripped to the waist and began to plant row after row of seed potatoes, which his father had carefully cherished throughout the winter. The two children played on the other side of the stream, building little planetoids in every bush, and pretending that Gripp was a monster from outer space.

The New Atlantis

Ursula K. Le Guin

Enthusiasts sometimes refer to science fiction writers as "the poets of our future," celebrating the art of the best science fiction in describing futures that are not only logically extrapolated but whose images and themes also move us on very basic levels. The following story is a superb example: its grim future is set in counterpoint to a utopian past that just might reemerge.

Ursula K. Le Guin is a writer of prose and poetry who has won high acclaim in both science fiction and general literature. Her best known novels are The Left Hand of Darkness and The Lathe of Heaven, which was adapted for presentation on PBS-TV early in 1980.

COMING BACK FROM my Wilderness Week I sat by an odd sort of man in the bus. For a long time we didn't talk; I was mending stockings and he was reading. Then the bus broke down a few miles outside Gresham. Boiler trouble, the way it generally is when the driver insists on trying to go over thirty. It was a Supersonic Superscenic Deluxe long distance coal-burner, with Home Comfort, that means a toilet, and the seats were pretty comfortable, at least those that hadn't yet worked loose from their bolts, so everybody waited inside the bus; besides, it was raining. We began talking, the way people do when there's a breakdown and a wait. He held up his pamphlet and tapped it—he was a dry-looking man with a school-teacherish way of using his hands—and said, "This is interesting. I've been reading that a new continent is rising from the depths of the sea."

The blue stockings were hopeless. You have to have something besides holes to darn onto. "Which sea?"

"They're not sure yet. Most specialists think the Atlantic. But there's evidence it may be happening in the Pacific, too."

"Won't the oceans get a little crowded?" I said, not taking it seriously. I was a bit snappish, because of the breakdown and because those blue stockings had been good warm ones.

He tapped the pamphlet again and shook his head, quite serious. "No," he said. "The old continents are sinking, to make room for the new. You can see that that is happening."

You certainly can. Manhattan Island is now under eleven feet of water at low tide, and there are oyster beds in Ghirardelli Square.

"I thought that was because the oceans are rising from polar melt."

He shook his head again. "That is a factor. Due to the greenhouse effect of pollution, indeed Antarctica may become inhabitable. But climatic factors will not explain the emergence of the new—or, possibly, very old—continents in the Atlantic and Pacific." He went on explaining about continental drift, but I liked the idea of inhabiting Antarctica and daydreamed about it for a while. I thought of it as very empty, very quiet, all white and blue, with a faint golden glow northward from the unrising sun behind the long peak of Mount Erebus. There were a few people there; they were very quiet too, and wore white tie and tails. Some of them carried oboes and violas. Southward the white land went up in a long silence toward the Pole.

Just the opposite, in fact, of the Mount Hood Wilderness Area. It had been a tiresome vacation. The other women in the dormitory were all right, but it was macaroni for breakfast, and there were so many organized sports. I had looked forward to the hike up to the National Forest Preserve, the largest forest left in the United States, but the trees didn't look at all the way they do in the postcards and brochures and Federal Beautification Bureau advertisements. They were spindly, and they all had little signs on saying which union they had been planted by. There were actually a lot more green picnic tables and cement Men's and Women's than there were trees. There was an electrified fence all around the forest to keep out unauthorized persons. The forest ranger talked about mountain jays, "bold little robbers," he said, "who will come and snatch the sandwich from your very hand," but I didn't see any. Perhaps because that was the weekly Watch Those Surplus Calories! Day for all the women, and so we didn't have any sandwiches. If I'd seen a mountain jay, I might have snatched the sandwich from his very hand, who knows. Anyhow it was an exhausting week, and I wished I'd stayed home and practiced, even though I'd have lost a week's pay because staying home and practicing the viola doesn't count as planned implementation of recreational leisure as defined by the Federal Union of Unions.

When I came back from my Antarctican expedition, the man was reading again, and I got a look at his pamphlet; and that was the odd part of it. The pamphlet was called "Increasing Efficiency in Public Accountant Training Schools," and I could see from the one paragraph I got a glance at that there was nothing about new continents emerging from the ocean depths in it—nothing at all.

Then we had to get out and walk on into Gresham, because they had decided that the best thing for us all to do was get onto the Greater Portland Area Rapid Public Transit Lines, since there had been so many breakdowns that the charter bus company didn't have any more buses to send out to pick us up. The walk was wet, and rather dull, except when we passed the Cold Mountain Commune. They have a wall around it to keep out unauthorized persons, and a big neon sign out front saying *COLD MOUNTAIN COMMUNE*, and there were some people in authentic jeans and ponchos by the highway selling macrame belts and sandcast candles and soybean bread to the tourists. In Gresham, I took the 4:40 GPARPTL Superjet Flyer train to Burnside and East 230th, and then walked to 217th and got the bus to the Goldschmidt Overpass, and transferred to the shuttlebus, but it had boiler trouble, so I didn't reach the downtown transfer point until ten after eight, and the buses go on a once-an-hour schedule at eight, so I got a meatless hamburger at the Longhorn Inch-Thick Steak House Dinerette and caught the nine o'clock bus and got home about ten. When I let myself into the apartment I flipped the switch to turn on the lights, but there still weren't any. There had been a power outage in West Portland for three weeks. So I went feeling about for the candles in the dark, and it was a minute or so before I noticed that somebody was lying on my bed.

I panicked, and tried to turn the lights on.

It was a man, lying there in a long thin heap. I thought a burglar had got in somehow while I was away and died. I opened the door so I could get out quick or at least my yells could be heard, and then I managed not to shake long enough to strike a match, and lighted the candle, and came a little closer to the bed.

The light disturbed him. He made a sort of snorting in his throat and turned his head. I saw it was a stranger, but I knew his eyebrows, then the breadth of his closed eyelids, then I saw my husband.

He woke up while I was standing there over him with the candle in my hand. He laughed and said, still half asleep, "Ah, Psyche! From the regions which are holy land."

Neither of us made much fuss. It was unexpected, but it did seem so natural for him to be there, after all, much more natural than for him not to be there, and he was too tired to be very emotional. We lay there together in the dark, and he explained that they had released him from the Rehabilitation Camp early because he had injured his back in an accident in the gravel quarry, and they were afraid it might get worse. If he died there it wouldn't be good publicity abroad, since there have been some nasty rumors about deaths from illness in the Rehabilitation Camps and the Federal Medical Association Hospitals; and there are scientists abroad who have heard of Simon, since somebody published his proof of Goldbach's Hypothesis in Peking. So they let him out early, with eight dollars in his pocket, which is what he had in his pocket when they arrested him, which made it, of course, fair. He had walked and hitched home from Coeur D'Alene, Idaho, with a couple of days in jail in Walla Walla for being caught hitchhiking. He almost fell asleep telling me this, and when he had told me, he did fall asleep. He needed a change of clothes and a bath but I didn't want to wake him. Besides, I was tired, too. We lay side by side and his head was on my arm. I don't suppose that I have ever been so happy. No; was it happiness? Something wider and darker, more like knowledge, more like the night: joy.

It was dark for so long, so very long. We were all blind. And there was the cold, a vast, unmoving, heavy cold. We could not move at all. We did not move. We did not speak. Our mouths were closed, pressed shut by the cold and by the weight. Our eyes were pressed shut. Our limbs were held still. Our minds were held still. For how long? There was no length of time; how long is death? And is one dead only after living, or before life as well? Certainly we thought, if we thought anything, that we were dead; but if we had ever been alive, we had forgotten it.

There was a change. It must have been the pressure that changed first, although we did not know it. The eyelids are sensitive to touch. They must have been weary of being shut. When the pressure upon them weakened a little, they opened. But there was no way for us to know that. It was too cold for us to feel anything. There was nothing to be seen. There was black.

But then—"then," for the event created time, created before and after, near and far, now and then—"then" there was the light. One light. One small, strange light that passed slowly, at what distance we could not tell. A small greenish white, slightly blurred point of radiance, passing.

Our eyes were certainly open, "then," for we saw it. We saw the moment. The moment is a point of light. Whether in darkness or in the field of all light, the moment is small, and moves, but not quickly. And "then" it is gone.

It did not occur to us that there might be another moment. There was no reason to assume that there might be more than one. One was marvel enough: that in all the field of the dark, in the cold, heavy, dense, moveless, timeless, placeless, boundless black, there would have occurred, once, a small, slightly blurred, moving light! Time need be created only once, we thought.

But we were mistaken. The difference between one and more than one is all the difference in the world. Indeed, that difference is the world.

The light returned.

The same light, or another one? There was no telling.

But, "this time," we wondered about the light: Was it small and near to us, or large and far away? Again there was no telling; but there was something about the way it moved, a trace of hesitation, a tentative quality, that did not seem proper to anything large and remote. The stars, for instance. We began to remember the stars.

The stars had never hesitated.

Perhaps the noble certainty of their gait had been a mere effect of distance. Perhaps in fact they had hurtled wildly, enormous furnace-fragments of a primal bomb thrown through the cosmic dark; but time and distance soften all agony. If the universe, as seems likely, began with an act of destruction, the stars we had used to see told no tales of it. They had been implacably serene.

The planets, however . . . We began to remember the planets. They had suffered certain changes both of appearance and of course. At certain times of the year Mars would reverse its direction and go backward through the stars. Venus had been brighter and less bright as she went through her phases of crescent, full, and wane. Mercury had shuddered like a skidding drop of rain on the sky flushed with daybreak. The light we now watched had that erratic, trembling quality. We saw it, unmistakably, change direction and go backward. It then grew smaller and fainter; blinked—an eclipse?—and slowly disappeared.

Slowly, but not slowly enough for a planet.

Then—the third "then"!—arrived, the indubitable and positive Wonder of the World, the Magic Trick, watch now, watch, you will not believe your eyes, mama, mama, look what I can do—

Seven lights in a row, proceeding fairly rapidly, with a darting movement, from left to right. Proceeding less rapidly from right to left, two dimmer, greenish lights. Two lights halt, blink, reverse course, proceed hastily and in a wavering manner from left to right. Seven-lights increase speed, and catch up. Two-lights flash desperately, flicker, and are gone.

Seven-lights hang still for some while, then merge gradually into one streak, veering away, and little by little vanish into the immensity of the dark.

But in the dark now are growing other lights, many of them: lamps, dots, rows, scintillations—some near at hand, some far. Like the stars, yes, but not stars. It is not the great Existences we are seeing, but only the little lives.

In the morning Simon told me something about the Camp, but not until after he had had me check the apartment for bugs. I thought at first he had been given behavior mod and gone paranoid. We never had been infested. And I'd been living alone for a year and a half; surely they didn't want to hear me talking to myself? But he said, "They may have been expecting me to come here."

"But they let you go free!"

He just lay there and laughed at me. So I checked everywhere we could think of. I didn't find any bugs, but it did look as if somebody had gone through the bureau drawers while I was away in the Wilderness. Simon's papers were all at Max's, so that didn't matter. I made tea on the Primus, and washed and shaved Simon with the extra hot water in the kettle—he had a thick beard and wanted to get rid of it because of the lice he had brought from Camp—and while we were doing that he told me about the Camp. In fact he told me very little, but not much was necessary.

He had lost about 20 pounds. As he only weighed 140 to start with, this left little to go on with. His knees and wrist bones stuck out like rocks under the skin. His feet were all swollen and chewed-looking from the Camp boots; he hadn't dared take the boots off, the last three days of walking, because he was afraid he wouldn't be able to get them back on. When he had to move or sit up so I could wash him, he shut his eyes.

"Am I really here?" he asked. "Am I here?"

"Yes," I said. "You are here. What I don't understand is how you got here."

"Oh, it wasn't bad so long as I kept moving. All you need is to know where you're going—to have someplace to go. You know, some of the people in Camp, if they'd let them go, they wouldn't have had that. They couldn't have gone anywhere. Keeping moving was the main thing. See, my back's all seized up, now."

When he had to get up to go to the bathroom he moved like a ninety-year-old. He couldn't stand straight, but was all bent out of shape, and shuffled. I helped him put on clean clothes. When he lay down on the bed again, a sound of pain came out of him, like tearing thick paper. I went around the room putting things away. He asked me to come sit by him and said I was going to drown him if I went on crying. "You'll submerge the entire North American continent," he said. I can't remember what he said, but he made me laugh finally. It is hard to remember things Simon says, and hard not to laugh when he says them. This is not merely the partiality of affection: He makes everybody laugh. I doubt that he intends to. It is just that a mathematician's mind works differently from other people's. Then when they laugh, that pleases him.

It was strange, and it is strange, to be thinking about "him," the man I have known for ten years, the same man, while "he" lay there changed out of recognition, a different man. It is enough to make you understand why most languages have a word like "soul." There are various degrees of death, and time spares us none of them. Yet something endures, for which a word is needed.

I said what I had not been able to say for a year and a half: "I was afraid they'd brainwash you."

He said, "Behavior mod is expensive. Even just the drugs. They save it mostly for the VIPs. But I'm afraid they got a notion I might be important after all. I got questioned a lot the last couple of months. About my 'foreign contacts.'" He snorted. "The stuff that got published abroad, I suppose. So I want to be careful and make sure it's just a Camp again next time, and not a Federal Hospital."

"Simon, were they . . . are they cruel, or just righteous?"

He did not answer for a while. He did not want to answer. He knew what I was asking. He knew by what thread hangs hope, the sword, above our heads.

"Some of them . . ." he said at last, mumbling.

Some of them had been cruel. Some of them had enjoyed their work. You cannot blame everything on society.

"Prisoners, as well as guards," he said.

You cannot blame everything on the enemy.

"Some of them, Belle," he said with energy, touching my hand— "some of them, there were men like gold there—"

The thread is tough; you cannot cut it with one stroke.

"What have you been playing?" he asked.

"Forrest, Schubert."

"With the quartet?"

"Trio, now. Janet went to Oakland with a new lover."

"Ah, poor Max."

"It's just as well, really. She isn't a good pianist."

I make Simon laugh too, though I don't intend to. We talked until it was past time for me to go to work. My shift since the Full Employment Act last year is ten to two. I am an inspector in a recycled paper bag factory. I have never rejected a bag yet; the electronic inspector catches all the defective ones first. It is a rather depressing job. But it's only four hours a day, and it takes more time than that to go through all the lines and physical and mental examinations, and fill out all the forms, and talk to all the welfare counselors and inspectors every week in order to qualify as Unemployed, and then line up every day for the ration stamps and the dole. Simon thought I ought to go to work as usual. I tried to, but I couldn't. He had felt very hot to the touch when I kissed him good-bye. I went instead and got a black-market doctor. A girl at the factory had recommended her, for an abortion, if I ever wanted one without going through the regulation two years of sex-depressant drugs the fed-meds make you take when they give you an abortion. She was a jeweler's assistant in a shop on Alder Street, and the girl said she was convenient because if you didn't have enough cash, you could leave something in pawn at the jeweler's as payment. Nobody ever does have enough cash, and of course credit cards aren't worth much on the black market.

The doctor was willing to come at once, so we rode home on the bus together. She gathered very soon that Simon and I were married, and it was funny to see her look at us and smile like a cat. Some people love illegality for its own sake. Men, more often than women. It's men who make laws, and enforce them, and break them, and think the whole performance is wonderful. Most women would rather just ignore them. You could see that this woman, like a man, actually enjoyed breaking them. That may have been what put her into an illegal business in the first place, a preference for the shady side. But there was more to it than that. No doubt she'd wanted to be a doctor too; and the Federal Medical Association doesn't admit women into the medical schools. She probably got her training as some other doctor's private pupil, under the counter. Very much as Simon learned mathematics, since the universities don't teach much but Business Administration and Advertising and Media Skills anymore. However she learned it, she seemed to know her stuff. She fixed up a kind of homemade traction device for Simon very handily and informed him that if he did much more walking for two months he'd be crippled the rest of his life, but if he behaved himself he'd just be more or less lame. It isn't the kind of thing you'd expect to be grateful for being told, but we both were. Leaving, she gave me a bottle of about two hundred plain white pills, unlabeled. "Aspirin," she said. "He'll be in a good deal of pain off and on for weeks."

I looked at the bottle. I had never seen aspirin before, only the Super-Buffered Pane-Gon and the Triple-Power N-L-G-Zic and the Extra-Strength Apansprin with the miracle ingredient more doctors recommend, which the fed-meds always give you prescriptions for, to be filled at your FMA-approved private enterprise friendly drugstore at the low, low prices established by the Pure Food and Drug Administration in order to inspire competitive research.

"Aspirin," the doctor repeated. "The miracle ingredient more doctors recommend." She cat-grinned again. I think she liked us because we were living in sin. That bottle of black-market aspirin was probably worth more than the old Navajo bracelet I pawned for her fee.

I went out again to register Simon as temporarily domiciled at my address and to apply for Temporary Unemployment Compensation ration stamps for him. They only give them to you for two weeks and you have to come every day; but to register him as Temporarily Disabled meant getting the signatures of two fed-meds, and I thought I'd rather put that off for a while. It took three hours to go through the lines and get the forms he would have to fill out, and to answer the 'crats' questions about why he wasn't there in person. They smelled something fishy. Of course it's hard for them to prove that two people are married and aren't just adultering if you move now and then and your friends help out by sometimes registering one of you as living at their address; but they had all the back files on both of us and it was obvious that we had been around each other for a suspiciously long time. The State really does make things awfully hard for itself. It must have been simpler to enforce the laws back when marriage was legal and adultery was what got you into trouble. They only had to catch you once. But I'll bet people broke the law just as often then as they do now.

The lantern-creatures came close enough at last that we could see not only their light, but their bodies in the illumination of their light. They were not pretty. They were dark colored, most often a dark red, and they were all mouth. They ate one another whole. Light swallowed light all swallowed together in the vaster mouth of the darkness. They moved slowly, for nothing, however small and hungry, could move fast under that weight, in that cold. Their eyes, round with fear, were never closed. Their bodies were tiny and bony behind the gaping jaws. They wore queer, ugly decorations on their lips and skulls: fringes, serrated wattles, feather-like fronds, gauds, bangles, lures. Poor little sheep of the deep pastures! Poor ragged, hunchjawed dwarfs squeezed to the bone by the weight of the darkness, chilled to the bone by the cold of the darkness, tiny monsters burning with bright hunger, who brought us back to life!

Occasionally, in the wan, sparse illumination of one of the lantern-creatures, we caught a momentary glimpse of other, large, unmoving shapes: the barest suggestion, off in the distance, not of a wall, nothing so solid and certain as a wall, but of a surface, an angle. . . . Was it there?

Or something would glitter, faint, far off, far down. There was no use trying to make out what it might be. Probably it was only a fleck of sediment, mud, or mica, disturbed by a struggle between the lantern-creatures, flickering like a bit of diamond dust as it rose and settled slowly. In any case, we could not move to go see what it was. We had not even the cold, narrow freedom of the lantern-creatures. We were immobilized, borne down, still shadows among the half-guessed shadow walls. Were we there?

The lantern-creatures showed no awareness of us. They passed before us, among us, perhaps even through us—it was impossible to be sure. They were not afraid, or curious.

Once something a little larger than a hand came crawling near, and for a moment we saw quite distinctly the clean angle where the foot of a wall rose from the pavement, in the glow cast by the crawling creature, which was covered with a foliage of plumes, each plume dotted with many tiny, bluish points of light. We saw the pavement beneath the creature and the wall beside it, heartbreaking in its exact, clear linearity, its opposition to all that was fluid, random, vast, and void. We saw the creature's claws, slowly reaching out and retracting like small stiff fingers, touch the wall. Its plumage of light quivering, it dragged itself along and vanished behind the corner of the wall.

So we knew that the wall was there; and that it was an outer wall, a housefront, perhaps, or the side of one of the towers of the city.

We remembered the towers. We remembered the city. We had forgotten it. We had forgotten who we were; but we remembered the city, now.

When I got home, the FBI had already been there. The computer at the police precinct where I registered Simon's address must have flashed it right over to the computer at the FBI building. They had questioned Simon for about an hour, mostly about what he had been doing during the twelve days it took him to get from the Camp to Portland. I suppose they thought he had flown to Peking or something. Having a police record in Walla Walla for hitchhiking helped him establish his story. He told me that one of them had gone to the bathroom. Sure enough I found a bug stuck on the top of the bathroom door frame. I left it, as we figured it's really better to leave it when you know you have one, than to take it off and then never be sure they haven't planted another one you don't know about. As Simon said, if we felt we had to say something unpatriotic we could always flush the toilet at the same time.

I have a battery radio—there are so many work stoppages because of power failures, and days the water has to be boiled, and so on, that you really have to have a radio to save wasting time and dying of typhoid—and he turned it on while I was making supper on the Primus. The six o'clock All-American Broadcasting Company news announcer announced that peace was at hand in Uruguay, the president's confidential aide having been seen to smile at a passing blonde as he left the 613th day of the secret negotiations in a villa outside Katmandu. The war in Liberia was going well; the enemy said they had shot down seventeen American planes but the Pentagon said we had shot down twenty-two enemy planes, and the capital city—I forget its name, but it hasn't been inhabitable for seven years anyway—was on the verge of being recaptured by the forces of freedom. The police action in Arizona was also successful. The Neo-Birch insurgents in Phoenix could not hold out much longer against the massed might of the American army and air force, since their underground supply of small tactical nukes from the Weathermen in Los Angeles had been cut off. Then there was an advertisement for Fed-Cred cards and a commercial for the Supreme Court: "Take your legal troubles to the Nine Wise Men!" Then there was something about why tariffs had gone up, and a report from the stock market, which had just closed at over two thousand, and a commercial for U.S. Government canned water, with a catchy little tune: "Don't be sorry when you drink/It's not as healthy as you think/Don't you think you really ought to/Drink coo-ool, puu-uure USG water?"—with three sopranos in close harmony on the last line. Then, just as the battery began to give out and his voice was dying away into a faraway tiny whisper, the announcer seemed to be saying something about a new continent emerging.

"What was that?"

"I didn't hear," Simon said, lying with his eyes shut and his face pale and sweaty. I gave him two aspirins before we ate. He ate little, and fell asleep while I was washing the dishes in the bathroom. I had been going to practice, but a viola is fairly wakeful in a one-room apartment. I read for a while instead. It was a best seller Janet had given me when she left. She thought it was very good, but then she likes Franz Liszt too. I don't read much since the libraries were closed down, it's too hard to get books; all you can buy is best sellers. I don't remember the title of this one; the cover just said "Ninety Million Copies in Print!!!" It was about small-town sex life in the last century, the dear old 1970s when there weren't any problems and life was so simple and nostalgic. The author squeezed all the naughty thrills he could out of the fact that all the main characters were married. I looked at the end and saw that all the married couples shot each other after all their children became schizophrenic hookers, except for one brave pair that divorced and then leapt into bed together with a clear-eyed pair of government-employed lovers for eight pages of healthy group sex as a brighter future dawned. I went to bed then, too. Simon was hot, but sleeping quietly. His breathing was like the sound of soft waves far away, and I went out to the dark sea on the sound of them.

I used to go out to the dark sea, often, as a child, falling asleep. I had almost forgotten it with my waking mind. As a child all I had to do was stretch out and think, "the dark sea . . . the dark sea . . ." and soon enough I'd be there, in the great depths, rocking. But after I grew up it only happened rarely, as a great gift. To know the abyss of the darkness and not to fear it, to entrust oneself to it and whatever may arise from it—what greater gift?

We watched the tiny lights come and go around us, and doing so, we gained a sense of space and of direction—near and far, at least, and higher and lower. It was that sense of space that allowed us to become aware of the currents. Space was no longer entirely still around us, suppressed by the enormous pressure of its own weight. Very dimly we were aware that the cold darkness moved, slowly, softly, pressing against us a little for a long time, then ceasing, in a vast oscillation. The empty darkness flowed slowly along our unmoving unseen bodies, along them, past them, perhaps through them; we could not tell.

Where did they come from, those dim, slow, vast tides? What pressure or attraction stirred the deeps to these slow drifting movements? We could not understand that; we could only feel their touch against us, but in straining our sense to guess their origin or end, we became aware of something else: something out there in the darkness of the great currents: sounds. We listened. We heard.

So our sense of space sharpened and localized to a sense of place. For sound is local, as sight is not. Sound is delimited by silence; and it does not rise out of the silence unless it is fairly close, both in space and in time. Though we stand where once the singer stood we cannot hear the voice singing; the years have carried it off on their tides, submerged it. Sound is a fragile thing, a tremor, as delicate as life itself. We may see the stars, but we cannot hear them. Even were the hollowness of outer space an atmosphere, an ether that transmitted the waves of sound, we could not hear the stars; they are too far away. At most, if we listened we might hear our own sun, all the mighty, roiling, exploding storm of its burning, as a whisper at the edge of hearing.

A sea wave laps one's feet: It is the shock wave of a volcanic eruption on the far side of the world. But one hears nothing.

A red light flickers on the horizon: It is the reflection in smoke of a city on the distant mainland, burning. But one hears nothing.

Only on the slopes of the volcano, in the suburbs of the city, does one begin to hear the deep thunder, and the high voices crying.

Thus, when we became aware that we were hearing, we were sure that the sounds we heard were fairly close to us. And yet we may have been quite wrong. For we were in a strange place, a deep place. Sound travels fast and far in the deep places, and the silence there is perfect, letting the least noise be heard for hundreds of miles.

And these were not small noises. The lights were tiny, but the sounds were vast: not loud, but very large. Often they were below the range of hearing, long slow vibrations rather than sounds. The first we heard seemed to us to rise up through the currents from beneath us: immense groans, sighs felt along the bone, a rumbling, a deep uneasy whispering.

Later, certain sounds came down to us from above, or borne along the endless levels of the darkness, and these were stranger yet, for they were music. A huge, calling, yearning music from far away in the darkness, calling not to us. Where are you? I am here.

Not to us.

They were the voices of the great souls, the great lives, the lonely ones, the voyagers. Calling. Not often answered. Where are you? Where have you gone?

But the bones, the keels and girders of white bones on icy isles of the South, the shores of bones did not reply.

Nor could we reply. But we listened, and the tears rose in our eyes, salt, not so salt as the oceans, the world-girdling deep bereaved currents, the abandoned roadways of the great lives; not so salt, but warmer.

I am here. Where have you gone?

No answer.

Only the whispering thunder from below.

But we knew now, though we could not answer, we knew because we heard, because we felt, because we wept, we knew that we were; and we remembered other voices.

Max came the next night. I sat on the toilet lid to practice, with the bathroom door shut. The FBI men on the other end of the bug got a solid half-hour of scales and doublestops, and then a quite good performance of the Hindemith unaccompanied viola sonata. The bathroom being very small and all hard surfaces, the noise I made was really tremendous. Not a good sound, far too much echo, but the sheer volume was contagious, and I played louder as I went on. The man up above knocked on his floor once; but if I have to listen to the weekly All-American Olympic Games at full blast every Sunday morning from his TV set, then he has to accept Paul Hindemith coming up out of his toilet now and then.

When I got tired, I put a wad of cotton over the bug and came out of the bathroom half-deaf. Simon and Max were on fire. Burning, unconsumed. Simon was scribbling formulae in traction, and Max was pumping his elbows up and down the way he does, like a boxer, and saying, "The e-lec-tron emis-sion . . ." through his nose, with his eyes narrowed, and his mind evidently going light-years per second faster than his tongue, because he kept beginning over and saying "The e-lec-tron emis-sion . . ." and pumping his elbows.

Intellectuals at work are very strange to look at. As strange as artists. I never could understand how an audience can sit there and *look* at a fiddler rolling his eyes and biting his tongue, or a horn player collecting spit, or a pianist like a black cat strapped to an electrified bench, as if what they *saw* had anything to do with the music.

I damped the fires with a quart of black-market beer—the legal kind is better, but I never have enough ration stamps for beer; I'm not thirsty enough to go without eating—and gradually Max and Simon cooled down. Max would have stayed talking all night, but I drove him out because Simon was looking tired.

I put a new battery in the radio and left it playing in the bathroom, and blew out the candle and lay and talked with Simon; he was too excited to sleep. He said that Max had solved the problems that were bothering them before Simon was sent to Camp, and had fitted Simon's equations to (as Simon put it) the bare facts, which means they have achieved "direct energy conversion." Ten or twelve people have worked on it at different times since Simon published the theoretical part of it when he was twenty-two. The physicist Ann Jones had pointed out right away that the simplest practical application of the theory would be to build a "sun tap," a device for collecting and storing solar energy, only much cheaper and better than the USG Sola-Heetas that some rich people have on their houses. And it would have been simple only they kept hitting the same snag. Now Max has got around the snag.

I said that Simon published the theory, but that is inaccurate. Of course he's never been able to publish any of his papers in print; he's not a federal employee and doesn't have a government clearance. But it did get circulated in what the scientists and poets call Sammy's-dot, that is, just handwritten or hectographed. It's an old joke that the FBI arrests everybody with purple fingers, because they have either been hectographing Sammy's-dots, or they have impetigo.

Anyhow, Simon was on top of the mountain that night. His true joy is in the pure math; but he had been working with Clara and Max and the others in this effort to materialize the theory for ten years, and a taste of material victory is a good thing, once in a lifetime.

I asked him to explain what the sun tap would mean to the masses, with me as a representative mass. He explained that it means we can tap solar energy for power, using a device that's easier to build than a jar battery. The efficiency and storage capacity are such that about ten minutes of sunlight will power an apartment complex like ours, heat and lights and elevators and all, for twenty-four hours; and no pollution, particulate, thermal, or radioactive. "There isn't any danger of using up the sun?" I asked. He took it soberly—it was a stupid question, but after all not so long ago people thought there wasn't any danger of using up the earth—and said no, because we wouldn't be pulling out energy, as we did when we mined and lumbered and split atoms, but just using the energy that comes to us anyhow, as the plants, the trees and grass and rosebushes always have done. "You could call it Flower Power," he said. He was high, high up on the mountain, ski-jumping in the sunlight.

"The State owns us," he said, "because the corporative State has a monopoly on power sources, and there's not enough power to go around. But now, anybody could build a generator on their roof that would furnish enough power to light a city."

I looked out the window at the dark city.

"We could completely decentralize industry and agriculture. Technology could serve life instead of serving capital. We could each run our own life. Power is power! . . . The State is a machine. We could unplug the machine, now. Power corrupts; absolute power corrupts absolutely. But that's true only when there's a price on power. When groups can keep the power to themselves; when they can use physical power-to in order to exert spiritual power-over; when might makes right. But if power is free? If everybody is equally mighty? Then everybody's got to find a better way of showing that he's right. . . ."

"That's what Mr. Nobel thought when he invented dynamite," I said. "Peace on earth."

He slid down the sunlit slope a couple of thousand feet and stopped beside me in a spray of snow, smiling. "Skull at the banquet," he said, "finger writing on the wall. Be still! Look, don't you see the sun shining on the Pentagon, all the roofs are off, the sun shines at last into the corridors of power . . . And they shrivel up, they wither away. The green grass grows through the carpets of the Oval Room, the Hot Line is disconnected for nonpayment of the bill. The first thing we'll do is build an electrified fence outside the electrified fence around the White House. The inner one prevents unauthorized persons from getting in. The outer one will prevent authorized persons from getting out. . . ."

Of course he was bitter. Not many people come out of prison sweet.

But it was cruel, to be shown this great hope, and to know that there was no hope for it. He did know that. He knew it right along. He knew that there was no mountain, that he was skiing on the wind.

The tiny lights of the lantern-creatures died out one by one, sank away. The distant lonely voices were silent. The cold, slow currents flowed, vacant, only shaken from time to time by a shifting in the abyss.

It was dark again, and no voice spoke. All dark, dumb, cold.

Then the sun rose.

It was not like the dawns we had begun to remember: the change, manifold and subtle, in the smell and touch of the air; the hush that, instead of sleeping, wakes, holds still, and waits; the appearance of objects, looking gray, vague, and new, as if just created—distant mountains against the eastern sky, one's own hands, the hoary grass full of dew and shadow, the fold in the edge of a curtain hanging by the window—and then, before one is quite sure that one is indeed seeing again, that the light has returned, that day is breaking, the first, abrupt, sweet stammer of a waking bird. And after that the chorus, voice by voice: This is my nest, this is my tree, this is my egg, this is my day, this is my life, here I am, here I am, hurray for me! I'm here!—No, it wasn't like that at all, this dawn. It was completely silent, and it was blue.

In the dawns that we had begun to remember, one did not become aware of the light itself, but of the separate objects touched by the light, the things, the world. They were there, visible again, as if visibility were their own property, not a gift from the rising sun.

In this dawn, there was nothing but the light itself. Indeed there was not even light, we would have said, but only color: blue.

There was no compass bearing to it. It was not brighter in the east. There was no east or west. There was only up and down, below and above. Below was dark. The blue light came from above. Brightness fell. Beneath, where the shaking thunder had stilled, the brightness died away through violet into blindness.

We, arising, watched light fall.

In a way it was more like an ethereal snowfall than like a sunrise. The light seemed to be in discrete particles, infinitesimal flecks, slowly descending, faint, fainter than flecks of fine snow on a dark night, and tinier; but blue. A soft, penetrating blue tending to the violet, the color of the shadows in an iceberg, the color of a streak of sky between gray clouds on a winter afternoon before snow: faint in intensity but vivid in hue: the color of the remote, the color of the cold, the color farthest from the sun.

On Saturday night they held a scientific congress in our room. Clara and Max came, of course, and the engineer Phil Drum and three others who had worked on the sun tap. Phil Drum was very pleased with himself because he had actually built one of the things, a solar cell, and brought it along. I don't think it had occurred to either Max or Simon to build one. Once they knew it could be done they were satisfied and wanted to get on with something else. But Phil unwrapped his baby with a lot of flourish, and people made remarks like, "Mr. Watson, will you come here a minute," and "Hey, Wilbur, you're off the ground!" and "I say, nasty mould you've got there, Alec; why don't you throw it out?" and "Ugh, ugh, burns, burns, wow, ow," the latter from Max, who does look a little pre-Mousterian. Phil explained that he had exposed the cell for one minute at four in the afternoon up in Washington Park during a light rain. The lights were back on on the West Side since Thursday, so we could test it without being conspicuous.

We turned off the lights, after Phil had wired the table-lamp cord to the cell. He turned on the lamp switch. The bulb came on, about twice as bright as before, at its full forty watts—city power of course was never full strength. We all looked at it. It was a dime-store table lamp with a metallized gold base and a white plasticloth shade.

"Brighter than a thousand suns," Simon murmured from the bed.

"Could it be," said Clara Edmonds, "that we physicists have known sin—and have come out the other side?"

"It really wouldn't be any good at all for making bombs with," Max said dreamily.

"Bombs," Phil Drum said with scorn. "Bombs are obsolete. Don't you realize that we could move a mountain with this kind of power? I mean pick up Mount Hood, move it, and set it down. We could thaw Antarctica, we could freeze the Congo. We could sink a continent. Give me a fulcrum and I'll move the world. Well, Archimedes, you've got your fulcrum. The sun."

"Christ," Simon said, "the radio, Belle!"

The bathroom door was shut and I had put cotton over the bug, but he was right; if they were going to go ahead at this rate, there had better be some added static. And though I liked watching their faces in the clear light of the lamp—they all had good, interesting faces, well worn, like the handles of wooden tools or the rocks in a running stream—I did not much want to listen to them talk tonight. Not because I wasn't a scientist; that made no difference. And not because I disagreed or disapproved or disbelieved anything they said. Only because it grieved me terribly, their talking. Because they couldn't rejoice aloud over a job done and a discovery made, but had to hide there and whisper about it. Because they couldn't go out into the sun.

I went into the bathroom with my viola and sat on the toilet lid and did a long set of sautillé exercises. Then I tried to work at the Forrest trio, but it was too assertive. I played the solo part from *Harold in Italy*, which is beautiful, but it wasn't quite the right mood either. They were still going strong in the other room. I began to improvise.

After a few minutes in E-minor the light over the shaving mirror began to flicker and dim; then it died. Another outage. The table lamp in the other room did not go out, being connected with the sun, not with the twenty-three atomic fission plants that power the Greater Portland Area. Within two seconds somebody had switched it off too, so that we shouldn't be the only window in the West Hills left alight; and I could hear them rooting for candles and rattling matches. I went on improvising in the dark. Without light, when you couldn't see all the hard shiny surfaces of things, the sound seemed softer and less muddled. I went on, and it began to shape up. All the laws of harmonics sang together when the bow came down. The strings of the viola were the cords of my own voice, tightened by sorrow, tuned to the pitch of joy. The melody created itself out of air and energy, it raised up the valleys, and the mountains and hills were made low, and the crooked straight, and the rough places plain. And the music went out to the dark sea and sang in the darkness, over the abyss.

When I came out they were all sitting there and none of them was talking. Max had been crying. I could see little candle flames in the tears around his eyes. Simon lay flat on the bed in the shadows, his eyes closed. Phil Drum sat hunched over, holding the solar cell in his hands.

I loosened the pegs, put the bow and the viola in the case, and cleared my throat. It was embarrassing. I finally said, "I'm sorry."

One of the women spoke: Rose Abramski, a private student of Simon's, a big shy woman who could hardly speak at all unless it was in mathematical symbols. "I saw it," she said. "I saw it. I saw the white towers, and the water streaming down their sides, and running back down to the sea. And the sunlight shining in the streets, after ten thousand years of darkness."

"I heard them," Simon said, very low, from the shadow. "I heard their voices."

"Oh, Christ! Stop it" Max cried out, and got up and went blundering out into the unlit hall, without his coat. We heard him running down the stairs.

"Phil," said Simon, lying there, "could we raise up the white towers, with our lever and our fulcrum?"

After a long silence Phil Drum answered, "We have the power to do it."

"What else do we need?" Simon said. "What else do we need, besides power?"

Nobody answered him.

The blue changed. It became brighter, lighter, and at the same time thicker: impure. The ethereal luminosity of blue-violet turned to turquoise, intense and opaque. Still we could not have said that everything was now turquoise colored, for there were still no things. There was nothing, except the color of turquoise.

The change continued. The opacity became veined and thinned. The dense, solid color began to appear translucent, transparent. Then it seemed as if we were in the heart of a sacred jade, or the brilliant crystal of a sapphire or an emerald.

As at the inner structure of a crystal, there was no motion. But there was something, now, to see. It was as if we saw the motionless, elegant inward structure of the molecules of a precious stone. Planes and angles appeared about us, shadowless and clear in that even, glowing, blue-green light.

These were the walls and towers of the city, the streets, the windows, the gates.

We knew them, but we did not recognize them. We did not dare to recognize them. It had been so long. And it was so strange. We had used to dream, when we lived in this city. We had lain down, nights, in the rooms behind the windows, and slept, and dreamed. We had all dreamed of the ocean, of the deep sea. Were we not dreaming now?

Sometimes the thunder and tremor deep below us rolled again, but it was faint now, far away; as far away as our memory of the thunder and the tremor and the fire and the towers falling, long ago. Neither the sound nor the memory frightened us. We knew them.

The sapphire light brightened overhead to green, almost green-gold. We looked up. The tops of the highest towers were hard to see, glowing in the radiance of light. The streets and doorways were darker, more clearly defined.

In one of those long, jewel-dark streets something was moving— something not composed of planes and angles, but of curves and arcs. We all turned to look at it, slowing, wondering as we did so at the slow ease of our own motion, our freedom. Sinuous, with a beautiful flowing, gathering, rolling movement, now rapid and now tentative, the thing drifted across the street from a blank garden wall to the recess of a door. There, in the dark blue shadow, it was hard to see for a while. We watched. A pale blue curve appeared at the top of the doorway. A second followed, and a third. The moving thing clung or hovered there, above the door, like a swaying knot of silvery cords or a boneless hand, one arched finger pointing carelessly to something above the lintel of the door, something like itself, but motionless—a carving. A carving in jade light. A carving in stone.

Delicately and easily the long curving tentacle followed the curves of the carved figure, the eight petal-limbs, the round eyes. Did it recognize its image?

The living one swung suddenly, gathered its curves in a loose knot, and darted away down the street, swift and sinuous. Behind it a faint cloud of darker blue hung for a minute and dispersed, revealing again the carved figure above the door: the sea-flower, the cuttlefish, quick, great-eyed, graceful, evasive, the cherished sign, carved on a thousand walls, worked into the design of cornices, pavements, bandles, lids of jewel boxes, canopies, tapestries, tabletops, gateways.

Down another street, about the level of the first-floor windows, came a flickering drift of hundreds of motes of silver. With a single motion all turned toward the cross street, and glittered off into the dark blue shadows.

There were shadows, now.

We looked up, up from the flight of silver fish, up from the streets where the jade-green currents flowed and the blue shadows fell. We moved and looked up, yearning, to the high towers of our city. They stood, the fallen towers. They glowed in the ever-brightening radiance, not blue or blue-green, up there, but gold. Far above them lay a vast, circular, trembling brightness: the sun's light on the surface of the sea.

We are here. When we break through the bright circle into life, the water will break and stream white down the white sides of the towers, and run down the steep streets back into the sea. The water will glitter in dark hair, on the eyelids of dark eyes, and dry to a thin white film of salt.

We are here.

Whose voice? Who called to us?

He was with me for twelve days. On January 28, the 'crats came from the Bureau of Health, Education, and Welfare and said that since he was receiving Unemployment Compensation while suffering from an untreated illness, the government must look after him and restore him to health, because health is the inalienable right of the citizens of a democracy. He refused to sign the consent forms, so the chief health officer signed them. He refused to get up, so two of the policemen pulled him up off the bed. He started to try to fight them. The chief health officer pulled his gun and said that if he continued to struggle he would shoot him for resisting welfare, and arrest me for conspiracy to defraud the government. The man who was holding my arms behind my back said they could always arrest me for unreported pregnancy with intent to form a nuclear family. At that, Simon stopped trying to get free. It was really all he was trying to do, not to right them, just to get his arms free. He looked at me, and they took him out.

He is in the Federal Hospital in Salem. I have not been able to find out whether he is in the regular hospital or the mental wards.

It was on the radio again yesterday, about the rising land masses in the South Atlantic and the Western Pacific. At Max's the other night I saw a TV special explaining about geophysical stresses and subsidence and faults. The U.S. Geodetic Service is doing a lot of advertising around town; the most common one is a big billboard that says IT'S NOT OUR FAULT! with a picture of a beaver pointing to a schematic map that shows how even if Oregon has a major earthquake and subsidence as California did last month, it will not affect Portland, or only the western suburbs perhaps. The news also said that they plan to halt the tidal waves in Florida by dropping nuclear bombs where Miami was. Then they will reattach Florida to the mainland with landfill. They are already advertising real estate for housing developments on the landfill. The president is staying at the Mile High White House in Aspen, Colorado. I don't think it will do him much good. Houseboats down on the Willamette are selling for $500,000. There are no trains or buses running south from Portland, because all the highways were badly damaged by the tremors and landslides last week, so I will have to see if I can get to Salem on foot. I still have the rucksack I bought for the Mount Hood Wilderness Week. I got some dry lima beans and raisins with my Federal Fair Share Super Value Green Stamp minimal ration book for February—it took the whole book—and Phil Drum made me a tiny camp stove powered with the solar cell. I didn't want to take the Primus, it's too bulky, and I did want to be able to carry the viola. Max gave me a half pint of brandy. When the brandy is gone I expect I will stuff this notebook into the bottle and put the cap on tight and leave it on a hillside somewhere between here and Salem. I like to think of it being lifted up little by little by the water, and rocking, and going out to the dark sea.

Where are you?
We are here. Where have you gone?

Young Love

Grania Davis

Among our possible/probable futures are some very depressing ones, as we've already seen. Still, what can overpopulation, lack of food and power sources, and rigid governmental controls avail against the euphoria of people in love? Very little, if they're lucky, as this clever and ironic story shows.

Grania Davis is a comparatively new writer who has published one "mainstream" novel, *Dr. Grass,* and has written a fantasy novel that will appear shortly.

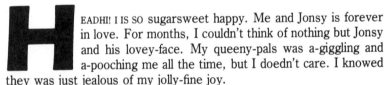

EADHI! I IS SO sugarsweet happy. Me and Jonsy is forever in love. For months, I couldn't think of nothing but Jonsy and his lovey-face. My queeny-pals was a-giggling and a-pooching me all the time, but I doedn't care. I knowed they was just jealous of my jolly-fine joy.

It were maybe ten months ago. A super-special day. Me and my queeny-pals, Mimi, Judy, and Sally gotted tickets to the beach, and we taked the rapid down super-early in the morning. It were a nice, bright, warmsy day, and it feeled jolly-fine to get away from the stuffy old commune for a bitsy.

Me and my queeny-pals hain't haved enough points for a outing for nearly two months before that, when we getted tickets for Golden Gate Park. But that were a real cold, blowy day.

So there we was, feeling super-spindly and wowsy. A-playing in the sand, and a-feeling of the sunny, and a-running in the shivery waves. And we was laughing and chittering, and smoking a little grassy. And Mimi alltimes so funny, when she feeling upper, she start mocking the commune-mommy:

"Come on now, queenies, line up for *bruncheon*. Do not push or *shove.* Do not take more food-a than you can *finish.* Wasters will get *demerits.* After bruncheon we will have bingo and checkers in the *aud.* Points for the *winners.* Demerits for *dragglers."*

When Mimi talk like the commune-mommy, it so hyster. We was all tearful with giggling, and getting sand in our mouths.

Soonly it were bruncheon time, and we was *starvy.* We dipped out the tokens what comed with our tickets, so we could get food-a at the beacheteria. We drawed straws, to see who haved to stand in liny to get it, and I losed. I groaned and chrised, but little doed I know it were my super-lucky day.

I glumphed along the beach with every's tokens, till I getted to the beacheteria, and there were a real *long* liny. I standed behind a old mommy and groaned and chrised somemore.

The singalong were playing "Riding on the Rapid" and "Old Man Moses." So I singed along, for a while, while the liny creeped up. Then I looked around, behind me, and feeled like I just won 100 points in the aud, cause behind me were the most lovey-faced tommy I never seed.

He gleamed at me, and I gleamed back. And soonly we forgetted all about the singalong and the liny, and just standed there, gleaming and gleaming.

Finally he said, "Hi, queeny, what's you name?"

My heart quicked up and I said, "Silvy, what's yours?"

And he said, "Jonsy."

And then we gleamed somemore, while the singalong played "Old Man Moses."

And then he said, "Where does you live?"

And I said, "At the Powell Street queeny-commune. Where does you live?"

And he said, "Oh, not so farsy, at the Eddy Street tommy-commune.

And then we gleamed somemore.

And then he said, "Maybe I could come to your aud, sometime, on fun-night, and we could have some fun."

And I said, "That would be headhi. Ours fun-night are on Friday, that tomarrio. You could come then."

But then the glumphy old mommy up ahead sharped, "Hey, you youngs, you is interrupting the singalong." So we quit chittering, and singed "Old Man Moses," but we still gleamed and gleamed.

Finally, the old mommy getted her food-a, and then it were my turn. I putted in my tokens and taked out four platies, and seed it were turkey-a, which are one of my super-yumyum favorites. I waited for Jonsy to get his, and we walked out together, in the warmsy sun.

They was some propers outside, like usual, reading newsy-bills to any what would listen. Some was from the Mother Mary commune, on Geary. And they was trying to get people to they Sunday lovelies. Other propers was from the Anti-Grass Group, and they was telling how grassy make the lungs all rotted, and how it should be against the law, like in the oldy days.

And they was somemore propers from the Real Food League, saying stuff about how food-a wreck brain cells and reflexes, so folks can't blink they eyes nomore.

But me and Jonsy was too deep in with each other to tune in on them. We jingled along, until we was nearly to my queeny-pals, and he said, "It were headhi chittering with you. Maybe we'll sees tomarrio."

And I said, "Jolly-fine."

And then he goed on to his tommy-pals. But I were thinking about him the whole day, and on the rapid, riding home, the singalong played "Old Man Moses," which maked my brain click right into before, and I singed so loud that my queeny-pals pooched me and giggled.

They clicked in that somesuch were weirdy with me, and wanted me to tell, but I just sitted at supper-time, chewing my stew-a and gleaming. But by sleepy-time, I couldn't seal it no more, so I telled. And Mimi mocked how the commune-mommy talked whenever any had a tommy guest, and that maked us all hyster in our room till lights-out.

We four was all so upped about it, the next day, we could hardly keep from hystering all through smart-time, which we do as in the morning. That day, we haved a cable-prog on how the Eskimos lived in the oldy days. Then the smarts-mommy readed us a newsy-bill what said how the white folks army were almost to Shanghai, which maked us clap and gleam. Then she turned to the singalong, what played "Hot Sunshine" and "Riding on the Rapid" and "Old Man Moses," and we all singed, though my brain were kind of buzzery.

At bruncheon, we haved bacon'eggs-a, what is very glumphy and rubbery, and not yumyum at all. We all groaned and chrised and Mimi mocked the Real Food League propers:

"This stuff is *poison*. It is all maked of *chemicals*. It is not meaned for human *beings*. It will rot your brains and *reflexes*. Become real folks, demand real *food!*"

But the bruncheon-mommy heared her and said how we was lucky to be in a nicey queeny-commune, with lots to eat, instead of being a freaky what couldn't find no room in a commune and gots to sleep in the streets, and are always hungry and eating garbage. Then the bruncheon-mommy give us each a demerit, what maked us hyster unhappily.

After bruncheon are play-time, and cause the day were warmsy, we doed it on the sun-roof, instead of the gym. Me and my queeny-pals played bangmitten against four queenies from another room, but we was so buzzery, they winned easy, and the play-mommy gived them each two points.

Then comed supper-time, and it were rosbeef-a, what are yumyum, but thiseve, my heart were quicking so fast, I couldn't hardly eat. Would he really come? Doed he really like me, or were he just pooching?

Finally it were time. Fun-time. The best time of the week. I doed my hair in fine curlies, and Judy letted me use some blue pawpaint. And Sally letted me wear her bestest tunic of red shinycloth, what she getted last year from all her points. I haved to for sure promise to be super-careful and not spill no punch-a on it. And I putted on some julies and some leggies and my queeny-pals said I were the most headhi queeny they never seen.

It were real hyster down in the aud. All the queenies from the whole commune was there and also a lot haved invited they tommy-pals from other communes and some haved invited they parents to come from the family-communes. Me and my queeny-pals hain't invited our parents for a long time, though we keeped thinking to do it soonly. But no juice for that *now*.

I goed over to the door of the aud where folks was waiting to get in. The aud-mommy only letted invited folks in, to keep out freakies. Were he there? Were he there? My heart quicked along.

Yes, he were there! There he were! And he gleamed when he seed me. And I gleamed right back. And after the aud-mommy letted him in, we just standed there, gleaming for a while.

Then the aud-mommy telled us to sit down and they showed a cartoon-prog what were real funny, about this dumdum cat, trying to catch this brainsy mouse, in the oldy days. And the mouse keeped on hitting the cat what gotted all grunchy and mangly, and other weirdy things what maked us hyster a lot.

And then we folded up the chairs, and all holded hands in a circle, and we doed folk dancies, like London Bridges and Here We Go Round the Rosy. But I couldn't hardly give them no juice cause of Jonsy being right next to me and a-holding of my hand, real tightsy, like no tommy never doed before, with his fingers slidded right up, between mine, and now and then a-squeezing and a-rubbing of them, so soonly my whole hand and arm was buzzering and I could feel the little brown curlies on his fingers, and rough places where his nails was bited, and it feeled so warm and good, like a platy of hot food-a.

And when the folk dancy were done, and the aud-mommy telled us to line up for punch-a and cake-a, he keeped ahold of my hand, and still rubbing and squeezing, till I were near hyster and the aud-mommy finally noticed and said we was to quit, or I'd get demerits.

So we drinked our punch-a and eated our cake-a, and I were super care not to spillsy on Sally's shinycloth. And then the singalong started and it were playing "Hot Sunshine" and "Old Man Moses," which was jolly-fine.

And then the aud-mommy readed us a special newsy-bill about how the white folks army were almost to Shanghai, what maked us gleam. But then fun-night were *over,* and all the guesties have to go away, what maked me feel super down, cept Jonsy gived my hand a quick, secret squeezy and whispered, "I got tickets for the ballsy on Wednesday. You wanna come?"

I getted so excity, I near hystered all over the shinycloth, and I said, "I sure does! That would be super-upper. No tommy never taked me ta the ballsy before!"

Then the aud-mommy helped him with his coat, and he gived my hand another squeezy and goed away. But I never feeled so headhi in my life, and I decided I were never gonna wash my hand again.

Oh, the week goed by so *super-slow.* Smart-time, with cable-progs on how birdies used to grow in eggs, and how Eskimos used to live in the oldy days. And the singalong. And bruncheons. Sometimes the food-a were yumyum, and sometimes it were glumphy. Play-time on the roof, or the gym, with bangmitten or pingypong. Then supper. Then game-time in the aud, with checkers or bingo, and the singalong, and then maybe a movie-prog with tommies and queenies holding hands and kissing, what maked me real hyster to think I doed that with Jonsy. And chittering with my queeny-pals. And lights-out.

Most times them things is jolly-fine. And I was glad I isn't one of them brainsy folks what thinks theys so upper, cause they gets to live in privapts, and eats real food sometimes and has privautos, and goes to privschools. They gots to spend all the day a-thinking and a-working and a-planning for the rest of us folks. They can't enjoy theyselves al-latimes, like me. Even the commune-mommies, what thinks theys so upper with they points and demerits and linies. Even them can't have as much fun, and doesn't get tickets out much moren me.

But this week I were wishing now I were a little brainsy, so I could think of something else cept *waiting to see Jonsy on Wednesday,* what were filling my whole brain.

But finally *Wednesday* comed, and I were near hyster the whole day, for fear he wouldn't come. But after supper, there he *were,* right at the door, and my heart roared like a rapid when I seed him. He showed the tickets to the door-mommy so I could get a pass to go, and she helped me with my coat. Headhi! Two outings in one week! I hain't never beed on so many. While we was walking to the rapid, he taked my hand again. My *other* hand, this time. What maked me hyster to think that now I couldn't wash neither hand nomore. And Jonsy asked how-come I were hystering, but I wouldn't tell.

And then he started to tell me how he weren't brainsy enough for school, of course, but he were maybe enough brainsy to pass the test for the army, and then he could have a semipriv room and more tickets for outings, and stuff like that. And he were asking how I'd like to have a tommy-pal what were brainsy enough for the army.

And I said I wouldn't like it, cause he'd have to work hard all a time, cleaning the streets and the rapid, and would maybe have to go to China.

But he said how most armytoms doesn't got to go to China, cause theys needed for all a jobbies here, what the robos can't do. The brainsy folks beed able to make robos to do most jobbies, but not ones where they has to move around by theyselves, like cleaning up, or watching folks like the mommies and daddies.

But Jonsy said how he thought it would be jolly-fine to walk around all day, doing something important, instead of staying in the stuffy old commune, with the commune-daddies telling him what to do.

And I said I doedn't like the commune-mommies, neither, but my queeny-pals was nice, and I sure hoped he doedn't got to go to China.

Then the rapid comed. And he taked my elbow to help me on. And I hystered to think I couldn't wash my elbow, neither. And there was two seats, what were a surprise, so we sitted down, and couldn't talk nomore, cause of the singalong, what were playing "Riding on the Rapid," and "Old Man Moses." But Jonsy putted his arm around my shoulder, what maked me get all red and sweaty, cause I could feel his muscles, all hard and strong, and his hand all a-rubbing of my shoulder. And my cheek a-leaning against his warmsy chest. I could feel the scratchycloth of his shirt against my cheek, and could even smell the soap and sweat and shave cream and other tommy-do, all mixed up, and a special, sugarsweet smell what were just himself. And I were feeling like a movie-prog star, until the rapid-daddy noticed us and told us to quit it, or he'd take our numbers for demerits.

So we sitted up and gleamed through the singalong. And I figured I'd *have* to wash my cheek and shoulder, else I'd get all pimply like.

At the ballsy park was more folks than I never seed before. The propers all a time tell us why we gots to eat food-a instead of real food is cause there's so much folks. But I never believed there was *so* much till now. I couldn't count them in a week.

And they is all drinking beer-a and punch-a, and sitting on rows and rows and *rows* of benches, piled high like a mountain, and all going in a big circle, round a little park. And in the park is a bunch a tommies in white leggies, and they shoulders maked *huge,* with maybe pillows in they tunics, which was red or white, and like potties on they heads. And they is throwing around a little bit of a ball and they is running and a-kicking and a-punching and a-hitting of each other, and Jonsy said how each side are trying to steal the ballsy for theyself, and them as manages to gets lots of points, but them as don't gets demerits. And that we was favoring the red tunics, but he didn't say why.

But then one of the white tunic tommies getted ahold of the ball, and started quicking along with it, up into the crowd, trying to get it out of the ballsy park. But some folks in they seats was trying to stop him and catch him and throw the ball back, while other folks was trying to stop *them,* and pretty soon there were a lot of fighting and yelling and folks was a-beating and a-stomping on each others.

And I getted kind of scaredy, but Jonsy laughed and said this were the funsy part and no one never getted too hurt, and besides it were headhi and pretty soon he were a-beating on some folks sitting near us, and they was a-beating back on him and I were hystering and trying to hide under the bench.

Then someone managed to throw the ball back into the park, and the tommies was fighting by theyselves somemore. And folks was watching and petting they sore places. And then, someone getted the ball again and folks was fighting somemore. And then, no one knowed where the ball were and so folks was running all around and into the park and a-grabbing and a-beating of each other and they was yelling and screaming and it doedn't seem so funsy to me. And Jonsy were gone someplace, a-fighting with the rest. And some old daddy falled back and stumbled over my legs, which I couldn't get all a way under the bench, and it were real cold and dirty under, so I started to hyster real loud and lots of other folks was hystering too.

And then a loud buzzerbell ringed and a voice said, from the singalong, *"The reds has taken the ballsy. I repeats, the reds has taken the ballsy. Go back to your benches, everyone. The reds has taken the ballsy. The game is over. Go back to your benches. The reds has taken the ballsy."*

And so on, while folks was sitting down again. And some was hystering happy, and some was unhappy cause they was all mangly or cause the reds winned all the points.

And I were worrying about Jonsy finding me again, but then I seed his lovey-face and it were all grunchy and blubby, and his clothes was all mangly, but he were all upper cause his side winned. And he helped me out from under the bench and said, "Weren't that jolly-fine?"

And I said, "Headhi," cause I were so glad to see him again.

And he said, "Its jolly-fine you thinks so, cause lots queenies too scaredy of the ballsy." And he gived my hand another squeeze.

212

For sure hearing him say that maked me feel sugarsweet, and I doedn't even care that my tunic and leggies was all torn and dirty and there were a grunchy on my ankle.

On the way back to the rapid, Jonsy putted his arm around my shoulder again, real super-tight, and his lovey-body were even warmer now cause of all the fighting and sweating, and he were breathing hard.

The rapid was super-crowded, cause of every going home from the ballsy. Folks was a-pushing and a-shoving, and lots was still hystering from being hurt or cause they side had losed. But the rapid-daddy said to quiet down, or we'd all get demerits. And there was no seats and we was packed standing, tight as could be, but we doedn't mind, cause it gived Jonsy a chance to hug me hard.

Then a weirdy thing happened. The singalong were playing "Old Man Moses," and it getted to the place where it says, "He climbed up the mountain." And the singalong getted *stuck* there, and it keeped singing, "He climbed up the mountain, he climbed up the mountain."

And for a while, no one gived it no juice, and we just keeped singing. "He climbed up the mountain, he climbed up the mountain."

And then some brainsy folks noticed and they starts to hyster and yell that the rapid weren't going nowhere and were stuck in the tunnel, and that howcome the singalong were stuck.

And other folks was hystering again, too, but the rapid-daddy yelled real loud that he would take our numbers for demerits sure, if we doedn't quit.

So soonly all was back to singing, "He climbed up the mountain, he climbed up the mountain, he climbed up the mountain, he climbed up the mountain."

And we keeped on singing it for a super-long time, and most folks was kind of downer about it, but not me and Jonsy. We just gleamed and gleamed at each other, and no one noticed how he haved both his arms around me, real tight.

And then, finally, the rapid gived a big jerk, and moved along again. And we getted to sing the next words of the song, "To chitter with Godsy, what gived him all the rules, so we wouldn't get demerits." And so on.

And the rapid-daddy gived us all passes for being late. When we getted off at the Powell Street stop, there were a tommy proper from the Real Food League. He were reading a newsy-bill about how eating food-a makes folks dumdum and ruins they reflexes so they eyes don't blink right, and they can't make babies, and sometimes they forgets how to breathe! This were making me feel real downer, but then Jonsy start to chitter with him.

"Howcome you knows this?" he asked the proper.

"Cause I is a brainsy, and gets to hear about it in school, and I doesn't like to see folks brains getting rotted."

"Well, what can we eat if we doesn't eat food-a?"

"We can eat real food, like in the oldy days."

"Where would we get the real food?"

"We gots to grow it in the parks."

"But how would we get to the parks without tickets, and how would folks know how to do the growing?"

"We gotta learn how again!"

"But how we gonna do that? And what is we gonna eat in the meantime?"

"I guess we'd eat food-a."

"Well, that what I's doing right now, so howcome I should do all this bothering? I doesn't think you is very brainsy at all!"

And then the proper getted real mad, and told Jonsy he were dumdum, and his brain were already rotted. And then Jonsy gived him a big grunchy in the face and said his brain were rotted, too. And then we runned away real fast, before someone seed us, and gotted us demerits for fighting. And I told Jonsy he were the most brainsy tommy I never meeted.

And he said, "Yeah, that's howcome I wanna get in the army, cause I is too brainsy to sit around the commune all a time."

And I said how I were sure he could pass the test. We seed some-more propers, from the Mother Mary commune, but we was too dozy to chitter with them. And we seed lots of freakies, laying around in the street, sleeping. I never beed out so late to see it before, even though the commune-mommy all a time tell us how we's so lucky our parents getted enough points to have us in a commune when we growed up, and how there aren't room for lots of folks what gots to sleep in the streets, and gots to stand in long lines for tiny bits of food-a with no flavor at all!

Some of them freakies waked up and tried to grab us, asking if we haved any food-a to give them, or any grass. But we telled them "No," and they goed away, cause they knowed it were true. But a couple of tommy freaks tried to pooch me, in a nasty way, and I were glad Jonsy were there, cause he gived them a kick, and they goed away.

It were after lights-out when we getted back to the commune, and we haved to bang super-loud at the door. While we was waiting to get letted in, Jonsy putted his both arms round me and pulled me super-close to him and kissed my curlies and said, "You is a sugarsweet queeny."

I thinked my head would buzz to bits with happy. When the commune-mommy comed to the door, she started to sharp, but I doedn't give her no juice. I just showed her the late pass from the rapid-daddy, and goed up to bed. But even though I were super-tired from the headhi day, I keeped clicking back to Jonsy, and I couldn't drowsy the whole night through.

The next day, I were drowsing at smart-time, and missed most of the cable-prog on how Eskimos lived in the oldy days. The smarts-mommy said if I doedn't quit, she'd send me to the nurse-mommy for a shot. That maked me hyster, unhappily. Folks mostly doesn't get sick now, like they doed in the oldy days, cause of all the vitas and trancs and antibods whats in the food-a. But sometimes the nurse-mommy gots to take care of folks grunchies, and also to give them a shot if they won't behave. So I tried harder to stay wakesy.

Anyhow, the next few weeks was mostly usual. Smart-time, bruncheon, play-time, supper, game-time and pooching, and chittering with my queeny-pals. The only thing that weren't usual were me, cause of all the time clicking into Jonsy. And fun-night, the best night of the week, and the only time I could see his lovey-face.

But it were hard now to give juice to the singalong, or the folksy, or the movie-prog, or the cake-a and punch-a, and all the other fun-night-do. Mostly we was busy trying to sit in a sneaky way, to hold hands without the aud-mommy seeing, or pretending to bump into each other, so he could give me a hug, or even a little kissy on the curlies, or to chitter together for a couple of minutes.

My queeny-pals noticed and pooched me a lot, but I knowed they wouldn't tell. Not even Mimi, whats so brainsy they is letting her take the test to be a commune-mommy. Nor even Judy, what were going to the Mother Mary lovelies a lot lately. And were all the time telling us to leave off smoking grass, and watching movie-progs and thinking of tommies, and learn to get upper from loving Jesus.

Judy were even thinking to put her name on the waity-list to *live* at the Mother Mary commune, what would be weirdy for us, cause we'd have someone new in our room. Maybe a youngling, fresh from her parents room, what would be all sobby, or, worse yet, a freaky from the street, what would be all smelly and dumdum and steal our pretties.

But anyhow, me and Jonsy was wishing and *wishing* how we could just be by ourselves, to chitter and touch and hug and kiss and, well, you *know*, queeny and tommy things, like in the movie-progs. And I were wondering if Jonsy were wishing the same thing. And I were meaning and chrising a lot about how we never gets to do what we wants, and my queeny-pals was saying how freakies gets to do what-ever *they* wants, with no mommies watching them, and I should be proper grateful. But I knowed they was just jealous.

Also, I were getting lots of demerits, from not giving enough atten-tion, and I knowed I wouldn't have enough points for no new pretties this year, what maked me glumph even more.

Then, one Friday night, the most sugarsweet thing in the whole world happened. Jonsy comed for fun-night, like regular. But I could tell, right away, he were headhi about something. First I thinked he maybe haved too much grass, or tickets for a outing. But it were even upper than that.

Minute he could, he whispered in my ear, "I passed the test for the army!"

"Oh, Jonsy," I hystered. The aud-mommy sharped me with her eyes. "You'll be able to get more tickets for outings," I said.

"Yeah, but there moren that," he said. "Soonly, I'll go to the army school, and learn how to clean the streets real good. Then I'll be ducted. And then, I can get me on the waity-list for a semipriv room at the army commune, *or,* Silvy, I can get me on the waity-list for a room at the army family-commune. We could get *married,* and jingle together every night, and chitter and hug and . . . and all kinds of jolly-fine things, just like the movie-progs. We could have a wedding in the aud, and maybe even a honey-trip, and stay headhi all the time!"

"Oh, Jonsy," I said, and I hystered so hard I couldn't stop, even when the singalong played "Old Man Moses," so I getted five demerits, but who cared, cause I were the upperest queeny in the aud.

The next week, at fun-night, the aud-mommy readed us a newsy-bill about how they isn't so much babies, nomore, cause of stricter controls, and so they will be less freakies sleeping in the streets in twenty years or so. And also how the white folks army were almost to Shanghai. And while all was gleaming and cheering, Jonsy whispered to me how there would maybe be a room in the army family-commune in maybe seven or eight months. And how we could get tickets for a *two-day* honey-trip in Yosemite Park, what are further away than any of us never been. And how a armytom can have punch-a and cake-a at they wedding, and they parents and pals can come and see. And lucky, all was cheering so loud from the newsy-bill, they doedn't hear me hyster.

Seven or eight months! It feeled like seven or eight years. I thinked I were dying from waiting for that sugarsweet day when me and Jonsy would be married folks and could do whatever we wanted.

In the meantime, every were usual. Smart-time, bruncheon, play-time, supper, game-time, lights-out. Just like always.

Only a couple differy things happened in that time. Like Mimi failed the test to be a commune-mommy, and were very sobby for a while.

Another thing what happened, were one time, all the food-a in this whole part of the city doedn't get sent to they communes. And we sitted two whole days in the aud, without nothing to eat. And they keeped telling us how it were OK, and the food-a would be here soonly, and they keeped the singalong and movie-progs on real loud. But we getted real starvy, and started to hyster, and finally we was all hystering so loud, you couldn't hardly hear "Old Man Moses" going. Finally the mommies telled us they didn't know howcome and we was all to do linies, cause we was going *outside,* to the depot where the freakies gets they food-a.

And we walked a long way. Longer than I never walked before. And we seed lots of broken-up buildings, and lots of other communes. And they folks was also marching out to the depot. And soonly they was a super-big crowd of folks, all over the street, and they was pushing and shoving, what aren't usual allowed, and I wondered howcome folks wasn't getting demerits. But then I seed how the mommies and daddies was also pushing and shoving cause they was starvy, too.

And soonly, they was so much folks on the street, that you couldn't keep no more linies, and I couldn't find my own queenies nomore, and I were in a super crowd of strange folks, all pushing real hard to try and get to the depot, but none knowed where it was, and so some was pushing one way, and some was pushing another.

And then one old mommy getted pushed down, and no folks would let her get up and she were yelling and screaming, and other folks was being pushed on top of her. And pretty soon, she were getting all grunchy and mangly. And this were happening to other folks, too. And all was hystering super-loud, cause of being starvy and scaredy, and not knowing the way to the depot.

And then some big privautos was coming along the streets with singalong speakers, and super-daddies was yelling, *"Go back to your communes. Food-a will be sent to your communes. Go back to your communes. Food-a will be sent to your communes. Go back to your communes. Food-a will be sent to your communes."*

So then, folks started trying to find the way back to they communes. But I doedn't know the way back and were hystering, superloud. And then, a smelly freaky queen grabbed my arm, and said if I were losed she would help me find my commune, but I haved to give her something. So I gived her my ear julies. She taken them, and runned away into the crowd. And I hystered even louder.

But then I seed a Mother Mary commune, and I thinked one of they propers could tell me the way back, so I goed inside, and they haved they own singalong, about Jesus and such, and good smellies in the air. And I sitted down, and singed for a while. But then I remembered how I was starvy and loosed, so I started to hyster. And then, the commune-daddy comed and said he would tell me the way home if I letted him look inside my leggies. So I doed that, and he telled me the way home.

When I finally getted back, lots was sitting in the aud, like before, singing "Hot Sunshine." But some haved manglies and grunchies and they tunics and leggies was torn. And some was still losed. I sitted down and singed, but were feeling awful buzzery from being so starvy.

But later on, a privauto comed to the door, and gived the mommy a big box of food-a. It weren't flavored, and looked kind of like a cleaning sponge, but we was glad to get it, and feeled a whole lot better, after.

Except for some of the queenies, what getted such bad manglies that they haved to go to the nurse-mommy. And three of them never comed back. And also, some of the queenies getted so losed in the crowd that they never comed back neither. So we getted some new queenies to fill they places. Lucky they was all sobby young ones from they parents communes and none was smelly freakies.

The only other differy thing what happened in them waiting months were Jonsy getted tickets to the museum, what I never beed to before, and were very excity to go.

All the way to the rapid, he holded my hand real tight and telled me about army school, and how he get to walk around in the streets all day, with a big bag on his shoulder and a broom and a stick with a point on the end, to pick up garbage. And he said how interesting it were seeing all the strange communes and folks, and stuff, and how he getted a super-tiny singalong to put in his ear, so he wouldn't get bored.

And he telled me how jolly-good it would be when we's married, with a room by weselves, every night. And our honey-trip, and maybe a outing every month, and maybe we could save points for a vacation trip someday. And how we'd get a baby, someday, just like the movie-progs, a real cute one, and we'd save points so it could go live in a queeny or tommy commune when it were twelve years old. And so on, till I nearly bursted with thrill.

And then, while we was waiting for the rapid, he putted his arms around me, super-tight, and gived me a rubby kiss, right on the mouth, and petted my back, real shivery like, and maked me feel all burny hot, and full of love-do.

The museum were jolly-fine. It were full of stuffed-up animals, showing how they used to live in the oldy days. Lions and tigers in the jungly, looking real scary. And birdies in trees with they eggies. And super-giant dinosaurs. And elephants and fishies and doggies and catties, what used to live right in communes with folks, and even super-teeny animals called buggies.

They was also stuffed-up folks what used to live in the oldy days. Eskimos, what I knowed right off, cause I once seed a cable-prog about them. And Americans and Chinese, and so on. All of them with funny, super-teeny communes what was called houses, and with trees all around, like it were Golden Gate Park, or something.

In the museum aud, we seed a scaredy film about all the awful things the red folks army do, and how they *eats* folks, and stuff. And we all gleamed a whole lot when the aud-daddy telled us not to worry, cause the white folks army were almost to Shanghai. And then they gived us punch-a and cake-a and played "Riding on the Rapid" and "Hot Sunshine" on the singalong.

When we walked back to the rapid, Jonsy telled me how he were glad to be in the army and how he wouldn't never let no red folks eat me. And he putted his arm around me again, and gived me another super-long and super-hard kiss. And I kissed him back, sugarsweet hard as I could.

Well, finally, after I couldn't hardly stand it nomore, Jonsy telled me the waiting were over. We could get our room in the family-commune. But first we'd get married, real good.

So the next day, I telled my counselor-mommy, and she were real glad I finded such a brainsy tommy, what's in the army, and getted tickets for a honey-trip in Yosemite, and all. And she said how we could get married next fun-night, and I could invite my parents.

I were glad about that, cause I hain't chittered with my parents in months, but when I phoned the Geary Street family-commune, where they lived, the daddy said how Mr. and Mrs. Andrews was still losed from the day when all a folks tried to get to the food-a depot, but if they getted finded again, he would tell them about my wedding. I hystered a little, but my counselor-mommy said they probably finded someplace else to live, or something, and I getted to choose chocolate or vanilla cake-a for my wedding, so I choosed chocolate, what are yumyum.

On that night, I weared my best tunic and julies and leggies and even some headpaint, and doed curlies up real fine. Jonsy comed with his three pals, and were wearing his new army tunic and leggies of bright green, what looked headhi. And his face and head, and even his eyebrowios was shaved. He looked so strong and handsome, I were stuffed up with lovedo from the sight.

The fun-night were just like usual, and I could hardly sit still, but then, just before the movie-prog, the aud-mommy getted up and said, "I got a special surprise for *you*. Our queeny-pal, Silvy, is gonna marry her tommy, *Jonsy*. And we got chocolate cake-a and cherry punch-a for a *treat*. Let's all sing the special wedding *song!*"

So they all singed,

> Happy wedding to you
> Happy wedding to you
> Happy wedding, dear Silvy and Jonsy,
> Happy wedding to you.

And then the aud-mommy said, "You is now man and wife."

And then we blowed out the candle on the cake-a, and Jonsy gived me a sugarsweet kiss, what maked me hyster to think every was looking.

And then they showed a excity movie-prog about this tom in the oldy days, with a mask, called the Lone Ranger, what killed baddy freakies. And Jonsy putted his arm around me for the whole thing.

When it were time for him to go home, he gived me another big kiss, and said, "I'll come and get you early tomarrio, for the honey-trip to Yosemite." And kissed me again, and the aud-mommy doedn't even tell him to quit, cause we was married folks now, and could do whatever we wanted. I were so buzzery that night, I couldn't drowse at all.

The next morning, right after bruncheon, I putted all my privy things in a bag, and he comed to get me. I said lots of hystery goodbyes to my queeny-pals, and even to the mommies, what I wouldn't never see nomore.

Jonsy helped me carry my bag. He said most all his privy things was already in our room at the family-commune. Our *own* room! I wouldn't see it till the next day, though, after our honey-trip.

We was going to take the rapid all the way to Yosemite, what takes nearly three hours! Yosemite are a super-big park. It got a mountain and a waterfall and lots of trees. And they is stuffed-up birdies living in the trees, just like the oldy days. And the stuffed-up birdies gots little singalongs inside them, cause oldy day birdies used to sing. But the stuffed-up birdies is better, cause they sing songs with words, what is more fun for folks to join in.

Inside Yosemite are a big family-commune, where folks from all northy Cal comes for they honey-trip, or, if they saves enough points, for they vacations.

The rapid ride were super-long. We was lucky to get some seats, after a hour. We was underground, of course, and couldn't see no scenery. But Jonsy said he thinked it were pretty much the same, all the way to Yosemite. Streets and communes and lots of broken-down stuff and queenies and tommies and parents and freakies. Lucky the singalong were playing "Hot Sunshine" and "Old Man Moses" and "Riding on the Rapid," so we doedn't get bored, and besides, Jonsy holded me close, all the way.

It were nearly dark when we getted there. But between the rapid stop and the commune was two trees, with the stuffed-up birdies singing "Hot Sunshine." They was also some Real Food League propers, saying how our reflexes was getting rotten, but we doedn't give them no juice.

We gived our tickets to the commune-daddy, what said we should go have supper. The communiteria were the biggest I never seed, with lots of strange folks chittering and laughing and hystering, happily. There were turkey-a for supper, what are my yumyum favorite. And after there were some bingo and singing, and then the daddy told us all it were bed-time, what maked me hyster to think of.

So we goed looking for our privroom. The first time I never been in one! We gotted to climb a bunch of stairs and go down a couple of halls, and keeped getting losed, but finally we finded it.

The room were little, but jolly-fine. It haved only two bunk-beds, instead of four, like my oldy room. And it haved a chair to sit on, and a pitcher of water-a and two cups. And it were right near the pissy. It doedn't have no window, but I doedn't care, cause I just wanted to look at my Jonsy.

Then we was both feeling a little buzzery and shy, and standed there, chittering and hystering a little. And finally, Jonsy said we should turn our backs and put our night tunics on. So we doed that, but it maked us hyster a whole lot, cause I never seed no tommy in his night tunic, and he never seed no queeny in one, neither.

Then he taked my hand, and we both sitted down on the lower bunk together. And he started to kiss me and hug me, and pat my back and my curlies and all kinds of other places, and I were kissing him and petting him, too, and it were just like a movie-prog.

Then he said, "I loves you, Silvy."

And I said, "I loves you super-much, and I feels headhi about us being married."

And he said, "I feels headhi, too. Just like a movie-prog."

And I said, "Me, too."

And he said, "Tomarrio, before we has to go back, we can take a walky, and we'll see the trees, and the waterfall, and the mountain, and we'll singalong with the birdies, and then we'll go back to our own family-commune and be together, just like now, doing whatever we want."

And I said, "That's the most sugarsweet thing in the world."

And then the speaker in the wall said, *"Its lights-out, go to your own bunk. No more chittering. Its lights-out. Go to your own bunk. No more chittering,"* and so on.

So then he said, "Well, we both haved a longy day, and better go dozy." So he climbed into the upper bunk. And I curled up, under the blanket on the lower bunk, what were super-comfy.

And he whispered, "Good night, lovey Silvy."

And I whispered back, "Good night, lovey Jonsy."

And then we both hystered to think we was chittering after lights-out, and was getting to sleep in the same room, together, like real married folks.

Then I heard him breathing and snory like, cause he were dozing, and even though I were headhi and buzzery, I started to feel dozy also. And super-glad, cause I were the luckiest queeny I knowed, and a real married folk, with the best tommy in the world, and tomarrio I could hear the stuffed-up birdies sing.

Whale Song

Terry Melen

We like to think that humans are the dominant intellectual species on Earth, but that's a matter of definition. We often think that big equals dumb, too, which may prove just the opposite, especially regarding whales. Who was here first, anyway? And who will be here last?

"Whale Song" is the first science fiction story by Terry Melen, who lives in Canada.

I

THE CONCUSSION is terrible.

Drifting pain.

I hang in a world of silence and blackness, and because the sea is never silent nor to me completely dark, I know that I have been blinded and my hearing taken from me.

But I am a land animal, so I think: Santa Lucia, Queen of Light, Lady of the Halo of Candles, guide me from the darkness. . . .

Consciousness returns, silence and pain; but this time there is light, blue light, the calm crystal blue of the level of the sea that I must inhabit, between the sunlit surface above and the black depths below. The sea is beautiful, the sea is home. When I am here I pity the land creatures in their dusty world of glaring sun and harsh, unfiltered colors.

Calmer now, I examine my situation and equipment. I hang at neutral buoyancy about thirty feet below the surface. My faceplate is cracked but not shipping water, the gill-pack on my back seems to be functioning properly, the water compressor under it still working to provide ballast. My right arm, however, is broken, as probably are several ribs, and my right leg is stiff and painful, all results of the collision with the saddle that the explosion caused. My nose is bloody and I can taste blood in my mouth, although whether this is from internal injuries or from biting my tongue I cannot tell. I am still completely deaf. The eliminatory slit on my wetsuit has popped open, and my right-hand glove has been torn off and dangles at the end of the sleeve, but otherwise the insulation appears to be intact. I do not feel cold. Power and communication telltales on my left arm have all gone red, however, so I am completely cut off from the outside. And where is Ka-dhrill?

The shark appears out of nowhere. It is a blue shark, some fourteen feet long, a dreadnought floating amid its flotilla of small striped pilot fish. It maintains a calm, almost lazy speed circling me, the powerful muscles on its great frame flexing slowly under sleek skin, its outline razor-sharp against the blue background haze. The five branchial clefts open and close slowly in the easy current, and just below them and under the shark's mouth, tiny remoras hang attached to it, waiting. Its great expressionless eye is forward near the long pointed snout, dark against the rich blue of its body, giving the shark an open-mouthed look of constant surprise. It moves with easy grace through the clear mid-ocean water, sending slow pressure waves toward me that I can sense more than feel. Its streamlining is extreme and utterly functional, and the long pectoral fins move only slightly to provide steering. Its stomach is flat and probably empty.

There is no certain way to predict what a shark will do, its size advantage over me is enormous, but the hereditary caution of its kind keeps it from attacking immediately, and it waits, considering. It is likely to continue circling for a while, gradually drawing closer and closer, then finally making its first attack. This could end in many ways; perhaps it will only bump against my leg—its method of tasting. This used to terrify divers who never realized that the disagreeable taste of the old neoprene wetsuits has probably saved more than one of them from losing a leg, although it is no sure deterrent to a hungry shark. Perhaps it will attack in earnest, and if I resist strongly enough it may retreat, or it could fly into a killing frenzy—in which case it will all be over. It may also give up the attack altogether and swim away, although this is unlikely. No, if its first attack fails it will continue to circle for a while and then make another, and another, until the end.

Noise is certain to attract its attention, so I hang silently, keeping it in sight, but making no unnecessary movements. It is closer now, its underslung jaw moving up and down, flexing perhaps in anticipation. I can see the old battle scars on its back, and the pressure wave is a palpable reality. With it come renewed sensations of pain in my arm and chest. I remain as still as possible and wait.

Time has passed; I'm not certain how much. I don't see the shark at first, but then I locate it circling farther out, moving faster now, the strange sideways motion of its powerful body more pronounced. Have I been unconscious? Has the shark already made a tasting run and then retreated to consider? Then I realize that I am nearer the surface now, the sunlight through the waves above casting strange, flickering patterns across the shark's back. This is wrong; the compressor on my back should be maintaining me at neutral buoyancy. Then I see the thin line of bubbles rising behind me; the gillpack takes oxygen directly from the water, but inside it there are several small bottles of compressed helium which allow me to dive down to six hundred feet, and evidently one or more of these, damaged in the explosion, has been leaking a slow giggle of bubbles, lightening my weight beyond the tolerance the compressor can handle. On the surface I will be completely helpless against the shark, if I am not that already.

Wait and watch. Several of the shark's dozen-odd pilot fish are swimming directly in front of it now, riding the pressure wave only inches from those huge jaws, but it pays them no attention. The eye is dark green and very large, seemingly out of proportion to the rest of its head. There is no sign of movement or personality in its stare, no hint to the complex set of patterns and influences that determine its behavior. A sonic resonator would drive it away, but of course I don't have one; it is the team that usually protects me, but they are gone, and I am rapidly becoming aware of my helplessness in this water-world without them.

Suddenly the shark gives a violent thrash of its notched tail and turns to charge at me head on. Instantly the symmetry is broken and there is only the ugly triangular cast of the three great fins around the gaping, tooth-lined mouth. Desperate, I twist around to put myself in a position to repel the attack. Pain ripples through me, and the utter futility of my gestures comes home on me. But then I remember how the attack will take place, and any thoughts of giving up without a fight leave. "Lucia," I say; "Santa Lucia."

Then, a bare couple of meters from me, the shark suddenly veers away and turns its left side to me. My head is spinning badly now and I don't understand what it is doing—then a gray streak flashes by me, buffeting me in its afterwave. It crashes with rending force into the side of the shark's head, crushing the branchial clefts, destroying the delicate gill structures, and impairing its ability to breathe. The shark wheels and twists savagely, emptying its bowels in shock and fury, and the dolphin has to dart away quickly to escape those massive jaws. But then another dolphin appears and drives its hard beak into the shark's pale abdomen, ripping apart delicate inner organs unsupported by ligaments as in most other animals. More team members appear and continue the attack, striking again and again in the same spot, giving their old enemy no chance to launch a successful counterattack. But the shark is intent only on fleeing now, deserted by its pilot fish, badly wounded. It is too late of course, for within minutes it will be dead. But it is outside my field of vision now, so I will not see its death throes. Which I do not mind in the least; I understand that the shark must die if I am to live, but I take no pleasure in watching.

Turrel, battle-scarred old dowager, leader of the dolphin team, darts about me, ruefully shaking her head as if in displeasure, but in reality carefully sonaring every inch of me and my equipment. Then she turns her great brown eye directly into my faceplate. She is probably speaking to me, using the trade language which is the only way men and dolphins can communicate, but with my hearing gone I cannot understand her. "Ka-dhrill . . ." I try to say, but the world has already become light and uniformly featureless, and with a quiet, faraway shudder I drift off into the greater darkness.

II

Waves lap against my back. I feel them, but can still hear nothing.

Two of the dolphins, flippers entwined under me, are supporting me face down on the surface, keeping the gill-pack out of the water to aid breathing. Their soft, rubbery bodies are warm even through the insulated wetsuit, and it is very comfortable hanging between them, the sun on my back and the blue-green darkness of the depths looming beneath me. They work their flukes slowly and in unison, bringing all three of us above the surface every couple of minutes to allow them to breathe, but otherwise trying to stay relatively still.

Kohleny, awash in the torrent of her love, begins to swing rapidly back and forth below us, almost panic-stricken, not knowing what to do to help, and sending pressure waves that make it difficult for the two supporting me to stay in position. Turrel intervenes, slapping Kohleny soundly across the head with her flipper and driving her away. She begins to circle farther out where her movements do not disturb us.

Turrel again moves close to my faceplate, and is probably saying something to me, although I cannot hear her.

"Ka-dhrill," I say in the whistling trade language, speaking into the breathing section of my faceplate. "Try to find Ka-dhrill; he may be injured." Turrel hesitates for a moment, perhaps wishing to handle the situation herself; but finally she turns and sends Kohleny to search for him, ordering Thine, a young male, to accompany her. Kohleny pauses for a few seconds, uncertain whether to go or not, then starts—

probably at a sharp rebuke from Turrel—and streaks away, Thine following close behind.

Turrel moves off to my left, holding most of her nine-foot body out of the water by the powerful thrashing of her tail. Returning, she wags her head quickly back and forth in front of me, not sonaring this time, but telling me with a gesture that she has picked up from me that the boat is nowhere in sight. Which is just as well since I do not feel much like continuing the battle. The herd, most likely scattered by the explosion, has had time to regroup, and my greatest fear is that the boat may have gone after them.

It was a small boat, an antiquated hydrofoil probably making a fast raid out of some South American port, hoping to secure a whale and haul it away before anyone was the wiser. This is illegal of course, both under U.N. law and the Sentients Treaty, and bears penalties up to life imprisonment. But the profits can be high also. Ka-dhrill and I had noticed them following the herd and had gone to investigate. The depth charges came down on top of us almost before we realized what they were. Ka-dhrill sounded, but not quickly enough to escape, and the concussion tore me loose from my harness and threw me against the saddle, possible injuring Ka-dhrill as well. If he is unconscious I am not sure what the dolphins—a third of his length and an even lesser fraction of his weight—will be able to do to help him.

Ka-dhrill is a true orc, *Orcinus orca*, and calling him a killer whale is both as accurate and as misleading as referring to me as a "killer ape." It is especially ironic that we should designate his species so, for the almost inbred affection that killer whales have for men despite the crimes of the past is still one of the great unsolved mysteries of the ocean. Ka-dhrill claims it is simply the ability of one sentient species to recognize and cooperate with another, and uses his own career as a good example. When he was still well short of his full manhood he applied for entrance at the Special Studies School at Kyoto University in Japan under a U.N. grant, although whether he was ordered to do so by his pod leader or whether he felt called upon to sacrifice to rescue his herd from the persistent pleas of the U.N. Sentients Committee he has never made clear. Once there, however, he studied for and received degrees in languages, marine biology, ichthyology, zoology, oceanology, delphinology, human psychology and physiology, and comparative anatomy as well as taking side courses in human beliefs and customs. The fact that he did so in shortly under three years is not really surprising; of the four sentient species thus far recognized on Earth, including man, killer whales have consistently proven to have the highest average I.Q.s. Ka-dhrill and I had collaborated on a paper before I left Sweden, but we first met at UCLA while taking postgraduate courses in ketaphonation, and when it came time to seek a U.N. marine research grant, it seemed only natural that we do so together. We were already recruiting our team when it came. The dolphins are nonspecialists, taught only to assist us in our experiments and observations, and to offer protection, mainly to me of course. Our field of study is the great sperm whale, *Physeter catodon,* and some sacrifices are demanded of both of us. I have to spend two-week periods inside an insulated wetsuit (metal shapes, such as a submarine, tend only to frighten the whales away), taking every third week off for rest and recuperation, and Ka-dhrill has to bear the indignity of the saddle. This contains most of our electronics equipment and apparatus as well as food concentrates, a gas supply, and a blowhole piece to allow Ka-dhrill to breathe underwater in an emergency. It is quite comfortable for him to wear, fitting on his back just in front of the tall dorsal fin and held in place by a type of static adhesion, but his hydrodynamic streamlining is highly specialized, and the drag from the saddle alone can cut his speed to a fraction of what it normally would be. The whales, however, when undisturbed usually cruise at not more than a few knots, so we have no difficulty in keeping up. Neither of us mind the inconveniences though; the insane butchery of the last century, even after it had been outlawed, has reduced the sperm whale population to a few thousand in all the oceans of the world, and even in our lifetime we may see the extinction of the species altogether. And the really insane thing about it is that it is so unnecessary.

Man will never build cities under the sea. Aside from the restrictions of the Sentients Treaty it simply doesn't make sense. Shelf-mining and -farming, in order to be carried out within ecological regulations, are primarily automatic, with only maintenance crews actually sub-surface. And even among them, hardships are extreme. It is a question of adaptation; man is a land animal, sight-oriented, while in the deep seas it is the cetaceans with their incredibly complex sonaric abilities who are best able to survive. Sight is of secondary use in a world where visibility at the best of times rarely exceeds a dozen yards. And besides, with the success of the terraforming projects on Mars and the hopes held out for atmospheric alterations on Venus, the need of new areas to colonize simply doesn't exist anymore. So with no need to compete for the living space of the sea, the harm man has done to its inhabitants can only be explained in terms of greed and stupidity.

My arm is beginning to ache unbearably now, and my entire chest hurts. Two other dolphins have arrived, so now there are five with me, Kohleny and Thine still off looking for Ka-dhrill. My efforts to reseal my seat flap have left me exhausted and my exposed hand is numb with cold despite the warmth of the water. Cold is the great enemy to man in the sea, and even the warmest water draws enormous amounts of heat from your body. This is the reason that there are no small cetaceans, no sea rabbits, for instance, and even the young of most whales suffer from the cold and have to be kept in warm equatorial waters while they grow their first insulating layers of blubber. I have no such layer and must depend on my thermostatically controlled wetsuit. In theory I can remain indefinitely in the sea in the wetsuit, although I usually find two weeks quite long enough; but for all the suit's engineering it can't seem to keep out the cold now, even with two warm dolphins beside me and the hot Pacific sun overhead.

There is no question about it, I am in deep trouble. The last contact I had with the outside was my hourly transmission to one of the research outposts off the Mexican coast; and while that was some time ago, it will probably still be a while before they begin to worry about me, and even then they will still have no exact reading on my location. The nearest land is almost eight hundred kilometers away, so there is little hope in making for shore. It was a stupid thing to try, going after a whaler all by ourselves instead of letting the U.N. Police investigate, but the thought of one of them being on the loose is enough to damage anyone's judgement. Whalers are mindless butchers, the scum and dregs of mankind, fully several notches below the fishermen who only rape and exploit the sea, putting nothing back for what they take, or sailors who foul the mid-ocean clarity with their wastes and illegal sludge. But it was stupid to go in alone. Ka-dhrill may be injured or dead, and if I do not get help soon, I may be also.

A cold uneasiness is growing throughout me, but the pain is subsiding a little, and gradually, like a deep blanket being drawn slowly across me, I drop off into unconsciousness again.

III

I dream of deserts, red deserts, and yellow and blue and black. Sperm whales raise their blunt heads out of the steaming sands, belly to belly, flippers entwined, copulating in the heat and blackness.

I wake in fever and dull pain. The dolphins still support me, another pair this time, taking turns. The sky has become overcast, and without the sun there seems to be little warmth in the upper air. When I lift my head above the surface the water seems thick and oily. Kohleny has returned and moves in slow, arching patterns around me and beneath me, a gray shadow against blackness. From her movements she may be trying to tell me something, but I am still deaf, and cannot understand her. She thrashes about, making unusual movements, perhaps trying to act out her meaning, but I am too tired to pay attention, and I can make little sense out of her movements. There is no sign of Ka-dhrill.

Kohleny abandons her efforts, and moving up to me, gently strokes my legs with her beak and flippers. Probably she understands my injuries better than I do; sound waves in water pass easily through skin and muscle, so what she understands of me from sonaring would essentially be reflections of my bones and the air-containing cavities of my body. She perceives her world in this manner as I perceive mine through the surface reflections of sight, having many times my acoustic abilities, and uses her excellent eyesight as a secondary means of gaining information. How odd I must appear to her, weak, ungainly, poorly adapted despite all my equipment, and yet she loves me. I don't know why. Yet love is a delicate and a rare thing, and I cherish it when it is given to me.

Turrel leaves off her perpetual circling and churns the water in front of me in a flurry of excitement, forcing the two supporting dolphins to struggle to maintain their positions. At first I think another shark is coming, but then I see great white flashes of underbelly and side markings moving up out of the darkness below me, and I know that everything will be all right; it is Ka-dhrill.

Later now; I hang in the harness of the damaged saddle on Ka-dhrill's back. Actually "saddle" is only a term of convenience, for I lie on my stomach, legs spread out on either side of the high dorsal fin, control panel under my face, air tanks and supply pouches strung out parallel to my chest on either side. Both the radio and the sonic telephone are out of commission, so no outside contact is possible even if I could hear. In fact, about the only thing that seems to be working at all is the weather satellite relay, and that is making dire predictions of an impending storm. If so, it will severely hamper rescue operations, so my troubles may be only just beginning. However, my right arm is now comfortably encased in a plastic water-splint, and having been shot full of drugs I at least feel no pain. Also, the oscilloscope on the control panel is working, so I am able to pick out certain phrases of trade talk that Ka-dhrill keeps repeating, and to a degree at least understand what has happened.

The concussion tore both me and the saddle loose from Ka-dhrill's back, ramming me against it in the shock wave. Ka-dhrill was stunned and drifted for a short while, hovering on the brink of unconsciousness, so that when he came to again, we had drifted several miles apart. He echo-located me almost at once, by that time safely surrounded by the dolphins, and decided to hunt for the saddle before it was completely lost. The ocean bottom here is about three miles deep, outside the diving range of even the sperm whales, but fortunately the saddle had

come to rest only a few hundred feet down on the edge of a thermo-
cline, and Ka-dhrill had little trouble in locating it. He sent Kohleny and
Thine back to tell me that he was all right and would soon be joining me
with the saddle. But once he had retrieved it he decided to make a brief
inspection of the herd first, and so it was later when he finally came.

All seven of the dolphins are becoming nervous now, knowing
without instruments that the storm is coming, and still no signs of rescue. I begin to hear strange ringings in my ears, just at the very edge
of perception, but the sea sounds are still lost to me, and for all intents
and purposes I am still deaf.

The waves are becoming choppy and a wind is rising out of the
northwest, and it will soon be time to dive in order to ride out the
storm. The air tanks on the saddle are undamaged, so even if my
gillpack fails both Ka-dhrill and I will be able to breathe without having to
surface. I feel strangely light-headed under the effects of the drugs, and
it takes considerable effort to carry out a complete check on our equipment. I keep remembering things out of my childhood, the forests and
farmlands around Lund, my studies at the University of Stockholm, the
first time I realized the difference between the sailor's surface sea of
waves and winds and the aquarian's sea, the rich, tinted world of sounds
and pressures, the peoples of its kingdoms, the wisdom of its ancient
knowledge. . . .

The waves are beginning to rise now, forming white sheets that
tear off and form ragged tatters in the wind, and walls of heavy rain
begin to fall. I crouch forward in the saddle and Ka-dhrill inhales quickly
several times and ducks below the surface. We dive to about forty feet,
well below the surface turbulence caused by the storm, and settle down
to begin a long, slow cruise. The extra pressure on the watercast
shoots a dull ache through my arm and shoulder, and suddenly I feel
chilled and very tired; but before doing anything else I loosen my harness and, easing forward, slip the breathing piece from the air tanks
over Ka-dhrill's blowhole, waiting while he delicately opens the triangular flap and takes it in. As I duck back into the saddle once again he
sends a great gush of bubbles out through the regulator, blinding me
momentarily in the murky water. My head swims for a minute, then
clears somewhat, but it is still with great effort that I strap myself back
down again before surrendering once more to the drug-induced darkness.

IV

The huge square head moves ponderously out of the murkiness
and bears directly down upon us, a scarred and wrinkled mountain of

moving flesh only partially lit by the churning cauldron that forms a ceiling over us. Coming out of the darkness it seems a menace difficult to envisage in its totality, but a good ten feet from us, having already carefully sonared us, it dips that massive head downward and dives under us, Ka-dhrill calmly riding the pressure wave up and over its back, being careful to pass well above those huge flukes. The world suddenly rings with dull sound, but the sea sounds, the clatter and crackle of the storm overhead and the low roars of the sperm whales all around us, those I do not hear.

We are moving now with the herd—or "family" to be more exact, a herd being comprised of several such groupings—its members moving like dark shadows all around us. There should be twenty-six members to it, although this number is constantly changing as the group splits up and re-forms following the callings of the seasons. Moving among them like this is unusual, for they are usually quite shy of us, but the racket of the storm has disrupted their continuous chatter back and forth, and they move on either side of us quite unconcerned by our presence. Even after all this time the effect on me is still stunning. We simply aren't trained on the land to think of animals this big. How do you comprehend something sixty feet long and weighing as many tons? The size, the sheer bulk of what you know to be an intelligent, thinking animal is very hard to grasp, much less explain to someone who has never experienced it. You expect that much mass to react like a speeding truck would, and yet they have repeatedly gone out of their way to avoid striking me when I have been among them, intent on some experiment or other, delicately lifting massive flukes so as to miss me when they pass by. All cetaceans seem to have this mysterious relationship with man, some more so than others, and it has never been adequately explained. Ka-dhrill for instance is not so bold to approach them as I can be, for they know him as a potential enemy, powerless without his herd, but still hardly to be trusted. Yet they have never gone out of their way to attack him, saving their ferocity for the battles with the giant squids that they feed on far beneath the surface.

They are making about four knots now, keeping in roughly the same pattern, and Ka-dhrill has little trouble in keeping up. No more than two or three of them are visible at any one time, but they try to stay close together during a storm, so I know that the others are not far away. Their movement is slow and almost sluggish, yet very graceful to watch, not like the sharp, muscular tail thrusts of a shark, but a calm, rhythmic undulation of their whole bodies that ends in a mighty sweep of wide, horizontal flukes that is impressive to watch.

Very little is known of their mental life, for they have not learned man-speech—unlike many of the lesser whales—and their own stereophonic language is as yet untranslated. They do have the largest brain of any animal on Earth, only a small fraction of which is put to use on the mundane efforts of surviving, so to what use the rest of it may be put is an open question. Many mysteries exist concerning them, the solution of which will probably not be seen in my time.

We pass diagonally across the path of a great bull, who is no doubt sonaring us intently, then Ka-dhrill slows his speed to allow him to pass. Once we are out of the way he gives a great thrash of his flukes and arches his square head upward to spout into the storm above. We are thrown about somewhat in the turbulence and sharp pains in my arm remind me that I have other concerns at the moment, and we dive again, seeking solace in the safety of the herd. I am weak now and terribly, terribly cold. I set the heating control on my suit to maximum, but I know that the cold is in my fever and not in the sea. I close my eyes and cling to the saddle, a frail monkey on the back of a whale, and as I have done so often in the sea, I wait.

V

Much later now. Night. The storm is long over and the dolphins have eaten, and sleep comes now, hanging just below the surface and moving only now and again to bob up without opening their eyes to breathe. Saddled with me, Ka-dhrill has neither eaten nor slept. He has released the blowhole piece, the tanks being almost empty, and must raise his head above the surface every few minutes. Otherwise he drifts slowly, moving only enough to keep his dorsal fin and the upper part of the saddle above water. Tiny waves slap gently against my faceplate and wash softly over the glowing instrument panel.

I raise my head and look around. The air feels warm on my bare right hand, long gone numb from the sea cold; with difficulty I swing it around in front of me, the water envelope clumsy and difficult to handle in the air. There is little or no wind and the sea is calm, glass-like almost, reflecting the stars and showing tiny pinpoints of phosphorescence around me. The whales are far off to my right, their angled spouts clearly visible in the still air. The world is calm now and very beautiful; the red glare of my suit and control panel telltales seems harsh and out of place.

The whales sing to each other. It is a deep song carried over to me on the wind and through the water, filled with high-pitched intricacies that I cannot quite hear but know are there. It has a quiet and reserved sound, far removed from their usual grunting communication or the crackling sounds they use for sonaring. The quiet slap of the waves against my chest come only faintly to me, but I can hear the whales clearly. Ka-dhrill speaks to me; at first I cannot understand him and tell him so, then he switches to humanese and says in a quivering falsetto: "How do you feel, Olaf?"

"Lightheaded," I reply, "but otherwise all right. How long do you think before they come?"

"Soon," he says, "soon. Are all the communicator lights still red?"

"Yes," I say, and for a long while we are silent, listening to the strange, moving music of the whales. "What are they doing?" I say at last. "Reciting," he replies, but he will not explain the remark when I ask. My arm begins to hurt and I lay back down on the saddle once again. "Rest now," he says. "I'll stay on the surface."

Seachange.
No, that's not right. . . .

The hotel bar is dark; the lights blue and cold and turned low. People are rushing by, but they look. . .different somehow. "Seachange" they keep saying, but that isn't the word they use, nor even its meaning. They are anxious to get there for there isn't much time. . . . She laughs, tosses back her head, her hair washing back like a breaking wave to settle gently on her bare shoulder. Estee, oh Estee. "Let's wait," she says. The ocean roars somewhere in the background.

Estee.

We have cocktails, then go up to our room, very North American; waves are breaking in the lobby. The hallway is shoddy, hung with trailing kelp, shelf kelp, which does not grow in the open seas. The room is wide and clean and the floor is sand. Outside we can hear the sound of people hurrying. Hurry.

Estee begins to undress and I mix drinks, light up a popper. Then we sit for a while shyly holding hands. I blow air bubbles that rise to the ornate ceiling and form clear upside-down puddles there.

Her eyes, I think to myself, are the slightly clouded light blue of the great whales. She arches her back, her breasts straining against the bounds of the gown. "It's all your fault," I say. Then I philosophize, saying, "People are always sorry afterwards, regardless of the fact that they do it anyway, although not meaning to. . . ."

We are in the streets hurrying to meet the change. The sea is higher, waves lapping against the buildings, foaming at plastic door jambs. There is singing.

Small monkey-like creatures dance back and forth in front of us: "Don't go," they cry, "don't go; come with us!" But we ignore them; we have already made our choice. . . .

Estee. She laughs, a high squealing trill, and tosses back her head, sending her long hair back over her shoulders and down past her dorsal fin toward her arched tail. She circles me in the water and the singing is louder now, more insistent. The Changemasters change themselves and go. . . . Estee circles me in the water, touching me with her flippers, rubbing her warm soft flank across my back. "You're confused," she says, laughing. . . .

"Confused," I say.

"Are you awake?" asks Donald Duck from somewhere.

Awake? Am I? "Yes," I say more to myself than to Ka-dhrill. The mask is unbearably hot, stuffy; difficult to breathe. I fumble at it weakly, trying to find the catch. Then things become clearer, and I relent.

The stars seem brighter now, and much closer. The whales are no longer singing, but my hearing is completely restored, and I can hear the quiet slapping of the water around me very clearly. I am very thirsty, but something keeps bothering me, something I want to remember. Then I know. "Dolphin," I say. "She became a dolphin."

"They have gone off to feed again," says Ka-dhrill, misunderstanding me. "There are no sharks around."

Sharks, I think; sharks . . .

It is very quiet. The stars are high and as yet no sign of dawn. Drugs are wearing off, pain returning, difficult to breathe. The water-splint heavy on my arm.

The whisper of the sea is wrong, ambience is wrong, something I sense but can't identify.

Something about cities . . . she became a dolphin and the city was sinking into the sea. And the people . . .

I fumble with my left hand in the med-pack and give myself another injection. Seachange. But it's not the right word. Seachange . . .

The sea is smooth, gleaming black, and the stars overhead are bright. A light mist hangs over the water, here and there lying in desolate tatters like the fading remnants of smoke from an autumn fire.

Ka-dhrill seems anxious; he bobs nervously above the surface and spouts rapidly, anxious to duck his head underwater again. I think: he feels that he should be doing something, but is forcing himself to be still. But that isn't it; he senses something. Sharks? I look for the dolphins, twisting around with difficulty, but cannot see them. Feeding again? Bottom-dwellers come up at night and feeding is usually good. But the surface seems too calm for that. Something is wrong. About to happen. Alice in Wonderland; something to happen.

On the horizon, hard to see at first, a glow, faint but growing stronger. Ka-dhrill is facing it, waiting. The whales are active now also, spouting and thrashing around, and I can sense their excitement even from here. The glow comes closer; miles wide, the mists lighting up with it and reflecting it back onto the sea. Then the first silver bodies begin to dart by, quick slashes that set the dark water on fire, and thousands follow.

They are Pacific albacore, a species of tuna running around thirty-five pounds each, moving in a vast, oval school that we are going to pass through the middle of. The pressure wave in front of each long body excites a cool phosphorescence out of the sea, and the wake they leave behind them bleeds with luminous purples and greens.

Ka-dhrill becomes frantic with excitement. He lunges forward, sending a glowing wake far out on either side and sending a sheet of water up over me, twisting my arm back painfully. He moves to intercept one of the tuna, positioning himself to be directly in its path. The fish feels the pressure wave he sets up and moves to dart aside, but Ka-dhrill has anticipated him, and with a sudden burst of speed he grabs the fish, a loud crunch, and the silver body has disappeared swallowed whole. Ka-dhrill grunts with satisfaction.

I in the meanwhile dangle on his back, thrown about in the harness like a rag doll by the force of his lunge, my mind dazed by the wild colorplay that lights up the night all around us, every drop of water or flash of silvered body fever-bright.

"One more," says Ka-dhrill in his quaking falsetto, "one more to take the edge off."

"Veto!" I shout, rousing myself. "No way! Starve! When I'm dead you can eat me!" But he is already tracking another streaking body.

VI

The school has passed and the sea is calm again, but still tingling with barely suppressed light, so that every movement brings forth its own tiny glow of color. Ka-dhrill has returned to his old stance on the surface, forcing himself to act relaxed, but he is still terribly excited. The whales are nowhere in sight, probably off chasing the tuna, gorging themselves on the rich, sweet meat, but the dolphins have returned and move cautiously around us, aware of Ka-dhrill's excitement and not wanting to take any chances.

My head is cleared somewhat, and I begin to consider the strange dream. Part of it was mine, the things about Estee, but another part of it, the setting and what was happening, that came from somewhere else. I'm certain that it came from what the whales were singing.

Translating the whale languages is not difficult if you have the proper equipment; understanding them is. The orientation is all wrong. Touch, for example, has social, sexual, and communicative overtones that simply don't exist in land creatures, and for another thing, much of what one whale says to another is in the form of altering the condition of the air cavities in their heads, synonymous with the way we read each other's facial expressions; but of course such sonic interplay has no meaning to a human, who lacks the physical equipment to join in. And since the messages almost always deal with present activities, the subtleties and shades of meaning can be almost limitless.

Yet these whales were not discussing the shade of the water but were recounting something, reciting, as Ka-dhrill said. . . .

"You know!" I say aloud. "You understood what they were saying, the whales before the albacore came." He does not answer, but his anxiety is readily apparent, and the dolphins, sensing it, quietly back away, leaving us alone to settle whatever it is that has come up between us.

Still he does not reply.

"You know," I say in a quieter voice, "you could understand what they were saying, the city sinking into the sea, the people becoming dolphins; I could understand it too, part of it, a word here and there, not consciously, but in my dream. But what was it? Do they tell stories to each other? All the human cities will be swallowed by the ocean and men will join them, become cetaceans? A reaction against the harm that man has done them? Do they have any such stories? Tell me, damn it! Why didn't you tell me you could understand their language?"

"I?" he says, giving a thrash with his tail that brings us well up out of the water, to sink back under the surface a moment later with battering force. "What am I? A bribe to satisfy the U.N., a freak, neither whale nor man, unable to assimilate with either. While with you I have to adhere to your ridiculous morality, and when I want a female I usually have to fight the pod bull and probably half of the other males as well. You at least can go back to your own world for your week-long orgies, but what can I do?"

But I recognize this tactic; he is stalling, dragging out self-pity as a shield against my questions. "So cry all over yourself later," I say. "But first tell me about these stories."

"They're not stories," he says, sounding like an angry Donald Duck. "They're . . . songs, I suppose." He pauses for several seconds, as if making up his mind about things, then calms down again, and returns to cruising just under the surface so that I ride just above it. "They're old songs," he says. "Only the big ones keep them. The language is old too; it's not the one they usually use. Sometimes they drag it out and repeat the old songs. I don't know why. They don't mean anything. . . ."

Old songs. Old? My arm and chest hurt, but I ignore them. How old? But then Ka-dhrill says, "It's nothing so unusual, you know; it's been known for a long time that we were once land animals who took to the sea. It's an old story anyway; nobody cares now. . . ."

But I am no longer listening.

The implications are stunning. Thirty to fifty million years ago the cetaceans were land animals. We know this, despite the fact that no fossils have ever been found of their land form, nothing except a small mammal that may have been a very remote ancestor. What Ka-dhrill is saying is that the cetaceans were sentient thirty million years ago, that they built cities, and that they still keep chronicles of those times, songs kept and repeated for thirty million years. "Impossible!" I say aloud. "It just can't be! The song was about land creatures changing themselves into sea mammals. Changemasters. That's genetic surgery on a vast scale, and thirty million years ago, perhaps even longer. It's ridiculous!"

He does not reply.

We drift in silence for a while. The eastern sky has begun to gray slightly, and a slight wind is rising. A new dawn rising; but symbolism always annoys me so I shrug off the idea and wait.

"They had to make a choice," he says at length. "Either to live your way, struggling, fighting, never enough food, always having to change, to adapt, never any rest, build and destroy, create and tear down; or to move into the warm, rich seas, where food is plentiful, and there is time to rest and play and enjoy the many sensations of existence. They were probably living half in the water anyway, the songs only tell about cities by the sea, so the final choice was easy."

"Thirty million years. And in all that time you never changed."

"Of course we changed: All things change. We adapted, we specialized, we became even better at living in the sea. But not much; once the major changes had been made, the rest was simply a matter of enjoying it. And we did; generation followed generation, and always the sea provided, the sea cared for us."

Small monkey-like creatures dance in front of us. . . . "Until we came along," I say.

"Yes," he says. "You came along. You evolved, you became too plentiful, too powerful, too efficient. Yet even faced with extinction, it's still terribly difficult for us to organize, to rouse ourselves to group action. The big ones don't seem to be able to do it at all. We "killer whales" are luckier; we have always liked men, cooperating with them was easier for us. That is why we work so well together, you and I."

"Why do you like men?" I ask.

He does not answer, so I go on: "They were semiaquatic even then, short-dwelling, sentient land mammals, not primates, but a differ-

ent racial group altogether, a species without the physical equipment to
do complex construction. They had the intelligence to, but they needed
hands to carry out the actual operations. Small, hairy hands, proto-
men who could be trained to do complex manipulation, like trained
dogs. . . ."

"No, not dogs," Ka-dhrill interrupts. "Your trouble is that you destroyed all of the slightly less intelligent creatures on the land; you still
have trouble conceiving of races with just slightly less intelligence than
your own. Besides which, they weren't men. Perhaps you evolved from
them, but . . ."

"But we look like them and you remember."

"Not remember. A racial memory perhaps, like your Garden of
Eden. Sometimes the big ones tell stories, sometimes we can understand them; we have little else in common with them, you know.
They're one of our food sources. Perhaps our ancestors were enemies
before the change. But we both feel kindly disposed toward men. You
remind us of something. Perhaps the way that you like small, furry
things. It was a long time ago, even for us. What difference does it make
now?"

But I am no longer listening. I am in the streets of a drowning city,
watching small nimble monkeys performing complex surgical operations
under the eyes and instructions of larger, clumsier, but more intelligent
beings. Changemasters.

The morning sun is hot on the water, for we are near the equator,
and the whales, bloated with albacore, are moving very sluggishly
through the warm currents, leisurely making their way south. We un-
hurriedly follow. Turrel is constantly bobbing up out of the water with
reports of sharks, coming to clean up after the feast, and the dolphins
stay close just in case, but I am not really concerned. No shark in his
right mind would attack a full-grown killer whale, even one saddled with
an injured man.

My chest is beginning to bother me quite a bit, and I am beginning
to worry about internal injuries: I have coughed up blood several times
this morning. I feel sick and very tired. Ka-dhrill has been moving nervously back and forth, as if getting ready to say something. Finally he
says, "Olaf?"

"Yes?"

But he does not ask. Damn the sea, I think; damn the stinking,
slimy sea and all the things that slither through it. I yearn for the
firmness of dry land, the smell of salt-free air. Racial pride is a terrible
thing. A dream of Estee.

"I won't tell anyone," I hear myself saying. "We'll talk about it when I get back." But his reply is lost in the swirl and whine of the hovercraft engine as it settles down beside us.

Under the Generator

John Shirley

Writers of science fiction have been both practical and bizarre in their suggestions for new energy sources. E. E. Smith published stories about atomic power as long ago as the 1920s, and Cleve Cartmill had worked out the essential process of nuclear fission in a 1944 story. On the other hand, Poul Anderson didn't hesitate to suggest using beer as fuel for a spaceship. He was joking, of course—and so is John Shirley, in a darkly humorous way, in this story about harnessing the power of entropy. But if we read it as metaphor, its statement becomes very pointed.

John Shirley's novels include Transmaniacon and City Come Awalkin'.

LOOKING INTO THE EYES of the woman who sat across from him in the crowded cafeteria, Denton was reminded of the eyes of another woman entirely. Perhaps there were secret mirrors hidden in the faces of the two women. He remembered the other woman, Alice, when she had said: *I just can't continue with you if you insist on keeping that damn job. I'm sorry, Ronnie, but I just can't. My personal convictions leave no room for those inhuman generators.*

He reflected, looking into the eyes of the second woman, that he could have quit the job for Alice. But he hadn't. Maybe he hadn't actually wanted her. And he had gone easily from Alice to Donna. He resolved not to lose Donna too because of his work with the generators.

"I used to be an actor," Denton said. Swirling coffee in his cup, he shifted uncomfortably in the cafeteria seat and wondered if the plastic of the cup would melt slightly into the coffee. . . . Working at the hospital, drinking coffee every morning and noon out of the same white-mold sort of cups, he had visions of the plastic slowly coating the interior of his stomach with white brittle.

"What happened to acting and how far'd you get?" Donna Farber asked with her characteristic way of cramming as much inquiry as she could into one line.

Denton frowned, his wide mouth making an elaborate squiggle across his broad, pale face. His expressions were always slightly exaggerated, as if he were an actor not yet used to the part of Ronald Denton.

"I was working off-Broadway, and I had a good part in a play I wrote myself. An actor can always play the part better if he wrote it. The play was called *All Men Are Created Sequels*. Tigner produced it."

"Never heard of it."

"Naturally it fell flat after I pulled out."

"Naturally." Her silver-flecked blue eyes laughed.

"Anyway, I felt that acting was stealing too much of my identity. Or something. Actually, I'm not sure just why I quit. Maybe it was really stage fright."

His unexpected candor brought her eyes to his. He remembered Alice and wondered how to discover just how Donna felt about his job, if she felt anything at all.

But the subject was primed by his black uniform. "Why did you quit acting to work in the generators?"

"I don't know. It was available and it had good hours. Four hours a day, four days a week, twelve dollars an hour."

"Yeah . . . but it must be depressing to work there. I mean, you probably still haven't been able to give up acting entirely. You have to act like there's nothing wrong around people who are going to die soon." There was no indictment in her tone. Her head tilted sympathetically.

Denton just nodded as if he had found sorrowful virtue in being the scapegoat. "Somebody has to do it," he said. Actually, he was elated. He had been trying to arouse interest from Donna for a week. He looked at her frankly, admiring her slender hands wrapped around her coffee cup, the soft cone of her lips blowing to cool the coffee, close flaxen hair cut into a bowl behind her ears.

"I don't entirely understand," she said, looking for a divination in her coffee, "why they didn't get the retired nurses or someone used to death for the job."

"For one thing, you need a little electronic background to keep watch on the generators. That's what got me the job. I studied electronics before I was an actor."

"That's a strange contrast. Electronics and acting."

"Not really. Both involve knowledge of circuitry. But anyway, not even experienced nurses are used to sitting there *watching* people die for four hours at a time. They usually let them alone except when administering—"

"But I thought you said all you had to do was sit and check the dials every so often. You mean you have to watch?"

"Well . . . you can't help it. You sit right across from the patient. Since you're there, you look. I'm aware of them, anyhow, because I have to make sure they aren't dying too fast for the machine to scoop."

She was silent, looking around the busy lunchroom as if seeking support from the milling, wooden-faced hospital employees. She seemed to be listening for a tempo in the clashing of dishes and the trapped rumble of conversations.

Denton was afraid that he had offended her, giving her the impression that he was a vulture. He hoped that she wasn't looking around for someone else to talk to. . . .

"I don't like it in here," she said, her voice a small life to itself. "I think it's because in most kitchens you hear the clinking noises of china and glass. Here it's scraping plastic." One side of her mouth pulled into an ironic smile.

"Let's go outside then," Denton said, a trifle too eagerly.

They discarded their trays in the recycling chute and walked to the elevator. Denton was silent as they rode to the ground floor of the huge hospital; he didn't want to converse, irrationally afraid that the giddy elevator box might trap their words in the sliding doors, to carry them off to strangers.

They emerged into the pastel curves of the hospital lobby, walking between artificial potted palms and people waiting with artificial expressions concealing worry. They went out the susurrating front doors, from the odor of disinfectant into June sunlight and the warm breathing of air-cars.

"I'm glad all the engines are turbines now," she remarked. "They're so quiet. No tires on the street squealing and no growling pistons and just air to wash my face in. All the noise of traffic used to scare me when I was little." They talked quietly of cars and the city and their jobs until they came to the park.

Sitting under a tree, plucking absently at the grass, they were silent for a while, feeling the ambience of the bustling park.

Until without provocation Donna began: "My parents died five years ago and—" Then she stopped and looked at him sideways. She shook her head.

"Were you going to say something else?"

243

She shook her head again, too quickly. He wanted to ask if they had put generators over her parents before they'd died; but he decided that the question might put him in a bad light.

They sat in the park and watched bicyclers and children sift through the plasphalt paths. After a while a slush vendor rolled a sticky white cart past, and Denton got up to buy two drinks. He was just returning from the vendor, about thirty feet from where Donna waited under the tree, when someone put a hand on his right arm.

"Can I talk to you?" A subdued tone. "Just for a minute?" It was a boy, perhaps sixteen, but at least three inches taller than Denton. The boy kept opening and closing his mouth pensively, questions anxious to spring from his lips. He was dressed in a denim body suit. His hands were thrust deep into his side-pockets, as if leashed. Denton nodded, glancing at the slushes to make certain that they wouldn't melt on his hands. Probably the kid was proselytizing for one of the burgeoning Satanic cults.

"You're a generator guy, aren't you? A compensator."

Denton nodded dumbly again.

"My father's under a generator; he's dying. And he ain't old or useless yet. He's still . . . needed." He paused to steady himself. "Can you . . . Maybe you could help him, turn off the machine for a while?" It was obvious that the boy wasn't used to asking favors. He resented having to ask Denton for anything.

Denton wished that he hadn't worn his uniform out of the hospital.

"I can't do anything for your father. I'm not a doctor. And there are dozens of generators in use at the hospital now. I've probably never seen your old man. Anyway, it isn't true that the generators steal strength from patients. It's an old wives' tale. It wouldn't do your father one bit of good if I turned it off. Sorry—" He began to walk toward Donna.

"What's your name?" the boy asked from behind, all respect gone from his tone. Denton could feel the boy's eyes on his back. He turned half around, miffed.

"Denton," he replied, immediately wishing that he had given a false name. He turned his back on the boy and walked back to Donna. He could feel an icy trail of slush melting over his hand.

"What did that kid want?" Donna asked, sipping her slush.

"Nothing. Directions to . . . the auditorium. He said he was going to the Satanist/Jeezus Freak confrontation."

"Really? He didn't look to be armed." She shrugged.

The boy was watching them.

Some of the slush had spilled onto Denton's leg. Donna wiped at the red stain on his black uniform with a white handkerchief.

He didn't want to think of work now. He had a date to take her to the Media Stew tonight. Finally: the first relationship he'd attempted since Alice.

But Denton decided it might be better to keep his mind on work. If he thought about her too much he would be nervous and contrived when he was with her. Maybe blow it. He tightened the belt around his one-piece jet uniform and went quietly into the arbiter's office. The arbiter of compensators was short, Jewish, and a compulsive caviler. Mr. Buxton smiled as Denton bent over the worksheet titled WEEK OF JUNE 19 THROUGH 26, 1986.

"What's your hurry, Denton? You young cats are always in a hurry. You'll be assigned soon enough. You might find it *too* soon. I haven't written into the chart yet."

"Leave me on Mr. Hurzbau's generator, sir, if you would. I get along well with Hurzbau."

"What is this 'get along' junk? We bend the rule a little that says no fraternizing with the patients under generators . . . but *familiarity* is strictly verboten. You'll go nuts if you—"

Not wanting to become embroiled in another of Buxton's lectures, Denton quickly capitulated. "I'm sorry, sir. I didn't mean to imply we knew each other well. What I meant was, Hurzbau doesn't worry me much, or talk to me past the usual amenities. Could I have my assignment now? I don't want the unwatched generator to overload."

"Somebody's watching the generator all the time, naturally. It can't over—"

"That's what I mean," Denton interrupted impatiently. "The guy who's watching it is going to overload if he has to work past his shift. He'll blame me."

"You should cultivate patience. Especially with your job." Buxton shrugged his wide shoulders and put a thick hand on his paunch. He regarded the chart, yawned, scratched his bushy black mustache, and began to fill his pipe.

Denton, still standing, shifted uncomfortably. He wanted to get his shift over with.

Buxton lit his pipe and blew gray smoke at Denton.

"Durghemmer today," Buxton said.

Denton frowned, dismayed. Durghemmer the leech.

"Durghemmer . . ." Denton spoke the name into the air so that it would permanently leave his lips. "No. No, really, Buxton, I—"

"Just as I thought. Another weakling. I can never find anybody willing to take care of Durghemmer's generator, but I'll be damned if I'll end up doing it myself. So, Denton—"

"I can't. Really. I have a date tonight. Very delicate Psychological

245

Balance involved. Durghemmer would ruin me." Denton looked with all his actor's pathos into his supervisor's eyes. Buxton stared at his hands, then relit his pipe.

"Okay. This time I let you off," he said. "Take Hurzbau. But don't talk to him unless it's absolutely necessary. I'm not supposed to, but I'll put Durghemmer's generator on automatic for tonight. It's dangerous but what the hell. But—Everybody's got to circulate sooner or later, Ron."

"Sure," said Denton, relieved. "Later." He took his punchcard from the rack on Buxton's office wall.

Denton read the dials punctiliously, reminding himself that this particular generator provided power for at least three hundred people. Amplitude was climbing. Poor Hurzbau. But thoughts like those, he told himself, were precisely tbe sort he didn't want. Good luck to Hurzbau.

Denton adjusted the position of the scoop over the bed. The scoop of the generator was a transparent bell enclosing the bed upon which Hurzbau rested. It was made of nonconductive fiberglass, veined with copper and platinum wiring which converged in a cable at its peak and twined like a thick metal vine through branches of metal supports into an opening in the cylindrical crystal in the generator's flat top.

The bulk of the rectangular generator transformer was opened in a honeycomb of metallic hexagons on the side facing the bed. On the other side Denton sat in his swivel chair, in his black uniform, in his controlled aplomb, behind his desk of dials and meters. Denton was officially the *compensator,* adjusting the rise and fall of energy absorbed by the generator so that a steady, predictable flow went out to the electrical transmitters.

Having checked the meters, Denton tried to relax for a while. He looked abstractedly around the room. The chamber was small, all white, with only the few paintings which Hurzbau's relatives had hung to cheer him up. The paintings were of pastoral scenes from places mostly now entombed in plasphalt.

Denton wondered why anyone had bothered with the paintings. Hurzbau couldn't see them except as vague blurs through the plastic scoop. Nothing extraneous to the function of the generator was allowed under the scoop. Not even bedclothes. Hurzbau's naked, cancer-eaten body was kept warm with heaters.

Half of Hurzbau's face was eaten away by cancer. He had once been overweight. He had gone from 220 pounds to 130 in four months. The right half of his face was sunken in to a thin mask of skin clinging to the skull, and his right eye was gone, the socket stuffed with cotton. He could talk only with difficulty. His right arm was withered and unusable, though his left was strong enough to prop him up on his elbow, allowing him to seek Denton's attention.

"Compensator . . . ," he rasped, barely audible through the plastic. Denton switched on the intercom.

"What can I do for you, sir?" He asked, a trifle brusquely. "Would you like me to call the nurse? I am not privileged to give out medical aid personally. . . ."

"No. No nurse. Denton? That your name?"

"Yes. Ronald Denton. I told you yesterday, I believe. How are—" He'd almost forgotten, but he caught himself in time. He *knew* how Hurzbau was . . . the invalid was in constant pain with six weeks to live, optimum. "Do you want to take some metrazine? That I can get."

"No. You know what, Denton?" His voice was a raven's croak.

"Look, I've been told I'm overfraternizing with the patients. That's not really my job. We have a capable staff psychiatrist and a priest and—"

"Who says you're not a priest, Denton? The other compensators don't talk to me at all. You're the only one who says a damn thing to me. . . ." Hurzbau swallowed, his dessicated features momentarily contorting so that the left half of his face matched the malformation of the right. "You know, Denton, I could have gotten the cancer vaccine but I thought I'd never have need for it. Not *me*." He made some sandpapery noises which might have been akin to laughter. "And it's a sure thing if you get the cancer vaccine you *can't* get cancer, and I turned down a sure thing. Too much bother."

Denton suddenly felt cold toward the dying man. He recoiled inwardly, as if Hurzbau were a deformed siren trying to lure him under the scoop. It was true in a way: Hurzbau wanted sympathy. And sympathy would mean that Denton would have to imagine himself in Hurzbau's place. He shuddered. He had worked at the generator for six months but never before had a patient confided in him. He had to cut it off, even if it was at Hurzbau's expense.

But he was deterred by a look in the old man's eye: a red light from the burning, blackened wick of Hurzbau's nerve-endings.

"Denton, tell me something. . . ." An almost visible wave of pain swept over Hurzbau's shrunken body; the parchment-thin skin of his face twisted as if it were about to rip. "Denton, I want to know. The generators, do they make me weaker? I know they . . . take energy . . . from my dying. . . . Do they . . . feed off me? Do they make me die so that—"

"*No!*" Denton was surprised at the stridency of his own exclamation. "No, you've got it turned around. It takes energies emitted because of your dying, but it doesn't come directly from *you*."

"Could you—" Hurzbau began, but he fell back on the bed, unable to keep himself propped up any longer. Drawn by inexplicable impulse, Denton got out of the control seat and walked around to the end of the bed. He looked down into the fading man's eyes, judging the advance of histolysis by the growth of an almost visible smoldering glow of pain. Hurzbau's mouth worked silently, furiously. Finally, tugging at the intravenous feeding tube imbedded in his left arm, he managed: "Denton . . . could you fix the generator if it broke down?"

"No. I don't know how it works. I just compensate for metrical oscillation—"

"Uh-huh. Then can you really say that it doesn't take away from my life if you don't know for sure how it works? You know what they *tell* you. But how do you know it's the truth?"

Hurzbau began to choke, spitting up yellow fluid. A moisture detector at the bedside prompted a plastic arm to stretch from the table of automatic instruments ensconced left of Hurzbau's head. The arm swabbed the pillow and Hurzbau's lips with a sponge. The light flared faintly in the dying man's eye and with his good arm he swiped angrily at the mechanical swab.

"Damn, damn," he muttered, "I'm not a pool ball." The plastic strut fled back to its clamp.

Denton turned away, deliberately breaking the minor rapport developing between the two of them. But doubts insinuated through his stiffly starched black uniform. Maybe Hurzbau had been a criminal whom they'd deliberately infected as an energy reserve—But, no, Durghemmer had been a respected politician, never convicted of anything; so how could one explain *his* interment under the generator? The man under the generator on the floor below had been a policeman. *No.* The principle behind the generators was taught in high school, and there were classes on the inner construction of the machines in vocational schools. There would be no way for the arbiters to hide anything from anyone. . . . There was no secret. But he understood Hurzbau's apprehensions. Even from his vantage point, perpetually on the bed, Hurzbau could see the two red dials side by side like mocking eyes, their needles climbing visibly whenever he got weaker.

He got weaker; the machine got stronger.

"Maybe it's something they're keeping under wraps, Denton," Hurzbau ventured suddenly. He spasmed then, rising almost to a sitting position, every muscle strained so that his skin was elasticized vitreously taut, making his withered frame mottle red. From between gritted teeth came Hurzbau's whisper, slightly metallic through the intercom: "How is there *room* for this much pain in this little body? There's enough to fill a warehouse. How does it all fit?" Denton turned off the intercom.

He rang for the nurse. The old man fell back, relaxing. Without wanting to, Denton glanced at the needle on the generator facing. It was climbing. He could hear the scoop humming. He ran around to the control panel and dialed to compensate for the upsurge in entropic energy. When the machine took in a great deal of energy at one time, it reacted with a high-frequency oscillating tone, very much like shrill laughter.

The generator chuckled, the old man grew weaker, the needles jumped higher. Hurzbau's body began to jerk and with each erratic rictus Denton's stomach contracted with revulsion. He had thought he was used to the onset of death.

Denton tightened the arm draped casually about Donna's creamy shoulders. She was asleep, or pretended to be. His casual posture lied about his inner turmoil. Inside, he seethed, remembering Donna's long boyish body like a graceful jet of water, thrashing with his. She'd responded only to the lightest touches. The visions of Donna alternated with memories of Hurzbau, which Denton strove to suppress. But Hurzbau had thrashed in agony as she had writhed in ecstasy. Denton sat abruptly up to light a cigarette, throwing a tobacco smokescreen between himself and the recollection of the dying man.

He glanced down at Donna, saw her looking at him out of slitted eyes. She smiled hastily and looked away.

"What time is it?" she asked, her voice weary.

"One A.M."

"What was your play about, anyway?"

"Do you want to read it? I have a copy—"

"No." Then she added, "I'm *interested*, but I don't like to read much these days. I had to read immensely before my internship. Medical textbooks ruined my appetite. I like live plays better. Why don't you perform it for me?"

He raised a hand melodramatically over her head and with an exaggeratedly visionary look that made her laugh, he quoth:

"'We have come to bury Caesar, not to praise him . . .'"

"Oh, I see. That's from your play? You wrote that, eh?"

"Well, it's one I wrote a few centuries ago—"

"SHUT UP IN THERE I GOTTA GET SOME SLEEP! YOU ALREADY MADE ENOUGH NOISE GRUNTIN' TO KEEP THE WHOLE BUILDING AWAKE TILL DECEMBER!" a male voice shouted from the next apartment.

"The walls are thin," Denton whispered apologetically. But Donna was crying. She was sitting up, taller than Denton by half a head, rocking back and forth. He put an arm on her leg but she pushed away and got out of bed, throwing the bedclothes askew.

"Listen," Denton said frantically, "I'm sorry about that creep next door. Let's go somewhere—"

"No, it's okay. I'm going home. I had a good time and all that, you're a good lover, only . . ."

"Only *what?*"

She had her suit on already; she was putting on her shoes. He wondered what he had done. Better stop her before she gets dressed or she'll feel obligated to leave once she's gone that far. She was putting on her coat.

"What is it?" he asked with growing anxiety. "What did I do wrong?"

"Nothing. I just don't know why I came here, really. I don't need anyone to tell me I'm human. It's not good to get attached, anyway." She was heading toward the door as she spoke.

"SHUT UP IN THERE ALREADY!" the man next door shouted.

"GO TO HELL!" Denton shouted back. He pulled on one of his uniforms. She went out the door, leaving him alone with all the noises of the city night rumbling through the open window like a hungry belly. "Damn!" Denton said aloud, fumbling at buttons.

Suddenly, apartments on three sides erupted, combining to grind the quiet evening into fine dust.

"ALL OF YOU CUT IT OUT!"

"I'LL BURN THIS HOLE TO THE GROUND IF YOU—"

"I'M GONNA CALL THE PIGS!"

Donna was stepping primly into the elevator just as Denton closed the door to his apartment behind him. He ran to the stairs and jogged swiftly down three flights, his footsteps echoing in the deserted concrete stairwell like the laughter of the generator.

He ran into the empty street. The night was muggy, warm with summer smugness. He spotted Donna halfway down the block to his left. He ran after her, feeling foolish, but shouting "Hey, wait! It's not that easy!"

She passed a black alleyway, turned the corner. He scuffled across the mouth of the alley, saw her disappear around the corner—

—something kicked his legs out from under him. He threw up his arms, felt the concrete edge of the curb crack an elbow, romancandling his arm; cheek striking the gutter grate; pain with snapping wires, cracking bullwhips. A hand pulled him roughly onto his back and he was looking at the twisted face of a teenage boy, ugly from barely repressed hatred. Someone else behind jerked Denton to his feet. His right eye was swelling and it hurt to squint, but with the other eye he saw that there were four hoods in all, each wearing transparent plastic jackets under which they were nude, muscular, and bristling with dark hairs. In sharp contrast to their hirsute lower parts, their faces and heads were shaved absolutely hairless. Their eyes burned with amphetamines. The drug made their maneuverings slightly spastic, like children flinching from expected blows.

Two of them held Denton's arms from behind. A third stepped in close with a knife. All four were strangely silent, almost pious. Denton saw the knife gleaming near his throat. He was paralyzed, numbed by what *should* have been unreality. He was watching viddy, he thought desperately. A commercial would come on in a moment. But one of the boys pulled Denton's head back by his hair with a violent twist that sent spotlights of pain into the growing darkness in his skull. The darkness congealed into abject fear. He was without volition. He remembered Donna. He looked around desperately without moving his head. Had she deliberately brought him here to meet these men? Had she set him up? What would they do with the knife?

One of the boys flicked quick fingers to unbutton Denton's shirt. He parted the folds of the black uniform slowly, almost formally, as if he were undressing a lover. Denton knew the night was warm but he felt the air in his open shirt cold as a knife blade. If he shouted for help they would probably kill him right away. The streetlight overhead hurt his eyes; his arms were cramping uncomfortably behind him. He tried to change position and was rewarded with a kneejab in the small of his back. He looked around for Donna as the knife cut open his undershirt (a very sharp knife, he noted; the fabric parted easily, as if it had been unzipped). Then he felt the knife on his navel, pain like a tiny point of intense light flaring up, and a trickle of warm blood. Already the warmth of shock enveloped him in surrender. He closed his eyes and bit his lips against the sting near his navel. The pain made him open them again.

The boy with the knife closed his eyes as if in anticipation of sybaritic satisfaction.

A blur of movement—

Then the boy with the knife screamed, his head snapped back, his mouth gaping, his back arched; he went rigid, yelling, "Damn! Who—"

He fell and Donna jumped easily aside and turned to face another. Denton felt the grip at the back of neck relax as the boy behind him ran to aid his companion lying on the ground in front of her. Donna shot her booted foot, heel first, straight up and out, catching the third tough in the throat. She was tall and her long legs held her in good stead as the other two tried to get in close with their knives. The first two were lying almost like lovers on the ground; the boy who'd threatened Denton with the knife lay with his eyes wide open, unblinking, staring upward. He was perfectly still. The other was on his hands and knees, coughing blood onto his supine companion, one hand on his own crushed windpipe, his face staring and fascinated, as if he were tasting real pain for the first time, exploring it as a new world.

Stopping another with a shoe-point in the groin, Donna spun and, without wasting momentum, came forward onto the foot and transferred the motion to her arm, striking the knife from his hand. The knife rang on the concrete, rolling in front of the boy with the crushed throat.

Denton was breathing in huge gulps, still unable to act: he was sure that he would only run up against a television screen if he tried to intervene. But without a weapon, the last standing tough turned and fled into an alley.

The other boy was still clutching his groin, rocking back and forth on his haunches, moaning, his face draining. Donna regarded him for a moment, then said in a low, calm voice:

"I suppose I should try to undo what I've done now. I've got some first-aid stuff in my purse. If I can find it . . ." Kneeling before the boy who still rocked, she looked with anomalous tranquility at the place between his legs where she'd kicked him.

Denton took a long breath, relaxing from his paralysis, an actor between scenes.

He put a hand on Donna's shoulder, felt her stiffen beneath his touch. He put his hand in his pocket, asking, "Where did you go when they jumped me?"

"I hid in a doorwell. I thought they were after me. When I saw them surround you I went around to the other side of the alley and came through it, and up behind them."

She turned from him to face the boy. "*Why?*" she asked.

Through grated teeth the boy answered, "Hurzbau . . ."

The name made Denton realize where he had seen the leader of the gang before: in the park, the boy who had asked about his father under the generator. He stepped toward the other tough, demanding, "Hurzbau *what?*"

"Hurzbau's father's in the hospital. Under the generator. He made us do it. He's our packleader. He said you were a vampire killing his father. He watched you, followed you. . . ."

Donna screamed shortly, the cry becoming a sigh as Denton heard her body hit the concrete sidewalk even before he turned around. A knife's black hilt protruded from her side, stuck from the back by the boy who stood, wavering, ready to fall, still coughing blood. Denton recognized Hurzbau's son, and he wondered: *Why her instead of me?*

The boy collapsed, crumpling limply, blood sliding between his skin and the transparent suit, the plastic making the blood seem orange and artificial.

Denton felt empathic pain in his own side as, sobbing, he ran to Donna. She was still breathing but unconscious. The knife was in to the hilt. He was afraid to pull it out and perhaps allow too much blood to escape.

"Here. Call an ambulance." The boy who had spoken before was standing, one hand still on his crotch, something like regret in his face. He handed Denton a public pocket-fone. Denton fumbled frantically to punch for EMERGENCY.

A small metallic voice responded, and he gave directions. When he had done he looked up and down the street, wondering that it was so deserted after all the noise. There were three bright streetlights on the block. Denton, Donna, and the remainder of the gang were visible and starkly outlined in the pool of light under the crowded skyscraper apartments lining both sides of the street.

The events of the past few minutes caught up with Denton when he felt blood warming the hand resting on Donna's still leg. He looked up at the boy who just stood there, face blanked.

"All of you are going to regret this, kid," Denton said in what he hoped was a steely, uncompromising tone.

The boy just shrugged.

He couldn't go to work now, to watch a man die under a generator scoop, knowing that Donna was dying under one just like it. He pondered the idea of quitting his job. Somehow he felt that losing his job at the generator would be a self-betrayal. It brought him a strange peace, as he sat in full health watching the patient wilt under the glass scoop like an ant burnt by a magnifying glass. Saying to himself: *I'm still strong, it passed me by.*

He decided not to go to work. He kept seeing Donna's name on the shift chart. They had expected *him* to tend her generator. No. No. He couldn't visit her, even, while off duty. She was in a coma. He had to get his mind off it. He hadn't slept at all that night and his eyes burned with exhaustion. He would go out and get something to eat and if Buxton decided to fire him because of his absence, then the decision to leave the job would be made *for* him.

He walked through the hospital lobby and into the glaring sunshine reflecting off the white buildings of the hospital complex. A growing tension was surmounting his composure. But he was an actor so no one could tell.

Not even Alice. Alice was standing on the steps to the hospital, handing out pamphlets. She saw him immediately, seeing first the black uniform she hated, and then her once-lover interred inside.

Denton hoped to avoid her, but before he could turn away she ran to him and, thrusting a pamphlet in his hand, embraced him. He pulled away, embarrassed, feeling tension about to break loose. The glare seemed to intensify, magnifying glass hovering over the ant. Alice laughed.

"Still working there? I think you must really like your job, Ronnie."

His mouth worked but his lines wouldn't come. He shook his head and finally managed, "I'd like to talk to you about it. Uh—welcome your opinion. But I've gotta go start my shift." He turned and hurried back into the coolness of the hospital, feeling her smug smile hanging onto the back of his neck.

It was suddenly important to him that he go to work. He had nothing to expiate.

In the elevator, alone, he glanced at the crumpled pamphlet. He read:

". . . if it is inevitable that a man must die, let him do it with dignity. Death has long been a gross national product, especially since United States intervention in the Arab-Israeli conflict. But a bullet through the heart kills quickly; death under the generator comes tediously. The common fallacy that entropic generators promote death has been proven untrue, *but what do they do to ease or inhibit death?* The presence of a generator is psychologically damaging to the dying, causing them to give up the fight for recovery before they normally would. . . ."

He remembered Hurzbau's words: *Can you say it doesn't take away from my life if you don't know how it works?*

"Mr. Buxton? Can I talk to you?"

Hardly looking up, Buxton demanded, "Well? What are you doing here? You were supposed to be in four-fifty-six twenty minutes ago."

"I want you to explain the principles of the entropic generator to me. I think it's my responsibility to know."

"Oh hell," Buxton spat, disappointed, "is that all? Look it up in the *Encyclopedia Britannica.*"

"I did. It was all in jargon. And they told us briefly and none too clearly when I was being trained for this job. But I never really cared to understand till now. But a . . . friend of mine is under—"

"Under the generator, right? And *now* you want to know. I've heard that one before too many times. Okay, Denton. I'll explain. Once. And you are going to be docked for the time it takes me to explain and the time you weren't working."

Denton shrugged, sat down across from Buxton. He felt like a boy going to confession.

Buxton sighed and began, playing with a pencil as he spoke: "The word *entropy*, literally translated, means *turning toward energy*. From our relative viewpoint we usually define entropy as the degree of disorder in a substance. Entropy always increases and available energy diminishes. So it seems. From our point of view, when we see someone's system of order decaying it seems as if the growth of entropy means a drop of energy. It appears that something is going away from us." He paused to organize his thoughts, began to doodle on scratchpaper.

Denton tapped his fingers irritably. "Yeah? So what? When people die they lose energy—"

"No, they don't lose it in the sense we're concerned with, and SHUT UP AND LISTEN because I'm not going to explain this to you twice. This is already the fourth time this month I've had to go through all this. . . . Now, when you get old, your eyesight fails so it appears as if you see less and less all the time. Things in this world are blotting out, blurring up. Actually, you're seeing something more than you could see before your eyesight failed. When your eyesight dims your entropy-sight increases. Objects look that way, blurred and graylike, in the other dimension, because they possess a form defined by where they are *not* rather than where they *are*."

"*What* dimension?"

Denton was lost.

"The dimension manifested concurrent with the accruence of entropy. We used to think entropy undid creation and form, but in its total sense, entropy creates a form so obverse to ours that it appears not to be there. It creates in a way we don't really understand but which we've learned to use." He cleared his throat, embarrassed by his lapse into erudition. "Anyway, the universe is constantly shifting dimensions. From entropic focus to our type of order and back again. When you get old and seem to be feeling and hearing and seeing less, you are actually perceiving the encroachment of that other universe."

They were silent for five breaths. The taciturn old Jew tapped his pencil agitatedly.

Denton wondered if his inability to comprehend stemmed from his youth. He wasn't decayed enough yet.

"What I'm trying to say," Buxton went on wearily, "is that entropy is a progression instead of a regression. When someone is walking past you it seems like they're regressing, in a relative way, because they are walking toward where you have already been, to what is behind you. But to them, they are *pro*gressing. There are two kinds of known energy, on a cosmic scale: electrical-nuclear energy causing form, and the negative energy of antiform. Nothing is really lost when you die. What occurs is a trade."

"You mean like water displacement? Going into *there,* some of it is forced into *here?"*

"More or less. The generators change the energy of death into usable electric power."

"But if you take energy from a dying person, doesn't that make them die faster?"

"WILL YOU PAY ATTENTION, FOR GOD'S SAKE!" Buxton was determined to get through. *"No.* It doesn't take anything from a dying person. It accumulates energy that's radiated as a result of dying. The negative energy is released into the inanimate environment whether the generator is there or not. The scoop doesn't come into contact with the patient himself . . . it reacts only to the side-effect of his biological dissolution." He took a deep breath. "The main idea is that entropy is not the lack of something, not a subtraction, but an addition. We learned how to tap it because the energy crisis forced us to put up with the temporary discomfort—purely psychological and rather silly—of having the scoop directly over a dying person. When it comes my time to go, I'll be damn proud to contribute something. None of my life is wasted that way, not even its end. One individual causes a remarkable amount of negative energy to be radiated as he dies, you know. We've only been using it practically for five years and there are still a lot of things we don't understand about it."

"So why do it to people? Why not plants?"

"Because various organisms have variegated patterns of radiating negative energy. We don't know how to tap all of them yet. We can do it with cattle and people now. We're working on plants."

"I don't know, I, uh . . ." Denton stumbled over his words, knowing that Buxton would be infuriated by the objection. "But couldn't a generator damage the morale of a person dying? Make him believe it's too late and prematurely give up? I mean, susceptibility to disease is largely psychological, and if you're under pressure by being under the scoop—" He cut short, swallowing, seeing Buxton's growing anger.

Hot ashes sprayed from Buxton's wagging pipe as he spoke. "Denton, all that is a lot of conjectural hogwash. And it is pure stupidity to babble about it in the face of the worst energy crisis the world has ever known. We may have the energy problem licked forever if we can learn to draw negative energy from the dying of plants and small animals and such. But people like you might just ruin that hope. And I want you to know, Denton, that I'm going to seriously consider letting you go, so if you don't want to clinch my decision you'd better get the hell to—"

"I can't go to my assigned shift, sir. I know the girl under that scoop."

"Okay then, that leaves Durghemmer. Take it or no more job."

Feeling drained, Denton nodded dumbly and left the office.

Durghemmer could wait. Denton called hospital information and was informed that Donna was still unconscious.

Denton went to see his only close friend. He took the bus to Glennway Park.

Donald Armor was a cripple in one sense and completely mobile in another. He had been a pro race-car driver for six years, several times taking national honors. During the final lap of the 1983 Indy 500 (the last one before the race was outlawed), while in second place, Armor's car spun out and bounced off the car behind it and went into the grandstands, killing five onlookers, maiming four. When gas-cars were banned and electric air-cars instituted in 1986, the authorities made an exception in Armor's case. He was allowed to drive his own car, the only vehicle on the streets with wheels, because he could drive nothing else. Part of the firewall of the racing car had been ripped loose by the impact of the accident, slashing deep into Armor's side, partially castrating him on the way and cracking his spine. Doctors could not remove the shred without killing him.

Armor was a rich man and he had a car built around him, customized to his specifications. It was a small sports car, but with the cockpit, firewall, steering wheel, and dashboard of the original Indy racer. He was now a permanent organ of the vehicle, living in it day and night, unable and unwilling to leave. Until he died. Excreting through a colostomy bag, eating at drive-ins, he was aware of the absurdity of his existence but he considered his predicament appropriate to the society in which he lived.

Denton sat in the seat next to Armor and, as usual, tried not to look at the thirteen inches of ragged steel protruding from the driver's right side to run to a ball-joint connecting him with the dashboard. The ball-joint gave him limited freedom within the car.

Armor had rudimentary use of his scarred and twisted legs, enough to gun the car down the boulevard with a speed and fluidity which never failed to amaze Denton. Armor drove without hesitation or false starts, always twenty miles in excess of the speed limit, knowing that no policeman would give him a ticket. They all knew him. Armor was famous, and he was dying. He had less than a year to live (long-range complications of the accident) but they could never install a generator over a moving car. He was the source of livelihood for some reporters who spent all their time trying to get interviews and photographs of him. He had no comforts; no radio or tape deck or juice dispensers. He didn't drink and he couldn't have sex.

"What's eating you today, Ron?" Armor asked in a voice like the distant rumble of a semitruck. He was dark and raw-boned and his bushy black brows sprouted alone on a scarred bald head. His hard gray eyes were perpetually lost in the spaces between the white dashes marking the abdomen of the road. "Something's messing you up," he said.

They had been friends since before Armor's accident. Armor knew Denton almost as well as he knew the road. Denton told him about Donna and his doubts concerning the generator.

Armor listened without comment. His eyes didn't leave the road—they rarely did—and his features remained expressionless aside from slight intensifications when the road called for more concentration.

Denton concluded, "And I can't bring myself to leave the job. Donna is still in the coma, so I can't talk to her about it. I almost feel like I'm working against her by continuing there. I know it's irrational. . . ."

"What is it you like so much that you can't quit?"

"It's not that. I . . . well, jobs aren't easy to find."

"I know where you can get another job."

He eased the car to a halt. They were parked in front of TREMMER AND FLEISHER SLAUGHTERING/PROCESSING. Below the older sign was, newly painted in black: GENERATOR ANNEX.

"My brother Harold works here," Armor said. He hadn't turned off the engine. He rarely did. "He remembers you. He can get you a job here. Go on up to the personnel office. That's where he works. You might like this job better than the other, I imagine." He turned uncompromising eyes from the hood of the car and looked at Denton with a five-hundred-horsepower gaze.

"Okay." Denton shrugged. "Anything you say. I can't go back to work now anyway." He opened the car door and got out, feeling his back painfully uncramping after the restriction of the bucket seat. He looked through the open door. Armor was still watching him.

"I'll wait here," Armor said with finality.

The bright light hurt Denton's eyes as he followed Harold Armor, brother to Donald, into a barnlike aluminum building labeled SLAUGHTERHOUSE GENERATOR ANNEX I.

Inside, the sibilance of air-conditioners was punctuated with long bestial sighs from dying cattle. There were two long rows of stalls, a bubble of the generator scoop completely enclosing each prostrate steer. The top of each scoop ducted into a thick vitreous cable joining others from adjoining stalls in a network of silvery wire like a spiderweb canopy overhead.

"Now these cattle here—well, some of 'em are cows what got old—they have a generator for the whole lot of 'em, and one compensator for every three animals," Harold intoned proudly. "And we've got some we've maintained there at just the right level of decay, you know, for six to eight months. And that's just plain difficult. They die a lot on us, though. A lot of 'em dying of old age. Most of 'em we bleed to death."

"You bleed them?" Denton was unable to conceal his horror. Seeing Denton's reaction, Harold stiffened defensively.

"Damn right we do. How else can we keep them at the right level of decay and still keep them alive long enough to produce? Sure, I know what you're going to ask. Everyone does when they first come here. The government shut the ASPCA up because of the power shortage. And of course part of your job as compensator here is you'll have to learn how to adjust their bleeding and feeding so they die at the right speed. It's a bit more work than at the hospital, where they die for you naturally. But it pays more than at the hospital. All you have to remember is that if they sneak back up on you and recover too much, you either have to bleed them more or feed them less. Sometimes we poison them some too, when they first come here, to get them on their way."

Denton stood by one of the cells and observed a fully grown bull with ten-inch horns, massive rib cage rising and falling irregularly, eyes opening and closing and opening and closing. . . .

"Now *that* one," Harold droned, "hasn't been here but a week and he ain't used to it yet. Most of them just lay there and forget they're alive after a few weeks or so. See, you can see marks on the stall where he's been kicking it and his hoof is bleeding—we'll have to patch that up, we don't want him to get an infection. Die too soon that way. You can see he's going to come along good cuz his coat is gettin' rough and fur startin' to come off. . . ."

The trapped beast looked at Denton with dulled eyes devoid of fear. It was lying on its side, head lolling from the stall opening. Three thick plastic tubes were clamped with immovable iron bands to its sagging neck. The steer seemed to be in transition between instinctual rebellion and capitulation. Intermittently it twitched and lifted its head a few inches, as if trying to recall how to stand.

From the *New York Times* review of Ronald Denton's only play, *All Men are Created Sequels:*
". . . like all so-called absurdism, Denton's play was an inert corpse albeit a charming one. This state of inflexible downbeat was probably intentional, and so, like all cadavers, the play began to decay well before the second act, as perhaps it was supposed to. By the end of the second act, the stage was a figurative miasma of putrid flesh,

squirming with parasitic irrelevancies. The least Mr. Denton could have done would have been the courtesy of a generator scoop hooked up to the audience so that we could glean something of value from the affair as the audience died of boredom."

Denton was looking out the window, wondering at the gall Armor had exhibited in arranging for him to see the slaughterhouse. He had known—

Durghemmer interrupted his thoughts.

"Come here, kid!"

Denton didn't want to go around to the other side of the generator. He didn't want to look at Durghemmer.

"*Comere,* boy!"

Denton sighed and stood up. "Yes?"

Durghemmer's face was round and robust. His eyes were bright buttons sewn deep in the hollows over his cheeks. He had a miniature round mouth, a wisp of white hair, and minimal chin. His jowls shook when he laughed. He pointed at Denton with a stubby finger. "You skeered of something, kid?"

"Shouldn't you be asleep, Mr. Durghemmer? It's past nine."

"Shouldn't *you* be asleep, kid? Sleep?" He laughed shrilly, cowbells filtering through the plastic bell of the scoop. He half sat up, grimaced, fell back.

Emanuel Durghemmer had come to the hospital three years before, dying of meningitis. He had been too far along for help; they had expected him to die within a week. A generator was immediately placed over him. He went into a month-long coma. When he woke, the needles jumped. According to the meters, he had come a substantial step closer to death by regaining consciousness. And according to hospital legend, he had sat up directly upon awakening from the coma, and *laughed.* The generator again had registered a drop in life-force and a corresponding gain in entropic energy. Each week for three years Durghemmer had shown signs of being on the verge of death. Always in pain, he delivered more negative energy than any other individual in the hospital. And he had developed a corrosive bedridden manner to counteract the doctor's bedside manners.

Denton was disquieted by Durghemmer's paradoxical joviality. But Denton had two hours left of his shift. He decided to make the most of it, find out what he could.

Somehow Durghemmer's attitude made Donna's imminent death seem ludicrous.

"You're wondering, aren't you?" Durghemmer asked, as if he were still a politician casting rhetoric. "You're wondering how I stay alive."

"No. I don't give a damn."

"But you do. You care for the simplest of reasons. You know you're going to die someday and you wonder how long you'll last under the generator and what it will be like watching the needle go up and down. Or maybe—if it's not you, is it someone else? Someone close to you dying, kid?"

No surprise that Durghemmer knew. The old parasite had been in the hospital for three years, a record by two and a half years for being under the generator. He could smell death a long way away.

"All right, but so what?" Denton said impulsively. "So you're right. It's a girl friend."

"She got cancer between the legs?" Hollow laughter reverberated inside the scoop. Lines of mirth on the old man's face meshed indistinguishably with lines of pain.

Denton wanted to smash the plastic of the scoop to get at the old politician's sour mouth with his fist. Instead, he said coolly: "No. She was knifed. I've got to see her. I heard she came around for a while this afternoon. Maybe I can . . ." He shrugged. "I've got to explain things."

"May as well write her off, kid. Nobody but me has ever figured out how to use it. I had training when I was mayor." He guffawed, coughing phlegm.

"What did you do to Burt Lemmer?"

"That kid that resigned? He was a short spit, only on my generator three weeks. Usually takes them at least a month." He closed his eyes. In a low, tense voice: "You know, sometimes pain sharpens things for you. It kind of wakes you up and makes you see better. You ever notice when your gut hurts and you feel like every sound and sight is too loud or bright for you to stand it? Everything makes you feel sicker because you're seeing it so well, so clearly. Sometimes people who haven't done anything with their lives become good painters when they get sick because the hurt *makes* them look at things. And sometimes—" He drifted off for a full minute, his eyes in limbo. Then he spoke conspiratorially, whispering more to himself than to Denton, "Sometimes I see things in the blossoms of pain. Useful things. Peeks into that other world. I go into it a little ways, then I come back here and I'm on solid ground. And I see these invisible wires connecting each man to the others, like puppet strings all mixed up."

Denton had lost interest in the old man's ramblings. He could see Donna's eyes smoldering with pain like the red dials of the generator.

Durghemmer's generator hummed into life as it began to absorb a flood of negative energy. The old man was tiring. The machine began to chuckle to itself. Durghemmer lay composed, a faint smile lost in the mazelike etchings of his face.

"Durghemmer," Denton said, standing. "I've got to see that woman. I've got to make sure she's all right. Now look, if I go, would you refrain from calling the nurse when I go out unless it's an absolute emergency? I've *got* to—"

"Okay, kid. But you can write off your girl friend. She hasn't lived long enough to learn. . . ." He had spoken without bothering to open his eyes.

Denton was alone with Donna; he had bribed the scheduled compensator. He peered through the scoop at her nervously, irrationally afraid that she might already be dead. Her elfin features, unconscious, blinked in and out of shadow with the strobing of the generator lights in the darkened room. Denton checked the dials, rechecked them, found a compensating factor he had missed the first time. He adjusted the intake of the scoop.

She was dropping. The needles were climbing.

He flipped on the intercom, walked around to the other side of the bed. "Donna? Can you hear me?" He glanced at the meter. It jumped. She was coming around but it took strength from her to awaken. Maybe talking to her would make her weak, perhaps cause her death, he thought abruptly. Something be should have considered sooner. His heart was a fist pounding the bars of his chest.

Her eyes opened, silver-blue platinum, metal tarnished with desperation.

He spoke hastily: "I'm sorry about everything, Donna. I don't know how you got involved in my problems. . . ." He waved his hands futilely.

She looked at him without comprehension for a moment, then recognition cleared her eyes.

"I shouldn't bother you now," he added gratuitously, "but I had to talk to you."

It came to him that he really had no idea what he wanted to say.

"Get out of here, Ron . . . you came for yourself, not for me." Her voice was thin as autumn ice. And like being awakened with ice-water, Denton was shocked into realization: It was true, he had been more worried about his own feelings than hers.

"You came here to apologize. Big deal. Maybe you should apologize to that Hurzbau kid. I heard that he died. I'm not moralizing. We killed him together." Her eyes fluttered.

"Donna?" She was giving up. Her voice trailed off. Get her attention, make her fight her way back. He buzzed for the nurse and shouted, *"Donna!"* His voice stretched wiry from hysteria.

She opened her eyes a crack and murmured, "They took a psychological test for you, didn't they? They tested you and knew you were right for the job."

The nurse bustled in then and Denton pressed the green button that lifted the scoop.

As he left he saw the needles, still rising. Rapaciously, the generator giggled.

He shuffled with great effort through the halls, two days' lack of sleep catching up to him. His arms and legs seemed to be growing softer, as if his bones were dissolving. He came to the window overlooking the parking lot. As he expected, Armor was waiting for him below, driving around and around and around without pausing, circling the parking lot in a loop of abeyance.

Denton left the window. He couldn't face Armor now. He scuffled down the antiseptic hallways. He fancied that he felt negative energy radiating from him like a dark halo. The penumbra grew darker as he sank deeper into exhaustion. His throat contracted till he could hardly breathe. He had memorized the exact shape of the trickle of blood on Donna's chin, the last thing that had caught his attention before the nurse had made him leave. It had runneled down from her nose onto her cheek, splitting into forks, a dark lightning bolt. He pictured the fine branchings of red multiplying in the atmosphere around him as if the air were filled with a skein of ethereal blood veins. The red lines connected the spectral orderlies and nurses rushing past, like the wires Durghemmer had described connecting the heads of everyone in the city. Denton walked slowly, plowing through molten wax to Durghemmer's room.

"I want to *know*, Durghemmer," he said to the old man, as he entered the sterile chamber. "I know you steal the negative energy of the scoop for yourself. I want to know *how*."

The old man grinned toothlessly. His gums were cracked and dried, making his mouth into the crumbling battlements of a ruined city. He sat up, and the needles rose again.

Denton leaned wearily on the generator, determined to come to terms with death.

"I figured you'd want to know, Denton." Durghemmer laughed, moths tumbling dustily in his throat. "I can see just by looking at you that the girl died."

Denton nodded. The movement might have been made by a scarecrow swayed by a breeze.

"Sure, lad, I'll show you just how I thrive in this hole. I'll show you how I keep an even keel under this scoop like a pheasant under glass. I'll show you just exactly and honest to God. You just watch me now."

"Watch you? You mean I can *see* how you do it?"

"Sure. You just watch now."

The dark room seemed to congeal with grains of opacity. The generator hummed happily to itself. Denton leaned forward, hands on the control panel, tired eyes locked desperately onto Durghemmer.

The decaying politician lay back and folded his hands on his chest. Then, he began to chuckle.

Denton was completely baffled. As far as he could see, the old man was doing nothing at all . . .

. . . except laughing.

The Ugly Chickens

Howard Waldrop

Vanishing species are by no means a product exclusively of the twentieth century, even if we confine the term to creatures being killed off by humans. The dodo comes immediately to mind. This story tells the odd history of their extinction, but goes farther, to suggest that perhaps not all of them died when we thought they had.

Howard Waldrop has written a number of highly regarded science fiction stories, and collaborated with Jake Saunders on the novel *The Texas-Israeli War.*

MY CAR WAS broken, and I had a class to teach at eleven. So I took the city bus, something I rarely do.

I spent last summer crawling through the Big Thicket with cameras and tape recorder, photographing and taping two of the last ivory-billed woodpeckers on the earth. You can see the films at your local Audubon Society showroom.

This year I wanted something just as flashy but a little less taxing. Perhaps a population study on the Bermuda cahow, or the New Zealand takahe. A month or so in the warm (not hot) sun would do me a world of good. To say nothing of the advancement of science.

I was idly leafing through Greenway's *Extinct and Vanishing Birds of the World.* The city bus was winding its way through the ritzy neighborhoods of Austin, stopping to let off the chicanas, black women, and Vietnamese who tended the kitchens and gardens of the rich.

"I haven't seen any of those ugly chickens in a long time," said a voice close by.

A gray-haired lady was leaning across the aisle toward me.

I looked at her, then around. Maybe she was a shopping-bag lady. Maybe she was just talking. I looked straight at her. No doubt about it,

265

she was talking to me. She was waiting for an answer.

"I used to live near some folks who raised them when I was a girl," she said. She pointed.

I looked down at the page my book was open to.

What I should have said was: That is quite impossible, madam. This is a drawing of an extinct bird of the island of Mauritius. It is perhaps the most famous dead bird in the world. Maybe you are mistaking this drawing for that of some rare Asiatic turkey, peafowl, or pheasant. I am sorry, but you *are* mistaken.

I should have said all that.

What she said was, "Oops, this is my stop." And got up to go.

My name is Paul Lindberl. I am twenty-six years old, a graduate student in ornithology at the University of Texas, a teaching assistant. My name is not unknown in the field. I have several vices and follies, but I don't think foolishness is one of them.

The stupid thing for me to do would have been to follow her.

She stepped off the bus.

I followed her.

I came into the departmental office, trailing scattered papers in the whirlwind behind me. "Martha! Martha!" I yelled.

She was doing something in the supply cabinet.

"Jesus, Paul! What do you want?"

"Where's Courtney?"

"At the conference in Houston. You know that. You missed your class. What's the matter?"

"Petty cash. Let me at it!"

"Payday was only a week ago. If you can't—"

"It's business! It's fame and adventure and the chance of a lifetime! It's a long sea voyage that leaves . . . a plane ticket. To either Jackson, Mississippi, or Memphis. Make it Jackson, it's closer. I'll get receipts! I'll be famous. Courtney will be famous. *You'll* even be famous! This university will make even *more* money! I'll pay you back. Give me some paper. I gotta write Courtney a note. When's the next plane out? Could you get Marie and Chuck to take over my classes Tuesday and Wednesday? I'll try to be back Thursday unless something happens. Courtney'll be back tomorrow, right? I'll call him from, well, wherever. Do you have some coffee?"

And so on and so forth. Martha looked at me like I was crazy. But she filled out the requisition anyway.

"What do I tell Kemejian when I ask him to sign these?"

"Martha, babe, sweetheart. Tell him I'll get his picture in *Scientific*

American."

"He doesn't read it."

"*Nature,* then!"

"I'll see what I can do," she said.

The lady I had followed off the bus was named Jolyn (Smith) Jimson. The story she told me was so weird that it had to be true. She knew things only an expert or someone with firsthand experience could know. I got names from her, and addresses, and directions, and tidbits of information. Plus a year: 1927.

And a place. Northern Mississippi.

I gave her my copy of the Greenway book. I told her I'd call her as soon as I got back into town. I left her standing on the corner near the house of the lady she cleaned up for twice a week. Jolyn Jimson was in her sixties.

Think of the dodo as a baby harp seal with feathers. I know that's not even close, but it saves time.

In 1507 the Portuguese, on their way to India, found the (then unnamed) Mascarene Islands in the Indian Ocean—three of them a few hundred miles apart, all east of Madagascar.

It wasn't until 1598, when that old Dutch sea captain Cornelius van Neck bumped into them, that the islands received their names—names that changed several times through the centuries as the Dutch, French, and English changed them every war or so. They are now known as Rodriguez, Réunion, and Mauritius.

The major feature of these islands was large, flightless, stupid, ugly, bad-tasting birds. Van Neck and his men named them *dod-aarsen,* "stupid asses," or *dodars,* "silly birds," or solitaires.

There were three species: the dodo of Mauritius, the real gray-brown, hooked-beak, clumsy thing that weighed twenty kilos or more; the white, somewhat slimmer, dodo of Réunion; and the solitaires of Rodriguez and Réunion, which looked like very fat, very dumb light-colored geese.

The dodos all had thick legs, big squat bodies twice as large as a turkey's, naked faces, and big long downcurved beaks ending in a hook like a hollow linoleum knife. Long ago they had lost the ability to fly, and their wings had degenerated to flaps the size of a human hand with only three or four feathers in them. Their tails were curly and fluffy, like a child's afterthought at decoration. They had absolutely no natural enemies. They nested on the open ground. They probably hatched their eggs wherever they happened to lay them.

No natural enemies until Van Neck and his kind showed up. The

Dutch, French, and Portuguese sailors who stopped at Mascarenes to replenish stores found that, besides looking stupid, dodos *were* stupid. The men walked right up to the dodos and hit them on the head with clubs. Better yet, dodos could be herded around like sheep. Ships' logs are full of things like: "Party of ten men ashore. Drove half a hundred of the big turkey-like birds into the boat. Brought to ship, where they are given the run of the decks. Three will feed a crew of 150."

Even so, most of the dodo, except for the breast, tasted bad. One of the Dutch words for them was *walghvogel,* "disgusting bird." But on a ship three months out on a return from Goa to Lisbon, well, food was where you found it. It was said, even so, that prolonged boiling did not improve the flavor.

Even so, the dodos might have lasted, except that the Dutch, and later the French, colonized the Mascarenes. The islands became plantations and dumping places for religious refugees. Sugarcane and other exotic crops were raised there.

With the colonists came cats, dogs, hogs, and the cunning *Rattus norvegicus* and the Rhesus monkey from Ceylon. What dodos the hungry sailors left were chased down (they were dumb and stupid, but they could run when they felt like it) by dogs in the open. They were killed by cats as they sat on their nests. Their eggs were stolen and eaten by monkeys, rats, and hogs. And they competed with the pigs for all the low-growing goodies of the islands.

The last Mauritius dodo was seen in 1681, less than a hundred years after humans first saw them. The last white dodo walked off the history books around 1720. The solitaires of Rodriguez and Réunion, last of the genus as well as the species, may have lasted until 1790. Nobody knows.

Scientists suddenly looked around and found no more of the Didine birds alive, anywhere.

This part of the country was degenerate before the first Snopes ever saw it. This road hadn't been paved until the late fifties, and it was a main road between two county seats. That didn't mean it went through civilized country. I'd traveled for miles and seen nothing but dirt banks red as Billy Carter's neck and an occasional church. I expected to see Burma Shave signs, but realized this road had probably never had them.

I almost missed the turnoff onto the dirt and gravel road the man back at the service station had marked. It led onto the highway from nowhere, a lane out of a field. I turned down it, and a rock the size of a golf ball flew up over the hood and put a crack three inches long in the windshield of the rental car I'd gotten in Grenada.

It was a hot, muggy day for this early. The view was obscured in a cloud of dust every time the gravel thinned. About a mile down the road, the gravel gave out completely. The roadway turned into a rutted dirt pathway just wider than the car, hemmed in on both sides by a sagging three-strand barbed-wire fence.

In some places the fence posts were missing for a few meters. The wire lay on the ground and in some places disappeared under it for long stretches.

The only life I saw was a mockingbird raising hell with something under a thornbush the barbed wire had been nailed to in place of a post. To one side now was a grassy field that had gone wild, the way everywhere will look after we blow ourselves off the face of the planet. The other was fast becoming woods—pine, oak, some black gum, and wild plum, fruit not out this time of the year.

I began to ask myself what I was doing here. What if Ms. Jimson were some imaginative old crank who—but no. Wrong, maybe, but even the wrong was worth checking. But I knew she hadn't lied to me. She had seemed incapable of lies—a good ol' girl, backbone of the South, of the earth. Not a mendacious gland in her being.

I couldn't doubt her, or my judgment either. Here I was, creeping and bouncing down a dirt path in Mississippi, after no sleep for a day, out on the thin ragged edge of a dream. I *had* to take it on faith.

The back of the car sometimes slid where the dirt had loosened and gave way to sand. The back tire stuck once, but I rocked out of it. Getting back out again would be another matter. Didn't anyone ever use this road?

The woods closed in on both sides like the forest primeval, and the fence had long since disappeared. My odometer said ten kilometers, and it had been twenty minutes since I'd turned off the highway. In the rearview mirror, I saw beads of sweat and dirt in the wrinkles of my neck. A fine patina of dust covered everything inside the car. Clots of it came through the windows.

The woods reached out and swallowed the road. Branches scraped against the windows and the top. It was like falling down a long, dark, leafy tunnel. It was dark and green in there. I fought back an atavistic urge to turn on the headlights. The roadbed must be made of a few centuries of leaf mulch. I kept constant pressure on the accelerator and bulled my way through.

Half a log caught and banged and clanged against the car bottom. I saw light ahead. Fearing for the oil pan, I punched the pedal and sped out.

I almost ran through a house.

It was maybe ten meters from the trees. The road ended under one of the windows. I saw somebody waving from the corner of my eye.

I slammed on the brakes.

A whole family was on the porch, looking like a Walker Evans Depression photograph, or a fever dream from the mind of a "Hee Haw" producer. The house was old. Strips of peeling paint a meter long tapped against the eaves.

"Damned good thing you stopped," said a voice. I looked up. The biggest man I had ever seen in my life leaned down into the driver-side window.

"If we'd have heard you sooner, I'd've sent one of the kids down to the end of the driveway to warn you," he said.

Driveway?

His mouth was stained brown at the corners. I figured he chewed tobacco until I saw the sweet-gum snuff brush sticking from the pencil pocket in the bib of his coveralls. His hands were the size of catchers' mitts. They looked like they'd never held anything smaller than an ax handle.

"How y'all?" he said, by way of introduction.

"Just fine," I said. I got out of the car.

"My name's Lindberl," I said, extending my hand. He took it. For an instant, I thought of bear traps, sharks' mouths, closing elevator doors. The thought went back to wherever it is they stay.

"This the Gudger place?" I asked.

He looked at me blankly with his gray eyes. He wore a diesel truck cap and had on a checked lumberjack shirt beneath the coveralls. His rubber boots were the size of the ones Karloff wore in *Frankenstein*.

"Naw. I'm Jim Bob Krait. That's my wife, Jenny, and there's Luke and Skeeno and Shirl." He pointed to the porch.

The people on the porch nodded.

"Lessee. Gudger? No Gudgers round here I know of. I'm sorta new here." I took that to mean he hadn't lived here for more than twenty years or so.

"Jennifer!" he yelled. "You know of anybody named Gudger?" To me he said, "My wife's lived around heres all her life."

His wife came down onto the second step of the porch landing. "I think they used to be the ones what lived on the Spradlin place before the Spradlins. But the Spradlins left around the Korean War. I didn't know any of the Gudgers myself. That's while we was living over to Water Valley."

"You an insurance man?" asked Mr. Krait.

"Uh . . . no," I said. I imagined the people on the porch leaning toward me, all ears. "I'm a . . . I teach college."

"Oxford?" asked Krait.

270

"Uh, no. University of Texas."

"Well, that's a damn long way off. You say you're looking for the Gudgers?"

"Just their house. The area. As your wife said, I understand they left. During the Depression, I believe."

"Well, they musta had money," said the gigantic Mr. Krait. "Nobody around here was rich enough to *leave* during the Depression."

"Luke!" he yelled. The oldest boy on the porch sauntered down. He looked anemic and wore a shirt in vogue with the Twist. He stood with his hands in his pockets.

"Luke, show Mr. Lindbergh—"

"Lindberl."

". . . Mr. Lindberl here the way up to the old Spradlin place. Take him as far as the old log bridge, he might get lost before then."

"Log bridge broke down, Daddy."

"When?"

"October, Daddy."

"Well, hell, somethin' else to fix! Anyway, to the creek."

He turned to me. "You want him to go along on up there, see you don't get snakebit?"

"No, I'm sure I'll be fine."

"Mind if I ask what you're going up there for?" he asked. He was looking away from me. I could see having to come right out and ask was bothering him. Such things usually came up in the course of conversation.

"I'm a—uh, bird scientist. I study birds. We had a sighting— someone told us the old Gudger place—the area around here—I'm looking for a rare bird. It's hard to explain."

I noticed I was sweating. It was hot.

"You mean like a good God? I saw a good God about twenty-five years ago, over next to Bruce," he said.

"Well, no." (A good God was one of the names for an ivory-billed woodpecker, one of the rarest in the world. Any other time I would have dropped my jaw. Because they were thought to have died out in Mississippi by the teens, and by the fact that Krait knew they *were* rare.)

I went to lock my car up, then thought of the protocol of the situation. "My car be in your way?" I asked.

"Naw. It'll be just fine," said Jim Bob Krait. "We'll look for you back by sundown, that be all right?"

For a minute, I didn't know whether that was a command or an expression of concern.

"Just in case I get snakebit," I said. "I'll try to be careful up there."

"Good luck on findin' them rare birds," he said. He walked up to the porch with his family.

"Les go," said Luke.

Behind the Krait house were a hen house and pigsty where hogs lay after their morning slop like islands in a muddy bay, or some Zen pork sculpture. Next we passed broken farm machinery gone to rust, though there was nothing but uncultivated land as far as the eye could see. How the family made a living I don't know. I'm told you can find places just like this throughout the South.

We walked through woods and across fields, following a sort of path. I tried to memorize the turns I would have to take on my way back. Luke didn't say a word the whole twenty minutes he accompanied me, except to curse once when he stepped into a bull nettle with his tennis shoes.

We came to a creek that skirted the edge of a woodsy hill. There was a rotted log forming a small dam. Above it the water was nearly a meter deep; below it, half that much.

"See that path?" he asked.

"Yes."

"Follow it up around the hill, then across the next field. Then you cross the creek again on the rocks, and over the hill. Take the left-hand path. What's left of the house is about three-quarters the way up the next hill. If you come to a big, bare rock cliff, you've gone too far. You got that?"

I nodded.

He turned and left.

The house had once been a dog-run cabin, as Ms. Jimson had said. Now it was fallen in on one side, what they call sigoglin. (Or was it anti-sigoglin?) I once heard a hymn on the radio called "The Land Where No Cabins Fall." This was the country songs like that were written in.

Weeds grew everywhere. There were signs of fences, a flattened pile of wood that had once been a barn. Farther behind the house were the outhouse remains. Half a rusted pump stood in the backyard. A flatter spot showed where the vegetable garden had been; in it a single wild tomato, pecked by birds, lay rotting. I passed it. There was lumber from three outbuildings, mostly rotten and green with algae and moss. One had been a smokehouse and woodshed combination. Two had been chicken roosts. One was larger than the other. It was there I started to poke around and dig.

Where? Where? I wish I'd been on more archaeological digs, knew the places to look. Refuse piles, midden heaps, kitchen scrap piles, compost boxes. Why hadn't I been born on a farm so I'd know instinctively where to search?

I prodded around the grounds. I moved back and forth like a setter casting for the scent of quail. I wanted more, more. I still wasn't satisfied.

Dusk. Dark, in fact. I trudged into the Kraits' front yard. The tote sack I carried was full to bulging. I was hot, tired, streaked with fifty years of chicken shit. The Kraits were on their porch. Jim Bob lumbered down like a friendly mountain.

I asked him a few questions, gave them a Xerox of one of the dodo pictures, left them addresses and phone numbers where they could reach me.

Then into the rental car. Off to Water Valley, acting on information Jennifer Krait gave me. I went to the postmaster's house at Water Valley. She was getting ready for bed. I asked questions. She got on the phone. I bothered people until one in the morning. Then back into the trusty rental car.

On to Memphis as the moon came up on my right. Interstate 55 was a glass ribbon before me. WLS from Chicago was on the radio.

I hummed along with it, I sang at the top of my voice.

The sack full of dodo bones, beaks, feet, and eggshell fragments kept me company on the front seat.

Did you know a museum once traded an entire blue whale skeleton for one of a dodo?

Driving, driving.

THE DANCE OF THE DODOS

I used to have a vision sometimes—I had it long before this madness came up. I can close my eyes and see it by thinking hard. But it comes to me most often, most vividly, when I am reading and listening to classical music, especially Pachelbel's *Canon in D*.

It is near dusk in The Hague, and the light is that of Frans Hals, of Rembrandt. The Dutch royal family and their guests eat and talk quietly in the great dining hall. Guards with halberds and pikes stand in the corners of the room. The family is arranged around the table: the King, Queen, some princesses, a prince, a couple of other children, an invited noble or two. Servants come out with plates and cups, but they do not intrude.

On a raised platform at one end of the room an orchestra plays dinner music—a harpsichord, viola, cello, three violins, and woodwinds. One of the royal dwarfs sits on the edge of the platform, his foot slowly rubbing the back of one of the dogs sleeping near him.

As the music of Pachelbel's *Canon in D* swells and rolls through the hall, one of the dodos walks in clumsily, stops, tilts its head, its eyes bright as a pool of tar. It sways a little, lifts its foot tentatively, one, then another, rocks back and forth in time to the cello.

The violins swirl. The dodo begins to dance, its great ungainly body now graceful. It is joined by the other two dodos who come into the hall, all three turning in a sort of circle.

The harpsichord begins its counterpoint. The fourth dodo, the white one from Réunion, comes from its place under the table and joins the circle with the others.

It is most graceful of all, making complete turns where the others only sway and dip on the edge of the circle they have formed.

The music rises in volume; the first violinist sees the dodos and nods to the King. But he and the others at the table have already seen. They are silent, transfixed—even the servants stand still, bowls, pots, and kettles in their hands, forgotten.

Around the dodos dance with bobs and weaves of their ugly heads. The white dodo dips, takes a half step, pirouettes on one foot, circles again.

Without a word the King of Holland takes the hand of the Queen, and they come around the table, children before the spectacle. They join in the dance, waltzing (anachronism) among the dodos while the family, the guests, the soldiers watch and nod in time with the music.

Then the vision fades, and the afterimage of a flickering fireplace and a dodo remains.

The dodo and its kindred came by ships to the ports of Europe. The first we have record of is that of Captain van Neck, who brought back two in 1599—one for the ruler of Holland, and one that found its way through Cologne to the menagerie of Emperor Rudolf II.

This royal aviary was at Schloss Negebau, near Vienna. It was here that the first paintings of the dumb old birds were done by Georg and his son Jacob Hoefnagel, between 1602 and 1610. They painted it among more than ninety species of birds that kept the Emperor amused.

Another Dutch artist named Roelandt Savery, as someone said, "made a career out of the dodo." He drew and painted the birds many times, and was no doubt personally fascinated by them. Obsessed, even. Early on, the paintings are consistent; the later ones have inaccuracies. This implies he worked from life first, then from memory as his model went to that place soon to be reserved for all its species. One of his drawings has two of the Raphidae scrambling for some goody on the ground. His works are not without charm.

Another Dutch artist (they seemed to sprout up like mushrooms after a spring rain) named Peter Withoos also stuck dodos in his paintings, sometimes in odd and exciting places—wandering around during their owner's music lessons, or stuck with Adam and Eve in some Edenic idyll.

The most accurate representation, we are assured, comes from half a world away from the religious and political turmoil of the seafaring Europeans. There is an Indian miniature painting of the dodo that now rests in a museum in Russia. The dodo could have been brought by the Dutch or Portuguese in their travels to Goa and the coasts of the Indian subcontinent. Or it could have been brought centuries before by the Arabs who plied the Indian Ocean in their triangular-sailed craft, and who may have discovered the Mascarenes before the Europeans cranked themselves up for the First Crusade.

At one time early in my bird-fascination days (after I stopped killing them with BB guns but before I began to work for a scholarship), I once sat down and figured out where all the dodos had been.

Two with van Neck in 1599, one to Holland, one to Austria. Another was in Count Solms's park in 1600. An account speaks of "one in Italy, one in Germany, several in England, eight or nine to Holland." William Boentekoe van Hoorn knew of "one shipped to Europe in 1640, another in 1685," which he said was "also painted by Dutch artists." Two were mentioned as "being kept in Surrat House in India as pets," perhaps one of which is the one in the painting. Being charitable, and considering "several" to mean at least three, that means twenty dodos in all.

There had to be more, when boatloads had been gathered at the time.

What do we know of the Didine birds? A few ships' logs, some accounts left by travelers and colonists. The English were fascinated by them. Sir Hamon Lestrange, a contemporary of Pepys, saw exhibited "a Dodar from the Island of Mauritius . . . it is not able to flie, being so bigge." One was stuffed when it died, and was put in the Museum Tradescantum in South Lambeth. It eventually found its way into the Ashmolean Museum. It grew ratty and was burned, all but a leg and the head, in 1750. By then there were no more dodos, but nobody had realized that yet.

Francis Willughby got to describe it before its incineration. Earlier, old Carolus Clusius in Holland studied the one in Count Solms's park. He collected everything known about the Raphidae, describing a dodo leg Pieter Pauw kept in his natural-history cabinet, in *Exoticarium libri decem* in 1605, seven years after their discovery.

François Leguat, a Huguenot who lived on Réunion for some years, published an account of his travels in which he mentioned the dodos. It was published in 1690 (after the Mauritius dodo was extinct) and included the information that "some of the males weigh forty-five pound. . . . One egg, much bigger than that of a goos is laid by the female, and takes seven weeks hatching time."

The Abbé Pingré visited the Mascarenes in 1761. He saw the last of the Rodriguez solitaires and collected what information he could about the dead Mauritius and Réunion members of the genus.

After that, only memories of the colonists and some scientific debate as to *where* the Raphidae belonged in the great taxonomic scheme of things—some said pigeons, some said rails—were left. Even this nitpicking ended. The dodo was forgotten.

When Lewis Carroll wrote *Alice in Wonderland* in 1865, most people thought he had invented the dodo.

The service station I called from in Memphis was busier than a one-legged man in an ass-kicking contest. Between bings and dings of the bell, I finally realized the call had gone through.

The guy who answered was named Selvedge. I got nowhere with him. He mistook me for a real estate agent, then a lawyer. Now he was beginning to think I was some sort of a con man. I wasn't doing too well, either. I hadn't slept in two days. I must have sounded like a speed freak. My only progress was that I found that Ms. Annie Mae Gudger (childhood playmate of Jolyn Jimson) was now, and had been, the respected Ms. Annie Mae Radwin. This guy Selvedge must have been a secretary or toady or something.

We were having a conversation comparable to that between a shrieking macaw and a pile of mammoth bones. Then there was another click on the line.

"Young man?" said the other voice, an old woman's voice, southern, very refined but with a hint of the hills in it.

"Yes? Hello! Hello!"

"Young man, you say you talked to a Jolyn somebody? Do you mean Jolyn Smith?"

"Hello! Yes! Ms. Radwin, Ms. Annie Mae Radwin who used to be Gudger? She lives in Austin now. Texas. She used to live near Water Valley, Mississippi, Austin's where I'm from. I—"

"Young man," asked the voice again, "are you sure you haven't been put up to this by my hateful sister Alma?"

"Who? No, ma'am. I met a woman named Jolyn—"

"I'd like to talk to you, young man," said the voice. Then, offhandedly, "Give him directions to get here, Selvedge."

Click.

I cleaned out my mouth as best I could in the service station rest-room, tried to shave with an old clogged Gillette disposable in my knap-sack, and succeeded in gapping up my jawline. I change into a clean pair of jeans and the only other shirt I had with me, and combed my hair. I stood in front of the mirror.

I still looked like the dog's lunch.

The house reminded me of Elvis Presley's mansion, which was somewhere in the neighborhood. From a shack on the side of a Missis-sippi hill to this, in forty years. There are all sorts of ways of making it. I wondered what Annie Mae Gudger's had been. Luck? Predation? Di-vine intervention? Hard work? Trover and replevin?

Selvedge led me toward the sun room. I felt like Philip Marlowe going to meet a rich client. The house was filled with that furniture built sometime between the turn of the century and the 1950s—the ageless kind. It never looks great, it never looks ratty, and every chair is com-fortable.

I think I was expecting some formidable woman with sleeve blot-ters and a green eyeshade hunched over a rolltop desk with piles of paper whose acceptance or rejection meant life or death for thousands.

Who I met was a charming lady in a green pantsuit. She was in her sixties, her hair still a straw-wheat color. It didn't look dyed. Her eyes were blue as my first-grade teacher's had been. She was wiry and looked as if the word *fat* was not in her vocabulary.

"Good morning, Mr. Lindberl." She shook my hand. "Would you like some coffee? You look as if you could use it."

"Yes, thank you."

"Please sit down." She indicated a white wicker chair at a glass table. A serving tray with coffeepot, cups, tea bags, croissants, nap-kins, and plates lay on the tabletop.

After I swallowed half a cup of coffee at a gulp, she said, "What you wanted to see me about must be important."

"Sorry about my manners," I said. "I know I don't look it, but I'm a biology assistant at the University of Texas. An ornithologist. Working on my master's. I met Ms. Jolyn Jimson two days ago—"

"How is Jolyn? I haven't seen her in, oh Lord, it must be on to fifty years. The time gets away."

"She seemed to be fine. I only talked to her half an hour or so. That was—"

"And you've come to see me about . . . ?"

"Uh. The . . . about some of the poultry your family used to raise,

277

when they lived near Water Valley."

She looked at me a moment. Then she began to smile.

"Oh, you mean the ugly chickens?" she said.

I smiled. I almost laughed. I knew what Oedipus must have gone through.

It is now four-thirty in the afternoon. I am sitting in the downtown Motel 6 in Memphis. I have to make a phone call and get some sleep and catch a plane.

Annie Mae Gudger Radwin talked for four hours, answering my questions, setting me straight on family history, having Selvedge hold all her calls.

The main problem was that Annie Mae ran off in 1928, the year *before* her father got his big break. She went to Yazoo City, and by degrees and stages worked her way northward to Memphis and her destiny as the widow of a rich mercantile broker.

But I get ahead of myself.

Grandfather Gudger used to be the overseer for Colonel Crisby on the main plantation near McComb, Mississippi. There was a long story behind that. Bear with me.

Colonel Crisby himself was the scion of a seafaring family with interests in both the cedars of Lebanon (almost all cut down for masts for His Majesty's and others' navies) and Egyptian cotton. Also teas, spices, and any other salable commodity that came its way.

When Colonel Crisby's grandfather reached his majority in 1802, he waved good-bye to the Atlantic Ocean at Charleston, S.C., and stepped westward into the forest. When he stopped, he was in the middle of the Chickasaw Nation, where he opened a trading post and introduced slaves to the Indians.

And he prospered, and begat Colonel Crisby's father, who sent back to South Carolina for everything his father owned. Everything— slaves, wagons, horses, cattle, guinea fowl, peacocks, and dodos, which everybody thought of as atrociously ugly poultry of some kind. One of the seafaring uncles had bought them off a French merchant in 1721. (I surmised these were white dodos from Réunion, unless they had been from even earlier stock. The dodo of Mauritius was already extinct by then.)

All this stuff was herded out west to the trading post in the midst of the Chickasaw Nation. (The tribes around there were of the confederation of the Dancing Rabbits.)

And Colonel Crisby's father prospered, and so did the guinea fowl and the dodos. Then Andrew Jackson came along and marched the Dancing Rabbits off up the Trail of Tears to the heaven of Oklahoma.

And Colonel Crisby's father begat Colonel Crisby, and put the trading post in the hands of others, and moved his plantation westward still to McComb.

Everything prospered but Colonel Crisby's father, who died. And the dodos, with occasional losses to the avengin' weasel and the egg-sucking dog, reproduced themselves also.

Then along came Granddaddy Gudger, a Simon Legree role model, who took care of the plantation while Colonel Crisby raised ten companies of men and marched off to fight the War for Southern Independence. Colonel Crisby came back to the McComb plantation earlier than most, he having stopped much of the same volley of Minié balls that caught his commander, General Beauregard Hanlon, on a promontory bluff during the Siege of Vicksburg. He wasn't dead, but death hung around the place like a gentlemanly bill collector for a month. The Colonel languished, went slapdab crazy, and freed all his slaves the week before he died (the war lasted another two years after that). Not now having any slaves, he didn't need an overseer.

Then comes the Faulkner part of the tale, straight out of *As I Lay Dying*, with the Gudger family returning to the area of Water Valley (before there was a Water Valley), moving through the demoralized and tattered displaced persons of the South, driving their dodos before them. For Colonel Crisby had given them to his former overseer for his faithful service. Also followed the story of the bloody murder of Granddaddy Gudger at the hands of the Freedman's militia during the rising of the first Klan, and of the trials and tribulations of Daddy Gudger in the years between 1880 and 1910, when he was between the ages of four and thirty-four.

Alma and Annie Mae were the second and fifth of Daddy Gudger's brood, born three years apart. They seem to have hated each other from the very first time Alma looked into little Annie Mae's crib. They were kids by Daddy Gudger's second wife (his desperation had killed the first) and their father was already on his sixth career. He had been a lumberman, a stump preacher, a plowman-for-hire (until his mules broke out in farcy buds and died of the glanders), a freight hauler (until his horses died of overwork and the hardware store repossessed the wagon), a politician's roadie (until the politician lost the election). When Alma and Annie Mae were born, he was failing as a sharecropper. Somehow Gudger had made it through the depression of 1898 as a boy, and was too poor after that to notice more about economics than the price of Beech-Nut tobacco at the store.

Alma and Annie Mae fought, and it helped none at all that Alma, being the oldest daughter, was both her mother's and her father's darling. Annie Mae's life was the usual unwanted-poor-white-trash-child's hell. She vowed early to run away, and recognized her ambition at thirteen.

All this I learned this morning. Jolyn Smith Jimson was Annie Mae's only friend in those days—from a family even poorer than the Gudgers. But somehow there was food, and a occasional odd job. And the dodos.

"My father hated those old birds," said the cultured Annie Mae Rawin, née Gudger, in the solarium. "He always swore he was going to get rid of them someday, but just never seemed to get around to it. I think there was more to it than that. But they were so much *trouble*. We always had to keep them penned up at night, and go check for their eggs. They wandered off to lay them, and forgot where they were. Sometimes no new ones were born at all in a year.

"And they got so *ugly*. Once a year. I mean, terrible-looking, like they were going to die. All their feathers fell off, and they looked like they had mange or something. Then the whole front of their beaks fell off, or worse, hung halfway on for a week or two. They looked like big old naked pigeons. After that they'd lose weight, down to twenty or thirty pounds, before their new feathers grew back.

"We were always having to kill foxes that got after them in the turkey house. That's what we called their roost, the turkey house. And we found their eggs all sucked out by cats and dogs. They were so stupid we had to drive them into their roost at night. I don't think they could have found it standing ten feet from it."

She looked at me.

"I think much as my father hated them, they meant something to him. As long as he hung on to them, he knew he was as good as Granddaddy Gudger. You may not know it, but there was a certain amount of family pride about Granddaddy Gudger. At least in my father's eyes. His rapid fall in the world had a sort of grandeur to it. He'd gone from a relatively high position in the old order, and maintained some grace and stature after the Emancipation. And though he lost everything, he managed to keep those ugly old chickens the Colonel had given him as sort of a symbol.

"And as long as he had them, too, my daddy thought himself as good as his father. He kept his dignity, even when he didn't have anything else."

I asked what happened to them. She didn't know, but told me who did and where I could find her.

That's why I'm going to make a phone call.

"Hello. Dr. Courtney. Dr. Courtney? This is Paul. Memphis. Tennessee. It's too long to go into. No, of course not, not yet. But I've got evidence. What? Okay, how do trochanters, coracoids, tarsometatarsi, and beak sheaths sound? From their hen house, where else? Where would you keep *your* dodos, then?

"Sorry. I haven't slept in a couple of days. I need some help. Yes, yes. Money. Lots of money.

"Cash. Three hundred dollars, maybe. Western Union, Memphis, Tennessee. Whichever one's closest to the airport. Airport. I need the department to set up reservations to Mauritius for me. . . .

"No. No. Not a wild-goose chase, wild-*dodo* chase. Tame-dodo chase. I *know* there aren't any dodos on Mauritius! I know that. I could explain. I know it'll mean a couple of grand—if—but—

"Look, Dr. Courtney. Do you want *your* picture in *Scientific American,* or don't you?"

I am sitting in the airport café in Port Louis, Mauritius. It is now three days later, five days since that fateful morning my car wouldn't start. God bless the Sears Diehard people. I have slept sitting up in a plane seat, on and off, different planes, different seats, for twenty-four hours, Kennedy to Paris, Paris to Cairo, Cairo to Madagascar. I felt like a brand-new man when I got here.

Now I feel like an infinitely sadder and wiser brand-new man. I have just returned from the hateful sister Alma's house in the exclusive section of Port Louis, where all the French and British officials used to live.

Courtney will get his picture in *Scientific American,* all right. Me too. There'll be newspaper stories and talk shows for a few weeks for me, and I'm sure Annie Mae Gudger Radwin on one side of the world and Alma Chandler Gudger Molière on the other will come in for their share of glory.

I am putting away cup after cup of coffee. The plane back to Tananarive leaves in an hour. I plan to sleep all the way back to Cairo, to Paris, to New York, pick up my bag of bones, sleep back to Austin.

Before me on the table is a packet of documents, clippings, and photographs. I have come across half the world for this. I gaze from the package, out the window across Port Louis to the bulk of Mont Pieter Both, which overshadows the city and its famous racecourse.

Perhaps I should do something symbolic. Cancel my flight. Climb the mountain and look down on man and all his handiworks. Take a pitcher of martinis with me. Sit in the bright semitropical sunlight (it's early dry winter here). Drink the martinis slowly, toasting Snuffo, God of Extinction. Here's one for the great auk. This is for the Carolina parakeet. Mud in your eye, passenger pigeon. This one's for the heath hen. Most important, here's one each for the Mauritius dodo, the white dodo of Réunion, the Réunion solitaire, the Rodriguez solitaire. Here's to the Raphidae, great Didine birds that you were.

Maybe I'll do something just as productive, like climbing Mont Pieter Both and pissing into the wind.

How symbolic. The story of the dodo ends where it began, on this very island. Life imitates cheap art. Like the Xerox of the Xerox of a bad novel. I never expected to find dodos still alive here (this is the one place they would have been noticed). I still can't believe Alma Chandler Gudger Molière could have lived here twenty-five years and not *know* about the dodo, never set foot inside the Port Louis Museum, where they have skeletons and a stuffed replica the size of your little brother.

After Annie Mae ran off, the Gudger family found itself prospering in a time the rest of the country was going to hell. It was 1929. Gudger delved into politics again and backed a man who knew a man who worked for Theodore "Sure Two-Handed Sword of God" Bilbo, who had connections everywhere. Who introduced him to Huey "Kingfish" Long just after that gentleman lost the Louisiana governor's election one of the times. Gudger stumped around Mississippi, getting up steam for Long's Share the Wealth plan, even before it had a name.

The upshot was that the Long machine in Louisiana knew a rabble-rouser when it saw one, and invited Gudger to move to the Sportsman's Paradise, with his family, all expenses paid, and start working for the Kingfish at the unbelievable salary of $62.50 a week. Which prospect was like turning a hog loose under a persimmon tree, and before you could say Backwoods Messiah, the Gudger clan was on its way to the land of pelicans, graft, and Mardi Gras.

Almost. But I'll get to that.

Daddy Gudger prospered all out of proportion to his abilities, but many men did that during the Depression. First a little, thence to more, he rose in bureaucratic (and political) circles of the state, dying rich and well hated with his fingers in *all* the pies.

Alma Chandler Gudger became a debutante (she says Robert Penn Warren put her in his book) and met and married Jean Carl Molière, only heir to rice, indigo, and sugarcane growers. They had a happy wedded life, moving first to the West Indies, later to Mauritius, where the family sugarcane holdings were among the largest on the island. Jean Carl died in 1959. Alma was his only survivor.

So local family makes good. Poor sharecropping Mississippi people turn out to have a father dying with a smile on his face, and two daughters who between them own a large portion of the planet.

I open the envelope before me. Ms. Alma Molière had listened politely to my story (the university had called ahead and arranged an introduction through the director of the Port Louis Museum, who knew

Ms. Molière socially) and told me what she could remember. Then she sent a servant out to one of the storehouses (large as a duplex) and he and two others came back with boxes of clippings, scrapbooks, and family photos.

"I haven't looked at any of this since we left St. Thomas," she said. "Let's go through it together."

Most of it was about the rise of Citizen Gudger.

"There's not many pictures of us before we came to Louisiana. We were so frightfully poor then, hardly anyone we knew had a camera. Oh, look. Here's one of Annie Mae. I thought I threw all those out after Momma died."

This is the photograph. It must have been taken about 1927. Annie Mae is wearing some unrecognizable piece of clothing that approximates a dress. She leans on a hoe, smiling a snaggle-toothed smile. She looks to be ten or eleven. Her eyes are half-hidden by the shadow of the brim of a gapped straw hat she wears. The earth she is standing in barefoot has been newly turned. Behind her is one corner of the house, and the barn beyond has its upper hay windows open. Out-of-focus people are at work there.

A few feet behind her, a huge male dodo is pecking at something on the ground. The front two-thirds of it shows, back to the stupid wings and the edge of the upcurved tail feathers. One foot is in the photo, having just scratched at something, possibly an earthworm, in the new-plowed clods. Judging by its darkness, it is the gray, or Mauritius, dodo.

The photograph is not very good, one of those 3½ x 5 jobs box cameras used to take. Already I can see this one, and the blowup of the dodo, taking up a double-page spread in *S.A.* Alma told me that around then they were down to six or seven of the ugly chickens, two whites, the rest a gray-brown.

Besides this photo, two clippings are in the package, one from the Bruce *Banner-Times,* the other from the Oxford newspaper; both are columns by the same woman dealing with "Doings in Water Valley." Both mention the Gudger family's moving from the area to seek its fortune in the swampy state to the west, and tell how they will be missed. Then there's a yellowed clipping from the front page of the Oxford paper with a small story about the Gudger Family Farewell Party in Water Valley the Sunday before (dated October 19, 1929).

There's a handbill in the package, advertising the Gudger Family Farewell Party, Sunday Oct. 15, 1929 Come One Come All. The people in Louisiana who sent expense money to move Daddy Gudger must have overestimated the costs by an exponential factor. I said as much.

"No," Alma Molière said. "There was a lot, but it wouldn't have made any difference. Daddy Gudger was like Thomas Wolfe and knew a shining golden opportunity when he saw one. Win, lose, or draw, he was never coming back *there* again. He would have thrown some kind of soiree whether there had been money for it or not. Besides, people were much more sociable then, you mustn't forget."

I asked her how many people came.

"Four or five hundred," she said. "There's some pictures here somewhere." We searched awhile, then we found them.

Another thirty minutes to my flight. I'm not worried sitting here. I'm the only passenger, and the pilot is sitting at the table next to mine talking to an RAF man. Life is much slower and nicer on these colonial islands. You mustn't forget.

I look at the other two photos in the package. One is of some men playing horseshoes and washer toss, while kids, dogs, and women look on. It was evidently taken from the east end of the house looking west. Everyone must have had to walk the last mile to the old Gudger place. Other groups of people stand talking. Some men, in shirt sleeves and suspenders, stand with their heads thrown back, a snappy story, no doubt, just told. One girl looks directly at the camera from close up, shyly, her finger in her mouth. She's about five. It looks like any snapshot of a family reunion that could have been taken anywhere, anytime. Only the clothing marks it as backwoods 1920s.

Courtney will get his money's worth. I'll write the article, make phone calls, plan the talk-show tour to coincide with publication. Then I'll get some rest. I'll be a normal person again—get a degree, spend my time wading through jungles after animals that will all be dead in another twenty years, anyway.

Who cares? The whole thing will be just another media event, just this year's Big Deal. It'll be nice getting normal again. I can read books, see movies, wash my clothes at the laundromat, listen to Johnathan Richman on the stereo. I can study and become an authority on some minor matter or other.

I can go to museums and see all the wonderful dead things there.

"That's the memory picture," said Alma. "They always took them at big things like this, back in those days. Everybody who was there would line up and pose for the camera. Only we couldn't fit everybody in. So we had two made. This is the one with us in it."

The house is dwarfed by people. All sizes, shapes, dress, and age. Kids and dogs in front, women next, then men at the back. The only exceptions are the bearded patriarchs seated toward the front with the children—men whose eyes face the camera but whose heads are still ringing with something Nathan Bedford Forrest said to them one time on a smoke-filled field. This photograph is from another age. You can recognize Daddy and Mrs. Gudger if you've seen their photographs before. Alma pointed herself out to me.

But the reason I took the photograph is in the foreground. Tables have been built out of sawhorses, with doors and boards nailed across them. They extend the entire width of the photograph. They are covered with food, more food than you can imagine.

"We started cooking three days before. So did the neighbors. Everybody brought something," said Alma.

It's like an entire Safeway had been cooked and set out to cool. Hams, quarters of beef, chickens by the tubful, quail in mounds, rabbit, butter beans by the bushel, yams, Irish potatoes, an acre of corn, eggplants, peas, turnip greens, butter in five-pound molds, cornbread and biscuits, gallon cans of molasses, red-eye gravy by the pot.

And five huge birds—twice as big as turkeys, legs capped as for Thanksgiving, drumsticks are the size of Schwarzenegger's biceps, whole-roasted, lying on their backs on platters large as cocktail tables.

The people in the crowd sure look hungry.

"We ate for days," said Alma.

I already have the title for the *Scientific American* article. It's going to be called "The Dodo Is *Still* Dead."

The Wind and the Rain

Robert Silverberg

Humanity is obviously in danger of extinction from many causes, all of our own doing. If we do disappear from the world, what might an alien research team millennia from now think of us, as they discover what happened? Remember, alien beings aren't likely to think just as we do—they might find something admirable, even esthetic, about our racial suicide.

Robert Silverberg is well known in science fiction for his dark visions of the future, and for his frequently wry tone. His new novel is Lord Valentine's Castle.

THE PLANET cleanses itself. That is the important thing to remember, at moments when we become too pleased with ourselves. The healing process is a natural and inevitable one. The action of the wind and the rain, the ebbing and flowing of the tides, the vigorous rivers flushing out the choked and stinking lakes—these are all natural rhythms, all healthy manifestations of universal harmony. Of course, we are here too. We do our best to hurry the process along. But we are only auxiliaries, and we know it. We must not exaggerate the value of our work. False pride is worse than a sin: it is a foolishness. We do not deceive ourselves into thinking we are important. If we were not here at all, the planet would repair itself anyway within twenty to fifty million years. It is estimated that our presence cuts that time down by somewhat more than half.

The uncontrolled release of methane into the atmosphere was one of the most serious problems. Methane is a colorless, odorless gas, sometimes known as "swamp gas." Its components are carbon and hydrogen. Much of the atmosphere of Jupiter and Saturn consists of methane.

(Jupiter and Saturn have never been habitable by human beings.) A small amount of methane was always normally present in the atmosphere of Earth. However, the growth of human population produced a consequent increase in the supply of methane. Much of the methane released into the atmosphere came from swamps and coal mines. A great deal of it came from Asian rice-fields fertilized with human or animal waste; methane is a byproduct of the digestive process.

The surplus methane escaped into the lower stratosphere, from ten to thirty miles above the surface of the planet, where a layer of ozone molecules once existed. Ozone, formed of three oxygen atoms, absorbs the harmful ultraviolet radiation that the sun emits. By reacting with free oxygen atoms in the stratosphere, the intrusive methane reduced the quantity available for ozone formation. Moreover, methane reactions in the stratosphere yielded water vapor that further depleted the ozone. This methane-induced exhaustion of the ozone content of the stratosphere permitted the unchecked ultraviolet bombardment of the Earth, with a consequent rise in the incidence of skin cancer.

A major contributor to the methane increase was the flatulence of domesticated cattle. According to the U.S. Department of Agriculture, domesticated ruminants in the late twentieth century were generating more than eighty-five million tons of methane a year. Yet nothing was done to check the activities of these dangerous creatures. Are you amused by the idea of a world destroyed by herds of farting cows? It must not have been amusing to the people of the late twentieth century. However, the extinction of domesticated ruminants shortly helped to reduce the impact of this process.

Today we must inject colored fluids into a major river. Edith, Bruce, Paul, Elaine, Oliver, Ronald, and I have been assigned to this task. Most members of the team believe the river is the Mississippi, although there is some evidence that it may be the Nile. Oliver, Bruce, and Edith believe it is more likely to be the Nile than the Mississippi, but they defer to the opinion of the majority. The river is wide and deep and its color is black in some places and dark green in others. The fluids are computer-mixed on the east bank of the river in a large factory erected by a previous reclamation team. We supervise their passage into the river. First we inject the red fluid, then the blue, then the yellow; they have different densities and form parallel stripes running for many hundreds of kilometers in the water. We are not certain whether these fluids are active healing agents—that is, substances which dissolve the solid pollutants lining the riverbed—or merely serve as markers permitting further chemical analysis of the river by the orbiting satellite system. It is not necessary for us to understand what we are doing, so long as we follow instructions explicitly. Elaine jokes about going swimming. Bruce says, "How absurd. This river is famous for deadly fish that will strip the flesh from your bones." We all laugh at that. *Fish?* Here? What fish could be as deadly as the river itself? This water would consume our flesh if we entered it, and probably dissolve our bones as well. I scribbled a poem yesterday and dropped it in, and the paper vanished instantly.

In the evenings we walk along the beach and have philosophical discussions. The sunsets on this coast are embellished by rich tones of purple, green, crimson, and yellow. Sometimes we cheer when a particularly beautiful combination of atmosphere gases transforms the sunlight. Our mood is always optimistic and gay. We are never depressed by the things we find on this planet. Even devastation can be an art-form, can it not? Perhaps it is one of the greatest of all art-forms, since an art of destruction *consumes* its medium, it *devours* its own epistemological foundations, and in this sublimely nullifying doubling-back upon its origins it far exceeds in moral complexity those forms which are merely productive. That is, I place a higher value on transformative art than on generative art. Is my meaning clear? In any event, since art ennobles and exalts the spirits of those who perceive it, we are exalted and ennobled by the conditions on Earth. We envy those who collaborated to create those extraordinary conditions. We know ourselves to be small-souled folk of a minor latter-day epoch; we lack the dynamic grandeur of energy that enabled our ancestors to commit such depredations. This world is a symphony. Naturally you might argue that to restore a planet takes more energy than to destroy it, but you would be wrong. Nevertheless, though our daily tasks leave us weary and drained, we also feel stimulated and excited, because by restoring this world, the mother-world of mankind, we are in a sense participating in the original splendid process of its destruction. I mean in the sense that the resolution of a dissonant chord participates in the dissonance of that chord.

Now we have come to Tokyo, the capital of the island empire of Japan. See how small the skeletons of the citizens are? That is one way we have of identifying this place as Japan. The Japanese are known to have been people of small stature. Edward's ancestors were Japanese. He is of small stature. (Edith says his skin should be yellow as well. His skin is just like ours. Why is his skin not yellow?) "See?" Edward cries. "There is Mount Fuji!" It is an extraordinarily beautiful mountain, mantled in white snow. On its slopes one of our archaeological teams is at work, tunneling under the snow to collect samples from the twentieth-century strata of chemical residues, dust, and ashes. "Once there were over 75,000 industrial smokestacks around Tokyo," says Edward proudly, "from which were released hundreds of tons of sulfur, nitrous oxides, ammonia, and carbon gases every day. We should not forget that this city had more than 1,500,000 automobiles as well." Many of the automobiles are still visible, but they are very fragile, worn to threads by the action of the atmosphere. When we touch them they collapse in puffs of gray smoke. Edward, who has studied his heritage well, tells us, "It was not uncommon for the density of carbon monoxide in the air here to exceed the permissible levels by factors of 250 percent on mild summer days. Owing to atmospheric conditions, Mount Fuji was visible only one day of every nine. Yet no one showed dismay." He conjures up for us a picture of his small, industrious yellow ancestors toiling cheerfully and unremittingly in their poisonous environment. The Japanese, he insists, were able to maintain and even increase their gross national product at a time when other nationalities had already begun to lose ground in the global economic struggle because of diminished population owing to unfavorable ecological factors. And so on and so on. After a time we grow bored with Edward's incessant boasting. "Stop boasting," Oliver tells him, "or we will expose you to the atmosphere." We have much dreary work to do here. Paul and I guide the huge trenching machines; Oliver and Ronald follow, planting seeds. Almost immediately, strange angular shrubs spring up. They have shiny bluish leaves and long crooked branches. One of them seized Elaine by the throat yesterday and might have hurt her seriously had Bruce not uprooted it. We were not upset. This is merely one phase in the long, slow process of repair. There will be many such incidents. Some day cherry trees will blossom in this place.

This is the poem that the river ate:

Destruction

I. *Nouns.* Destruction, desolation, wreck, wreckage, ruin, ruination, rack and ruin, smash, smashup, demolition, demolishment, ravagement, havoc, ravage, dilapidation, decimation, blight, breakdown, consumption, dissolution, obliteration, overthrow, spoilage; mutilation, disintegration, undoing, pulverization; sabotage, vandalism; annulment, damnation, extinguishment, extinction, invalidation, nullification, shatterment, shipwreck; annihilation, disannulment, discreation, extermination, extirpation, obliteration, perdition, subversion.

II. *Verbs.* Destroy, wreck, ruin, ruinate, smash, demolish, raze, ravage, gut, dilapidate, decimate, blast, blight, break down, consume, dissolve, overthrow; mutilate, disintegrate, unmake, pulverize; sabotage, vandalize; annul, blast, blight, damn, dash, extinguish, invalidate, nullify, quell, quench, scuttle, shatter, shipwreck, torpedo, smash, spoil, undo, void; annihilate, devour, disannul, discreate, exterminate, obliterate, extirpate, subvert; corrode, erode, sap, undermine, waste, waste away, whittle away (*or* down); eat away, canker, gnaw; wear away, abrade, batter, excoriate, rust.

III. *Adjectives.* Destructive, ruinous, vandalistic, baneful, cutthroat, fell, lethiferous, pernicious, slaughterous, predatory, sinistrous, nihilistic; corrosive, erosive, cankerous, caustic, abrasive.

"I validate," says Ethel.

"I unravage," says Oliver.

"I integrate," says Paul.

"I devandalize," says Elaine.

"I unshatter," says Bruce.

"I unscuttle," says Edward.

"I discorrode," says Ronald.

"I undesolate," says Edith.

"I create," say I.

We reconstitute. We renew. We repair. We reclaim. We refurbish. We restore. We renovate. We rebuild. We reproduce. We redeem. We reintegrate. We replace. We reconstruct. We retrieve. We revivify. We resurrect. We fix, overhaul, mend, put in repair, retouch, tinker, cobble, patch, darn, staunch, caulk, splice. We celebrate our success by energetic and lusty singing. Some of us copulate.

Here is an outstanding example of the dark humor of the ancients. At a place called Richland, Washington, there was an installation that manufactured plutonium for use in nuclear weapons. This was done in the name of "national security," that is, to enhance and strengthen the safety of the United States of America and render its inhabitants carefree and hopeful. In a relatively short span of time these activities produced approximately fifty-five million gallons of concentrated radioactive waste. This material was so intensely hot that it would boil spontaneously for decades, and would retain a virulently toxic character for many thousands of years. The presence of so much dangerous waste posed a severe environmental threat to a large area of the United States. How, then, to dispose of this waste? An appropriately comic solution was devised. The plutonium installation was situated in a seismically unstable area located along the earthquake belt that rings the Pacific Ocean. A storage site was chosen nearby, directly above a fault line that had produced a violent earthquake half a century earlier. Here 140 steel and concrete tanks were constructed just below the surface of the ground and some 240 feet above the water table of the Columbia River, from which a densely populated region derived its water supply. Into these tanks the boiling radioactive wastes were poured: a magnificent gift to future generations. Within a few years the true subtlety of the jest became apparent when the first small leaks were detected in the tanks. Some observers predicted that no more than ten to twenty years would pass before the great heat caused the seams of the tanks to burst, releasing radioactive gases into the atmosphere or permitting radioactive fluids to escape into the river. The designers of the tanks maintained, though, that they were sturdy enough to last at least a century. It will be noted that this was something less than one percent of the known half-life of the materials placed in the tanks. Because of discontinuities in the records, we are unable to determine which estimate was more nearly correct. It should be possible for our decontamination squads to enter the affected regions in eight to thirteen hundred years. This episode arouses tremendous admiration in me. How much gusto, how much robust wit those old ones must have had!

We are granted a holiday so we may go to the mountains of Uruguay to visit the site of one of the last human settlements, perhaps the very last. It was discovered by a reclamation team several hundred years ago and has been set aside, in its original state, as a museum for the tourists who one day will wish to view the mother-world. One enters through a lengthy tunnel of glossy pink brick. A series of airlocks prevents the outside air from penetrating. The village itself, nestling between two craggy spires, is shielded by a clear shining dome. Automatic controls maintain its temperature at a constant mild level. There were a thousand inhabitants. We can view them in the spacious plazas, in the taverns, and in places of recreation. Family groups remain together, often with their pets. A few carry umbrellas. Everyone is in an unusually fine state of preservation. Many of them are smiling. It is not yet known why these people perished. Some died in the act of speaking, and scholars have devoted much effort, so far without success, to the task of determining and translating the last words still frozen on their lips. We are not allowed to touch anyone, but we may enter their homes and inspect their possessions and toilet furnishings. I am moved almost to tears, as are several of the others. "Perhaps these are our very ancestors," Ronald exclaims. But Bruce declares scornfully, "You say ridiculous things. Our ancestors must have escaped from here long before the time these people lived." Just outside the settlement I find a tiny glistening bone, possibly the shinbone of a child, possibly part of a dog's tail. "May I keep it?" I ask our leader. But he compels me to donate it to the museum.

The archives yield much that is fascinating. For example, this fine example of ironic distance in ecological management. In the ocean off a place named California were tremendous forests of a giant seaweed called kelp, housing a vast and intricate community of maritime creatures. Sea urchins lived on the ocean floor, one hundred feet down, amid the holdfasts that anchored the kelp. Furry aquatic mammals known as sea otters fed on the urchins. The Earth people removed the otters because they had some use for their fur. Later, the kelp began to die. Forests many square miles in diameter vanished. This had serious commercial consequences, for the kelp was valuable and so were many of the animal forms that lived in it. Investigation of the ocean floor showed a great increase in sea urchins. Not only had their natural enemies, the otters, been removed, but the urchins were taking nourishment from the immense quantities of organic matter in the sewage discharges dumped into the ocean by the Earth people. Millions of urchins were nibbling at the holdfasts of the kelp, uprooting the huge plants and killing them. When an oil tanker accidentally released its cargo into the sea, many urchins were killed and the kelp began to reestablish itself. But this proved to be an impractical means of controlling the urchins. Encouraging the otters to return was suggested, but there was not a sufficient supply of living otters. The kelp foresters of California solved their problem by dumping quicklime into the sea from barges. This was fatal to the urchins; once they were dead, healthy kelp plants were brought from other parts of the sea and embedded to become the nucleus of a new forest. After a while the urchins returned and began to eat the kelp again. More quicklime was dumped. The urchins died· and new kelp was planted. Later, it was discovered that the quicklime was having harmful effects on the ocean floor itself, and other chemicals were dumped to counteract those effects. All of this required great ingenuity and a considerable outlay of energy and resources. Edward thinks there was something very Japanese about these maneuvers. Ethel points out that the kelp trouble would never have happened if the Earth people had not originally removed the otters. How naive Ethel is! She has no understanding of the principles of irony. Poetry bewilders her also. Edward refuses to sleep with Ethel now.

In the final centuries of their era the people of Earth succeeded in paving the surface of their planet almost entirely with a skin of concrete and metal. We must pry much of this up so that the planet may start to breathe again. It would be easy and efficient to use explosives or acids, but we are not overly concerned with ease and efficiency; besides, there is great concern that explosives or acids may do further ecological harm here. Therefore we employ large machines that insert prongs in the great cracks that have developed in the concrete. Once we have lifted the paved slabs they usually crumble quickly. Clouds of concrete dust blow freely through the streets of these cities, covering the stumps of the buildings with a fine, pure coating of grayish-white powder. The effect is delicate and refreshing. Paul suggested yesterday that we may be doing ecological harm by setting free this dust. I became frightened at the idea and reported him to the leader of our team. Paul will be transferred to another group.

Toward the end here they all wore breathing-suits, similar to ours but even more comprehensive. We find these suits lying around everywhere like the discarded shells of giant insects. The most advanced models were complete individual housing units. Apparently it was not necessary to leave one's suit except to perform such vital functions as sexual intercourse and childbirth. We understand that the reluctance of the Earth people to leave their suits even for those functions, near the close, immensely hastened the decrease in population.

Our philosophical discussions. God created this planet. We all agree on that, in a manner of speaking, ignoring for the moment definitions of such concepts as "God" and "created." Why did He go to so much trouble to bring Earth into being, if it was His intention merely to have it rendered uninhabitable? Did He create mankind especially for this purpose, or did they exercise free will in doing what they did here? Was mankind God's way of taking vengeance against His own creation? Why would He want to take vengeance against His own creation? Perhaps it is a mistake to approach the destruction of Earth from the moral or ethical standpoint. I think we must see it in purely esthetic terms, i.e., a self-contained artistic achievement, like a *fouetté en tournant* or an *entrechat-dix,* performed for its own sake and requiring no explanations. Only in this way can we understand how the Earth people were able to collaborate so joyfully in their own asphyxiation.

My tour of duty is almost over. It has been an overwhelming experience; I will never be the same. I must express my gratitude for this opportunity to have seen Earth almost as its people knew it. Its rusted streams, its corroded meadows, its purpled skies, its bluish puddles. The debris, the barren hillsides, the blazing rivers. Soon, thanks to the dedicated work of reclamation teams such as ours, these superficial but beautiful emblems of death will have disappeared. This will be just another world for tourists, of sentimental curiosity but no unique value to the sensibility. How dull that will be: a green and pleasant Earth once more; why, why? The universe has enough habitable planets; at present it has only one Earth. Has all our labor here been an error, then? I sometimes do think it was misguided of us to have undertaken this project. But on the other hand I remind myself of our fundamental irrelevance. The healing process is a natural and inevitable one. With us or without us, the planet cleanses itself. The wind, the rain, the tides. We merely help things along.

A rumor reaches us that a colony of live Earthmen has been found on the Tibetan plateau. We travel there to see if this is true. Hovering above a vast red empty plain, we see large dark figures moving slowly about. Are these Earthmen, inside breathing suits of a strange design? We descend. Members of other reclamation teams are already on hand. They have surrounded one of the large creatures. It travels in a wobbly circle, uttering indistinct cries and grunts. Then it comes to a halt, confronting us blankly as if defying us to embrace it. We tip it over; it moves its massive limbs dumbly but is unable to arise. After a brief conference we decide to dissect it. The outer plates lift easily. Inside we find nothing but gears and coils of gleaming wire. The limbs no longer move, although things click and hum within it for quite some time. We are favorably impressed by the durability and resilience of these machines. Perhaps in the distant future such entities will wholly replace the softer and more fragile life-forms on all worlds, as they seem to have done on Earth.

The wind. The rain. The tides. All sadnesses flow to the sea.

Virra

Terry Carr

Ultimately, there's no question that we will come to the end of life on Earth, since the sun itself will inevitably gutter and die. In the last days, when humans have evolved into beings who need very little energy to feed their life processes, what should their attitude be toward the final night that awaits them?

Terry Carr's writing includes the novel Cirque and a collection of his shorter stories, The Light at the End of the Universe.

at the last
judgement we will all be trees

—MARGARET ATWOOD

AM WALKING; I am leaving my family, stepping past them day by day with hardly time for talk. Soon I shall be beyond them all, alone in fields where no roots touch.

I enter the dim clearing caused when Morden fell, bringing down with him three others of the family. Morden was one of our oldest, a giant who commanded the sun for thirty meters around. Lightning wounded him; years later he fell.

He is not dead. Fresh limbs reach straight up from his side while all others are crumbling and covered with ice; he has put all his blood into these new limbs. As I skirt his roots I see that two are still in place, still feeding. I trip over one, underground.

"Who is it?" asks Morden drowsily. "Who are you?"

"Wesk. I am Wesk." (I am dreadfully afraid of him. From earliest memory I have been told Morden would strangle the sun if I angered him.)

"Are you such a child, Wesk, that you are unable to feel when roots are near?" His voice is like winter blood, slow and thick.

"No, sir. I apologize for disturbing you. I was hurrying, and I am . . . afraid of you, sir."

Morden's laughter shakes his few leaves. "Then if you are not young, you lack understanding. How could one so old as I harm you? I lie on my side, catching the sun of noon, in shade the rest of the time. As the family grows over me, they take away even the noon."

I continue to move around him, feeling more carefully now as I slip my roots into the soil. Touching shallowly, barely penetrating the crisp ice that covers the ground even in summer.

"I am only passing," I say. "I shall not steal your sun."

"Where are you going? Is there more sun nearby?"

"No," I say, "but there was one who carried the sun with her. I am seeking her."

"Phaw! No one carries the sun; your roots are feeding in a cavern, your thoughts are starved."

I am nearly past Morden now, and I take courage. "But I saw her as she passed. She moved so quickly! She was small and unable to reach up for sun, but she carried light in her leaves. Her name is Virra."

Morden laughs deeply, causing my roots to tremble. I pause while I regrip the soil.

"So the quick ones still live," he says sardonically. "Beware of them, child; they are leftovers of the past. You might as well chase insects."

I move away from his root-drainage, but I hesitate and take time to feed in the soil. The sun is overhead now, and I stretch my branches upward; energy makes me giddy and foolish. "Insects exist only in tales for children," I say challengingly.

Morden shifts a limb with surprising swiftness in my direction; it intercepts the sun and I am left in shadow. "There *were* insects," he says. "I saw one during my second ring. The creature was hardly the size of a bud, but it flew faster than sight. Then it fell, and died. I believe it was the last."

"If you could not see it, how could you know of it?" I ask, edging away. There is another patch of sunlight nearby.

Again his root-shaking laughter comes, but I am further away now and it hardly touches me. "I saw it when it had fallen. Later I ate it."

My curiosity is aroused. "What did it look like? Is it true that the insects had no leaves at all, no limbs?"

"It was ugly." The soil ripples around my roots: is Morden shuddering? "It searched my leaves for blossoms, and its touch was disgusting. We once reproduced by making leaves of pretty colors, you know, and scents like the whores of legend. We needed the insects then, to carry our seed, but no more."

He is rambling, as so many of the aged do. They love to talk of the past, and they seem to take special delight in grotesque tales. I drink the sun, and say respectfully, "How awful for you to be touched by such a thing."

"Yes, but the insect got nothing from me, or anyone. It fell, they all fell, and our pure seeds fed on the ground they enriched." Morden's voice is growing dimmer as the sun passes; he says dreamily, "The one of whom you speak is like the insects—fast-movers, strangers to peace. They will soon be gone."

I walk on, refusing to believe this. Virra was too beautiful for me to conceive of her dying. I remember the day she passed by me, moving so quickly she was almost gone before I could hail her. Smaller than a sapling, she moved with sureness and grace, holding her supple, leaf-clustered limbs away from any touch with the rest of us.

"Wait," I called after her. "What are you?"

"I am Virra," she said. "And I can't wait; I'm returning to the field, where giants don't steal all the sun."

"We do not steal!" I cried; but she was nearly out of hearing range. She moved like limbs dancing in wind, her tiny roots touching the soil so shallowly that she seemed a mass of drifting leaves. But she was bright with inner-held sun. "Wait!" I called again. "I want to talk, to know you!"

"Then come to the field."

So I am walking, going on a journey longer than anyone in my family has made. I am still young; I can do it. Already I have passed Morden, who has grown silent in his shade.

The way is easy, for every year there are fewer of the family; there is always much room between us, and only the decaying bodies of fallen ancestors to block my path. I skirt them easily, for their roots have long since passed back into the earth. Mindless ferns offer no resistance to my passage.

I speak to no one for three days, moving quickly past the elders who stand dreaming in the sun, feeding in the earth below the ice. I pause for an hour here or there when I find unused sun. There is enough to replenish my energy, but my roots are becoming brittle and frayed from so much exposure to the air, and I notice I am leaving sap in my back-trail of rootings. Perhaps this journey will be more difficult than I thought.

I come to the place where Querca stands: she whose drainage extends for scores of meters from her trunk. Old as she is, she has recently dropped acorns; they punctuate my path, and several have melted through to the soil where they may take root. But I am fearful now because my own roots are bleeding. So I do not skirt her ground; I pause hardly an hour in sun before hurling myself across her shade.

I have traversed little more than half of it when she notices me. "Who is it?" she rumbles. "I can see you are young—have you no respect?"

Frightened, I blurt, "Have you seen one passing who carried sunlight in her leaves?"

I am able to take several more root-steps before I hear Querca chuckle (she drops an acorn that is still green), and she says, "You mean a *bush?*"

I shiver at the scorn in her voice and grip underground stones to steady myself. "I do not know her family, only that she lives in the field. What is a 'bush'?"

"Nothing; a bush is nothing. The ferns serve more purpose—at least they feed us when they die."

"But this . . . bush . . . has a mind. Her name is Virra."

Querca moves roots languidly, easing into soft, fresh earth. "Bushes have no memory. They have no need to remember, because they die so soon. What does it matter that this creature has a mind, if she cannot remember?"

Anxiety strikes me, and I pause in my traversal of Querca's icy shade. "Do you mean she will not remember me when I find her?"

"Hah! Remember you?" Querca slowly bends down over me, mingling her brittle branches with my young ones; I draw back involuntarily at the touch of dry, aging leaves. "The bushes have no past, nor any future. They have been driven from the family and must live alone in the open field. They sprout and die almost while we sleep."

"But she did *think!*" I am approaching the edge of Querca's shade now, and I take courage. "Even her thoughts were full of sunlight, and she did not hoard it as the old ones of the family do."

"Exactly," says Querca. "They throw away their thoughts and do not think them again." Her limbs lift away from mine as I pass from beneath her. "They waste the past just as they waste the sun. The sun is old; it was not always small as it is now. We have a duty to use its energy wisely, but *bushes* have no care for that."

"I shall ask her about wasting the sun," I say, moving at last out of Querca's shade and stepping carefully along a slope strewn with the crumbling remains of ancient ancestors. "But must we talk so much about the past?"

This rouses anger in Querca. "*Yes,* we must talk of it, for we used up the sun! We were so different—creatures that ran and ran, burning the sun within us till it was almost gone. The bushes are still like that: they are enemies!" She dips a giant bough. "How are you named?"

"I am Wesk. You do not know me."

"I shall know you in the future," Querca promises.

Her words are like frost, but I continue walking. I am free of Querca's shade and her voice now. I continue across the sun-dappled slope; the ancients of the family only glance at me. There are fewer of them than before, farther apart; I am coming to the family's edge, to the beginning of the field.

There is a strange form of life here, one that we see seldom in the deeper forest-family. Slim green trunks rise from the ground; they are only centimeters high, and they have no limbs. Their very trunks are their leaves. In that way they are like the ferns, but they are much simpler creatures. Ancient tales call them grasses, and this is as good a name as any, since, like the ferns, they cannot think and tell us a name for themselves.

Here too are the hermits, those who stand away from the edge of the family and think only to themselves. They spread great limbs wide and luxuriate in the energy of the red sun; but their roots feed on the shallow loam of grasses, and it is said within the family that the hermits must one day return to our ground for sustenance.

My roots stumble across one of the hermits, for it lies shallow in the ground, and I wake her from a morning sleep. "Go away," she grumbles, still half dreaming. "Whoever you are."

I wonder briefly if she will ever be able to return to the family, since I have felt how stiff her roots are. "My name is Wesk. Have you seen the bush who recently visited the forest-family?"

"No. Go away from me." She spreads her limbs even more wide, hoping to induce me to move off in search of sun.

"Her name is Virra," I say, obediently hurrying toward the edge of the hermit's shade.

"I have nothing to do with bushes. I have nothing to do with anyone."

"Then farewell," I say as I reach the sun again, "and may your thoughts of yourself be rewarding." I intend this as an insult, for I am annoyed by the hermit's rejection, but as I move on I feel only contentment from her.

Night comes and goes before I reach the next hermit in my path; he stands alone on a small hillock held together by his roots, and so I surmise that he is old. I skirt his cold roots, which are surprisingly wide, and say, "I am seeking the bush named Virra; if you know where she is, tell me and I shall travel on more quickly."

I feel his roots move slowly as he rouses. "Virra?" he says sleepily. "Always Virra." He begins to lift his limbs to the morning sun. "Continue on your path and you will find Virra."

The blood surges within me and I press forward through the shallow grasses, giddy with the full sunlight of the field. There are rocks and boulders here, many more than there are within the family; some thrust up out of the ground as though they could draw life from the sun. I come to a small creature, a being of leaves like Virra but no more than a summer old.

"I search for a bush who is named Virra," I say, hoping that this young creature will understand me.

"I am a bush," he says. "I am Virra."

"No. You are not the same Virra; you are too small, and you are male."

"Then go further into the field," he says, "and you'll find your Virra."

I move off, in a hurry now that I am nearing the end of my journey, but the young bush is too fast for me: "What are you?" he asks.

"I am Wesk. I am a tree."

The rocks and gravel of the ground are hard on my roots, and the surface ice reaches deeper than that in the family, but I hurry on, using the abundant energy of the sun in open air. There are harsh winds out here, too, and they stir my leaves though I try to hold each to the sun.

"A tree?" says the young bush. "Do trees walk?"

Impudence! I say with calm hauteur, "Trees are the world's nobility; we do whatever we wish." I continue away from this ignorant creature, but my roots are tired and sore again from the hard ground. The bush moves after me, and I am startled by his agility.

"Are you really a tree?" he asks. "Yes, you must be—you're so *big!* Are you older than the rocks?"

I try to ignore him, striding on in silence. I notice with a touch of pride that the back-trail where my roots have sunk into the ground is deep and definite, the sign of a giant stalking the earth.

The bush moves in front of me and stops. *"Are* you? Are you older than rocks?"

"Rocks are not people," I say shortly, altering my course to move around him. "Rocks are dead things."

He laughs suddenly, his ridiculous tiny leaves shaking. "Then *they* are older! Everyone knows the old things are dead, and only the younger ones still living." He studies me critically as I begin to step around him. "But you move so slowly! Are you sick, or do all trees move like invalids?"

Anger courses through me; my leaves quiver and I reach out with my longest limbs to cover him with shade. "Go away."

He does not seem to mind, and I notice that he too, like the Virra I seek, can hold the sun in his leaves. He even turns to follow me as I pass.

"Old creatures are ill-tempered, too," he says. "I've heard that the really ancient people, the wonderful meat creatures, were so dissatisfied with the world that they lifted their roots—if they had roots—and flew into the clouds." He giggles. "But when the clouds were gone, so were they."

"I am not a meat creature. Some of them went away, as you say, but those who remained either died or became trees. So you see which of us is the more wonderful: they became us."

I am stepping more rapidly now, as the noon sun softens the ground, but I am still not fast enough to escape this bush. He moves once again, and stands before me.

"You're bad to say such things about the meat creatures. They were so very wonderful; they moved like winter winds and thought great thoughts. You mustn't say bad things about them!"

"Let me pass!" I rumble, stirring the ground so violently with my roots that the bush is pushed backward. I am furious; I reach deliberately for his roots, seize one, and hold him still with my greater strength. I move in on him, intending to drop my limbs around him till he is forced into sleep.

But he does an unthinkable thing: he pulls away from his trapped root, deliberately breaking it off as he scurries back beyond my reach. He stops in the sun, slightly uphill from me, and I see his limbs trembling. (Limbs! They are hardly more than twigs!)

We stare at each other for long minutes, until he says, "All right then, go away. You bore me anyway with your slowness."

I regard him a little while longer, wondering if I can somehow reach him before he escapes again. But he would feel my massive roots pushing toward him underground, and in any case my anger is fading: he is, after all, only an ill-mannered child. Without further word I move on, sinking my roots deep through the surface of ice, drinking what sustenance there is in this rocky soil. My bleeding roots ache but I pay no mind, retaining my dignity. Before night comes, he is out of sight behind me.

I choose this night for sleep. It has been days since I rested, and without the surrounding protection of my family I am chilled by the winds of the field. Besides, bushes are so small: I might walk right past Virra in the dark without seeing her.

In the morning, when the dim rays of the sun touch my highest leaves, I wake refreshed, though my roots seem afire with pain when I free them from the ice and resume walking. The pain passes into a dull ache; I walk till the sun touches my naked trunk, and then I notice that I am being followed.

No, I am being chased. It is a bush, larger than the one I met yesterday, and female. She is lovely, holding her tiny leaves proudly in the morning breeze, stepping delicately past my deeply dug path. In minutes she overtakes me, for I have paused to wait for her. She settles lightly into the ground near me but not in my shade; I study her.

Her leaves are the color and shape I remember; her branches quiver with controlled excitement, just as Virra's did. The light in her leaves is glorious, each a miniature green sun.

"My name is Virra," she says. "Were you looking for me?"

Her voice in my mind is both familiar and strange. Have I forgotten how she sounded, or has she changed since I saw her among the family? Time must pass more quickly for these swiftly moving creatures, after all.

"I believe I have been searching for you since I was born," I say. "But I did not know it until I saw you."

She laughs, and her rustling leaves make music. "But you're a tree. You must be so *old!*"

"No, I have only fifteen rings."

"Fifteen?" Again her rustling laughter. "Then you've lived twice as long as I have. How could you have been looking for me before I was born?"

My blood pulses through me; I feel giddy. "I suppose I believed in you before I ever saw you."

Her leaves are still for a moment. She says in a strangely subdued tone, "Do trees foresee the future, then?"

"No, but we dream. We have time to think, and there are not so many things in the world to think about. So I think of things that do not exist."

"These are dreams?"

"Waking dreams. I think of things I would wish to exist—people filled with light and joy, like you." I pause, embarrassed.

But she does not seem to resent my familiarity; instead, she lifts her leaves to the sun and turns before me, preening. "Am I as beautiful as you dreamed?"

"Even more beautiful. I could never imagine the way you move, so lightly and surely. You amaze me."

She laughs, and the sound is like light rain in my highest branches. "You're silly," she says. "Are all the trees like you?—No, they can't be; the trees I've seen wouldn't even talk to me."

"My family considers me irresponsible," I admit. "I see you agree with them."

"No!" She stops moving and stands before me sedately now. I see her delicate roots sink into the ground, taking sure purchase. "I think you're wonderful. To be able to think of things you've never seen! How

302

fascinating your conversations with your family must be!"

"Alas, no. None of the others ever talk to me of dreams. They tell me to think only of what is real—if not now, then in the past." I sigh, remembering how stern my elders have been with me. "They talk so often of things past. . . . These are their dreams, but they are not mine."

"Then your dreams are more real than theirs," she says, amused. "You dreamed of me, and here I am."

"Yes, here you are." I am suffused by joy as I realize that I really have found her, at last we are together. The winds of the open field stir my leaves and the ground at my roots seems to shift.—No, it is not the ground that moves: Virra has extended a slender root to touch one of mine. Her touch is as gentle as a caress; hesitantly I reach toward her.

Abruptly she grasps my root and tugs sharply. I recoil, startled rather than hurt, and her root slips away. She backs off quickly, and her laughter rustles softly.

"You're so strong! I've never touched a tree before, but I should have known you'd be strong!"

I am confused by her sudden shift of mood. "Are you mocking me?"

"Oh, no! I'm so tiny beside you, I wouldn't dare! Anyway, you're wonderful and wise, and I'm sure you're gentle, just from seeing how you walk—so calm and dignified. How could I mock you?"

She holds her limbs still as she speaks, as though I were an elder of her family. I feel oddly uncomfortable at this.

"I am simply a tree," I say. "We are a proud family, but I see wonders in you that are new to me. My family descended from the meat people, but yours must have too. No doubt they were different kinds of people who chose to become trees or bushes, but our heritage is the same. . . . I try to resist my family's pride; please do not tempt me with adulation."

(Yet I remember my scornful rebuke of the ill-mannered bush yesterday. Is this modesty any more appropriate?)

My thoughts are interrupted by another tweaking of my roots: Virra has moved underground again to grasp and jerk at me. She dances lightly away before I can react, and now her laughter is a brook.

"But you're so *serious*!" she cries. "Don't you know you mustn't be serious with bushes?" She pauses. "Have you a name?"

My roots stir the rocks beneath me, but I mutter, "Wesk."

"You're named Wesk? Then please don't be so gloomy, Wesk; you're not in the forest now, you're in the sunlight! Be happy with me —oh, please!"

There is such a note of appeal in her voice that I must respond, confused and doubtful as I am. "What should I do?"

"Play with me!" She begins to dance around me, her roots scarcely touching the icy ground; I think of acorns bouncing down a hillside. I look at her in wonder: this is how the swift meat people must have moved when the sun was young.

(I hear Querca's voice in memory: "They waste the sun, but bushes have no care for that.")

"What shall I do?" I ask.

She continues to circle me. "Do you think you can catch me?"

"No, I could never catch you." I recall yesterday's young bush. "And if I could catch you, I could not hold you."

She edges in closer to me; she is actually standing partly in my shade now. "But you're so clever, Wesk. You know so much. Are you trying to trick me? I know you trees have thoughts so deep they could penetrate boulders."

"Hardly," I say, but I take her cue and stealthily lower my limbs as she advances toward me. She is completely inside my shade now, and perhaps I can trap her before she can retreat. "You are flattering me again, Virra. If you really thought me so wise, you would not challenge my mind."

She continues moving forward, stepping lightly over my roots; I hold them still so that she will not try to flee yet. I continue to lower my limbs, and now they are nearing the ground. She does not seem to notice, for her voice is unconcerned as she says, "We're only playing, Wesk. It's a game—surely even trees play games."

"No, never. I was taught to be serious about all things."

My branches are fully lowered now, my leaves lying flat on the ground behind her. She is trapped; she could never force her way through.

"Then I can teach you about games!" she cries, and suddenly she sprints forward, barely touching the base of my roots as she passes my trunk, her bright leaves brushing against me. She dashes on toward the edge of my shade on the other side, and though I lower the rest of my limbs as quickly as I can, she gains the sun before I can catch her.

She stands quivering as my limbs belatedly strike the ground, my branches and leaves crashing into the grass. I let them rest there as she begins to giggle. I am mortified to have been tricked so easily.

By the time I have lifted my limbs again, I have recovered some composure. Virra has ceased her laughter, but she dances back and forth in delight. I say, "You *were* mocking me, I see."

"No no, oh no! You *are* clever or you could never have thought of trapping me that way when you've never played a game before! But I'm used to games, you know; so I realized what you might do."

"You are clever too, Virra, though you pretended you were not."

She notices the ruefulness in my voice, for she says quickly, "We each played tricks, but I started mine first—it was *my* game, after all. Oh, please don't be angry with me. It was a *game.*"

"Games must give more joy to those who are successful at them," I say.

"Well of *course* it's more fun to win! But it wouldn't be any fun at all if you couldn't lose." She rustles her leaves playfully at me. "I'll bet you trees never take any chances at all. You just sit there in your forest trying to stay alive. What for? It's such a waste!"

I am shaken by her words. She is right: so many of us do nothing but dream of the past while trying to live longer into the future— separating ourselves further from the time of ancient joys. It seems a paradox, yet my entire life's teachings go against what she says.

I notice that she stands directly over my longest root, and cautiously, reaching deeper into the rocky ground of the field, I extend the root until it reaches past her. I am not sure why I continue to play this game; perhaps it is to please her.

Yet I promised Querca that I would question Virra's way of wasting the sun, and if I keep her talking perhaps she will not notice that I am trying to capture her. "You should not accuse me of waste," I say, "for you burn the sun's energy each hour of each day. The sun is dying; you must know that. My family gathers its energy, and if we live for a long time we may preserve the fruit of the sun for centuries after final darkness falls."

This brings leaf-shaking laughter from Virra. "The sun may be dying, but we'll die much sooner. Does it matter what may happen centuries from now?"

I do not reply immediately; I am raising the tip of my root to the surface. She takes my silence for agreement, and goes on, "You think of the ancient past, days that are dead, and you think of the future, days that may never come. Don't you ever think of *now*?"

There is surprising passion in her speech. While her attention is distracted, I break the icy ground silently with my root and suddenly reach to grasp her slender trunk. At the last moment she sees me reaching for her and tries to spring away, but I grasp and hold her tightly. She writhes in my grip, but I am too strong for her; and she cannot tear away from her main body.

After a minute she subsides, though I continue to hold her fast. In the silence that follows I say, "We are capable of thinking of now. As you see."

Quietly she says, "All right, you've caught me. You *are* clever, Wesk, just as I said. This time you've won; now let me go."

"No. I shall continue to hold you, and in this way I shall remain the victor."

Her body trembles with pent energy; I feel that I am holding life trapped forever. But abruptly the tension is gone, as she relaxes completely. "You really don't know anything at all about games, do you?" she says. "You can't win just by holding on to something. If you could, you might as well chase rocks."

She says no more. I continue to hold her but she does not try to move. Eventually I loosen my grip and withdraw my root into the cold ground.

I feel suddenly morose. "Then what use is victory? Time eats everything, it seems; the past is a monster that follows us everywhere."

Her voice is gentle: "You're right—our past is enormous, greater than anything in the world. But while we keep moving, it can't reach us."

"Then we can only run away from it." The thought is ice reaching down to my roots.

But again her mood changes. "Oh, no, Wesk, we can move in so many ways that aren't running! Let me show you!"

She begins to dance. I have seen her do it before, the graceful motions of roots and limbs, leaves swaying without wind; when she walked through my forest-family she moved like this. I recognized it as something wonderful then, and perhaps it was this that caused me to follow her so far. She dances in a circle around me and I watch in awe; gradually I begin to notice patterns in her movements, repeated figures, slight dippings of her branches, and even a kind of sound among her leaves that is rustling, but more than that—is she singing with her body?

She returns to the point where she began her dance, and pauses. "You see? I'm back here again, but the past is gone; it's chasing me, but it will never catch up."

My branches feel as though they are swaying, though I can feel that they are still. The winds of the field seem warm. "You are so lovely," I murmur. "Does beauty hypnotize the past, then?"

"No, it isn't like that. Don't you see, Wesk? Dancing *is* beautiful, if you want to call it that—it's happiness. Can you dance too? Oh, of course you can! Come dance with me, dear Wesk!"

"I cannot. I am too slow."

"You *can*. Be stately, be dignified; it doesn't matter. Just move and be happy. I'll show you."

She begins to dance again, this time in a leisurely, languorous way. Her tiny branches sway gently like those of the great sun-gatherers; her roots caress the frost-crusted soil. I watch her, and her rhythms penetrate to my heart.

Hesitantly I begin to dance too. I make a step toward her, and another step with a different root. The icy ground grips me but I ignore it; I imitate her movements. I feel foolish and clumsy, but joy spreads in me.

"There!" she says. "You see?" She turns a complete circle where she stands, leaving delicate marks where she has touched the ground. "Can you do that?"

I try; jerkily and with great effort I withdraw my roots from the ground and turn. The winds rush through my branches, confusing me because they seem to come from all directions at once. I have to stop then, for I am exhausted and overcome by vertigo; I sink one long root directly down into the soil for strength, hoping she will not notice.

I find that I am laughing. It is an utterly strange feeling, yet delicious. The ground around me trembles and the surface ice cracks in a thousand tiny lines.

"You *can* dance! I knew you could!" Virra's branches raise into the air; the emerald light of her leaves is silhouetted by the deepening red of the late-afternoon sky.

"But not for long," I say faintly.

"Oh, yes! You can dance whenever you want, and for as long as you want!"

She is wrong. I am no bush who can drink surface frost and store sunlight in my leaves. My roots ache and bleed, and I can no longer hold my branches up to the sun. I stand motionless; I am finished, and the winds become cold again.

Virra sees the way my limbs bend, and she ceases her dance. The sun is almost set; I could gather no more energy from it anyway. She moves to me, stepping as lightly as ever past my roots. I sink them into the ground to allow her easier passage, then continue to reach for the warmer earth beneath the surface. Soon I am deeply rooted, and the sun is completely gone, and Virra stands at the very base of my roots, her small branches wrapped around my trunk.

"You're very brave," she says. "I didn't know trees could still be brave."

I feel her roots reaching down into the soil and wrapping around one of mine; they feel warm.

"I can dance," I say in wonder. "Though I know I do it badly."

"You'll get better when you've practiced a while."

The night is freezing cold. "If I do more, it will bring me to death," I tell her.

Her leaves are the only spots of light left. She keeps them wrapped around me and I catch what energy I can from them. Is she deliberately feeding me? My family would call it madness.

"I'd never cause you to die," she says softly.

Exhaustion and cold are sending me inexorably into sleep, but I manage to say, "I love you."

Then I do fall asleep, and I know nothing more till late the next morning, when I wake slowly and raise my limbs to the sun, and move my roots as I begin to loosen the frozen earth, and discover that Virra is gone.

At first I wait patiently for her to return, convinced that she has merely gone off on some unpredictable bush-whim. Perhaps she has; but she does not come back, though I stand rooted and drinking, spreading my limbs and gathering energy to dance again if she wishes. The red disk of the sun reaches zenith and begins to descend; I am anxious now but I remain where she left me. In a way I am grateful to have this time to mend and grow strong again. I remember her laughter, and the way she danced and played with me, and at times it seems I am dreaming.

When the sun sets I lower my limbs, drawing them in as close to me as I can, holding what warmth I have for as long as I can. In the dark, still watching for her, I begin to remember things she said:

Am I as beautiful as you dreamed? . . . But you're so *serious!* Don't you know you mustn't be serious with bushes? . . . You can't win just by holding on to something. If you could, you might as well chase rocks.

I watch for the light of her leaves, but she does not come. The night grows colder, and I sleep.

In the morning I wake early, and see a bush nearby. The sun's light is still dim, but I see tiny glowing leaves. "You've come back!" I cry.

"No."

That one word chills me more than ice, for it is not her voice.

"I've never seen you before," the bush says. "What are you doing so far out here? You're a tree!"

Without knowing why, I explode with anger at this . . . accusation. "Trees own the world! We are the final product of all history, the greatest of creatures!" I tremble so violently that ice shards fall from my limbs and the ground is shattered around me.

The bush moves quickly away from me. "You're as ridiculous as the rest. How did you get here?"

"I walked! Trees can walk—we can even dance. We can do anything!" My blood is rising now, filling my trunk and limbs; it brings pain even as the night frost falls away. I shake my leaves at the bush, though it is not wholly a voluntary act.

The bush laughs at me. It is the size of Virra; it is even female like her. But its laughter holds ridicule. "If you can dance, then show me. Oh, I'd love to see you dance! Will boulders dance next?"

"I dance only for Virra." My voice is as cold as the morning wind.

"*I'm* Virra. Dance for me."

Enraged, I try to leap after the bush, lifting three roots at once from the ground and flailing clumsily. Rocks and wedges of ice fly through the air. The bush retreats further, and I am caught by my remaining roots, which are sunk so deep that I must pause to work them loose.

"Is that what you call dancing?"

I stretch my free roots toward her, but she is too far away. I would grasp and rend her, strip her leaves, smother her with my own, and gather ice from the ground to heap upon her.

"You are *not* Virra! Where is she?" But my voice cannot rumble and threaten as I want: it pleads.

The bush laughs again. "Of course I'm Virra. We're all Virra."

Something touches me that is not frost, but it is cold. The young bush I first met said he was Virra too. "What do you mean?" I ask, still struggling to free my deep-sunk roots.

She stands oddly still, and her voice is softer when she speaks again. "You don't know, do you? *All* the bushes are called Virra—why should we care about names?"

I am bewildered, though something in me says I should have known this. The bushes live so briefly; they move around so that they have no ground of their own; they hold on to nothing, not even names.

Not even to love. Least of all to loving me.

I force myself to speak: "There was one of you who came to me and gave me joy. But she went away, and I have to find her."

The winds of the field continue to rush by us. The bush asks, "How long ago?"

"Two days. Less."

The emerald glow of this person's leaves is as bright as Virra's— the real Virra's. "Then you'll never catch up to her."

Even the voice of this Virra sounds like hers now. It is an unreal world here in the great open field; nothing it as it should be.

I have at least freed my remaining roots—I can walk now, but I do not know in which direction to search. Confused and fearful, I look for the tiny root-tracks Virra must have left. But the ground is covered with frost.

Hopelessly I say, "You must know where Virra went. Tell me."

"How could I know? I don't even know which Virra you mean; we're alike to each other." She hesitates, seeing my leaves shake. "Anyway, she must have gone so far by now that you'll never find her."

"I *will!*" The force of my cry frightens the bush, and she runs. In minutes she has disappeared over a low hillock. I watch her disappearance as though she were hope itself, for I realize that she is right: I could never overtake Virra even if I knew in what direction to go.

I hold my limbs up to the chill sun and consider my situation. I have only two chances: either Virra will return to this spot, or I must hope to find her by a blind search of the field. Neither possibility seems likely, but I must do something. So I begin.

I walk through windy fields strewn with rocks and chunks of ice. I search for Virra while the dim red sun rises and sets, rises and sets more times than I bother to count. I have no direction; I turn to left or right when hopelessness strikes me, and I continue though all I find are the mindless grasses, and rocks and empty ground, and occasionally a traveling bush.

"I search for one called Virra. Are you Virra?"

"We're all Virra."

I go on, hopeless but hoping.

Several times I return to the place where I stood when Virra left. But she is never there, and there are never any tracks except my own deep root-holes. Each time I think: She will see them if she comes, and she will be able to find me.

But she never does, and though the memory of trees is greater than that of any other beings who have lived, I am beginning to forget what Virra was like. Bright green in her leaves, yes, but precisely what color? Her laughter rustled with life, but what was its sound?

One thing I do remember clearly. The last words Virra said to me were, "I'd never cause you to die." I believed it was a statement of love, but it must have been something else.

It was high summer when I left my family, but I can feel the ground growing cold at deeper levels as the sun dims toward winter. Walking is harder each day, yet I continue. My roots have become tough, lacerated by stones but covered now with something that is almost bark. I move ever more slowly.

One day I find myself at the edge of the forest-family. The hermits stand silent and I do not disturb them; perhaps they are already in their winter sleep. Beyond them is darkness, and the warmth of hundreds of my family huddled together. I recall how the ground moves within the family, stirred constantly by our roots.

I look once more at the great empty field, filled with winds and strangers. My soul is utterly silent as I step carefully into the shade of an unmoving hermit, skirt her roots, and move on into the forest. I step painfully from one patch of sun to another; the trees grow more numerous and closer together, and after a while I begin to hear their vague dreams, but I ignore them.

Then a voice comes: "Well. Did you find her?"

It is Querca, who promised she would remember me when I came again. Aged and great Querca, who once filled me with fear. Now I feel nothing.

"Yes, I found her."

Querca's brittle leaves rustle. "A creature who kills the sun. How did she explain that?"

I stop and sink my roots deep; deliberately I drink the soil that Querca has owned since before I was born. Querca is too old to object, or perhaps it is the coming of winter that keeps her still.

"She said the sun's energy is for life, and for joy. She said we waste it if we do not use it." I feel Querca's contempt stir the ground, but before she can speak I add, "I believe she is right."

"Then why are you returning?"

There is no way to explain what happened. "I lost her," I say.

"I see. Of course."

There is silence, as there usually is in the family during winter. Finally Querca asks, "How was the soil there? Rich and soft, as it is here?"

Her words cause me to move my roots in the deep loam of the family. "There were rocks. The soil everywhere was dry beneath the ice."

"As bad as I thought," says Querca. "They will not remain much longer."

"But while they remain, they *live!*"

Querca suppresses laughter in her roots before it can reach her leaves and cause them to fall. "When the end comes, there will be no bushes left," she says. "We shall inherit all."

Suddenly I am flooded by emotion, and it takes me several minutes to realize what it is: I feel pity for Querca.

I withdraw my roots from her soil and turn toward the field. Stepping carefully away, I say, "Then let the end come."

And now I am walking again toward the edge of the family. I shall find a place outside the forest, beyond the hermits and perhaps touching the stones of the field. If Virra—any Virra—comes to me, I will try to dance again.

Acknowledgments

FORTUNE HUNTER by Poul Anderson. Copyright © 1972 by Lancer Books, Inc. From *Infinity Four*, by permission of the author and his agents, Scott Meredith Literary Agency, Inc., 845 Third Avenue, New York NY 10022.

MY LADY OF THE PSYCHIATRIC SORROWS by Brian W. Aldiss. Copyright © 1977 by Terry Carr. From *Universe 7*, by permission of the author.

THE NEW ATLANTIS by Ursula K. Le Guin. Copyright © 1975 by Ursula K. Le Guin. From *The New Atlantis*, by permission of the author and her agent, Virginia Kidd.

YOUNG LOVE by Grania Davis. Copyright © 1974 by Damon Knight. From *Orbit 13*, by permission of the author and her agent for that story, Virginia Kidd.

WHALE SONG by Terry Melen. Copyright © 1974 by The Condé Nast Publications Inc. From *Analog*, September 1974, by permission of the author.

UNDER THE GENERATOR by John Shirley. Copyright © 1976 by Terry Carr. From *Universe 6*, by permission of the author.

THE UGLY CHICKENS by Howard Waldrop. Copyright © 1980 by Terry Carr. From *Universe 10*, by permission of the author.

THE WIND AND THE RAIN by Robert Silverberg. Copyright © 1973 by Roger Elwood and Virginia Kidd. From *Saving Worlds*, by permission of the author and his agents, Scott Meredith Literary Agency, Inc., 845 Third Avenue, New York NY 10022.

VIRRA by Terry Carr. Copyright © 1978 by Mercury Press, Inc. From *Fantasy and Science Fiction*, October 1978, by permission of the author.